That
Thing You Do

WHISPERING BAY ROMANCE BOOK 1

maria geraci

More from Maria Geraci

That
Thing You Do

Author's Note

Welcome to Whispering Bay, where smart heroines and hot heroes collide to find love and their happily-ever-afters! To find out more about this series and my other books, please visit my website. There, you may sign up for my newsletter if you'd like to be kept in the loop about releases, contests, and other fun stuff. You can also find me on Facebook, Twitter and Pinterest.

http://mariageraci.com

Acknowledgments

First off, thank you to all the members of my Facebook Street Team page and my awesome review team. You're the best! Hugs to my husband Mike, who supports me in this crazy writing endeavor and to Jamie Farrell, my awesome critique partner. I'd also like to do a great big shout out to my lovely agent, Deidre Knight, and to everyone at The Knight Agency, and to Jia Gayles and Jamie Schlansky for all the hard work they put into this book.

Chapter One

ALLIE GRANT AIMED HER flashlight at the padlocked door to the Margaret Handy Senior Center. On the surface, the abandoned building appeared like any other ranch-style structure built in the nineteen-fifties. Lots of brick, lots of windows, lots of deterioration. But this wasn't just any crumbling building. According to her anonymous source, this building was haunted.

Unfortunately, it was also locked up tighter than the Spanx she'd worn on her last date. Which was so long ago that Allie could barely recall the details, the only memorable part of the evening being when she took off those Spanx. Alone. Right before crawling into bed with a Snickers bar and the worn-out copy of *Anne of Green Gables* Buela had given Allie on her seventh birthday.

She stifled a yawn. She wouldn't mind being in bed right now. It was nearly midnight and she'd been up since dawn. But she was a journalist in need of a story and a haunted building (as hokey as that sounded) was a potential goldmine in magazine advertising revenue. It was also the kind of story that could get a freelancer like herself a cover byline. Better yet, it was the sort of story that could land her a permanent job at *Florida!* magazine.

She raised her flashlight above the door, illuminating a huge NO TRESPASSING sign. The way Allie saw it she had two options.

The first involved going to her brother Zeke's house, getting a decent night's sleep, and then waking up bright and early to seek out The Person In Charge. She'd make an impassioned (yet logical) plea on why she had to spend time inside the building, and The Person In Charge would comply, because, really, why wouldn't they?

Under normal circumstances, that's exactly what she'd do. She simply couldn't help herself. Buela taught her early that good girls finish first. A thought that had remained stuck in her head the way her Cuban grandmother's lumpy cheese grits used to stick to Allie's ribs on a cold January morning. Although she'd been gone over twelve years now, Allie could still hear Buela's voice telling her what to do. Right now, however, that voice was being drowned out by yet another sign stating that the building was scheduled for demolition at nine a.m. tomorrow, giving Allie basically zip time to contact The Person In Charge.

Bringing her to option number two.

An option Buela would definitely not have approved of. Not to mention Zeke, who also happened to be Whispering Bay's current chief of police. Nope. Allie was beyond certain Zeke wouldn't take too kindly to his baby sister committing a B&E.

But was it really a crime to break into a deserted building scheduled for demolition in less than nine hours?

A shiver skated up her spine.

It wasn't cold. Not really. It was October and still seasonally warm enough for the Florida panhandle, but the building was isolated from the rest of the ocean strip by at least half a mile. That on its own made it creepy enough, and then of course, there was that *haunted* thing.

Maybe she should channel the lion from *The Wizard of Oz* and begin chanting *I don't believe in ghosts... I don't believe in ghosts...*

But there was something to be said about Patrick Swayze and Demi Moore and that whole pottery wheel scene.

Hopeless Hollywood romanticism? No doubt. It was lovely to believe that even after death there was something so powerful about the feelings we had while we were alive that they pulled us back to the people and places we once loved.

All corniness aside, though, she was a journalist, and at the behest of *Florida*! magazine's editor, Emma Frazier, Allie had just driven nearly six hours to investigate a story on what most people (herself included) would consider the flimsiest of leads. But if Emma wanted a ghost story, then that's what Allie would give her. Impressing Emma Frazier was the key to landing her dream job, which happened to be Goal Number Three on Allie's four-part Life Plan. So despite the NO TRESPASSING sign, she wasn't leaving until she got her story. A padlocked door was beyond her capabilities, but no building this old could be burglarproof.

Using her flashlight to guide her, Allie made her way through a patch of weeds to study the windows on the side of the building.

Bin-go! Jalousie glass panes. Popular in Florida during the last century before central air-conditioning became standard. Those windows might provide excellent ventilation but they looked easy as all heck to break into. Not that Allie had any experience sneaking in or out of windows. Once upon a time, that had been Zeke's forte. Before he'd cleaned up his act, of course. Nowadays, there wasn't anyone more upstanding than her big brother.

She noticed the window in the middle was missing several of its glass panes. Had someone already broken inside? Maybe. Or more likely, those panes had fallen out over time, and since the building was scheduled to come down, it wouldn't have made sense to fix them.

Which brought Allie to her third option—it wasn't really a B&E if she didn't actually break anything. Yes, there was that big NO TRESPASSING sign but the window was practically open. Some people might consider that an invitation.

Ha. Her brother would call that delusional thinking. Fuzzy morality, at best. But what were her options? Despite the late hour, she was now fully awake.

She sent up a silent apology to Buela (Zeke, she would deal with later) and went into action. With the flashlight tucked beneath her arm, she knocked the flimsy metallic screen out of the way. Balancing her bottom on the open window ledge, she lowered one sneakered foot inside—when the tinny-sounding ring tone version of Adele's "Rumour Has It" startled her into falling butt first onto a hard wooden floor.

Her cell phone flew out of her shorts pocket. Allie scampered on all fours to retrieve it, causing her right knee to encounter something sharp. *Ouch*! She ignored the pain and glanced at her cell phone's caller ID telling her (warning her) that it was her roommate, Jen.

"Where are you?" Jen asked.

"Check the fridge." Allie had purposely left Jen a note taped to the refrigerator door. It was the first place

Jen always went when she got home from her evening shift at the hospital where she worked as a respiratory therapist.

After a slightly too long pause in which Allie imagined Jen not only finding the note, but last night's leftovers as well, Jen said, "You're in Whispering Lakes? Isn't that where you grew up?"

"Yep, but it's Whispering Bay." Allie went on to explain about the email that had caused her to jump in her car and make the six-hour drive to her hometown.

"So, let me get this straight," Jen said. "Someone sent you an anonymous email telling you there's a *ghost* inside the building? And you, what? Jumped in your car and drove up there? Just like that?"

Yes, just like that, she wanted to say, but something warm and wet trickled down her shin, distracting her. She pointed the flashlight on her leg to investigate. *Blood*! The sight of blood (especially her own) made her light-headed. Allie took a shaky breath. "Are ghosts attracted to blood?"

"That's zombies. Or is it vampires? Yep, it's definitely vampires. *Wait.* Did you say *blood*? Allie, whose blood are we talking about here?"

"Mine. I kind of cut my knee going in through the window." No need to mention the knee incident had occurred because of Allie's own clumsiness. Of course, that clumsiness was the result of Jen's poorly timed phone call, but Allie wasn't one to point fingers.

"Ooh! You broke into the building? How very Woodward and Bernstein of you. But if you get arrested, don't expect me to bail you out of jail. I have a hot date tonight, and driving all the way up to Whispering Pines to save your butt isn't on my agenda," Jen said.

A hot date at this time of night was code for a booty

call from Jen's boyfriend, Sean. For the first time this evening Allie was glad she wasn't home tucked away in bed. She wasn't sure what Jen and Sean were into, but they'd met at a Tarzan yodeling contest. If Sean spent the night, it meant Allie didn't get any sleep unless she wore earplugs.

"It's Whispering Bay," Allie said, unable to stop from correcting Jen. Allie hadn't called Whispering Bay home since she was eighteen, but the only family she had in the world lived here, and she still visited frequently enough that she was on a first-name basis with most of the town's population. It was only natural she felt protective of the place.

"Whatever. You're so uptight. You know, you could use a hot date yourself. Hey, maybe the ghost is male."

"And probably like eighty years old. This place used to be a senior center. Plus, I kinda like my guys alive. Jen, listen, I really have to go—"

"Alive does come in handy. *So...*the reason I called is we just got a notice saying our electricity is going to be turned off in two days. Didn't you pay the bill?"

"I thought it was your month to pay the bill."

"I paid it last month," Jen said. "I'd pay it, but I'm kind of short. Plus, you know, *it is* your turn."

Allie was positive she'd paid the electricity last month, but without checking her online bank statement, she had no proof.

Argh. Why did money (or the lack of it) always seem to pop up at the most inconvenient times? At this point in her life, Allie should have been well on track with Life Goal Number Three—a permanent job with benefits. But Life Goal Number Two had taken her longer (and been more expensive) than she'd originally thought, putting her woefully behind schedule. Which meant she was still freelancing, which meant she lived article-to-article.

Translation: Paycheck-to-paycheck.

Hence, she had to supplement her income with the second oldest profession known to womankind. *Waitressing.* Weekdays, she lived her dream job. Weekends? Not so much. But the tips she made waiting tables at The Blue Monkey, a hipster Vegan restaurant in downtown Tampa, had saved her carnivorous butt from starving on more than one occasion. There was no way around it, in order to pay the electric bill she'd have to transfer money from that pathetic creature she called a savings account.

The sound of crunching gravel made Allie stop in her tracks. "Jen," she whispered into the phone, "I think I just heard something."

"Like what? Moaning? Chains rattling?" Jen's voice hitched with excitement. "Sounds like my kind of place. And why are you talking so low? I can barely make out what you're saying. It's not like the ghost couldn't hear you if it wanted to. It can probably even read your thoughts."

If Allie hadn't been so creeped out she would have laughed. "What are you, a ghost expert?"

Another sound. This time *it did* sound like a chain rattling.

Blimey. A ghost after Jen's own kinky heart!

"Jen, I gotta go—"

"But the electric bill—"

"I promise I'll pay it tomorrow online."

"Okay. Awesome! So, good luck with that ghost. And don't do anything I wouldn't do!" She hung up, leaving Allie to wonder exactly what those last words meant.

Keeping herself as still as possible, Allie slipped the

cell phone back into her shorts pocket. The building was now eerily quiet. No gravel crunching. No chains rattling. Had she imagined it? Probably. Allie let out a pent-up breath. She didn't know whether she was relieved or disappointed. Both, maybe.

She waited a few minutes so that her vision adjusted to the darkness. Years ago, she'd been inside this building. Buela had brought her here after Allie had graduated high school, proud of the granddaughter about to go off to college that she'd raised almost single-handedly. Back then, the senior center had been alive. Full of noise and energy. Now, the place just looked sad. Empty, with bits of scattered trash strewn on the floor.

Something small and dark scurried past her.

Correction: Not exactly empty.

Cockroaches!

The place was probably crawling with them. Allie was a native Floridian, so she should be used to all manner of creepy crawly things, but sorry, she'd never get used to cockroaches. Best to get this over with as quickly as possible.

"Hello?" she called out. Unable to help herself, she giggled. More out of nerves than a comedic response, because it wasn't as if she expected someone to answer.

A chain rattled—louder than before—followed this time by a distinct clang.

This was no product of her imagination.

Her mouth went dry. She squeezed the flashlight in her hand, nearly cutting off the blood flow to her fingers.

She tried to concentrate on the rattling sound but all she could hear was the soft whoosh of waves lapping onto a beach. Was her mind playing tricks with her? Because it would be impossible to hear the ocean from inside the building.

Then she remembered the window she'd crawled through.

Of course. The sound was coming though the now-open window.

A rush of air swept through her. But instead of the cool night air she'd expected, this was a warm tropical breeze. A pleasant smell assailed her nostrils. Slightly sweet, and vaguely comforting. Lemons, maybe? Her arms erupted in goose bumps. But strangely enough, she was neither cold nor frightened.

A door slammed behind her. She spun around just in time to see a shadow dash across the room. The warm lemony smell vanished, replaced by a voice inside telling her that she was in big trouble. The door was padlocked. Which meant that whatever had gotten inside the building had bypassed the lock. Which was…*impossible.*

Allie tried to scream, but her throat wasn't cooperating.

Luckily, her legs weren't so chicken shit.

She turned to run but something charged at her, smacking her solidly in the chest. The air flew from her lungs. Her last thought before hitting the floor was that ghosts weren't supposed to make physical contact. They needed Whoopi Goldberg for that!

She struggled to roll out from under whatever had attacked her, but it was no use. The thing on top of her was composed of solid bone and muscle.

"Hold still," hissed a deep voice. For a second there, it sounded like… *No,* that too was impossible. "I told you the next time I caught you breaking into the place I'd call the cops."

Allie nearly swallowed her tongue. She *knew* that voice. Hot, dark, male. And definitely *alive.*

"I think you have me confused with someone else," she gasped.

The body above her stilled. Did he recognize her voice, too?

A light shone directly in her face, temporarily blinding her. Enough was enough.

She found the flashlight clutched in her hand and aimed it in retaliation at the two-hundred-pound mass pinning her to the ground. "Hey, can you stop with the *Dragnet* treatment?"

It was almost worth being crushed to death to see the incredulous look on Tom Donalan's face. "*Allie*? Allie Grant? What the hell are you doing here?"

"First things first. I'll drop my flashlight if you drop yours. And if it's not too much to ask, maybe you could get off me while you're at it? You're not exactly made of air, you know."

He jumped off her like she was on fire.

After a few long and tortuous moments, he reluctantly extended his hand. Considering that she was flat on her ass, she should have taken it. But it would be a snowy day in Florida before she accepted help from Tom Donalan. She pushed herself up on her elbows and rose as gracefully as possible under the circumstances.

It had been twelve years and two months since she last saw, talked, or even thought about Tom Donalan. Not that Allie had been counting. Six hours ago, he'd been nothing more than an unpleasant memory. Like a pimple on the chin on prom night, or a lost library book racking up fines. Okay, so maybe she had thought about him *some*.

The fact was she couldn't cross over the Choctawhatchee Bay Bridge without thinking of him, and she couldn't get to Whispering Bay without crossing that bridge. Hence, he was the first thought (regret) she had whenever she drove home for a visit. The last she'd heard of Tom Donalan he'd made it big in Atlanta. Some kind of hot shot in the construction business, recently divorced from his perfect hometown sweetheart.

Allie tried not to stare, but it was impossible. This certainly was *not* the Tom Donalan of her fantasies. The ones she had (only occasionally) after eating too much Ben and Jerry's Chunky Monkey. In that world Tom Donalan had a beer belly, was bald, and missing a couple of front teeth. A lot of deterioration for only twelve years, but, hey, a girl could dream, right?

This Tom Donalan, on the other hand, had far superseded the promise made by his high school boyish good looks. Tall. Broad shouldered. With a full head of dark blonde hair and piercing blue eyes. He stood there staring at her with his arms crossed over his chest like he was Captain Friggin' America in charge of the planet.

He looked angry, which didn't make sense. She was the wronged party here! He'd practically attacked her, for Pete's sake.

She took a deep breath and tried to act as if running into her ex was an everyday occurrence. "Well, well, well, if it isn't Tom Donalan. I see you still have all your teeth."

He blinked and shook his head. "What?"

I see you still have all your teeth.

Argh!

Of all the Tom Donalan scenarios she'd played in her head over all the years, this was *not* what she was supposed to say to him. She was supposed to be witty. Charming. He was supposed to be dumbstruck by her brilliance. He was at a loss for words, all right.

Allie pasted a smile to her face and tried again. "You

need to be more specific. *What*, as in, what's my favorite color, or what do I have programmed on my DVR for tomorrow night, or what—"

"*What*, as in, what are you doing inside this building?"

"I could ask you the exact same question. Where'd you come from anyway?"

"I was driving by and I saw a car in the parking lot. So I stopped to investigate. Now it's your turn. What are you doing back in town? I thought you lived in Tampa."

He knew where she lived? "I don't need a reason to come back home. Certainly not one I need to run by you, anyway. And I thought *you* lived in Atlanta."

"Things change," he said.

"Right. Things change."

"So are you going to answer me or not?"

The way he stared at her made Allie squirm. Instinctively, she went to run a hand through her hair, then remembered that she'd pulled it back in a ponytail. She didn't need a mirror to know exactly what she looked like. Ratty shorts, skinned-up knee, no makeup. Her when-I-see-Tom-Donalan-again revenge fantasy was officially zero-for-two now.

"I don't have to explain myself to you," she said.

He shrugged in a way that made her want to punch him. How could she have ever thought the two of them were kindred spirits?

"Suit yourself," Tom said. "But you have about three minutes before the cops show up, and if you don't want me to press charges you better have a damn good reason for breaking into my building."

Chapter Two

OF ALL THE ABANDONED buildings in all the towns in all the world, she walks into mine. Tom Donalan had known when he moved back to Whispering Bay it would only be a matter of time before he eventually ran into Allie Grant. He just hadn't expected it to be tonight. Or to be so damn unprepared for it.

Kismet was truly a bitch.

Allie's brown eyes sizzled. Which wasn't the only thing hot about her. Those legs that had nearly caused him to flunk AP chemistry were still going strong.

"*Your* building?" she said. "I thought this was public property."

"Public property that's about to come down to make way for progress. And I'm the guy in charge." He sounded like an asshole, but he couldn't seem to help himself.

What was she doing here?

His gaze cut to the broken glass on the ground, leading him to the metallic screen on the floor beneath an open window. "You broke in through the window?"

"I can explain—"

"The place is practically falling down on its own. You get hurt in here, it's my responsibility."

"And we all know how *big* you are on responsibility."

Her eyes went wide, like she hadn't planned on saying that out loud.

Leave it to Allie Grant. The girl had no filter. Together less than five minutes and she'd already thrown down the gauntlet.

A blue police light flashed through the window.

"*Captain Crunch*," she muttered. "You really did call the cops, didn't you?"

Only Allie Grant would think the name of a kids' breakfast cereal constituted some kind of cuss word. The first time he'd heard her say it was after she'd botched a chemistry experiment. Almost immediately, she'd turned beet red. Her grandmother, she explained, had encouraged her to use the expression to replace saying something not as nice. It had been cute at the time. He remembered the last time he heard her say it. It hadn't been so cute then.

"I thought you were the same kids who've been sneaking around here all week." He shrugged, and added, "Sorry." Only he wasn't sorry he'd called the cops because this building was turning into a real pain in the ass. He was only sorry that... What? That it was Allie Grant he'd found inside?

The door burst open. "Hands in the air!" shouted a uniformed officer. It was Rusty Newton, a member of Whispering Bay's finest, and he was waving a gun like he'd just stepped into a real live version of *Die Hard*.

Tom put his hands up in the air. "Whoa. Take it easy, Rusty. No one here is armed."

Other than the Bruce Willis routine, Tom had to admit he was awful glad it was Rusty who'd answered the call. He wasn't the brightest bulb on the Whispering Bay Police force but he was a good ol' boy and could be reasoned with.

Rusty holstered his weapon. "What's going on, Tom? You call in a B&E?"

Allie waved her arm in the air to get the deputy's attention. "Hey, Rusty. What's shakin'?"

Rusty did a double take. "Allie? *Damn*, girl, what are you doing here? Does Zeke know you're in town?"

"I'm hoping to surprise him," she said.

"By getting yourself thrown in jail?" Tom asked. There he was, being an asshole again. He should shut his trap, lock up the place, and let Rusty deal with her. God knew he needed to get at least a few hours' sleep. He doubted that was possible, though. At least not until he found out what Allie Grant was doing inside his building.

She ignored his sarcasm and gave Rusty a sweet smile. A smile Tom instinctively knew was fake. "Actually, I'm here following a lead for a story," she said.

Rusty frowned. "What's that got to do with the old senior center?"

"Have you heard any rumors about a ghost haunting this place?" Allie asked.

Rusty's eyes popped wide. "A ghost? Here? Golly, Allie, *no way*."

"Yep. That's what I'm here to investigate. A real, honest-to-life ghost."

Rusty glanced nervously around the room. "But...if it's a ghost, then it isn't alive. Right?"

Allie's gaze met Tom's. Just for a second. But long enough for him to know exactly what she was thinking, because he was thinking it, too. Somehow he managed to keep a straight face.

"I was just using a figure of speech, Rusty," Allie said.

"Oh, yeah. Sure, sure. So..." Rusty lowered his voice

to a near whisper. "Did you see or hear anything...*weird* in here?"

"Well, I did get a sort of warm and fuzzy feeling, but it disappeared the minute Dirty Harry here came charging in."

Rusty looked momentarily confused, until he realized Dirty Harry was none other than Tom. "Oh. Just took for granted you two knew one another. Allie, this here is Tom Donalan, he's the site foreman for Pappas-Hernandez Construction. He's in charge of taking down the building and putting up the new town rec center."

"Allie and I already know each other," Tom said. "We—"

"Went to high school together," she quickly clarified.

They knew each other a lot better than that, but Tom let it slide.

"High school, huh? Go Wolverines!" Rusty thrust three fingers in the air to form the letter W. He waved the symbol above his head just like all the kids did during high school football games. Only for Rusty, that must have been at least twenty-five years ago.

Once again, Tom caught Allie's gaze. This time, she held it a little longer and for an instant, it was as if they'd been transported back to their first shared smile, back to the first day of senior year AP Chemistry. As small as Whispering Bay High was, it had been the first time in their entire four-year high school career they'd shared a class. Not that Tom hadn't always been aware of her. At five foot ten with a set of legs that went on forever, a teenage boy would have to be dead not to have noticed Allison Grant.

She turned and gave Tom an appraising look that bordered on the hostile. "You're really the person in charge, huh?"

"You better believe it."

Her right eyelid twitched. "So," she said, ignoring him to address Rusty, "back to the Ghost of Whispering Bay. Haunting the old senior center at night, roaming the halls of the abandoned building searching for the people he or she once loved in life. What can you tell me about that?"

"Unbelievable," Tom said. "Please don't tell me you actually believe that malarkey."

"*Malarkey*?" She fisted her hands on her hips. "Do people still use that word?"

"What word would you like me to use?"

Rusty glanced between the two of them. "Um, Tom, Allie, we're all friends here, right?"

"Sure, Tom and I are *great* friends," Allie said.

Rusty still looked confused. Not that Tom blamed him. You'd have to be an idiot to not pick up the tension between them.

"Look, Donalan, I take it from your attitude that you don't believe in ghosts, but I have proof that someone does," Allie said.

"Oh yeah? What kind of proof?" Cause he'd love to see that.

She reached inside the pockets of her tight little shorts to produce a folded-up sheet of paper. "Go ahead and see for yourself," she urged. "It's a copy of an email I received six hours ago."

Tom unfolded the paper and began reading while Rusty hung over his shoulder.

To: EmmaFrazier@Florida!magazine.com
From: ConcernedCitizen@zmail.com

Dear Ms. Frazier,
I am writing to tell you how much I enjoy your

magazine and the many entertaining articles I've had the privilege to read over the years. My particular favorite is the one about Perky the Duck, who was shot by a hunter, presumed dead, and then later "came to life" and ended up being adopted by the wildlife people. What a heartwarming story! The author of the article seemed to have such empathy for her subject matter and, after giving this some deliberation, I decided she was the perfect person to write about the current situation plaguing us here in Whispering Bay. In case you've never heard of it, it's a small town located on the panhandle between Panama City and Destin. I will be blunt, Ms. Frazier, there is a ghost haunting the old Whispering Bay Senior Center. I think this would be a perfect story for your magazine, but please hurry. The senior center is scheduled to be torn down any day now and it would be a shame if the story disintegrated into the ashes along with it.

Sincerely,
A Concerned Citizen

PS I've tried contacting the author of the Perky the Duck story directly, but all my correspondence has gone unanswered. Perhaps you could forward this to her?

"Let me guess," Tom said. "You're this infamous author. The one who wrote about a duck coming back to life? Why didn't you get in touch with this Concerned Citizen yourself?"

She snatched the paper from his hands. "I'll have you know that story was picked up by the Associated Press. And as for why I didn't contact Concerned Citizen, that's...none of your business."

"I *love* that duck story," Rusty said. "Made me look

at huntin' a whole different way. To tell the truth, almost made me quit altogether." His voice cracked. "Sorry, Allie, I tried, but I just couldn't give it up."

"That's okay, Rusty. I understand."

"Yeah, well, I'll have to read it sometime, but for now, let me get this straight," Tom said. "You received a tip from someone you don't know telling you the building is haunted. And you just, what? Jumped in your car and raced up here? Did it ever occur to you the whole thing might be some kind of hoax?"

"Why does everyone keep asking me that? I didn't just *jump* in my car on some whim. And in case you've forgotten, the letter was addressed to my editor. I'm here at her request on official *Florida!* magazine business, pal."

So now he was *pal.* He wasn't sure but it sounded a step down from being called Donalan.

"Naturally," she continued, "I called my brother to try to validate the story but he didn't pick up."

"That's probably because he's at the big police convention in Tallahassee," Rusty said.

Allie nodded like this was information she already knew. "So when I didn't hear back from Zeke, I called Mimi and she filled me in. She hadn't heard anything about a ghost but she told me the building was scheduled for demolition. I had no choice, really. It was either come investigate now or lose the story."

Mimi was Allie's sister-in-law. Tom had run into her at the Piggly Wiggly just last week. His son, Henry, and Allie's nephew, Cameron, were becoming fast friends. No doubt about it. Moving back to Whispering Bay meant his life and Allie's would eventually intersect. Was she married? He didn't think so or he would have heard about it. But she had to be seeing someone.

19

"You know, Tom, maybe Allie's onto something," Rusty said. "We've gotten a few calls reporting some strange noises here late at night. Never occurred to me it might be a ghost."

"Christ," Tom muttered. "Rusty, there's no ghost. It's just some local kids breaking in looking for a place to get drunk. Here, let me show you."

They followed him outside the building to a dumpster located at the edge of the parking lot. Tom stuck his hand in the garbage to fish out a grocery bag filled with empty beer bottles. "I drove by last night and chased some teenagers off the premises. Confiscated a couple of six packs and told them if I ever caught them here again I'd call the cops." He shrugged. "Sorry, but there's your ghost, Allie."

She looked back to study the building; a glimmer of disappointment shadowed her eyes. He could almost feel sorry for her. If he weren't so tired. He should have hired a security guard, but Tom had tried to keep the budget for this project as lean as possible, so instead, he'd personally spent the past four nights patrolling the building to keep out trespassers. At the moment it was damn near impossible to feel sorry for anyone except himself.

"Look," Tom said, "it's late. Let's just call this a big misunderstanding."

"Does that mean you're not pressing charges?" Rusty asked.

"Sure. No charges. Let's all go home and get a good night's sleep and forget this ever happened."

Rusty looked relieved. "Good idea."

"But I still need to do my investigation," Allie said. "According to the sign in front, the building is scheduled to be torn down tomorrow. Which means tonight is all the time I have left to—"

"To what?" Tom said. "Make contact with a ghost that doesn't exist?"

She took a deep breath like she was struggling to keep her cool. "So you're a non-believer. I get that. But what would it hurt to let me spend the night? I'm thinking I could write an exposé." Her voice rose with excitement. "My own personal experience of a night spent in a haunted building *à la American Horror Story*. The readers will eat it up."

Rusty's eyes grew impossibly large. "That's real brave of you, Allie. Real brave."

Allie gave Rusty another sweet smile. Only this time, the smile was for real and Tom couldn't help but feel envious. Once, he'd been the recipient of those smiles. He doubted she would ever smile at him like that again. At least not in this lifetime.

His gaze drifted back to those legs he'd been trying not to stare at. A thin trickle of blood ran down Allie's right shin. He pointed to her skinned-up knee. "That happen on your way inside?"

"It's just a scratch." But her voice sounded hollow.

"That could have just as easily been a cut requiring stitches or a broken skull. The fact is that if you stay the night, then I have to stay, and that's not going to happen. It's already close to midnight and I have to be back here in less than nine hours to supervise the demolition."

"But once this building gets torn down, it will be impossible to ascertain the validity of the ghost. Can't you delay things? Just for one day?" she asked.

He wanted to say yes. Partly for old time's sake, and partly for...shit. He didn't know what for, except when she looked at him like that it was hard not to give her whatever she wanted. But he wasn't eighteen anymore.

And she'd been right earlier. Except for the one time he'd screwed up, he'd always been the responsible one. Twelve years hadn't changed that. If anything, the years had reinforced it.

"Sorry, but postponing the demolition means going off schedule, which means going off budget." And going off budget meant no bonus, and he wasn't about to let that happen.

"Maybe the ghost will relocate somewhere else?" Rusty suggested. "There's lots of old buildings in this town."

"Don't encourage her, Rusty."

"He can encourage me all he wants," Allie shot back.

They stared at one another, neither of them backing down at first, then after a few long seconds she began to shift from leg to leg, like she was nervous. "Okay, buddy, obviously, I need to go above your head on this. Maybe your boss will be a little more accommodating."

So now he was *buddy*. Definitely a step down from pal.

"My boss is Steve Pappas. Go ahead and give him a call. Tell him you need him to delay the demolition on the building so you and Casper can have a one-on-one."

"All right, I will. And I'll be sure to tell him you suggested it." She pulled out her cell phone. "Um, you don't happen to have his number, do you?"

She had hutzpah; he'd give her that. "Sorry, I'm not about to give you my boss's personal cell phone number so you can ask him to delay a job that he's already doing pro bono. But hey, I'm sure Rusty here will be happy to give you his home address if you ask real nice."

She looked ready to spit.

God, he could be a dick. He didn't mean to be. And he normally wasn't. His momma had taught him early on how to talk to a lady. But there was something about Allie Grant that pushed all his buttons. The bad ones, as well as the good.

Rusty looked alarmed. "Allie, I know you're Zeke's sister and all, but I really can't give you Steve Pappas's home address."

"I know that, Rusty," she said, sounding sincere again. "But thanks anyway."

"Good! So, if Tom isn't pressing charges, then yeah, we're all done here. Except I should probably run your license and give you a verbal warning. Only cause that's what I would do for anyone else. Don't want Zeke to think I'm giving his kin any special treatment. Considering you did actually break into the place."

"No problem." She limped over to her car to retrieve her driver's license then handed it to Rusty.

"This will just take a sec," Rusty said. "Then it will be all nice and proper." He gave her a friendly wink and trotted off to his police cruiser.

Now that they were alone again, she seemed to have lost some of her earlier steam. He tried to think of a way to ease some of the awkwardness. "So you work for *Florida*! magazine, huh?" Tom asked, mostly because he was genuinely interested, and hell...what else were they going to talk about?

"I freelance for them. Why? You a subscriber?"

"I pick it up every now and then at the grocery. Good fishing articles."

"Yeah, I don't write those."

"What do you write?"

She batted her eyelashes at him. "Ghost stories."

He fought back a grin. He'd always liked that she never took crap from anyone. His gaze honed in on her knee again. "Wait right here." He walked over to his

23

truck to get the first aid kit he kept in the glove compartment, then crouched in front of her to inspect the cut on her leg.

She eyed him suspiciously. "What are you—Oh, no need to go all Florence Nightingale on me," she squeaked, realizing what he was about to do. "I'm perfectly fine."

"You're bleeding all over the parking lot. *My* parking lot, remember?"

"*My* parking lot. *My* building. You sound like a two-year-old. Is there anything here that isn't *yours*?"

He decided to ignore that and instead moistened a piece of gauze with antiseptic then pressed it against her knee.

"*Hey*! That hurts." She tried to pull away, but he secured her leg by placing his other hand firmly behind her calf. Her skin felt firm and smooth. What had she said earlier? That she'd gotten a warm and fuzzy feeling inside the building? Yeah, he was feeling pretty warm and fuzzy, too. But it didn't have anything to do with any bogus ghost.

"Hold still," he said.

"I think you're enjoying this a little too much." A thin line of blood oozed from beneath the gauze. She gulped, then quickly looked away.

He pressed tighter to staunch the flow. "Still can't stomach the sight of blood?"

She whipped her head around. "How did you remember—never mind. It doesn't matter."

"It matters," he said, catching her eye.

Then she started doing that thing she did whenever she got nervous. She began to talk non-stop. She asked him about his parents, his older sister, Katie, who was married and now lived in Daytona Beach, his grandparents, his aunt and uncle. She asked about his entire family. Except the most obvious member.

"How's Brandy doing? Still stealing food from the garbage can?"

"Brandy's dead."

"Dead?" She looked stunned.

"She was a beagle and twelve years old when you knew her. So, yeah, she's been gone awhile now."

"Oh, yes, of course," she muttered. Then she cleared her throat and finally asked, "How's Lauren? I was sorry to hear about your divorce."

Was she really sorry? Or just being polite? If anyone had a right to gloat over his failures, it was Allie. He could hear the unasked question in her voice. *What happened to your marriage?* He'd been asked that a lot lately, but he never gave anyone a straight answer. It was nobody's business but his and Lauren's. He considered telling Allie the truth. But she hadn't asked out loud, and besides, what was the point? In the end, he picked the easiest response. "Thanks. And Lauren's fine."

"And Henry?"

"He's eleven and grows about an inch a day." He finished bandaging her knee, then stood and faced her. The parking lot was dark but there was enough light from the nearby road that he could see her cheeks were flushed. A result from her line of questioning? Or had she been affected by his touch? The same way he'd been affected by touching her.

Rusty came back from his cruiser looking like he'd swallowed a hornet. "Um, Allie, did you know your license has been suspended?"

"*What*? No." She laughed nervously. "Run it again, Rusty."

"I already did," he said miserably. "Three times."

"But that's impossible. I'd know if my license was suspended, wouldn't I?"

"Not exactly. Happens all the time. Think back. You get stopped by a cop recently?"

"No—well, I did take a right on a red illegally. But the sign was so out of the way, I mean, really, *anyone* would have been confused. And the cop was just so dang nasty. Not nice, like you would have been, Rusty." Rusty rewarded her flattery with a smile. "I gave him my license but I couldn't find my proof of insurance, but… I mean, I do *have* insurance and I told him that, but he still tacked on another fine. I paid the ticket so everything should be cool. Right?"

"Did you go to the courthouse and show them your insurance papers?" Tom asked.

She pressed her lips into a tight line.

Rusty took off his cap and scratched the top of his head. "There's the problem."

"All right, well, I can take care of that when I get back to Tampa."

Rusty went silent. Tom had a bad feeling he knew exactly where this was going. Allie must have, too, because she laughed again, sounding even more nervous than before. "You're not going to arrest me, are you?"

"No, no, not gonna arrest you. But I can't let you drive, Allie."

"Oh, come on! This is ridiculous. You know me, Rusty. I'm not some criminal."

"Sure, sure, of course not. But I can't bend the rules just because you're the boss's little sister. I'm real sorry, Allie."

Her shoulders slumped in defeat. "It's not your fault, Rusty." She glanced at the VW bug parked in the center of the parking lot. "How am I supposed to move my car if I can't drive?"

"Golly, Allie, I sure would like to help you with that, but with Zeke gone, I'm in charge and I'm the only patrol car on this side of town tonight. Can't let down the citizens of Whispering Bay. They're all counting on me."

"You can move your car in the morning," Tom said.

Rusty nodded his head in agreement. "Good plan." Then he frowned, like he just realized the other part of Allie's predicament. "You're staying at Zeke's tonight, right? I bet Tom wouldn't mind giving you a ride."

"I can walk," she blurted, looking horrified by Rusty's suggestion.

"I'm afraid I can't let you do that," Tom said. Without asking her permission, he went to her car and pulled the suitcase from the backseat. "This all you got?"

The struggle on her face was clear. Walk two miles in the middle of the night or get a ride with him. She might not like him but she wasn't dumb. Without saying another word, Allie Grant locked up her car then climbed into the front seat of his pickup truck.

Chapter Three

THE HORROR OF HER current situation was not lost on her. For the first time in twelve years, Allie was completely alone (as clichéd as it sounded) with The One Who Got Away. Or rather, The One Who *Ran Away,* tossing pieces of her broken heart along the highway.

Okay, so maybe that was a tad bit dramatic.

She watched Tom Donalan out of the corner of her eye. His big hands gripped the steering wheel—strong, and masculine, and…lovely. It was an odd trio of words to describe a man, but there it was. Tom was gorgeous. Always had been. And probably always would be, no matter how much Ben and Jerry's she overdosed on.

Allie forced her attention to the road in front of them. She had no business thinking about his hands. Or any other part of him. He was a Class A jerk. Best not to forget that.

She settled back in the truck's leather seat and tried to relax. *Ten minutes.* If she could spend eight hours on her feet wiping down tables and pretending she loved dishes with the name of Tofu Surprise, she could certainly do ten minutes in a car with Tom Donalan.

Relax. Concentrate. On anything but him.

She discreetly took in her surroundings. The inside of the truck was clean, not fancy or new, but well kept. No empty McDonald's wrappers or beer cans strewn on the floor. A faint hint of *him* lingered in the air. Sniffing things out had always been a talent of hers. Some people remembered faces. Allie remembered smells. *Eau de Tom Donalan* was a mixture of ocean air, soap, and aftershave. Clean and sexy, not too overpowering. In other words, just right.

Growing up, Zeke had grudgingly nicknamed her The Nose. She'd been able to smell Buela's *picadillo* halfway down the block. But a more practical trick had been her ability to sniff out any lingering traces of pot (no matter how much Zeke had tried to mask it). Sibling blackmail had helped finance the ten-speed bicycle she'd used for beach transportation the summer before middle school.

Had she imagined the lemon smell back at the senior center? She didn't think so. But where had it come from?

Tom glanced at her. "So, how are you?"

"Well, let's see. My license is suspended and some twit won't let me spend a few hours in an abandoned building so I can make a living. But other than that, just peachy."

He shifted in his seat. "No, I mean, how have you *been*?"

"You mean, as in the past twelve years?"

He nodded.

"I've been great, Donalan. Really. I mean, other than the night you took a blowtorch to my heart, I've been just *great*. Of course, there was that year I spent in rehab after taking all those pills. But I hardly ever relapse anymore."

He looked mortified.

Or ready to laugh.

She couldn't tell which (or which she preferred). Mortification, she decided. After all, why shouldn't Tom Donalan feel bad for the way he'd dumped her? And a mighty dumping it had been. But she didn't want his pity. Or anything else from him, either.

Correction: She did want something from him. She wanted to spend time inside his precious building.

"Relax. It was just a high school romance. I was over you within two weeks."

He didn't say anything, not that she expected a response, but it felt even more awkward now than before. So she began to babble, because that's what she did whenever she got nervous. And it was hard not to be nervous around the guy she had practically begged to take her virginity. She wished she could say this was an exaggeration, but unfortunately, it wasn't.

Tom, please, just do me.

Had she really said those words to him? *Yep.* She most certainly had. The Night of The Great Humiliation Part One, as she liked to call it. Over the years the sting should have eased some. But it hadn't.

She kept her eyes on the road ahead and told Tom all about her current life back in Tampa. Her part-time job at The Blue Monkey, her roommate, Jen, and her crazy antics, which elicited a laugh from him and startled her into glancing his way. She was shocked to find that the truck was parked in front of her brother's house.

How long had they been here?

It was only a ten-minute drive but she'd managed to talk non-stop. He, on the other hand, hadn't gotten in one word. *Geez.* She'd probably bored him to death.

Only, he didn't look bored. He looked—

"So what about you? Are you happy?"

He broke eye contact. "Happy enough."

Allie waited for him to elaborate, but he didn't. She'd practically spilled out her entire life for him and all she got in return was two words?

Great! She was happy.

He was happy *enough.*

They were good. *Move along, people, there's nothing more to see.*

"I hate to ask again, but is there any way you can postpone the demolition on the building? Just for one more day?"

"I know you think I'm a dick, and I don't blame you. But it's not up to me. We can't build the new rec center until the old building comes down. There's a schedule—"

"And a budget, yeah, yeah, I know." It was like talking to a brick wall. She decided to try another angle. "You must have spent time in the building. Have you ever seen or heard anything strange? Anything that might lead you to think the place might be haunted?"

"Trust me. There's no ghost, Allie."

Trust him?

Strange as it seemed, on this, she did trust him. At least, she believed that *he believed* what he was saying. Funny, even after all these years she could still read his expressions. When he said he knew nothing about a ghost, he meant it.

Which meant there was nothing left for her to do but reach into the back seat of his truck and pull out her overnight bag. Tom got out of the vehicle and opened the door for her. Gentlemanly enough, she supposed, but she also had the feeling he was going to try to walk her to the front door.

"I got this," she said, but he ignored her and kept

walking alongside her anyway. There was probably no use in arguing, so Allie let it slide.

The front porch light snapped on, which meant her sister-in-law knew she was here. Knowing Mimi, she was probably peeking out the window as well. Allie tested the door and found it unlocked, but before she could twist the knob, Tom placed his hand over hers, stopping her cold. "Hold on. I want to say something."

She glanced down at their hands then lifted her gaze to meet his. For the first time tonight, he looked nervous. Oh, this was golden. Tom Donalan was about to apologize for breaking her heart. *Ha! It's just a little too late for that, buddy!*

"I was really sorry about your grandmother," he said quietly. "I wanted to come to the funeral. But under the circumstances, I thought it was best I stayed away."

Allie snatched her hand from his. *He was apologizing for missing Buela's funeral?*

Buela died three days after The Night of the Great Humiliation. Her death had been unexpected. The doctors said it was a heart attack, but it had taken Allie a long time to come to grips with that diagnosis.

A part of her wanted to shove Tom in the chest. To knock him off her brother's front porch. But that was silly. Buela's death hadn't been his fault. Just like she knew it hadn't been hers, either.

In the immortal words of the Beatles, "Ob-La-Di, Ob-La-Da." Life goes on. The lyrics to the song began playing in her head. Quiet and warm and oddly familiar.

Allie frowned.

Where had *that* come from?

Allie had never in her life quoted the Beatles. Either out loud or in her head. She rubbed her arms up and down.

Tom frowned. "You cold?"

"No... I just..."

Weird.

He looked concerned, so she straightened back her shoulders and tried to sound normal.

"No worries about Buela's funeral. That was twelve years ago, and yeah, you were right. It was best you stayed away." Allie didn't think she could have handled seeing Tom at the funeral. And Zeke? He would have punched Tom's lights out. "It's nice that you remembered her, though. After all this time," she added.

Neither of them said anything for a few long seconds. *Oh God.* They were having a *moment.* She didn't expect to ever get an apology from Tom for leading her on that summer after high school. What happened was twelve years ago, for God's sake. She was a grown woman. As much as she wanted to, she couldn't hate Tom Donalan.

"About your car. You'll have to move it before nine. Because—"

"Yeah, I know. The building is coming down. Don't worry. I'll get Mimi to help."

He looked distracted, but he nodded. "So long, Allie. It was really good seeing you again."

Strangely, she realized that a part of her (a very tiny part, maybe) thought it was good to see him again, too.

The Beatles were right. *Life does go on.*

Running into Tom Donalan hadn't been as terrible (or as satisfying) as she'd always envisioned. She hadn't fallen into a puddle at his feet. Or thrown a grenade at his head (another fantasy courtesy of Chunky Monkey).

Maybe this was the closure she'd subconsciously needed all these years.

He walked to his truck and turned around one last time, pausing before he got inside. Like he was trying to memorize what had just happened. Like it was good-bye forever.

Did he think she'd give up that easily?

If he did, then he never really knew her, because despite the fact that she didn't think either one of them was particularly eager for a repeat meeting, Tom Donalan would be seeing her again a lot sooner than he could ever imagine.

Chapter Four

OTHER THAN HER BROTHER, Zeke, and her niece and nephew, Mary Margaret Grant (known to everyone who was anybody as Mimi) was the one person in the world Allie loved best. Mimi had married Zeke at the tender age of eighteen after discovering she was pregnant. Allie was fourteen at the time and although Mimi was only four years older, she'd seemed so sophisticated and beautiful. Mimi had always been incredibly kind to her and there wasn't anything in the world Allie wouldn't do for her sister-in-law.

"Sorry to show up so late." Allie pulled out the pale blue sheets with the faded polka dots from the hall closet and held them up to her nose. Sachet of roses, with a little fabric softener for good measure. She gingerly laid them on the foldout couch in the den.

Mimi picked up a worn-out pillowcase and frowned. "There's a set of new sheets on the top shelf."

"I don't want new sheets. I want these. And in case you're getting any ideas, don't you dare throw these out. They're my favorite."

Mimi yanked on the mattress to smooth down a corner and asked in a deceptively mild voice, "Was that Tom Donalan who dropped you off?"

"You were looking through the window, so you know it was."

"Where's your car? And how on earth did you run into *him* of all people?"

Allie filled Mimi in on everything that had happened since they'd spoken earlier in the evening. Her breaking into the senior center (at which Mimi visibly cringed), her run-in with Tom, and then finally Rusty and the license suspension.

"Zeke will be back in a couple of days. I'm sure he can help you get the license thing straightened out," Mimi said.

"I hope I didn't wake up the kids."

"They're eleven and sixteen. They both probably went to bed with their iPods glued to their ears. Only an act of God could wake them up."

"I still can't believe Claire is sixteen. Makes me feel old," Allie joked.

"Sixteen going on thirty." Mimi pointed to her right temple. "See that? I'm going gray because of that girl."

Allie playfully threw a pillow at her. "You are not!"

Mimi caught the pillow, then laid it across the top of the bed, giving the covers one final tug to smooth them in place. "Wait till you have a teenager of your own."

Mimi was right, Allie observed with a tender eye. Her sister-in-law was sporting a hint of silver at the temples. But other than that, it was hard to believe Mimi was old enough to have a teenage daughter. Despite their somewhat shaky beginning, Mimi and Zeke were the poster couple for marriage with a capital M. Even after sixteen years, they were still crazy about one another, with their two-point-zero kids in a house they had bought twelve years ago and were still renovating. Mimi carted the kids around all day in her eight-year-old minivan while Zeke kept Whispering Bay free from crime. They could be a reality TV show on the perfect family.

Mimi sat on the edge of the bed and patted the space next to her in invitation. "That must have been weird for you. Seeing Tom again after all this time."

Allie avoided Mimi's shrewd gaze. Her sister-in-law was the only person in the world who knew *every* detail of Allie's short-lived romance with Tom Donalan. At times, that had been a blessing. Tonight, it felt more like a curse. There would be no sleep until Mimi was satisfied she knew every second of Tom and Allie's ill-fated reunion.

"It was inevitable we would see each other again one day." Allie knew that after their divorce, Lauren Donalan had returned to Whispering Bay. But she'd had no idea that Tom had followed her. She tried to sound casual. "Did you know Tom was back in town?"

"I ran into him and Henry at the Piggly Wiggly. Henry is the spitting image of him. He and Cameron are in the same grade."

Seeing Tom again had been disorienting enough. What would it be like to run into a kid version of him? Luckily, she wasn't going to be around long enough to find out.

"So what's Lauren up to?" She remembered the look on Tom's face when she'd asked about his ex-wife. He had seemed...conflicted by the question. "Still petite, blonde, and beautiful?"

"Naturally. She just opened up a sixties vintage boutique next door to The Bistro. Very cute."

"Well, good for her. She was always into all that fashion stuff." Although Allie had always thought of Lauren as more Lilly Pulitzer than retro.

Allie began pulling at the edge of her bandage. Why had she let Tom bandage up her knee? He had remembered how she hated the sight of blood. And she had hated the fact that he remembered. Did he remember the reason behind it? Instinctively, she knew he did. She had read it in his eyes.

It was embarrassing to think how a virtual stranger (and that's what they were now—strangers) knew that oh-so-most-personal thing about her. Mimi probably suspected the reason behind Allie's aversion to blood, but they'd never spoken about it. There were only two people alive who knew that story. Zeke, because he'd been there. And Tom, because *she'd told him*.

"Tom and Lauren have been divorced, what, about a year now?" Allie said. "Do you think he regrets it? I mean, do you think he followed her here to win her back? Not that I care or anything, but you have to admit, it's kind of fascinating, in a Dr. Phil kind of way. Man follows ex-wife back to their hometown, blah, blah, blah."

"Fascinating, huh?" Mimi looked as if she wasn't buying it, but nevertheless she continued. "I'm not one to gossip, but in this case, I don't think I'm going to tell you anything you don't already know. All these years everyone thought Lauren and Tom had this solid marriage, but according to Pilar, if it wasn't for Henry, they would have never gotten married to begin with."

Pilar Diaz-Rothman was one of Mimi's closest friends, as well as a member of Mimi's Bunco group, more affectionately known around town as the Bunco Babes. They met every Thursday night to play Bunco, drink margaritas, and gossip. Death or relocation were the only reasons a Babe gave up her spot at the weekly dice game and permanent admission was strictly by group invitation only. Pilar's father, Dr. Diaz, had been their family dentist since forever. Plus, he and his wife were two of the few native-born Cuban-Americans in town, which had made them instant friends with Buela.

Mimi made a face. "Do you think people in town wonder about Zeke and me?"

"Wonder what?"

"If we would have gotten married if I hadn't been pregnant with Claire?"

"Are you serious? Of course you would have gotten married."

"Well, this is a small town and people like to talk about stuff like that."

"What is this? The nineteenth century? Hence, one of the reasons I'm glad I now live in Tampa," Allie muttered.

Mimi didn't look one hundred percent convinced. "So, back to Tom and Lauren. According to Pilar, who heard it from Tom's cousin, Tom thought everything was coming up roses until one day out of the blue Lauren just up and asked him for a divorce. Before he knew what had happened she'd moved herself and Henry back here to Whispering Bay."

Allie let this information sink in. Had Tom really been as clueless about the state of his marriage as Mimi's story painted him? Ha! So he'd been sucker punched. It should have brought a smile to her face. You reap what you sow, and all that. Still, Allie couldn't help but feel a little sorry for him. "And how exactly did that land Tom back in town?" she asked.

Mimi was about to answer when instead she pointed to Allie's leg. "You're bleeding."

Allie quickly glanced down, then away from her scraped-up shin. She must have worked off the bandage during their conversation. She didn't think she'd pulled at it hard enough to dislodge it, though. She gulped. "It's just a scratch."

"Yeah, but I know how you hate the sight of blood." Mimi went to the bathroom and returned with a first aid kit. She made fast work of cleaning up Allie's cut, replacing the bandage Tom had applied with a fresh one. God Bless Mimi. Her maternal instinct was spot on.

"Where was I?" Mimi continued. "Oh yeah, after the divorce Lauren came back here to be near her parents. You know she's a Handy and they all stick together like they were bonded with superglue."

Mimi was a Handy as well through her mother's side. She and Lauren were something like second cousins. A fact Allie was about to remind her sister-in-law of, but she didn't want to interrupt the flow of the story.

"Lauren's daddy set her up in that nice little shop I told you about. And I think Tom was tired of only seeing his son on a long distance basis, so last month he moved back to town."

"And took a job with Pappas-Hernandez Construction," Allie finished.

"You catch on fast." Mimi's gaze softened. "What are you going to do?"

Allie pulled the rubber band from her hair and shook out her ponytail. "Get some sleep, then get up bright and early and try to figure out a way to stop that building from coming down before I get a chance to investigate my story."

"Not about the building, silly! About Tom. He's single now. And you're still single. I've always thought maybe the reason you never found anyone was because you were still kind of hung up on him."

Allie's jaw dropped.

"Well, you have to admit—"

"Tom Donalan is the last man on earth I'd ever go for. That ship sailed a long time ago."

"But—"

"Sailed and sunk. Like the Titanic. Never to be resurrected again." She reached inside her shorts pocket and pulled out the printed copy of the anonymous email. "Right now this is the only thing that interests me. Can you read this and tell me who you think might have written it?"

It was obvious from the look on Mimi's face that she wanted to continue talking about Tom, but Allie tapped the paper to get her attention back on track. Mimi gave in and quickly scanned the contents.

"It sounds kind of formal. Like an older person might have written it," Allie said. "Don't you think?"

Mimi glanced up from the paper. "What makes you say that?"

"The language, I guess. I bet it's one of the Gray Flamingos. Especially since they're the ones who've spent the most time inside the senior center."

The Gray Flamingos were a local senior citizens activist group. They liked to march around town in matching T-shirts and spout off about the rights of the elderly. A very cool group as far as Allie was concerned. If they'd been around when Buela was alive, Allie was sure she would have been a member.

"Mmm…well, maybe," Mimi said. "It says here that this Concerned Citizen tried to contact you directly?"

"Something like that." Allie tried to brush it off but Mimi kept staring at her. "Okay, so yeah, I got a few emails, but honestly? A ghost? Don't tell me you believe that malarkey."

"Malarkey?" Mimi giggled.

"It's a perfectly legitimate word," Allie said. *Dang.* Thirty minutes with Tom Donalan and she was already emulating him.

"If you don't believe in ghosts, then why did you drive all the way up here to investigate this?"

"Because my editor at *Florida!* magazine said so, that's why."

Mimi glanced at the email again. "You have to admit, this is pretty intriguing. And it's sort of clever, don't you think, using this Concerned Citizen moniker?"

"Clever? All that says is that someone is too embarrassed to use their own name. Either that or they're hiding something."

Mimi blinked. "Well, all I can say is that nothing this exciting has happened in Whispering Bay since the big robbery at Black Tie Bunco last year. Maybe when Zeke gets back from his police conference he can help you figure this out."

"Maybe, only I can't wait a couple of days to start working on this. I think I'll start by interviewing everyone who's spent time in the senior center, get their take on what they think. Once word spreads that there's a journalist investigating the story, hopefully Concerned Citizen will make themselves known. As for the building, Tom has pretty much told me in no uncertain terms that it's coming down tomorrow. But if I can get one of the owners of the construction company to—"

"Allie!" Mimi jumped off the bed. "Steve Pappas is the owner of Pappas-Hernandez construction."

"I know. Tom told me. But I'm not sure I can find a way to reach him before nine in the morning, in which case—"

"Steve Pappas," Mimi interrupted again, "just so happens to be married to Kitty Burke. You remember

Kitty, don't you? She's a realtor here in town and her grandmother was very big into the Gray Flamingos."

"She's in your Bunco group, too, right?"

"Yep." Mimi folded the paper and handed it back to her. "First thing in the morning I'll call Kitty and ask her to ask Steve to postpone the demolition. At least for a day or so."

For the first time tonight, Allie began to feel hopeful. "You think she'll do it?"

"Of course she'll do it. What I can't promise is that Steve will be able to hold off on that building, but if Kitty asks him, I just don't see how one more day can make a difference."

"And I won't have to deal with Tom Donalan again." Allie stood and gave her a hug. "You're the best sister-in-law in the world. You know that?"

"Of course I know that." Mimi's eyes softened. "I'm so glad you're home."

"I was just here a few months ago."

"Exactly. Way too long as far as I'm concerned. Do you ever think about moving back? Zeke and the kids would love it. And of course, I'd be over the moon."

There was a wistful tone to Mimi's voice that made Allie pause. In the past, Mimi had hinted about Allie coming back to Whispering Bay, but she'd never been so blatant about it.

Allie chose her words carefully. "It isn't that I wouldn't like to move back here, but there's really not much for me in the way of work. You know?"

"But you're still freelancing, right? Couldn't you do that from anywhere?"

Yes, but she didn't want to tell Mimi that. "I guess Tampa has me a little spoiled. Small town living just isn't my thing anymore. Plus, if I do a good enough job with this haunted building story, maybe Emma can expedite a permanent job at the magazine for me."

Mimi's shoulders slumped. "Life Goal Number Three."

"I promise, I'll try to come home more often," Allie said. And she meant it. So what if Tom Donalan (and his DNA) were running around town? It wasn't as if they'd ever have to cross paths again. At least, not after this thing with the senior center was resolved.

After Mimi went to bed, Allie tried to sleep, but she was too pumped up, so she pulled out her laptop and began an email to Emma at *Florida!* magazine.

Mimi had gotten it right. Allie's Life Goal Number Three was all about stability. But it wasn't just about *any* job. It was about working in an environment in which Allie could grow her journalistic career. Allie freelanced for several periodicals, but *Florida!* magazine was far and beyond her number one choice for a permanent position. It was an award-winning upscale monthly journal that celebrated the beauty of the Florida lifestyle (the magazine's tagline). But the real attraction for Allie was *Florida!*'s editor, Emma Frazier. No one got Allie's writing like Emma did.

Times being what they were, however, the magazine had been in a hiring freeze for the past year. According to Emma, Allie was number one on the list to be hired whenever a full-time position opened, so for now, she was biding her time, writing the best stories she could find. Which would include this ghost story (if someone stubborn wasn't standing in her way).

She sent Emma a brief recap of the night's events, including her plan to try to stop the demolition. Despite the late hour, Emma immediately responded.

Good work. Keep me in the loop.

They emailed back and forth for a few more minutes, and then Allie slipped under the covers and turned off the lights. She was exhausted and strangely exhilarated at the same time. Not to mention just a bit conflicted.

The exhilaration came from being on the brink of getting her story. The confliction? That wasn't too hard to figure out. A ghost story was fluff. Not that there was anything wrong with writing fluff, especially if it had Emma's seal of approval, but it reminded Allie too much of her Perky the Duck story, and *that* had been the real reason she'd blown off Concerned Citizen.

Despite almost seven years of writing stories that dealt with environmental concerns and women's issues, it was that dang duck story that anyone ever remembered.

Ironically, it had started out as an anti-hunting piece, controversial enough for a magazine like *Florida!*, whose reading demographics included a heavily southern male population. But somehow the story had evolved into something lighter. And it was that something that had captured the attention of Emma Frazier, as well as hundreds of other readers who had taken the time to email Allie telling her just how much they loved her article.

So while she was certainly grateful to Perky, she didn't envision herself writing that type of story for the rest of her career. It was like accidentally tripping over a rock and discovering that everyone thought it was the best thing since sliced bread, and now wanted you to continue finding rocks to trip over when what you really wanted was to scale mountains.

The trick was to somehow turn this "haunted" house thing into a credible story that would sell magazines *and* keep her journalistic integrity intact.

She sighed and burrowed further under the covers. She'd need her sleep to deal with whatever happened tomorrow.

Would Tom be upset that she'd gone over his head? Probably. But that wasn't her problem. After all, he was the one who suggested (rather sarcastically) that she go to Steve Pappas in the first place, so she was just taking his advice. The fact that she was going through his wife would hopefully work in Allie's favor.

And if Allie was being honest, there was a tiny part of her that would love to see the look on Tom's face when he found out his precious schedule was being turned over in favor of her story.

Chapter Five

ALLIE FELT THE BED vibrate. Was that an earthquake? Impossible. This was Florida. Hurricanes, yes. Earthquakes, *no*. She opened her eyes to see her niece staring down at her.

"Wake up, Aunt Allie. Mom says she's supposed to take you to get your car this morning." Claire sprang off the mattress with all the enthusiasm that only a sixteen-year-old could muster. "Are you staying till Friday? Because if you are then you can go to the football game and watch me cheer. I'm co-captain this year."

Allie blinked away the sleep in her eyes. Dear God. Her last visit had been Fourth of July weekend. Only three months and Claire had grown at least two inches. And there were now *boobs*. Claire Bear had boobs!

"Who is this evil Victoria's Secret model interrupting my beauty sleep?"

Claire glanced down at her chest with a mixture of awe and pride. "I know! It's like they just grew overnight!"

"That is definitely a gift from your mother's side," Allie muttered. She took a longer look at her niece. Claire wore a tank top and a tiny denim skirt that was way too short for anyone other than a toddler. But then,

Claire Bear was still a little girl. At least, she was in Allie's mind. She'd given her niece the nickname Claire Bear after Allie had babysat her one weekend and Claire had insisted on watching her *Monsters, Inc.* DVD non-stop.

Allie got out of bed and shuffled her way to the bathroom but the door was locked.

"Cameron's in there. The little shit takes all morning to get ready. I think he has a GIRLFRIEND," Claire said loud enough for Cameron to hear through the door.

"Little stinker," Allie said, automatically correcting Claire's use of profanity. Buela had drilled it into Allie that young ladies of good breeding simply did not use four letter words (despite the fact that an occasional *caramba* had been heard from Buela's lips). So Allie had come up with appropriate alternatives, like *Captain Crunch*.

She'd seen the look of amusement on Tom's face when she'd uttered the expression last night. Maybe he thought she was weird. Or maybe he'd remembered her using it before. Whatever. It didn't matter to her what Tom Donalan thought.

Mimi appeared in the hallway looking like a general ready to lead the troops into battle. She pointed to Claire's little denim skirt. "You're not wearing that outfit to school."

"But there isn't time to change."

"Then make time."

"You don't think this skirt is too short, do you, Aunt Allie?" Claire looked at Allie like she was Obi-Wan Kenobi and the fate of the galaxy rested on her shoulders.

She hated to play the adult card, but in this case, Allie had to agree with Mimi. "Kiddo, I haven't had my coffee yet, so, er, please, just listen to your mom."

"Fine!" Claire stomped off to her bedroom.

Yikes. It looked like Claire Bear had gotten hormones along with those boobs. This new parent-teenage dynamic hadn't been in play three months ago. Did things really change that quickly? Allie now understood why Mimi's hair was beginning to gray.

Mimi handed Allie a mug of steaming hot coffee, which Allie gratefully took. "Claire's right about the bathroom. You'll never get in there. Feel free to use mine. But you only have about five minutes."

Allie took a big swig of the java and moaned in ecstasy.

"It's almost seven-thirty," Mimi continued. "And we have lots to do. We need to drop the kids off at school, swing by The Bistro, pick up Kitty, and then head to the senior center to get your car."

"You already talked to Kitty?"

"Yeah, and she talked to Steve. Unfortunately, Steve says that although it's his company, this is Tom Donalan's project and he's the guy in charge. Says he was really lucky to get a guy with Tom's experience to come work for him, so he's not going to undermine him on this. Which means the only person who can stop this demolition is Tom himself."

"*Flippity Flop.*"

"My thoughts exactly. Sorry."

"Thanks anyway for trying." Allie finished her coffee, but it didn't taste nearly as good as it had a few seconds ago.

She'd known the thing with Steve Pappas wasn't a done deal, but she'd thought there was a good chance he'd stop the demolition. At least for a day. Especially since it had been his wife making the request on her behalf. Begrudgingly, she had to admire that Steve had enough respect for Tom not to interfere with his business decisions. She just wasn't sure if that made Steve a good boss or Tom a really valuable employee.

"Did you say Kitty's meeting us at The Bistro?"

"She's going to drive out with us to the senior center to help move your car. Since you can't drive it yourself."

That last part hadn't been said with any rancor, but Allie still cringed at the reminder that her license was suspended. She mentally put that on her list of things to take care of today. Right after she emailed Emma to let her know the ghost story probably wasn't going to pan out.

Allie searched her mind for some way around this demolition thing, but she came up blank. Maybe the story could still be salvaged, but she'd have to be satisfied with interviews and secondhand accounts (if she could find anyone who'd actually seen this ghost, of course). Because there was no way she was going to debase herself and ask Tom Donalan for yet a third time to help her out. *Nope.* Not happening. She'd rather swallow nails.

She quickly got dressed and out to the garage to find Mimi and the kids waiting for her. How had she overslept this morning of all important mornings? She couldn't believe how much Mimi had accomplished, and it was only seven-thirty. The army had nothing over motherhood.

Claire was now wearing a pair of extremely tight jeans but it was still better than the little skirt. Thank God Cameron was still the same pudgy cutie pie with the freckles and wire-rimmed glasses he'd been a few months ago. He was wearing braces now, but it was the only thing different about him.

Allie ruffled the top of his curly head.

"Why are you here?" he asked her.

Claire punched her brother in the shoulder. "That's so rude, you little dweeb. Aunt Allie doesn't need a reason to come visit."

"Did you see that? Mom! She hit me."

"Oh my God. I barely touched you!"

Mimi was completely unfazed by their screeching. "Do you want to drive to school or not?" she asked Claire.

Claire instantly appeared contrite. "Yes, please."

Mimi handed her the keys. "Then behave."

Allie climbed into the minivan's back seat. "Claire's driving?"

"I just got my license last week," Claire said proudly.

Allie mentally winced at the irony that was her life. Her niece, who just yesterday (it seemed) was wearing pigtails and watching *Sesame Street*, could legally drive and had better boobs than her.

Coffee. She needed more coffee.

Mimi strapped herself in the front passenger seat and watched Claire with an eagle eye as she went through the ritual of readjusting the car's mirrors.

Cameron turned to face Allie. "Is Dad gonna throw you in jail?"

Mimi smiled apologetically. "He wanted to know why your car wasn't here so I, *um*, explained your situation."

Allie grinned at her nephew. "Yeah, I'm in trouble, big guy. Think I can throw myself on my brother's mercy?"

Cameron thought this over a second. "Did you ever call him a dweeb when you were growing up?"

Claire eyed Cameron through the rearview mirror. "Shut up or I'll make you sit in front with me."

Cameron's face visibly paled.

"That's enough," Mimi warned.

Claire backed out of the driveway and they took off down the road. Allie gripped the doorknob to keep from getting jostled in her seat. She now understood Cameron's reaction to Claire's threat. But everyone had been a novice driver at one point, right? Claire just needed more practice.

Cameron yakked all the way to his middle school, which was only a five-minute drive. Allie forced him to kiss her good-bye on the cheek, but she didn't have to push too hard. Apparently, eleven was still a sweet age for pre-adolescent boys. She caught a whiff of freshly brushed teeth, Clearasil, and...Old Spice cologne. Claire was right. Cameron had a girlfriend! Scratch the pre-adolescent part. Why was everyone in such a hurry to grow up?

Claire drove on to the high school and parked (rather badly) into a space in the second row of the student section. Allie hadn't been back to Whispering Bay High in ages. There were kids everywhere in the parking lot, rushing to get to class before the first bell. The hair was different and the clothes were definitely different (had Allie ever dressed this hoochie in high school?), but the rest was the same. Bright young faces and pimply chins and lots of laughter and roughhousing.

A vision of Tom and her eating lunch while sitting on the hood of his red Crown Victoria popped into her head. It was the way they'd spent almost every lunch period their senior year.

Claire waved good-bye and disappeared among a gaggle of giggling girls, shaking Allie out of her reverie.

"Okay, first stop, The Bistro," Mimi said, back in control of the wheel.

Chapter Six

THE NICE THING ABOUT growing up in a small town was that things rarely changed. Yes, an occasional strip mall might pop up, or a new seafood joint might give the few restaurants in town some competition, but somehow, Whispering Bay had managed to avoid the fate of most Florida beach towns. With no condos or vacation resorts, it was a sleepy hollow of ten thousand residents, a middle class bedroom community comprised of almost equal parts young families and retirees.

The downside to small town living meant no Starbucks. But that was fine with Allie because Whispering Bay had something better. The Bistro by the Beach, owned by Frida Hampton, another Bunco pal of Mimi's, was a cute little coffee house located just a few miles from the senior center and a major meeting place for the town's citizens. The coffee was strong, the muffins were fresh, and it had a first-rate view of the water. Deputy Rusty was there, along with a dozen or so regulars and the usual handful of tourists from nearby Seaside.

Rusty smirked at Allie in acknowledgement, then gave Mimi a deferential nod. Although cerebrally Allie knew that Zeke was Whispering Bay's Chief of Police, she couldn't help the sudden wave of pride that washed over her. If you'd told her twenty years ago, when she was ten and Zeke was sixteen, that her pot-smoking, juvenile delinquent brother would one day be The Law in this town she would have spit up her Fruit Loops from laughing so hard.

Kitty Burke Pappas met them by the counter. Her brown hair was pulled back in a low ponytail and her makeup was impeccable. She wore an apricot sheath dress that fit her perfectly and complemented her lightly freckled skin. She wasn't a great beauty, but there was something about the way she carried herself that made Allie feel like a total slouch next to her. She wished she'd had more than five minutes to pull herself together this morning.

Allie ordered the biggest café latte on the menu. "Thanks for talking to your husband for me. Even though it didn't work out, I really appreciate it."

"I can't believe Steve is being so stubborn." Kitty shook her head. "*Men*," she said in a way that made Allie smile. "But we're not done yet. I want you to meet some friends of mine that might be able to help." She led Allie to a table in the back of the restaurant where four seniors were in the middle of a lively discussion. Allie immediately recognized one of the women as Buela's old friend, Viola Pantini.

There were three types of senior citizens living in Florida. There were the natives, those born and bred Floridians who'd lived here all their lives. The snowbirds who came from up north for the winter to avoid the cold. And the retirees, those who decided to live out their golden years in the Sunshine state.

Viola was a native. Kitty reached out and placed a hand on the older lady's arm in a gesture of affection.

"Allie, I'd like you to meet the executive board of the Gray Flamingos."

"Executive *flock*," corrected a woman wearing a visor with a Tampa Bay Rays logo. Her accent, however, hinted at a previous Boston Red Sox affiliation. Definitely not a native.

Viola stood and hugged Allie. "Sweetie! I haven't seen you in ages. You look fabulous! How's the writing going?" She turned to the other members of the table and went through a swift round of introductions. "Allie was Barbara Alvarez's granddaughter. *She's* the one who wrote the Perky the Duck article."

The table erupted in murmurs of appreciation.

"I *love* that article," said the woman with the Rays visor, whose name was Betty. "How is Perky, anyway?"

Allie plastered the well-worn smile she used whenever Perky came up in a conversation. "Thank you, and Perky is still alive and well and living at the Tallahassee Junior Museum."

Betty nodded. "Good to hear." She looked Allie up and down. "So, you're the chief's sister, huh?" She let out a predatory growl. "Good-looking man, if you ask me."

Okay, that was definitely weird.

"Uh, yep, Zeke's my older brother." Not sure what else to say, Allie turned to an attractive older man who'd been introduced as Gus Pappas. "Any relation to Steve Pappas?"

"My nephew. But I don't hold much influence over his business decisions. If Kitty here can't convince him to let you investigate that old building, then no one can."

"Yes, apparently the whole thing is up to his grumpy foreman," Allie said.

Gus smiled sympathetically. "We heard you got kicked out of the senior center last night."

"*What*? How did you hear that?"

"Got one of those police scanners," said the last member of the table, a gentleman with an impressive set of eyebrows who'd been introduced as Roger Van Cleave. "Also heard how your license was suspended." He tsked. "Same thing happened to my grandniece. Of course, she's barely eighteen and doesn't know any better."

Allie smiled weakly.

"Kitty called me this morning and said you had an urgent situation," Viola said, her blue eyes curious. "So I called an emergency meeting of the flock."

Allie reached into her tote and pulled out a copy of the email from Concerned Citizen, then passed it around the table. "Do any of you know who might have written this?"

All four seniors began talking at once.

"A ghost?" Betty said. "*That's* why you broke into the building?"

"Who's this Concerned Citizen?" Gus asked.

"That's the million dollar question," Allie said.

Viola frowned. "You really have no idea who wrote this?"

"I was kind of hoping one of you would know."

"If it had been someone from our group, I'm sure the rest of us would have heard about it," Viola said. "There's about fifty of us active Flamingos, but honestly, I just don't see any of us writing this anonymously."

Roger glanced around the restaurant. "Who else have you shown this to?" he asked in a hushed voice.

"Just the four of you, and my sister-in-law, Mimi. And Rusty Newton and Tom Donalan, who's in *charge of the building*." Allie used her fingers to make air quotation marks on that last part.

"It's imperative that you don't show this to anyone else," Roger warned.

"What do you care who she shows this to?" Gus asked Roger.

"Roger's right," Betty said. "We shouldn't show this to anyone. This ghost is probably trying to warn us and we don't want to start a panic in town."

"What kind of panic?" Allie asked.

Betty looked at her as if she were an idiot. "Ever hear of the end of the world?"

Viola and Gus moaned.

"Betty, *enough* with the end of the world stuff," Gus said.

"Just because the Aztec calendar thing didn't pan out doesn't mean the world isn't coming to an end soon. If there's a ghost haunting the senior center then it's someone we all knew. Someone who's trying to come back from the dead to tell us something. Now, I ask you, what's so important to come back to warn people about *except* the end of the world? All I can say is that if the apocalypse is around the corner then I need to know pronto."

"Betty Jean Collins, you already have a garage full of generators and enough bottled water for the entire town! What more do you need?" Viola asked.

"*That* was in preparation for this year's hurricane season. Which didn't go the way those forecasters thought it would. We barely got enough rainfall this past summer, and hardly any high winds. Hell, my electricity didn't even go out once."

"You sound disappointed we didn't have a major disaster," Gus said.

"Of course I'm not disappointed," Betty grumbled. "But a dozen generators and a few hundred cases of bottled water aren't going to be nearly enough if the apocalypse is coming. Don't want to get caught with my pants down."

"Yeah, nobody wants to see that," Roger muttered.

Allie tried to hide her smile. She should probably keep her mouth shut, but she couldn't help herself. "Um, if the world is going to end, then what does it matter?"

Betty threw her arms up in the air. "That's the problem with your generation! Always flying by the seat of your pants. If the world is coming to an end, I need to be ready."

"If the world is coming to an end, then I need to go to Confession," Gus said. He caught Allie's gaze and winked.

She giggled, but Betty scowled, so Allie quickly wiped her expression clean.

Viola leaned over and whispered in her ear, "If you haven't figured it out by now, Betty Jean is one of those preppers."

"How can we help?" Gus asked, making Allie smile at him in gratitude. Talking about the end of the world was all good and fine, but she had business to take care of.

"Have any of you ever seen or heard anything strange while in the senior center? Anything that would make you think it was haunted?"

"The building's been closed up since summer," Viola said. "Up to then I'm probably the one who's spent the most time there. I used to teach seniors yoga, you know," she added proudly, "but I never came across anything strange."

Sigh. This wasn't the news Allie had hoped to hear.

"Can I ask a favor then? Would you hold on to this copy of the email and pass it around to the rest of your group? Maybe one of them might have heard something and just didn't think it was important enough to share."

Betty and Roger began to protest, but Viola silenced them. "How are we going to help Allie solve this mystery if we keep this letter to ourselves?" She turned to Allie, all business-like. "Send me the original email and I'll forward it on. We communicate strictly through email or texting. It's much faster that way."

"Oh, yeah, of course." Now why hadn't she thought of that? Allie pulled out her smartphone and forwarded the letter to the address Viola had given her.

"Got it!" Viola's thumbs flew through her phone's tiny keypad. A few seconds later, the rest of the group's phones began pinging. She winked at Allie. "Just because we're retired doesn't mean we're technically challenged. If I hear anything from one of the Flamingos, I'll send you a text."

Mimi walked up to the table. "Sorry to interrupt, but I've got to get Allie to her car before it gets demolished by a wrecking ball."

Allie thanked them and said her good-byes. Hopefully, with any luck, one of the Gray Flamingos would know who had sent the email. She stepped outside to get in the van, when her gaze zeroed in on the shop next door to The Bistro, causing her to come to a halt. This had to be Lauren Donalan's retro shop.

A sign made of whitewashed driftwood stenciled in bright pink and lime green letters highlighted the store's name, Can Buy Me Love (Lilly Pulitzer meets The Beatles!). She took a few seconds to peer through the glass window. A trio of mannequins dressed like something out of a Partridge Family nightmare formed the store's front-end display.

Once again, Allie was struck by how odd it seemed that Lauren would own this kind of place. But then, she really hadn't known the former Mrs. Tom Donalan all that well in high school.

She was about to step inside the van when Roger Van Cleave dashed out the door. He discreetly slipped her a piece of paper. "Didn't want to give you this in front of the others, but call that number. I promise; you *won't* be sorry."

He disappeared back inside the restaurant before Allie could think of a response. She climbed into the back seat of the minivan and stared down at the scribbled number. *Good Grief.* Was Eyebrows making a move on her?

"What did sweet old Mr. Van Cleave want?" Mimi asked.

"I think he just hit on me."

Mimi met her gaze in the rearview mirror. "Seriously?"

Kitty turned around to face her and said gravely, "You'll have to let him down gently. He's very fragile. His wife passed away last year." Allie wished she knew Kitty well enough to know if she was joking. The twinkle in her brown eyes said she was.

"Okay, so he's probably not hitting on me," Allie said, feeling foolish.

Mimi and Kitty laughed, and then Mimi put the car in motion.

"Mr. Van Cleave is a cool old guy," Kitty said. "You should call him. He used to be a journalist, or something. Maybe he has some advice for you on your article."

The last thing Allie needed was tips from some wannabe news reporter. If Roger Van Cleave didn't have any direct knowledge about the ghost, then Allie wasn't sure how he could help her, but she slipped the paper into her purse anyway. She'd call him later, just to be polite.

Mimi and Kitty began gabbing about their Bunco group, which gave Allie an opportunity to check her cell phone for messages.

There was a text from Emma. ***How's the story going?***

Not so good. Allie responded.

Her cell phone broke out into Adele. Allie sighed. She was really going to have to change her ring tone to something more upbeat.

"What do you mean not so good?" Emma said before Allie could even say hello.

Best to get the bad news over with pronto.

"The senior center is definitely being demolished this morning." Allie went on to explain how Steve Pappas had refused to intervene on her behalf. "I can still resurrect the piece," she said, trying to sound professional and optimistic. "I plan to interview all the locals. It'll come together, I swear."

"Oh, I know you'll make it work. You always do. It's just, the story would have so much more *pizazz* with the whole spending the night in the haunted house angle. Are you sure you still can't swing it? Because I think you need to know that I've just got the go ahead from Ben to hire another full-time writer." Ben Gallagher was Emma's boss and the publisher for *Florida*! magazine. This was the break Allie had been waiting for.

"That's great!" Allie's enthusiasm was met with silence. "Um, isn't it?"

"You're definitely my number one candidate, but Ben... Well, he thinks to be fair we need to post the job, do interviews, that kind of stuff. He wants the candidates to submit three articles of their choice to an editorial committee. I was thinking you would include your Perky the Duck article, which *everyone* loves, and of course, the follow-up story on the BP oil spill, which is a lot meatier and more serious and a really well-written piece."

Allie let Emma's words sink in.

It made sense that Ben wanted to post the job. There was probably some kind of company HR policy on that, but still. She really thought the next opening at *Florida!* was hers, no questions asked. In retrospect, that had been naïve of her. Nothing in this world was guaranteed. Especially a rare job with a sought-out publication. Allie tried her hardest to squelch her disappointment. "And you think this ghost story would be a good third piece?"

"Well, here's the catch. He wants the third piece to be an original. Something never published before. I think if you can take this story to the next level it would be perfect."

The next level?

"Do you know who my competition might be?"

There was a long pause that made Allie's throat go dry.

"I'm not going to lie to you. Chris Dougal is looking for a full-time job and he's working on this big illegal immigration piece. Its effect on the Florida economy, that kind of stuff."

In other words, *serious* stuff. The kind of stuff Ben loved. If it sold magazines, that is. Ben Gallagher was all about the bottom line. Chris Dougal had written several books on Florida politics. Boring stuff, to be sure. Stuff that didn't sell so well, but he had the kind of credentials that gave Ben an editorial hard-on. If Chris could write a story that would interest their readers enough to buy magazines then Allie was toast. *Burned*. To a crackly crunch.

She now knew exactly what Emma meant by the next level. This ghost story needed to be the best thing she'd ever written. Even better than the Perky the Duck story, which seemed near to impossible. Chasing this bogus ghost story to please Emma Frazier was one thing, but having her career ride on it was something altogether different.

"Here's the thing, I can find another story to write. As a matter of fact, before you sent me that anonymous email I was doing research for a piece on the history of St. Augustine, and I think—"

Emma moaned. "St. Augustine has already been done. One too many times as far as I'm concerned. No, I really think this ghost story is so *you*. And the magazine has never done anything like it before, so it will be fresh."

"But—"

"I guarantee you," Emma continued, "if you can take this ghost story and wring the emotion out of it—get it to really zing—then I'm positive I can swing Ben to your side."

Allie had no choice. If she wanted to elevate this story to the next level, to make it *zing*, as Emma said, she was going to have to make this story personal. Which meant she was going to have to experience this "ghost" for herself. Which meant she needed to keep this building from coming down. Which meant... She was going to have to throw herself at the mercy of The Person In Charge. Who, number one, didn't believe in ghosts, number two, was on a schedule, and number three, was the last person on earth Allie wanted to ask for a favor.

She didn't get it. She was a good person. She smiled at strangers, didn't cheat on her taxes, and recycled religiously. So how could fate be this cruel? In all her Tom Donalan fantasies, *he* was the one begging her for something. Not the other way around.

Chapter Seven

TWELVE YEARS AGO, FOR one glorious summer, Tom Donalan had been Allie's first boyfriend. Her first love. Her first...everything. Although technically, he was never her first lover because they never actually "did it." It was not, however, for her lack of trying.

She'd wanted in Tom Donalan's pants. Badly.

Not that she'd been one of those girls. Just the opposite. At eighteen, Allie had been a complete dork. She'd been on the volleyball team and the swim team and a pretty decent student but she'd never been one of the popular girls. She'd never even kissed a guy before Tom, unless you counted playing spin the bottle at Julie Howard's end-of-the-year eighth grade party.

Tom, on the other hand, had been the kind of guy every girl dreamed of when she imagined her first big love. Handsome, smart, funny, kind. By senior year, he'd been practically a Whispering Bay High legend. There wasn't anything he couldn't do better than anyone else. Star quarterback, starting pitcher for the baseball team, senior class president, Merit Scholar. All the guys wanted to be him. And all the girls wanted to be with him.

When he'd singled Allie out that first week of AP

chemistry as his lab partner, she'd been flattered. And nervous and flustered. But they had quickly become genuine friends. Tom was the only other person Allie knew who loved *Star Wars* as much as she did. Even Buela adored him, and Buela wasn't the type of woman who'd been easily fooled.

Then, one day out of the blue, something spectacular happened. Tom's steady girlfriend, Lauren Handy, broke up with him.

Lauren Handy had been the female version of Tom. With long blonde hair, terrific boobs, and a tight butt, she had most of the male population of Whispering Bay High salivating after her. And the crappy thing was, she was nice. So you couldn't even hate her. They were the dream couple (gag). They were supposed to be Prom King and Queen. But the day after the senior awards banquet, a mere week before prom, Lauren dumped Tom cold.

Allie had spun by his house the instant she'd heard the news, ready to console him with her best friend shtick, which in those days consisted of a swiped six-pack of beer from Zeke's refrigerator and a shoulder to lean on.

But instead of being upset, Tom was relieved (or so he had said). They then proceeded to watch the full *Star Wars* trilogy on his parents' brand new DVD player and down the beers (and no, Tom's parents weren't home). Sometime after the second beer, Tom asked Allie to be his prom date.

Her! Allison Isabel Grant, the too-tall girl with no boobs, was going to prom with Tom Donalan, the guy every girl in their senior class dreamed of. It was almost too good to be true. Which should have been her First Big Clue.

So Tom and Allie went to prom, a night that ended in

her first real kiss. Which then led to an entire summer where they were joined at the hips, or the lips, or whatever other body part they had pressed against one another. When they weren't working at their summer jobs trying to save money for college, they were at the beach, or at his parents' house watching movies, or finding places to go make out.

Their favorite make-out spot had been the back seat of Tom's nineteen eighty-seven Crown Victoria, which they'd park along the end of the bay bridge. But just about any place they could be alone would do. It was during one of those make-out sessions that The Great Humiliation Part One happened.

They were naked, all alone in an empty house, huddled beneath the covers of Tom's too-small twin-sized bed. Allie was trying to be quiet (just in case his parents came home unexpectedly), but it was impossible. Tom's fingers were nestled between her thighs, doing something Allie had never even *thought* of on her own. Where had he learned to do that?

"Don't stop," Allie moaned. The words were no sooner out of her mouth that she realized she didn't want him to stop at all. As in, she wanted him to take the next step. As in, the *big* step. "Tom, please, just do me."

Oh. My. God. Did she say that out loud?

He laughed, but it sounded strained. "Allie, I don't think you mean that."

Yep. She'd said it out loud. But she wasn't embarrassed.

She sat up, taking the covers with her. "I do mean it. I...I love you, Tom."

He looked startled.

She gulped. Should she not have it said it first?

Then he grinned, and a wave of relief washed over her. Of course he loved her. He just wasn't ready to say it yet. He sat up and tucked a long stand of hair behind her ear, then leaned down to gently kiss her. "You make me crazy. You know that, right?" he whispered against her mouth.

Her mind immediately jumped to Lauren, Tom's-ex. She shouldn't compare herself to anyone else, but it was hard not to wonder what exactly had gone down between them. They'd dated almost a year. Had he said those same words to her, as well?

Allie tried not to think about anything other than the two of them. If he wanted Lauren, then he'd have tried to win her back. But he hadn't tried. *Not one little bit.* "Not as crazy as you make me," she whispered back. She glanced over at his nightstand.

He followed her gaze and shook his head. "I don't have any condoms."

She sighed. What eighteen-year-old boy given the proverbial green light refused sex? Tom Donalan. Mr. Responsible, that's who. Allie should be grateful he wasn't reckless enough to engage in intercourse without protection. It was just... She mentally shook her head. Didn't he want her as much as she wanted him?

He jumped up from the bed, and Allie couldn't help but sit back and enjoy the view. Six foot three, and all those lovely muscles. Allie hadn't fallen in love with Tom because of his looks, though. Initially, yes, she'd been attracted to him for all the usual reasons, but it went far beyond that. He was the one person in the world she felt comfortable saying anything to, and the only person in the world who knew what happened the day her mother died. Allie had never been able to talk to anyone about it. Not grief counselors, not even Buela. But Tom? There was something so natural about their relationship. It was like there was this *thing* between them that didn't exist with anyone else.

He began pulling his clothes back on. "My parents should be home any minute," he warned.

"I thought church lasted till at least nine. Doesn't your dad believe in long sermons?"

"It's a meet and greet, not a service," Tom said.

"Well, I wouldn't want the Reverend Donalan's son to be found in a compromising position," she joked. Reluctantly, Allie began pulling her clothes back on as well.

He playfully swatted her on her ass then pulled her against his chest. "Were you serious?"

"About…going all the way?" She nodded.

"I don't want to rush you," he said.

"We've been going out for three months now. Besides…" She let her next words drift off. She was going to say she loved him again. But she didn't want to put him in a position where he said it just because she'd said it.

He cupped her chin with his fingers and stared down into her eyes. "I'm not very good at this. But… I've never felt about anyone the way I do about you. You know that, right?"

It was as if the sun had knocked down the walls to his bedroom and was shining down on top of them. They were all the words Allie needed to hear. She shamelessly rubbed herself against him, making him go hard.

He groaned. "Allie, are you sure?"

"Positive. And…we could use Zeke's house. He and Mimi are taking Claire to Disney World tomorrow, so their house will be empty. And guess who has a key?"

"I don't get off work till after eight."

"I'll meet you there at nine," she said.

He slowly nodded, then smiled. "Sounds like a plan."

She smiled back. "Bring a condom. No wait, on second thought, bring two."

On his nights off from the police force, Zeke worked security at The Harbor House, Whispering Bay's fanciest restaurant. That connection had helped Allie land a summer job bussing tables. In exactly two weeks, she'd be moving into her dorm at Florida State. The money she'd made this summer would help offset some of her living expenses. Eight more shifts and she'd be done here. Eight more hours and she'd be in the process of losing her virginity.

Was Tom a virgin, too? Allie had never asked him and he had never volunteered the information. But considering his only real girlfriend before her had been Lauren Handy (little Ms. Perfect who never once colored outside the lines) then the answer to that was probably a resounding *yes*.

During her lunch break, Allie drove into Destin and stopped by the Target store. She picked out the sexiest pair of white panties she could find, and tried not blush when the cashier rang them up. On her way out of the store, she decided to call Tom at his job.

"Ace Hardware," answered Dell, Tom's boss.

"Hey, Mr. Kutchens, it's Allie Grant. Is Tom available?"

"Well, hey there, Allie. Sorry, hon, but Tom called in sick today."

"Oh, okay, sorry to bother you."

She immediately called Tom's house. His mother answered. Geez! Talk about embarrassing. Allie hoped there was nothing in her voice that would make Betsy Donalan suspicious. "Hi, Mrs. Donalan, it's Allie. Is Tom all right?"

"Allie?" she said it like Allie was the last person on Earth she'd expect to be calling. Considering that Allie had been dating her son all summer… Okay. His mother was definitely acting weird. *Oh God*. Allie hoped she hadn't found the condoms Tom was supposed to buy for tonight. "Um, how are you, dear?"

Whew. That was more normal. "Oh, I'm great."

"Tom is… He's not able to come to the phone right now."

"Can you please tell him I called? And that I hope he's feeling all right."

Allie drove back to work and finished the rest of her shift. By eight, she still hadn't heard from Tom, which was definitely not like him. Maybe he was so sick he couldn't even come to the phone. Should she drive by his house? It seemed like the logical thing to do. But when she rang the doorbell, no one answered. Allie could hear Brandy, the Donalans' beagle, barking from the back of the house. She rang the bell a second time, just for good measure, then got back in her car.

Her only option was to go back home. Or she could go to Zeke's and wait. Just in case. So she drove to her brother's and let herself in with the spare key he had given her. She tried not to feel guilty, but she knew Zeke wouldn't be thrilled to know that his baby sister was planning on using his house as her own personal love shack.

An hour went by and no Tom. Confused (and more than just a little worried), Allie went to lock up, when the house phone rang. She checked the caller I.D. It was Tom!

"Oh, thank God! What's going on? Are you okay?" she said, rushing through all the words.

"I'm okay," he said, but he sounded even weirder than his mother had this afternoon.

"I went by your house but there was no one there. I was afraid they had to take you to the hospital."

"Allie...can you meet me by the bridge?"

"Now?"

"Yeah, there's something really important I have to tell you."

"Okay, I can be there in ten minutes." She locked up the house and jumped in her car. The bridge was their favorite parking spot. The place where he'd shown her his acceptance letter to the University of Florida. Where they'd shared almost everything about each other. But why meet her there now?

Allie's hands began to tremble. She gripped the steering wheel and tried her hardest to drive within the speed limit, but she was nearly giddy with anticipation. There could only be one reason Tom had canceled their date to meet her at the bridge. It was the perfect place to tell her that he loved her, too!

It was dark, but she could still make out his car overlooking the water. She parked her car next to his and ran out to hug him. "I was so freaked out when I heard you were sick!"

He held onto her tightly. Too tightly.

"Um, Tom, you're kind of squishing me here." She disentangled herself from his arms and looked him over. His eyes looked hollow and there was a strange expression on his face that made Allie's heart leap to her throat. "Oh, God, you *are* sick. Should you be out? Shouldn't you be—"

"Allie, I'm getting married."

Her heart came sliding back into her chest as she laughed with relief. "Okay, so that's kind of funny, but—"

He caught her hand. "I'm serious. Lauren's pregnant...and I'm the father, and..." He shrugged.

Her heart shifted around again. Only this time it began to fall south. "This is a joke, right? I mean, you do know you have to have *sex* to get pregnant."

He wouldn't look her in the eye. "I'm sorry, Allie. I'm so damn sorry, but...I have to do the right thing here." His voice cracked.

She knew Tom too well not to know that he was completely one hundred percent telling the truth.

"The right thing? Are you friggin' kidding me?" Allie pulled her hand from his grasp. She began pacing the grassy strip next to the water. This didn't make any sense! She stopped and whirled around to face him. "How far along is she?"

"Four months." He looked so miserable that Allie wanted to put her arms around him and tell him everything would be okay. But it wasn't going to be okay. It was never going to be okay again.

Tears welled in her eyes. "Do you love her?"

He hesitated, then for the first time tonight, met her gaze square on. "A part of me does."

"A *part* of you? Let me guess which part. Captain Fucking Crunch, that's just peachy."

He flinched. "I don't blame you for hating me."

Hate him? She didn't hate him. She... *Oh, God.* When she thought about all the things she'd let him do to her. And all the things she'd *wanted* him to do her. Her face felt like it was on fire. How could she have been so stupid? He was getting married because he'd knocked up Lauren Handy. If the whole thing wasn't so ridiculous, she would have laughed.

Anger oozed like a river of lava through every vein in her body. She wanted to yell at him. To tell him to go fuck off. But somewhere beneath it all, she could hear Buela's voice telling her to hold on to her pride.

She straightened back her shoulders. She wasn't going to ask for any more explanations. And really, what more explanation did she need? He hadn't wanted to sleep with her, but he had no problem screwing perfect little Lauren.

"Congratulations, Tom." He started toward her but Allie put up her hand to ward him off, stopping him dead in his tracks. "No really, have a great life. Maybe I'll see you around sometime."

They arrived at the senior center. Mimi parked her van along the side of the road. The parking lot was abuzz with activity. There were all kinds of big machines and lots of men in hard hats milling about, but it was still easy to spot Tom. He had an air of authority about him that made him stand out.

Allie weaved her way through the parking lot teaming with construction workers.

"Lady!" yelled a guy in a hard hat. "You can't be here. We're about to tear down a building."

"Yeah, yeah, I know, but that's my car right there." She pointed to the VW bug parked in the middle of the lot.

He looked her up and down. "So you're the Flaky Biscuit who broke into the building last night. Boss says I'm supposed to bring you to him when you show up."

Flaky Biscuit?

Was that Tom's terminology or Hard Hat's?

She took a deep breath of the crisp gulf air and tried to stay calm.

You can do this, Allie. Part Three of her Life Plan depended on it.

Hard Hat escorted her to Tom, who was busy talking on the phone. In the bright sunshine, Tom's eyes looked impossibly blue. He wore snug bleached out jeans, a black T-shirt that stretched over his broad shoulders, and ankle-high, steel-toe boots. He couldn't have looked yummier, even in a tux.

She might be a flaky biscuit, but she had to admit begrudgingly Tom was definitely what she'd call a *tasty* biscuit. If you liked tall, handsome, and ridiculously stubborn. Which, thank God, she was immune to in his case.

Tom slipped his phone in the back pocket of his jeans then picked up a clipboard from a nearby makeshift table. "Thanks for coming early."

"Sure, no problem. I've got Kitty Pappas and my sister-in-law here to help me move my car."

"Great. I appreciate that." Tom didn't react to the mention of Kitty's name, but Allie had to wonder what he thought about the fact that his boss's wife was here. Or if he even knew that Kitty had tried to intervene on Allie's behalf by going above his head.

She couldn't help but think for the umpteenth time how much simpler all this would be if Steve Pappas had just shut things down for one day. But nothing in life worth having was easy.

Tom glanced down at his clipboard, effectively dismissing her.

Okay, she got it. He was a very important person and he had work to do.

But so did she.

A trickle of perspiration ran down her spine. She didn't have to do this. There had to be *some* other way to get this story. Unfortunately, she just couldn't think of one right now.

A vision of Chris Dougal sitting at his desk typing away at his big illegal immigration piece jumped into her head. Allie couldn't begin to imagine what he did to research that but she wouldn't put it past him to have gone undercover, big show-off that he was. Ben was probably salivating at *Florida*! headquarters, waiting for Chris's article to come across his desk. Despite Emma's support, Allie's little ghost story didn't stand a chance. Especially since there was no such thing as ghosts.

Maybe she could drive to Tallahassee and do a follow-up on Perky. She could see the byline now. *Perky the Duck, Three Years Later...*

It sounded pathetic. But what where her choices? Too bad there wasn't some manatee trapped in a reef somewhere. Or a flock of endangered pelicans or some sick sea turtles to write about. Or better yet, a dolphin in trouble. People loved dolphin stories. Especially if it had a happy ending.

But no. Emma wanted a ghost story. And Emma was her chief supporter at *Florida*! so this was a no-brainer. Her only other option was to bow out of the competition gracefully. But Allie had wanted this job at *Florida*! for so long and just giving up was unthinkable. She'd been stuck in the middle of Life Goal Number Two for far too long now.

She swallowed past the lump of pride swelling her throat. "Tom, do you think, maybe, I could have a word with you?"

Hard Hat raised a brow and made a great big gurgling

noise like he was about to spit out tobacco or something, which Allie certainly hoped was not going to happen. Her stomach felt queasy enough already. "We need to get going, Boss. The guys have already had their morning coffee."

Tom frowned, although she couldn't tell if his displeasure was meant for Hard Hat or her. Probably her. "I'm busy, Allie. Can this wait till later?"

"I just need a minute. But it definitely can't wait until later."

Tom glanced at his wristwatch. "Okay, you got one minute." He handed the clipboard off to Hard Hat. "Do me a favor, Keith, tell the guys to be ready. I'll meet you in front of the building as soon as I'm finished here."

He placed his hand on her elbow and led her to the edge of a trailer where they were essentially hidden from the rest of the parking lot's occupants. "What did you want to talk about?"

She tried to think of something compelling, something that would convince him that delaying the teardown on the building was in everyone's best interests, but all that came out was, "Kitty asked Steve to delay the demolition, but he says it's all up to *you*. I know I'm asking a huge favor here, because this is your job and you're on a tight schedule. I get that. I really do. But all I need is one night. Just one more day so that I can spend tonight in the building and write my story."

"Allie—"

"Don't say no. Because I really need this. And because…because you owe me."

She blinked.

Then he blinked.

And then no one said anything.

Because you owe me. Talk about hitting an all-time low!

The trickle of perspiration running down her back was now a river. It was barely eight-thirty and already humid, but nowhere near hot enough for her to be sweating like this.

She followed Tom's gaze to all the waiting men, at the big machines primed and ready to tear down the building. What she was asking was not only impossible, it was impractical. Expensive. And crazy. She was asking him to put his job on the line. And for what? For a girl he knew back in high school. A girl he'd used as a rebound fling. A girl he hadn't seen or talked to or probably even thought about in over twelve years.

He was going to laugh in her face and say no. And Allie couldn't blame him.

"You know, I wouldn't ask for your help if I didn't need it." Those words wouldn't change anything, but at least it allowed her to save a bit of pride.

He frowned and shook his head. "What did you just say?"

Great. He was going to make this even harder for her.

"You heard me, Donalan. I need your help here."

Instead of answering, he turned and shouted to a nearby group of workers, "Hey! Turn down the radio."

The men all stared back with blank expressions.

Okay, that was a little freaky.

"What are you talking about? There's no radio," Allie said.

He whipped around. "What do you mean? You don't hear the music?"

"What music?"

He closed his eyes for a second and shook his head as

if to clear his thoughts. "Did you just say you need my...*help*?"

She frowned. Tom wasn't faking this clueless routine. There had been a time when Allie could have read his mind; they'd been that close. It might have been over a decade since she'd last seen him but no one changed that much. Maybe after all these years of working construction sites he'd gotten hit on the head one too many times by a rogue ply board.

"Are you okay?" she asked.

There were dark smudges under his eyes like he hadn't slept well. What had he said last night? That he'd been "patrolling" the senior center?

He took off his hard hat and squinted up into the sun as if searching for something.

"Donalan, you're kind of scaring me here. You look tired. Maybe you should go lie down."

This seemed to pull him out of whatever trance he was in. "I'm fine."

He didn't seem fine, but he also seemed irritated by her questioning. "All right, so are you going to help me or not?"

"Okay, okay." He threw up his hands in surrender. "You win. I'll give you twenty-four hours."

"You mean it?"

"Sure I mean it." He glanced around apprehensively. After a few seconds, he let out a big breath and muttered, "Thank God."

Allie wasn't sure what God had to do with it. Or what had just happened. Not that she was complaining, but this sudden reversal of his seemed almost too good to be true.

"Twenty-four hours," Allie repeated, wanting to make sure she'd heard him right. Because honestly?

Tom still looked a little disoriented. "This building is staying intact for the next twenty-four hours. You promise?"

"Yeah," he said. "But you have to promise me something in return."

Was he serious? She'd promise him just about anything right now. Well, almost anything. "Name it."

"This is it. No matter what happens. Ghost or no ghost, and I can pretty much guarantee it's going to be no ghost, but one more day, that's all the time I can give you because tomorrow the building comes down."

"Sure, sure! I promise. No more delays. Twenty-four hours, that's all the time I need. I'll even toss the first wrecking ball myself," she said, giddy with relief. "So, I can go in the building now?"

"Not now," he said, looking more like the old Tom. In control again. "I can't let you in the building unsupervised and if I'm going to call off this demolition then I've got to get this crew off to another work site."

Yikes. Was she putting all these men out of work for the day? Her Catholic guilt tried hard not to think about that. "All these workers? They're still going to get paid, right?"

"Would it matter if they weren't?" Before she could answer, he said, "We have a project going on in Mexico Beach that's short of workers. If I can get the crew out there in time then no one will lose a work day." He stared at her hard. "You can get in tonight at eight. Not a second before."

"Works for me," she said, trying to sound humble. Because despite the fact that she'd hated asking him, she was grateful that he'd capitulated. She should be ecstatic. Except... "Can I ask you a question? What made you change your mind?"

For a long time Allie didn't think he'd answer. Then he did this twitchy thing with the corner of his mouth that she'd seen him do once, twelve years ago, when he'd lied to his mother about where they were going. "You're right. I owe you."

Chapter Eight

KITTY DROVE ALLIE'S CAR, while Mimi followed them in her minivan. The plan was to then drive Kitty back to The Bistro so she could get her own car. All this brouhaha because Allie couldn't be bothered to read the back of a traffic citation. She was embarrassed by all the trouble she'd caused, but she was more stunned by what had just happened back at the senior center.

Apparently, so was Kitty. "I can't believe Tom postponed the demolition. I mean, that's great for you and all, but I really got the impression... Why do you think he did it?"

"Who knows? I'm just glad he did." As casually as she'd just answered, Allie had been racking her brain with the same exact question, but she hadn't been able to come up with any sort of answer that made sense.

Why had Tom changed his mind?

The only logical answer was that she had guilted Tom into giving her a break. She should probably feel ashamed for using their angsty teenage history against him. But she didn't. Especially since she was pretty certain their history had nothing to do with his reasoning. The only thing Allie was one hundred percent sure of was that he'd been all ready to say no, and then suddenly, he'd said yes.

"Do you think he's still into you?" Kitty asked.

"*What*?"

"Mimi told me the two of you used to be a hot item. First love, and all that. And now that he's divorced—"

"That was twelve years ago." *First love. Ha! What a joke*. First love implied a reciprocal relationship. "I'm pretty certain he has absolutely no romantic feelings toward me whatsoever. And I feel exactly the same toward him."

"Sorry, I don't mean to be nosy. It's just, I can't help myself. I'm a hopeless romantic."

"Hopeless would be the key word in any relationship between Tom and myself."

Kitty suddenly looked uncomfortable, making Allie regret her last words. She sounded bitter. What happened to last night's love, peace and *que sera, sera* moment? Maybe she should try to channel the Beatles again. Although, she hadn't consciously channeled them last night...

"What I meant to say was Mimi exaggerated. Tom and I dated one summer. You could pretty much say I was a rebound for him. Honestly, I'd forgotten all about it," Allie said, forcing a smile.

"A rebound, huh?"

Normally, Allie would brush Kitty off. Talking about her sad little past with Tom Donalan wasn't something she enjoyed. But Kitty seemed genuinely interested and she owed her. Not only had Kitty gone out of the way to try to help her with this ghost story, she was now giving up her morning to help chauffer Allie around town.

"It's kind of a long story," Allie said. "But basically, it's a case of girl and boy date heavily all senior year of high school, then one week before prom girl breaks up with boy and boy turns around and asks his best friend to the dance, which then ends up in a summer romance. Best friend falls hard. Boy, not so much. Then two weeks before everyone goes off to college, girl discovers she's four months pregnant and boy goes running back to her and they get married. Best friend ends up with a 'Hey, it was nice, but...'" She shrugged.

Kitty frowned. "So Tom would be boy, you would be best friend, and Lauren is... *Oh*. I get it."

"Yep. Then girl ends up divorcing boy and somehow, girl, boy, and best friend all end up back in Whispering Bay like some bad alignment of the planets. Sorry to burst your bubble, but that's it in a nutshell. Not much to resurrect in the form of a romance, I'm afraid."

If Kitty doubted her, she was polite enough not to say so. "How long do you plan to stay in town?"

"Probably just until I get the story." And fix her suspended license, of course.

"If you're still here on Thursday, you should play Bunco with us. It's at my house this week." Kitty smiled proudly. "Most groups only play once a month, but we manage to meet every Thursday. Of course, some nights we don't even play. It's a great excuse to get out for a girls' night and to gorge on Shay Masterson's super-secret margaritas, which are the best you'll ever drink."

Allie nodded politely.

Mimi was always going on about Bunco night. When Allie was younger it had sounded like a suburban nightmare. But now she could see how it would be a nice diversion from her sister-in-law's regular routine of picking up kids and doing housework. "Sounds fun, but I'm not sure what my schedule is going to look like," she said, not wanting to make a promise she couldn't keep.

"Sure, but if you're available, we'd love to have you. We always need subs."

Mimi left to go to the grocery store, leaving Allie home alone to do research. The first thing she did was call Emma with the good news. "So you plan to spend the entire night in the senior center? By yourself?" Emma asked.

"Just me, my camera, and I."

"Ooh! Do you really think you can get a picture of this ghost?"

Well, first she'd actually have to find one. "Why not?"

"I thought ghosts didn't like being photographed and that's why they always end up looking like these funny-looking orbs. You know, like little white blobs."

"Oh, yeah, sure." It occurred to Allie that she knew almost nothing about the paranormal.

"Whatever you can get, I'm sure it will be great. I filled Ben in on what you were working on." *Pause.* "He's really excited to read the piece."

Oh Lord. Emma was an even worse liar than Tom. Ben was so *not* enthusiastic about her little ghost adventure.

"So what made this guy, what's his name, the head of the construction crew—"

"Tom Donalan."

"Yeah, him. I thought you said he was a jerk. What made him change his mind and delay the demolition to let you spend the night in the building?"

"Well, that's the million dollar question."

"Maybe he's not such a jerk after all."

"Maybe." She thought about the guilty conscience

theory then dismissed it. Tom was more of a responsibility junkie. Which made his decision to postpone the demolition all the more confusing. But who was she to look a gift horse in the mouth?

Allie promised to call Emma back in the morning and was ready to dive into her research when her cell phone rang.

"I can't believe you got your driver's license suspended," Zeke said.

"Well, hello to you, too."

"You'll be happy to know I looked into this mess for you. There's a hefty fine and you have to present proof of insurance at a courthouse before you can drive again. You can do it locally and we can fax the information to Hillsborough County, which should take care of the suspension."

"Excuse me, but isn't this a little out of your jurisdiction?"

"Yeah, and you can thank me later." Beneath Zeke's gruffness lay an undercurrent of affection making it impossible for Allie to resent his interference. Besides, who was she kidding? She needed his help here.

"How about I get this over with now? You're the best big brother in the world and I love you more than anything."

"That's more like it. You know, if you're short on funds, I could pay the fine."

"Absolutely not. I'm thirty years old. I pay for my own mistakes."

Speaking of which, she had to pay that overdue electric bill. She said good-bye to her brother then whipped out her computer and logged onto the electric company site, then nearly emptied what was left of her checking account. But Allie wasn't going to wallow in self-pity. Buela had been a firm believer in the old adage God helps those who help themselves. And getting a permanent job at *Florida!* seemed like the perfect first step in helping herself.

She rummaged through the kitchen, grabbed a piece of the best zucchini bread she'd ever tasted, then set up her laptop on the dining room table and fired away.

Unfortunately, what Allie knew about ghosts was limited to the stuff she'd seen on TV and in the movies, neither of which were credible sources. Of course, neither was Wikipedia, but it was a start. She read the definition aloud: "A ghost was the soul or the spirit of a person or animal that was once alive and now managed to make itself known to the living."

Okay. Nothing she didn't already know there.

Next, she perused a list of websites, but most of them looked sketchy and absolutely none of them gave her any more information beyond what she'd learned from watching those ghost hunter shows.

A couple of weeks ago, Jen and Sean had an *American Horror Story* marathon. They got the first three seasons from Netflix and stayed in all day on a Saturday, eating popcorn, drinking mojitos, and laughing. Yes, *laughing.* Since they were watching TV in the living room of their small apartment, Allie couldn't help but absorb a few episodes. While Jen and Sean had found the whole thing humorous, Allie literally had the crap scared out of her. She'd come down with a stomach flu that night and had had to sleep with her bedroom light on.

It occurred to Allie that Jen, of all people, might be able to help with her research. She hit her roomie's number on speed dial. After a few rings, Jen picked up. "Did you pay the electric bill?"

"Doesn't anyone start a conversation with a simple hello anymore?"

"What's that supposed to mean?"

Sigh. "Nothing. And yes, I paid the electric bill."

"Good. Because I mean, you know, *it is* your turn."

"This ghost story is going to take me a little longer than I originally thought, so I'll be sticking around Whispering Bay for a while." She left off the part about her suspended license. In order to pay the fine she'd have to wait for her next paycheck from The Blue Monkey. Thank God she had it automatically deposited. Still, that wasn't till Friday, which meant she'd be here for at least four more days. "I'll probably be here till the weekend."

"No problem," Jen said, sounding unusually happy, which probably meant Sean had spent the night. Allie envisioned Sean walking around their little apartment in nothing but a loincloth. *Oh no.* She should have had more than coffee for breakfast.

"Uh, one more thing. I know this sounds kind of crazy but I was wondering if you had any idea where I might be able to get some general ghost information. Other than what I can find on Wikipedia."

"I *love* Wikipedia," Jen gushed, "but yeah, probably not the most reliable source. Have you tried contacting any mediums?"

"Is that like a psychic?"

Jen sighed impatiently. "Psychics are people with ESP—extra sensory perception."

"Like the little boy in *The Sixth Sense*?"

"No, he saw dead people, which would make him a medium. Which is *exactly* what you need. Only he's fictional and you need someone real."

"How do I find someone? I mean, I can't very well

advertise." It was T-minus ten hours, which barely gave her enough time to do computer research let alone search for a reputable ghost expert.

"Aren't you the Queen of Google?"

"You think I should do a Google search for ghost mediums?"

"Why not? The Internet knows everything, right? Hey, listen, Sean's here. Gotta go!" Jen hung up before Allie could pick anymore of her brain.

She stared at her blank computer screen. Jen had a point. What could it hurt to do a Google search? She typed "Ghost Mediums in North Florida" into the subject line. Several pages popped up. Allie scrolled through the links. There were numerous sites for ghost societies, ghost hunters, psychics, and even a group that claimed to sunbathe with ghosts.

Wouldn't Tom Donalan just love to hear that one?

Wait. Who cared what Tom Donalan thought? And why was she thinking about him anyway? She had work to do. Thank God she was no longer attracted to him.

She went back to studying the links.

Now she had the opposite problem of just a few minutes ago. With so many potential sources to ask for help, where did she start? She clicked several of the links, but without more information, she was more confused than ever.

What if she called one of these places and they went to another media source? She could have her story ripped out right from under her. What she needed was someone she could trust. Or at least, someone who might share her interests. Maybe she should call Viola Pantini and ask if any of the Gray Flamingos had gotten in contact about the anonymous email. She thought back to their meeting this morning and how Roger Van Cleave had reacted when she'd produced the email, and the way he'd been all ninja stealth-like when slipping her his phone number.

She dug in her purse to retrieve the paper and dialed his number. It immediately went to voice mail: "*BOO! Thank you for calling The Sunshine Ghost Society. All of our investigators are currently busy, but your haunting is very important to us, so please leave a brief message and a number where we can reach you. And remember, ghosts are people, too.*" This was followed by an eerie sounding cackle. "*At least...they used to be.*"

Chapter Nine

WHAT? **THE SUNSHINE GHOST** Society? Allie immediately hung up. She thought she'd been calling Roger. But it was no coincidence that the number he'd given her belonged to a ghost investigation group.

Allie checked the names of the groups from her Internet search. The Sunshine Ghost Society was one of the groups she'd put on her short list. Their website described them as a non-profit organization dedicated to the investigation of the paranormal. Allie had to admit, she rather liked the name. It sounded almost…friendly.

She thought about it a few minutes, then called again and got the same message. The voice on the phone sounded like a cross between Kathleen Turner and Harvey Fierstein.

She waited until the beep.

"Um, yes, this is Allison Grant. I'm a journalist for *Florida!* magazine and I got this number from Roger Van Cleave. I'd appreciate it if someone could give me a call back." She gave her cell phone number then hung up.

She briefly thought about contacting one of the other groups from her Google list, but eliminated that idea. She didn't want anyone else stealing her scoop, so it was best not to get too many people involved. Hopefully someone from the Sunshine Ghost Society would call her back ASAP.

Next, she Googled the Margaret Handy Senior Center but, unlike her search for mediums, this one produced only a few links, all from the *Whispering Bay Gazette*, a local paper that used to come out daily, but now only printed once a week. She called their number and got a recording saying that their office was open till one p.m. Since she couldn't drive without breaking the law, she'd have to wait till Mimi got home and throw herself on her sister-in-law's mercy. Thankfully, Allie didn't have to wait too long.

"This is actually kind of fun," Mimi said, backing out of the driveway.

"What? Playing chauffer to your husband's ditzy little sister?"

"Investigating ghosts. Maybe you can give me a byline?"

"If this article lands me a permanent gig with *Florida!* then you can have whatever you want. Just name it. Champagne? Chocolate? Eternal baby-sitting duties?"

"I hardly need a babysitter anymore, but chocolate sounds pretty good right about now. Of course, you know what they say about chocolate."

"That it's a substitute for sex?" Allie snorted. "In that case, I need a couple of crates." She glanced at her sister-in-law. "Everything is cool between you and my brother, right?"

"Why do you ask?"

"I thought maybe the chocolate thing…"

"Zeke and I have been married sixteen years. We're not kids anymore."

"But you're happy?" Funny, she'd asked Tom that same question just last night. Irrationally, she stiffened, as if preparing herself for an answer she might not want to hear.

"Sure we are," Mimi said in a perfunctory way. Then she smiled, and Allie relaxed. Of course Zeke and Mimi were happy. They were the most in-love couple Allie knew.

They arrived at the offices of the *Whispering Bay Gazette*, where they were greeted by the receptionist, who happened to be none other than Boston Betty, the Prepper.

"Nice to see you again," Allie said, inwardly cringing. Not that Betty didn't seem like a nice enough lady. Except she was so…negative.

Betty immediately honed in on Mimi. "Hey there, Mrs. Chief of Police. You bring your hottie husband with you?"

"Zeke is at a police conference in Tallahassee."

"Too bad. I could have used some pretty scenery around here today."

Mimi smiled as if she were used to this kind of thing.

Allie coughed. "Um, yeah, Betty, I was wondering if you could help me?"

"I take it this visit has something to do with that anonymous letter and the ghost?"

It occurred to Allie while she was doing her computer research that Concerned Citizen might have contacted other journalists with a similar version of that anonymous letter. Her vanity hated to think that, (after all, Concerned Citizen *did* state they'd chosen her because of the Perky the Duck story) but the pragmatist in her had to consider that a slightly different version of that letter could be in circulation.

"I was wondering if maybe the *Gazette* had received a similar letter."

"Would have told you this morning if we had," Betty said, cracking her knuckles. "Anything else I can do for you?"

"Do you know of anything unusual that ever happened in the senior center? Something that would inspire a person, or, I guess a former person, to come back and haunt the place?"

"That's it?" Betty said. "Sounds like you don't have much to go on."

"I have other leads. This is just one facet of my investigation," Allie said, putting a little steel in her voice. But Betty was right. Allie had precious little to go on. "So, back to the information I need. Can you recall anything dramatic happening in the building?"

Betty perked up. "Like a murder?"

"Um, well, I was thinking more along the lines of a heart attack or something. But yeah, a murder. That would be unusual, all right. Especially for Whispering Bay."

"I'll say. This town is about as boring as it gets." She warmed up her computer and went through the files but all Betty came up with was some general background information on the building. Nothing Allie didn't already know. Not that Allie was surprised. If anything as sinister as a murder had ever occurred in Whispering Bay, she'd have heard of it. No matter how long ago it had occurred. What she was looking for was probably something much simpler and less...evil. Of course, the ghost (assuming there *was* a ghost) could be attached to the senior center because he or she just liked hanging out there while they were alive. The journalist in her, however, wanted to scratch out that possibility. One, because it opened the field to too many potential ghosts, and two, it simply wasn't as good a story.

Betty provided her with a few old black-and-white snapshots of the original building that could prove helpful if the piece ever made it to print, as well as some more recent photos.

"These are really good," Allie said, studying one photo in particular. It was a candid shot of Viola and Gus along with another couple playing cards. They were sitting in the building's back porch with the gulf in the background. The blues from the water and the bright sky were muted causing the viewer to focus on the subjects' faces. Both couples looked happy and somehow younger than what Allie knew them to be.

She stuffed the photos in her leather tote, next to her story notes, and promised to mail a waiver for their use.

"Good luck," Betty said. "Sounds like you're going to need it."

"Sorry that wasn't more helpful," Mimi said. She slipped a key into the van's ignition. "Any more ideas?"

"Unfortunately, I'm fresh out of those."

"In that case, I need to go by Doc Morrison's office to pick up an immunization form so Cameron can play soccer."

Doc Morrison was Whispering Bay's only medical doctor. Most of the town's population drove to nearby Panama City or Destin for their medical care, but there was a staunchly loyal core the community who wouldn't dream of going to anyone but Doc. Including the Grant family. To Allie's surprise, there was a new and familiar name on the office door.

Dr. Nathanial Miller, MD, Family Practice.

Allie had gone to high school with Nate. She knew he'd gone to medical school but she had no idea he'd moved back home to practice.

The waiting room was packed with a mixture of senior citizens, children, and everything else in between. Mimi went to the front desk to get the paperwork she needed. They were about to leave with the forms when Allie came up with an idea. She pulled out a business card, scribbled on the back of it, and handed it through the little glass window to the receptionist. "Would you mind giving this to Dr. Miller? I went to high school with him and I'd like to pick his brain about something."

"What was that all about?" Mimi asked once they were back in the car.

Allie shrugged. "Just a long shot."

Ten minutes later, she got a call from Nate Miller. He was about to break for lunch and wanted to get together to talk over old times. They agreed to meet at The Bistro by the Beach. She'd no sooner hung up on Nate that her cell phone rang again.

"You're popular," Mimi joked.

Allie glanced at her phone screen. The number was blocked.

"Hello," she said tentatively.

"Is this Allison Grant?" asked a gravelly voice.

Allie's heart did a somersault. It was the voice from the Sunshine Ghost Society recording.

"Yes, this is she."

"Phoebe Van Cleave, here. President and current top investigator for the Sunshine Ghost Society."

"Van Cleave?"

"Roger's little sister. He's already filled me in on your ghost. *Please* tell me you haven't been foolish enough to have contacted any other agencies."

"You're the only one. So far," Allie admitted.

"Excellent!" Phoebe's voice dropped. "Are you alone? Can you talk freely?"

Allie glanced at Mimi, who was looking at her with a *what's going on* face.

"Sure. Go ahead."

"Because it's imperative that you keep this between us," Phoebe said. "Lots of kooks out there. Yes, siree. But here at the Sunshine Ghost Society we're strictly one hundred percent legit. If this ghost is a fake, we'll know right away and that's what you want, right? To know if this is a legitimate haunting? Or are you one of those journalists who don't care if the story is for real? One of those hacks who'll print anything for a nickel?"

"Of course I want to know if this is for real."

"Don't get all huffy. I was just testing you. If you're a legitimate journalist then the Sunshine Ghost Society is who you're looking for. You won't find anyone better than us."

There was something about this Phoebe Van Cleave that Allie didn't like. Of course, it was probably the threatening know-it-all tone to her voice. But Phoebe seemed eager to investigate. Other agencies might not be available. Plus, there was the time factor to consider. As in, Allie didn't have a lot of that.

"Is there a fee involved?"

"Nope. We receive our payment in knowing that we've helped someone from the other side make contact. It's what we live for."

"Okay," Allie said. "I guess that sounds all right. So what happens now? I have permission to stay inside the building tonight but it's scheduled for demolition tomorrow morning."

"Tomorrow? That doesn't give us much time."

"Sorry for the short notice but it couldn't be helped. I only found out about this ghost yesterday," Allie said.

"The thing is my top crew is going to be over in Destin this evening. We're going to try to make contact with the Dolphin Ghost."

"The what?" Could animals come back as ghosts, too? According to the Wikipedia definition, then yes, they could.

"Surely you've heard of him? He's the guy who jumped off the harbor bridge a few years ago and drowned? He's been seen swimming with a pack of dolphins. Don't tell me this is your first ghost investigation," Phoebe added suspiciously.

"Oh, *that* Dolphin Ghost, well, of *course* I've heard of him," Allie lied. *Good Grief.* This took the old adage 'fake it till you make it' to a whole other level. "So, back to my ghost—"

"My team is already on it. Don't worry, if there's a ghost inside that old senior center, we'll find out. Expect to hear from me soon. Phoebe Van Cleave, over and out."

Chapter Ten

MIMI DROPPED HER OFF at The Bistro. Allie got a table in the back and was about to sit down when Nate Miller walked in. Even though it had been twelve years, she'd have recognized him anywhere. In high school, he was tall and gangly and wore wire-rimmed glasses. He was still on the thin side, but the glasses were designer and his shaggy brown hair was cut short, emphasizing a surprisingly strong jaw. He'd also filled out in the shoulders.

They hugged awkwardly then laughed about it.

"You look great," he said.

"Thanks, so do you."

"You haven't changed a day since high school."

Allie winced. "Ouch."

"Hey, that's a compliment." He smiled and an appealing set of twin dimples came on display. Did he have those back in high school?

They ordered sandwiches at the counter and sat at a table facing the water. Frida brought them their drinks. "I had a crush on you, you know," Nate said to Allie.

She struggled to keep the Diet Coke from squirting out her nose. "No you didn't!"

"Senior year AP chemistry class. You probably don't remember I sat across from you."

"Of course I remember." The truth was she didn't. But it wasn't because she hadn't liked Nate. AP Chemistry had been the class she'd shared with Tom. Matt Damon could have sat across from her and she wouldn't have remembered him either.

"You had the longest pair of legs I'd ever seen. I almost flunked out first semester because of them." He said it without the slightest hint of flirtation, as if he were reciting the menu.

Allie laughed, thoroughly charmed by the adult Nate.

"I tried everything I could to get your attention but you only had eyes for—"

"Tom Donalan," she said with a sigh.

"*That* would be the guy."

Did everyone know about her mega crush on Tom back in high school? Probably, she thought glumly.

"So, Nate, are you married? Seeing anyone?"

"Not married. At least, not yet. But I'm hoping to rectify that soon." He told her about his girlfriend, Jessica, whom he had met while he was in med school at FSU. She had studied law and was now a practicing attorney in Miami.

"That's a woozy of a long-distance relationship," Allie said.

"I think an engagement ring will convince her to move up here."

"You're not interested in moving to the big city?"

"I've always wanted to come back home and practice family medicine. I couldn't imagine living anywhere else."

"Whispering Bay is lucky to have you." Allie put down her sandwich. Running into Nate seemed almost too good to be true. She decided to follow her instincts. "Would you be willing to do an interview? For a potential article? The future of health care in Florida and the lure of returning to your roots to practice medicine, that sort of thing? You know, life as a small town doctor."

"Don't you think…I'd be a little boring?"

"Not at all." She smiled. Nate Miller was technically single, handsome, and intelligent. Not to mention he was a doctor. He was like catnip to ninety-nine percent of the female population. But what made him really attractive was that he didn't seem to have a clue. Allie hoped his girlfriend knew how lucky she was.

"Is that what you wanted to talk to me about?" he asked.

"Not exactly." She told Nate all about her ghost story and how she'd tried to find out if anyone had died in the senior center. "So, what I'm looking for is any evidence that someone might have had a heart attack or a stroke inside the building. I know it sounds ghoulish, but according to my research, ghosts tend to haunt places that held deep meaning to them, and a life-threatening event sounds pretty deep to me."

"And you want me to go through Doc Morrison's records to see if I can verify that?"

"I would never ask you to go through records. That would be too time consuming. But I thought maybe you could ask Doc if he remembers anything that would fit that description."

He shook his head. "Even if he was willing to share that information with me, I couldn't relay that on to you. HIPAA violation and all that."

"Oh, yeah, sure." Well, there went that idea.

The door to The Bistro opened. Nate glanced up. He stuck a finger inside his shirt collar to loosen his tie, like it was too tight all of a sudden.

Allie turned to see Lauren Handy, or rather, Lauren Donalan, standing at the food counter. Lauren's gaze drifted through the small dining room. She spotted them and froze, but quickly recovered her surprise and waved, leaving Allie no choice but to wave back.

"Looks like a high school reunion," Nate said. He wrapped up what was left of his sandwich and stood. "I hate to run, but I got to go. Sorry I can't help with your research but I enjoyed catching up. Maybe we can do it again before you leave town." He took her business card and promised he'd think about doing an interview.

Allie noticed that Nate didn't stop to speak to Lauren on his way out of the restaurant. It wasn't that he particularly snubbed her, but he didn't take the time to stop and say a simple hello, either. Maybe they hadn't interacted all that much in high school. Or maybe he was in a big hurry to get back to his patients.

Allie took a few bites of her sandwich, willing herself to stay calm. Not that she was nervous at the thought of running into Lauren; she just didn't know what she'd say to her if she—

"Hi, Allie." Lauren's soft voice cut through her thoughts. "I'd heard you were back in town. It's good to see you again."

"Hi there, yourself." So much for not knowing what to say to Lauren Donalan!

Lauren looked different from the way Allie remembered her in high school. Gone was her signature long Barbie hair. Instead, she sported a jaw-length cut with side-swept bangs. Not many women could get away with hair that short, but on Lauren, it looked terrific. It made her blue eyes bigger and her pink lips plumper and everything else about her seemed more intense. Despite having had a baby she still looked like she could fit into her cheerleading outfit, but today she looked like she'd stepped straight out of a sixties fashion magazine. She wore a bright yellow unbuttoned raincoat over an orange shift with tiny purple flowers. Lauren also wore galoshes, which was a little weird because it was probably about eighty degrees and sunny outside. Allie had never seen anyone but little kids wear galoshes. The whole thing should look ridiculous. But it didn't. Not on Lauren.

"You look great," Allie said, still a little in awe.

"Thanks!" Lauren held back the edges of her raincoat to give Allie a better look. "I just got this at an estate sale a few weeks ago. I was going to sell it, but I couldn't resist." There was a shy excitement to her voice that instantly won Allie over. "You look great, too. But then, you always did."

It was just like high school all over again. She wished she could dislike Lauren. But she couldn't. The whole thing seemed unfair somehow.

"Thanks," Allie said, searching for something to say. "So, you own the shop next door?"

"I'm renting for now, but yeah, the shop is mine."

"Congratulations." And then because it would seem strange not to mention it, she said, "I was sorry to hear about you and Tom getting a divorce."

"It was hard on Henry, but Tom is a great dad." She fidgeted with the hem of her raincoat. "He's made everything a lot easier by following us back here to Whispering Bay."

"You didn't like Atlanta?"

"Oh, I liked it enough. But it wasn't home, you know?" She seemed pensive for a few seconds, then brightened. "Cameron is a sweetheart. You must be really proud of him."

At the mention of her nephew, Allie smiled. "I hear he's in the same class as your son."

"And the same soccer team," Lauren said. "I was relieved when Henry made a friend. Moving is always hard on kids."

Allie nodded, not sure what else to say.

"So are you back home permanently?" Lauren asked.

"Work assignment. Tampa is home. For now."

"What kind of work assignment?"

Allie shrugged. "Just following up on a lead." For some reason, she didn't want to get into the ghost thing with Lauren. She didn't know what Lauren's attitude might be toward the paranormal, and on the chance that she agreed with Tom's opinion, Allie didn't want the former Mrs. Donalan thinking she was a quack.

"I'd love to stay and talk but I really need to get back to the shop." Lauren hesitated, then rushed out her next words. "Maybe you'd like to come next door to see it?"

"Sure," Allie said. Lauren stared back at her expectantly. "You mean, as in right *now*?"

"There's no time like the present. You can pick out anything you want. On me."

"Oh, well, thanks, that's really generous, but I have a lot of work to do on this article I'm writing…and Mimi should be back here any minute to pick me up." Nothing against Lauren and her shop, but it all sounded a little too cozy for Allie. She wasn't about to be BFFs with Tom's ex.

Lauren nodded, like she had expected to be turned down, but she still had the good manners to look disappointed. "Promise me you'll stop by before you leave town. There's something I'd love to show you."

Allie wasn't into vintage clothing. Nor could she afford it. And she wasn't about to take a freebie. But

Lauren had been nice and she didn't want to seem rude. "Thanks. Maybe I will," she lied.

Lauren went to the counter to pick up her order and waved good-bye on her way out the door. "Don't forget your umbrella. It's going to rain tonight!"

Allie glanced out the window and frowned. There wasn't a cloud in the sky. Where was Lauren getting her information?

She'd just finished her lunch when her cell phone pinged. It was a text message from Tom. *Wait.* How had he gotten her number?

Then Allie remembered they'd exchanged phone numbers after he'd promised to let her spend the night at the senior center. For logistical purposes, he'd said.

I'll pick you up at eight p.m. Read the text.

Pick me up? She texted back.

You're not thinking of driving, are you? Did you fix your suspended license?

No, darn it. But she didn't want to admit that to him.

It's a beautiful night. I plan to walk.

It's going to rain.

What are you, The Weather Channel? What she really wanted to ask was if he'd been talking to his kooky ex-wife. Nope. Not gonna go there.

Tom ignored the Weather Channel dig. *Who do you think is going to let you into the senior center? Or have you managed to swipe a key?*

Ha! Don't give me any ideas.

She waited a few minutes to see his response, but none came. Allie was about to put her cell phone back in her purse when her phone pinged again.

What ideas would you like me to give you?

She stared at the tiny phone screen. Was Tom Donalan *flirting* with her? She really shouldn't answer.

But then, she couldn't very well ignore him, could she? Before she had a chance to fashion a response, he texted her again.

Cold front coming in after the rain. Dress warm. I'll bring extra blankets.

Okay, this she could certainly answer. *Thanks, but I'll bring my own blankets.*

He texted back: *Extra blankets are for ME.*

Allie almost dropped her cell. *For you?*

You didn't think I was going to let you stay the night alone?

Her fingers flew faster than she would have thought humanly possible. *I'll be perfectly fine.*

Yeah, but the company's insurance won't allow it. Either I stay the night or the deal is off.

That's ridiculous. I don't need a babysitter.

Afraid to be alone with me?

What? No!

I'm not afraid of you. She texted.

Good. He texted back. *Because I'm not afraid of you either.*

Chapter Eleven

TOM OPENED THE DOOR to Can Buy Me Love and stepped back into the nineteen-sixties. Dionne Warwick's "Walk On By" played in the background on the record player Lauren had bought at a garage sale last month. Initially, the record player had seemed defective—until Tom had suggested a simple cleaning, turning the old machine almost as good as new. Along with the record player, she'd bought about a dozen or so vinyl albums featuring everything from The Beatles to Herb Alpert and the Tijuana Brass. Stuff his grandparents had listened to.

Funny, how Lauren was into all this retro stuff. Even as teenagers she'd been quirky. She loved old movies. Old music. Old things in general. Always going to estate sales and poking around Goodwill shops. Tom had thought it was a hobby she'd outgrow, but she'd turned it into a kind of obsession, going so far as to dress like she lived in another decade.

He spotted her behind a rack of mini-skirts. She wore a short dress with lots of bright flowers. On another woman it might have looked dumb, but not on Lauren. Looking at her now, humming along to the music as she transferred skirts from one rack to another, it was hard to imagine her as the scared eighteen-year-old girl who'd come to him that night twelve years ago in tears. She'd managed to turn her love for vintage clothing into a business. One he hoped like hell worked out for her. She deserved success. But then, she deserved a lot of things. Especially the things he hadn't been able to give her.

She glanced up and spotted him. "Tommy!" Besides his mother, she was the only other person who ever called him that.

She came over and stood on tiptoe to give him a hug, then stepped back to inspect him. Despite the fact that he stood a full foot taller, she still managed to make herself look almost formidable. "How much sleep have you had this week?"

He rubbed his palm against the scratchy five o'clock shadow covering his jawline. "Do I look that bad?"

"You look tense." She narrowed her eyes at him. "When was the last time you got laid?"

"Why? Are you offering?"

Lauren snorted. "In your dreams." Then her expression softened. "I'm worried about you. Henry says you've been working night and day on this new rec center project. You know, you don't have to prove anything to anyone."

"I got kids poking around at all hours of the night messing with that old building. It's a real insurance nightmare. But come tomorrow morning that building comes down. Then things will get back to normal."

"You mean the building's still intact? I thought it was supposed to be demolished today." Only she didn't really sound surprised.

"It's complicated."

"Complicated, huh?" She resumed loading skirts onto the rack. "Guess who I ran into this afternoon? Allie Grant. Did you know she was back in town?"

He felt like one of those lab rats who'd been tricked into going into a maze they couldn't get out of. "She's the reason I'm here. I need a favor."

"*Oh?*"

There were a dozen questions loaded into that one word. He knew from experience there was no use fighting it so he gave her the lowdown on the events of the past twenty-four hours.

"A ghost? *Well,* that's certainly interesting. And you're helping Allie with the investigation?"

Helping wouldn't be the way Allie would put it. In her eyes, she'd probably say he was more like hindering. "Don't tell me you believe in ghosts."

"Of course I do. Just because I've never seen one doesn't mean they don't exist."

Tom squelched a moan.

"She looks great, doesn't she?"

"Who?"

She rolled her eyes. "Who do you think? Allie Grant."

"I guess." Allie looked better than great. But despite the good relationship he and Lauren had managed to maintain since the divorce, he didn't think it very gentlemanly to discuss another woman with his ex.

"She's still into you, you know."

"I highly doubt that."

"No, really. It's pretty obvious."

He stilled. "The two of you talked about me?"

"Of course not. But a woman can always tell when another woman is interested in something she's *had.*" Lauren wiggled her eyebrows suggestively.

"This conversation isn't natural."

"But then we aren't the typical divorced couple, are we?"

"I like to think we're friends."

"Oh, we're more than that, Tommy. I'm crazy in like with you."

"You're just not *in love* with me," he said, repeating the worn-out cliché she'd used when she'd asked him for a divorce.

"Just like you're not in love with me. Besides, crazy in like is better than love. It lasts longer."

Before he could respond, she waved a hand through the air. "I know how uncomfortable all this makes you. Talking about *feelings* and *emotions* and all that *stuff.* Let's get back to something more interesting. Let's talk about sex."

"How about we talk about money, instead?"

She gave him a look that said she knew exactly what he was doing. He might be uncomfortable discussing his emotions, but she was equally as uncomfortable when it came to more practical matters. Like how she planned to pay the rent each month.

"You still haven't cashed any of my checks," he said.

"Your child support goes directly into my bank account. I don't know what other checks you're talking about."

He glanced once more around the shop. This time noting the lack of customers. "How are you paying for the overhead on this place? Because I know for a fact you're not taking any money from your parents."

A flash of anger shot through her baby blues. But only for a second. Her daddy didn't call her his Sweet Tea for nothing. Lauren Handy Donalan couldn't stay mad for longer than you could slice a hot knife through butter. Even when you stuck your nose where she didn't think it belonged.

She straightened back her shoulders and gave him a debutante smile her momma would be proud of. "I'm doing just fine, Tommy. I'm all grown up now. I can take care of myself."

"Just because you didn't ask for alimony doesn't mean you don't need it or deserve it. Girl, we were married for eleven years. You don't think I worry about you?"

She stood up on tiptoe once more and kissed him on the cheek. "Please stop sending those checks, Tommy. I don't need them. And I don't want them. But I'll make you a deal. If *you* ever need any money, just ask. I'll be happy to bail you out."

Tom knew when he'd been outplayed. Might as well get on with why he'd stopped by in the first place. "I know it's short notice, but do you think you can take Henry for the night?"

"So you can spend the night at the senior center? With Allie Grant? Why didn't you say so in the first place? Of course—" Her face clouded over and took on a serious look. "I almost forgot; Momma and I are taking Daddy to Pensacola this evening. He has an appointment with a neurologist at eight a.m., so we're driving over to spend the night."

"How's your daddy doing?"

"Not great. But I'm hoping this new doctor might have a few tricks up his sleeve."

As an only child, it had been hard for Lauren living away from her parents, especially when her daddy had begun to show early signs of dementia. After their divorce, Lauren had taken Henry and left Atlanta to move back to Whispering Bay to help her mother. Tom had admired her for that. But he'd missed Henry too much, so he'd quit his job and followed them back home. They might be divorced, but they were still a family. She was the mother of his child and he'd always be here for her. No matter what.

Tom wished he had something encouraging to say, but he didn't. So instead, he tried to give her a reassuring nod. "Good luck tomorrow. And no worries about Henry. I'll try my mom. I'm sure she'd love to have him for the night."

Betsy Donalan was taking an apple pie out of the oven when Tom walked through the kitchen door. She carefully placed it on a cooling rack and stepped back to admire her culinary genius. No one made pie better than his mother. He was tempted to reach out and tear a piece of crust off the edge but that would only earn him a rap on the knuckles.

"Put your fangs back in your mouth. This is for the church meet and greet tonight." She stretched up to give him a kiss. "You look terrible."

"Et tu, Mother?" She frowned, so he clarified. "Lauren just told me the same thing."

She paused as if digesting that information, then opened the top door of the double oven to produce a second pie. "This one is for you," she said with a smile in her eyes.

This time he did reach out to tear off a piece of crust. It scalded the roof of his mouth but he didn't care.

"Oh, for crying out loud, Tom, let it cool off." But there was no real conviction in her voice. "To what do I owe this unexpected visit?"

"Can you keep Henry tonight?"

"You know I'd love to, but your daddy and I are going to be at the church till late. If you don't think Henry would mind tagging along?"

Henry was eleven, which meant yes, he'd definitely

mind, but Tom didn't want to hurt his momma's feelings. "Don't worry about it. I can make another arrangement."

"What's Lauren up to?"

"She and her mom are taking Dan to Pensacola for a doctor's appointment."

"Tell Lauren I'm keeping him in my prayers." Tom reached out to swipe another edge of piecrust when she said, "This doesn't have anything to do with that ghost, does it?"

"What ghost?" This time he managed to get some of the apple filling along with the crust. *Score.*

"You know what ghost. The whole town is talking about it! I was at the Piggly Wiggly this morning when I heard it from Doc Morrison's receptionist. You know, Janie Fairfax, the cute brunette? Not married. I think she heard it from Betty Jean Collins who works at the *Gazette*. You should ask her out sometime. Plus, you know, she's a member of your daddy's parish."

He couldn't help himself. "You don't think Betty Jean's too old for me?"

"Ha ha, Mister Smarty Pants. You know very well I meant Janie Fairfax. But frankly, at this point I wouldn't care who you asked out, as long as you asked out someone. *Anyone.*"

Ridiculously, Tom realized he actually preferred talking about the ghost. "Ma, you know better than anyone else there's no such thing as ghosts."

"I certainly do *not* know that."

"Yeah, well, there's no ghost."

"So you haven't seen anything strange in the building?" she asked.

"Nope."

She turned her back to him so that he couldn't see her

face and began emptying the dishwasher. "I heard Allison Grant was back in town. But of course, you know that since you saw her last night."

Hell. Did anyone get any actual shopping done at the Piggly Wiggly? This definitely called for more pie. He picked up a knife and tried his best to stealthily slice himself a wedge.

"What a sweet girl! And so pretty. Her grandmother was such a lovely lady. Barbara Alvarez. Catholic, but she always donated one of her delicious flans to the parish festival bake sale booth. You remember her, don't you? Well, of course you do. I mean, you *did* date her granddaughter."

She turned around and caught him with the knife in his hand. "Tom! You need to let that cool off." She shook her head at him like he was three. "If you insist on eating a slice this instant and burning the roof of your mouth, at least let me cut it for you." She sliced him a generous piece of pie, eyeing him the whole time like he was some leery wolf she was ready to spring a trap on.

"Spit it out," he said.

She smiled sweetly. "I was just thinking. It's been over a year since the divorce and you haven't dated anyone." The smile vanished. "You haven't dated anyone, have you?"

"I'm sure you'll be the first to know when I do."

"Humph. Well, anyway, it just seems like perfect timing. You and that sweet Allison together again. I always felt so *terrible* about the ways things ended between you two. Not that it could have been helped under the circumstances, but now that the two of you are single again—she is still single, isn't she?"

Tom almost choked on his pie. "Ma, I appreciate the thought but I'm happy with my life exactly the way it is."

"Happy? How can you be happy being alone?"

"I'm not alone. I have Henry. And my job. And you and Pops."

"Your *job*? Well, I hope that keeps you nice and warm on a cold winter's night."

"We live in Florida."

"You know what I mean."

First Lauren, now his mother. The women in his life needed to get their own lives. For the first time he wondered if Lauren's prodding him to date meant that she herself was dating. He hoped so. Just as long as she dated a good guy. Not that Tom had any worries on that account. Despite her quirkiness, Lauren had always been sensible.

"So why can't you keep Henry tonight?" she asked.

"Gotta work," he said, swallowing down the rest of the pie she'd sliced him. If Betsy Donalan knew he planned to spend the night in the senior center with Allie Grant, she'd be calling the *Whispering Bay Gazette* to announce their engagement.

He thought back to their text conversation. He hadn't meant to flirt with her. It had just come naturally, but flirting or anything else that might come equally as naturally with Allie was a bad idea.

He kissed his mother and said a quick good-bye before she could get another word in.

I'm happy enough. Those had been his exact words to Allie last night. He thought it over a second. Was he happy? Hell, he wasn't unhappy.

Why did women always overthink everything?

Chapter Twelve

OKAY, SO MAYBE ALLIE was just a *tiny* bit afraid of Tom Donalan.

No, not Tom Donalan exactly. It was the whole set up that had her squirmy. And then of course, there was the problem of what to wear. She was *not* dressing up for tonight's sleep-in at the senior center. Allie chanted this to herself while she got ready. It was like a mantra of sorts to remind her that tonight was strictly business.

Still, that little fantasy she'd been holding onto for the past twelve years, the one where she saw Tom again for the first time? In that fantasy she was a goddess to be reckoned with. Her long dark hair was straight and shiny, her brown eyes were made up to look smoky and sexy, and her perfect curves were accentuated by a designer gown.

In other words, she was Sophia Vergara.

Eat your heart out, Fat and Bald Tom Donalan.

Of course, in reality Tom wasn't fat, nor was he bald, and she certainly didn't look anything like Sophia Vergara. Allie's long brown hair was straight and maybe just a tad bit shiny (shampoo had a tendency to do that), but her eye makeup was minimal, and as for the perfect curves? Not even close. She was more Olive Oyl than sexy Latina star.

Her legs were her best body part, but she couldn't justify wearing a short skirt tonight. Plus, she'd only packed a couple days' worth of clothes, so she had to work with what she had. Jeans, white T-shirt, a red sweater and her cowboy boots. The boots were turquoise leather with a *fleur-de-lis* cream embroidery and a conservative two-inch heel making her almost six feet tall. Allie had never felt comfortable in girly heels, but if the temperature ever went below sixty (chilly for native Floridians), she'd be in these boots. Lauren had been right about the rain. It poured for a couple of hours straight, instantly bringing cooler weather.

She sprayed some cologne along the inside of her wrist and did a quick inspection in the mirror. It was exactly the look she was going for. Casual, slightly hip, and semi-attractive journalist who hadn't put much thought into what she looked like (ha!).

Both Mimi and Claire remarked on her appearance over dinner.

"You look great," Mimi said.

"No, she doesn't. She looks *hot*. Can I borrow your boots?" Claire asked.

Allie helped herself to some of Mimi's homemade lasagna. "My sixteen-year-old niece thinks I look hot. Should I be flattered or am I being played for a pair of boots?" she mused aloud.

Cameron snickered.

"Both," Mimi said.

Claire flushed. "I mean it. You look awesome, Aunt Allie."

"You're great for my ego, kid. Maybe I *should* move back to town."

"Well, you already know how I feel about that," Mimi said.

The rest of dinner went by quickly with the majority of the conversation devoted to talk of Allie's upcoming ghost adventure.

"I think it's really cool what you're doing," Cameron said, as he loaded the last of the dirty plates into the dishwasher. "Can I see your phone?"

"Cameron," Mimi said. "We've been through this before. You're not getting a cell phone."

"All the kids at school have a phone. And Claire has one."

"You're not all the kids at school. And Claire is sixteen and driving. She needs a basic phone for security reasons. When you learn to drive, then you'll get a phone, too."

Cameron looked at Allie with those big brown eyes that looked exactly like Zeke's. *He's going to be a heartbreaker.* She didn't envy Mimi one bit.

She pulled out her phone and checked it for incoming messages but there was nothing. She'd hoped by now she would have heard something from Phoebe Van Cleave and The Sunshine Ghost Society, but either Phoebe wasn't as interested as she'd first sounded, or there was nothing to report. It looked like Allie was going to be on her own tonight. She handed Cameron her phone. "It can't hurt him to look at it," she said to Mimi.

Cameron studied the phone for a few seconds. "Can I play a game on here?"

"Sure. Just don't mess with my settings."

Mimi gave Cameron the stinky eye. "Did you finish your homework?"

"Yep." He ran into the living room, taking Allie's phone with him.

"Thank God Zeke will be home tonight," Mimi said, putting the leftovers in the fridge. "Oh, before I forget, take this." She handed Allie a large wicker basket.

Allie opened the lid. Inside were candles, a lighter, a woolen blanket, cheese, crackers, and a thermos. "Gee, all that's missing is a bottle of wine and some mood music."

Mimi smirked. "Don't think I wasn't tempted."

"This is all great, but I'm not going there to have a picnic."

"Of course not, but you might get hungry. And there's coffee in the thermos with a little zing added."

The doorbell rang.

"I'll get it!" Claire yelled.

"It's Mr. Donalan!" Cameron chimed in a few seconds later.

Allie steeled herself. She could do this. She was, after all, a professional, and tonight could be the biggest night of her journalistic career. She picked up her backpack and Mimi's basket of goodies and headed into the living room.

Tom wore jeans and a black turtleneck sweater and he looked...*good*. Too good as far as Allie was concerned. The stubble he'd been sporting this morning was gone, which meant he'd shaved for the occasion. Most men looked sexier with stubble but Tom looked equally fine with or without it.

Claire stood behind him and mouthed WOW.

Yeah, my thoughts exactly.

Mimi shooed Claire away and that was when Allie noticed that Tom wasn't alone. Standing next to him was a miniature version of him whom Allie could only assume must be Henry. No one seemed surprised to see him. Well, no one except her, that is.

"Thanks for letting Henry spend the night," Tom said to Mimi.

"Henry's welcome here any time," Mimi said, smiling down at Tom Donalan's progeny.

Cameron grabbed Henry's overnight bag and the two of them were about to take off for Cameron's bedroom when Tom interrupted them. "Hey, it's rude not to say hello," he said to his son. Tom turned to her with an expression Allie couldn't read. "Henry, this is Cameron's aunt, Allison Grant. She's a journalist doing a story on the old senior center."

As well as my ex-girlfriend, Allie thought he might have added. Probably wouldn't have been appropriate, though.

Henry politely extended his hand. "Nice to meet you, Mrs. Grant."

"That's Miss Grant," she said, shaking Henry's hand. "And…it's nice to meet you, too."

She was meeting Tom Donalan's son. It was like she was in a real live version of the *Twilight Zone*.

Mimi must have known all along that Henry was coming over tonight. The fact that she hadn't said anything…

A myriad of emotions washed over Allie. Confusion, betrayal (for the love of God, Mimi could have warned her!) and strangely enough, a tiny bit of pride. Although why she should feel proud, Allie didn't have a clue. Except that although she'd just met him, she could see Henry was a terrific kid. Handsome, polite, well-spoken. The kind of kid Mimi and Zeke would be happy to include among Cameron's friends.

Allie stood there, frozen, listening to Mimi and Tom talk about the upcoming soccer season, and then Tom mentioned calling Zeke to set up a potential father/son camping trip for the four of them. Talk about cozy! Her ex was wiggling his way into her family's life and there was nothing she could do about it.

Four more days and she could get back to her old life in Tampa.

It couldn't happen soon enough.

"You ready?" Tom asked her.

She tamped down whatever emotion she hoped wasn't showing on her face and nodded.

Cameron handed her back her cell phone. "When you get a chance, check your apps," he whispered so that only she could hear.

She grabbed the rest of her things and followed Tom out the door.

Tom unlocked the door to the senior center and handed Allie a flashlight. "I'll get the rest of the stuff out of my truck."

"Look, I know this is a huge imposition. You really don't have to stay the night. I promise I'll be a good girl. No broken windows this time. Scout's honor." She used her finger to make the cross symbol over her chest and even smiled at him. Just to show him she meant it, which she did, of course.

"Sorry, like I said, it's an insurance thing."

Gone was the flirtatious mood Allie thought she'd detected from their text messages this afternoon. Right now, Tom was all business. Which was good because she needed to be all business, too. Only she really didn't want to spend the next twelve or so hours alone with him. All business or not.

She brought in her belongings, careful to keep her

flashlight aimed at the ground. Hopefully the cockroaches would make themselves scarce tonight. She found a clear space in the center of the main room and set down Mimi's picnic basket, then opened up her backpack and checked the contents: laptop, cell phone (which had a pretty decent camera), and a yellow legal pad for note-taking.

The building looked exactly the way it had last night except the window she'd broken into was now patched over with clear vinyl sheeting and duct tape. Did Tom do that?

Allie couldn't help feeling just a tad bit guilty over the trouble she'd caused him. She wondered again for the umpteenth time exactly what had made him change his mind about delaying the demolition. Maybe tonight, if the timing was right, she'd ask him again. And maybe this time, he'd tell her the truth.

Tom lugged in more supplies. He had a broom, a blow-up mattress, blankets, and a few kerosene lamps. He'd also brought along a radio, which he immediately set to a station carrying a baseball game. "Hope you don't mind. The Braves are playing tonight." He swept over a large area to clear it of debris, then squatted down and began inflating the mattress with a hand pump.

Allie watched as the mattress filled with air. Queen size, she'd guess. She hadn't given a thought to actually sleeping tonight. No, the mattress was all his. She was here to work.

She pulled out her cell phone to check the camera setting when she noticed there was a new app on her phone. She clicked the icon and the small screen opened up to reveal...*a ghost detector*. No wonder Cameron had been so pleased with himself!

She read the directions then casually held her phone

out in the palm of her hand. On the screen, a yellow band went round and round in a circle, like those radar things from a submarine movie. According to the instructions, a blip would come across the yellow band in the presence of "extra energy," *aka* a ghost.

Tom would probably laugh at this bit of technology, but Allie was thrilled. Not that she really believed it might work, but hey, you never knew unless you tried, right? Plus, it would give her something to do besides watch Tom set up camp for the night. A queen-sized air mattress, blankets, and Mimi's secret basket of goodies all combined were way too cozy as far as Allie was concerned.

"I'm going to walk around," she said.

He barely glanced up at her. "Go for it."

With the flashlight in one hand and her cell phone in the other, she slowly walked the perimeter of the main room. She glanced down at her phone screen. No blips, no beeps. She made her way down the hall facing the entrance to two rooms that had once been used as classrooms. The rooms were dark and strewn with the same scattered trash she'd encountered last night.

She randomly picked the room on the right and went inside. Since Tom couldn't see her all the way back here, there was no point in hiding what she was doing, so she held the phone out in front of her, allowing it to guide her steps. The yellow line continued round and round in the same circle.

Nothing.

She should probably be disappointed, but she wasn't. After all, it wasn't as if she expected the thing to work. Fighting off a fit of the giggles, she repeated the routine in the next room. All she needed to complete the ridiculousness was the *Ghostbusters* theme playing in the background. She was about to give up when her phone made a strange sound. Allie glanced down to find a red blip on the screen.

She shook the phone. Just to make sure she wasn't imagining it. The blip was still there.

This was priceless! Too bad Cameron wasn't here to share in the fun.

All of a sudden the room went warm. The smell of lemons hit her like a slap in the face. It was the same sensation she'd experienced last night. Allie had almost begun to believe that she'd imagined it, but this was as real as the ground beneath her boots. Her hand trembled, making it difficult to concentrate on the screen. She willed herself to take a deep breath.

The blip became bigger and the lemon smell stronger. It should have gagged her, but it didn't. Instead she wanted to drown in it. To sink against its warmth, like a fire on a cold winter day. She shook away that ridiculous thought and concentrated on her phone screen. According to her location, whatever was making the ghost radar go off was standing directly behind her.

Chapter Thirteen

TOM WATCHED AS ALLIE held her phone in her hand like her life depended on it. Whatever she was looking at had distracted her enough that she hadn't heard him enter the room.

"What are you doing?"

She jumped around, her brown eyes wide. "You scared the heck out of me!"

"Sorry." He hadn't meant to sneak up on her, but he'd wanted to make sure she was all right. "Why are you holding your phone that way?"

"No reason," she said as if he couldn't tell when she was lying.

He glanced down at her phone. She tried to hide it behind her back but then it began to beep.

"Oh my God. Hold still." She aimed the phone in his direction. "Dang! It disappeared!"

"What disappeared?"

"Nothing." She stared at her phone like it was going to explode.

"Are you going to tell me what's going on?" he asked.

"Believe me, you don't want to know."

"Yeah, actually, I do want to know. I can't have you

going around in the dark where you can fall and get hurt again."

"I only fell last night because I lost my balance going through the window." He opened his mouth to say something but she cut him off. "And yes, I know it was my fault because I was trespassing."

"I wasn't going to say that."

"But you thought it."

She was right. It had been exactly what he'd been thinking. "Look, I'm here for the night so I might as well help you."

"What about your baseball game?"

"The game's over."

She thought it over for a few seconds, then shrugged. "All right, if you really want to know what I'm doing, I'm using a ghost detector. Cameron downloaded it for me." She handed him her phone and pointed to the screen. "See? It's searching for any disturbance in the quantum flux. Which just occurred. According to this, there was a ghost right where you're standing." Her tone dared him to contradict her. He wondered if she knew how damn adorable she looked right now.

"The quantum flux?"

"I know, it sounds hokey, but basically it's a disturbance in the force. And please no *Star Wars* or *Back to the Future* jokes."

"According to this…ghost detector, there was a ghost," Tom said. "Right where I'm standing now?"

"Well, there was *something* there. Something with enough energy to make this thing go off. I mean, besides you." She glared at him. "Maybe you scared it away."

"*I* scared it away?"

"Or maybe it just doesn't like you."

More like *she* didn't like him. Not that he blamed her.

Tom studied her phone for a few minutes. "Henry would get a kick out of this." He handed her back her phone then pulled out his own cell and downloaded the app. "Now we both have one. You want to start back in the main room?"

"Are you kidding? You're really going to help me?"

"The Braves just won their division playoff so I'm feeling pretty good right now. Besides, there's not much else to do, is there?"

"Nope, nothing else to do," she said, which of course, immediately made him think of the one thing he did want to do.

Especially with Allie Grant.

Exclusively with Allie Grant, if he were being honest.

When was the last time you got laid?

If anyone other than Lauren had asked, he would have told them it was none of their fucking business. The thing was she had a point. After the divorce, he'd slept around a little. Not enough to put him in the man-whore category, but enough to satisfy his newly divorced fragile ego. Since moving back home, though, he'd been living like a monk. Working a sixty-hour week, relieved only by an occasional fishing trip with Henry or a Sunday night dinner with the folks.

Maybe his mother was right and it was time to start dating again. Not the kind of dating she had in mind. He wasn't ready for anything serious. He had too many responsibilities. A son. An ex-wife to support, even if she didn't want to take a penny from him. A new job. And a bonus to collect. If he could ever get this new rec center project off the ground, that is.

No, what he needed was something more casual. If the right sort of woman were to come along. As

Maria Geraci

tempting as Allie Grant was, she was definitely the wrong woman. For one thing, there was too much history between them. Sure, he'd been a teenager and dumb as rocks but there were some things in life you couldn't take back. Besides, she had to be dating someone. She was gorgeous. Smart. Funny. Even if she was willing to overlook their past, there was no way she was available.

They spent the next hour scouring the building with their "ghost detectors" in hand, but both their phones had gone silent. They ended up back in the center's main room.

"I swear this thing really did go off." Allie tossed her phone into her bag in disgust.

"I believe you."

She threw him a look that said, *Liar*.

"No, really, I believe you saw something on that phone." He didn't want to add that the ghost radar was probably programmed to go off if it encountered too much dust in the air or something else equally hokey.

He glanced at his watch. It was nearly midnight. He shook out a couple of the blankets and spread them on the inflatable mattress, then pocketed his cell phone and sat down. "What do you got in there?" He pointed to the picnic basket.

"Goodies. Made by Mimi Grant herself. Since you've been such a good boy, I might even be inclined to share." Although there was plenty of room on the mattress, he noticed that she chose to sit on a blanket she'd tossed on the floor. "Want some coffee?" Without waiting for his response, she poured them each a cup.

Tom took a swallow. "Whiskey?"

Allie didn't look surprised. "So that's what Mimi meant when she said she added some zing." She raised

134

her drink in salute. "Here's to Mimi." She downed it, then immediately refilled both their cups. Because she was cold and wanted the warmth the coffee offered? Or because she was nervous and needed the fortitude supplied by the whiskey?

Either way, he didn't plan to mess this up. He was alone with Allie Grant and neither of them was going anywhere. It was a chance he thought he'd never have. A once in a lifetime opportunity to really talk to her.

"So why journalism school?" he asked. Twelve years ago she'd wanted to become a lawyer. What had changed her mind?

"Because I flunked out of nursing."

He smiled at the joke. The Allie Grant he knew in high school would never have gone to nursing school. There was that blood thing, after all. She smiled back, knowing he'd gotten it. And then her smile turned pensive and he realized they were remembering the same thing.

Allie had just finished whooping his ass at the bowling alley. She tossed her long brown hair over one shoulder, and began doing a little victory dance in the parking lot. "I beat you—I beat you—" she chanted, then laughed. Two guys came out the front door of the Bowlarama and stopped to stare. Allie, as usual, was oblivious. Did she really not know how fucking gorgeous she was?

"Admit it, Donalan, you let me win," she said, her dark eyes glittering with happiness.

He grinned. "Never." And it was the truth. He was a decent bowler, but Tom hadn't been able to concentrate on his game. Not when he knew what they would be doing afterward.

They got in his car and went through the drive-thru at McDonalds before heading toward the bridge. Allie was feeding him a french fry—and still gloating over her victory—when out of nowhere, a white pickup truck tried to run him out of his lane.

"Shit!" Tom swerved to the right, causing his car to go off the road. Food went flying everywhere. He slammed his foot on the brake just in time to avoid plowing into a fruit stand.

"God damn it!" He jumped out of the car and ran down the road to try to get a look at the pickup truck, but it was already speeding away. "Come back here, you fucker!" he yelled.

Not that anyone could hear him, but it felt good to let out some of the steam. He paced back and forth in front of the car, then after he'd calmed down, he inspected the driver's side for any damage. He'd saved all his money from his part-time job at Ace Hardware to buy this car. A shiny red 1987 Ford LTD Crown Victoria that he'd bought from one of his dad's parishioners—the proverbial little old lady who only drove her car to church on Sunday. He'd just detailed it this morning. Luckily, there were no scratches or dents that he could see, which was a good God damn thing, or he'd track that son-of-a-bitch from here to the ends of the earth.

He got back in the car. "Man, I wish I'd gotten his license plate. Too bad your brother wasn't here to—" Allie was lying on her side, her long legs tucked beneath her in the fetal position. Fuck! He was an idiot. It had never occurred to him that she'd been hurt.

He reached out and touched her arm. It was late June

and still at least eighty degrees outside, but her skin felt like ice. "Baby, are you okay? What happened? Did you hit your head?" His gaze searched frantically for any signs of blood, but there was none that he could see. Fear swamped through his veins, making him break out into a sweat. "Allie, you need to talk to me. Where does it hurt?"

She shook her head. "I'm...okay."

"The hell you are." He turned on the ignition and got back on the road, going as fast as he could. "It's going to be all right. I'm taking you to the hospital."

She sat up slowly, still looking dazed. "No, I'm okay. Honest."

He glanced at her out of the corner of his eye. She looked pale, and she was still shaking.

"You're in shock. You need to see a doctor."

"*No*," she said with a little more vigor. "I'm okay; I was just...scared, is all." She reached down to the floor of the car and began picking up bits of scattered food and stuffing it back into the McDonald's bag with an eerie sort of calm precision that should have reassured Tom. Instead, it did the opposite.

He eased off the accelerator. "Are you sure you don't need to go to the hospital? Do you want me to take you home?"

"No, I want to go to the bridge. *Please.*"

He slowed down to ten miles under the speed limit, trying his best to keep his eye on both her and the road at the same time. She seemed better, but he was still a little freaked out by her reaction to the near-accident. Despite her protests, maybe he should take her to the hospital anyway. Or at least, back home, where she could lie down. Her breathing seemed normal, though, so he decided to go along with her. For now. But if she started going pale on him again, he'd take her straight to the hospital, no matter what she said.

He parked his car in their spot and killed the engine. Neither of them said anything, so he pulled her trembling body next to his and wrapped his arms around her. "It's okay, baby, I was scared, too. I thought that asshole was going to ram right into us."

She shuddered. "I just need to calm down a little."

He tucked her head into his shoulder and held her. Her skin was beginning to warm up. He'd held her like this before, but not to comfort her. She sighed and shifted closer. He tightened his arm around her. He knew her mother had died in a car crash when she was seven. But they'd never talked about it. Is that what this was? Was she remembering her mom's accident?

"What happened?" he asked quietly.

He could feel her shudder all the way through his own body, almost as if they'd melded into one person. "I was sitting behind her in the back seat, coloring. I had my seat belt on, but... I wasn't happy about it. Zeke was in the front, next to her. He was...happy, though. He'd just made the baseball team and he was talking non-stop when all of a sudden... I don't know; it was weird. I didn't even see it. Not really. It was like a bomb exploded or something. At least, that's what I thought."

She didn't say anything for a few long seconds.

"I found out later we'd been T-boned. The driver from the other car was hurt pretty badly, but he survived. He ran a red light. Not on purpose, though. He was having chest pain, a heart attack. Kind of weird, huh? I guess you could say my mom was killed by some other guy's heart attack."

Her attempt at levity made his throat go tight. As a pastor, this must be the kind of stuff his dad listened to all the time. What would he say? How would he help her? Tom's mind came up a big fucking blank. You'd think maybe some of his dad's genes would have rubbed off on him. Instead, all he'd been able to think about tonight was getting a blowjob. He was worthless.

"Zeke went unconscious, but I didn't know that. I thought he was...dead. I kept screaming for Mom to help him, and then I realized that she couldn't because she was hurt, too. There was all this blood oozing from her chest and she kept trying to reach out and hold my hand."

Her body began shaking again. Only this time it was accompanied by great big sobs. He'd never heard anyone cry like that before. He kissed the top of her head, only because he had no clue what else to do. After a few minutes, the sobs began to space out.

"It took the EMTs a long time to get her out of the car. Zeke... He was on the side that hadn't been smashed, so they got him out right away. He'd hit his head on the dashboard, but they told me he'd be okay. But Mom and me... They had to get us out through the other way, because our side of the car was all crumbled up. And all that time, she kept trying to grab my hand, but I couldn't reach her."

She tried to shift away and Tom realized that he was probably crushing her. He reluctantly loosened his grip around her shoulders. Allie took a deep breath. "If the other car had hit us just a little more to the rear, I would have been the one crushed in the car. Everyone told me afterward how lucky I was." She glanced down at her hands. "And I know it could have been worse. Zeke could have been killed and then I wouldn't have anyone. Well, except Buela."

Tom had always wondered what happened to Allie's

father. He'd asked her once, but she'd brushed it off and he hadn't wanted to press her. "What happened to your dad?"

"After Mom died, he tried to take care of us, but he was messed up pretty bad, too. Emotionally, I mean. So Buela moved up from Miami. My grandfather had passed away the year before, so I guess taking care of us helped her overcome all that grief. At least, that's what she said."

"Where's your dad now?"

Allie shrugged. "I don't know, and I don't care."

Neither of them said anything more. They sat there in his car, listening to the water lap gently on the shore. After a long time, Tom realized it had grown late. Way past Allie's curfew. He didn't want her to get in trouble, so he gently disentangled his stiff arm from around her shoulder. "I'm really sorry, Allie." It sounded dumb, but he couldn't think of anything better to say.

She nodded, then smiled. Her color looked normal again and the shaking had disappeared a long time ago. "Thanks, Tom."

At eighteen, he hadn't been able to offer more than a mumbled "I'm sorry." At thirty, he still didn't know what to say. Watching your mother bleed to death... How had she overcome that?

He took another swig of the whiskey-laced coffee and waited for her to continue.

"Well, you know I planned to go to law school after getting my BA in Journalism, but I don't know," she said. "Law school was something Buela always wanted for me but I never really saw myself in a suit working for some firm." She narrowed her eyes at him. "What about you? I thought you wanted to be an architect."

"Construction Management was a more practical way to go at the time. I had a family to feed. It just made more sense."

She glanced at him sideways. "What ever happened to that red Crown Victoria of yours? I thought you were going to drive it to the day you died."

He laughed. "I really loved that car. I traded it in for an SUV with enough room for a car seat and a Pack 'N Play and all the other stuff we used to haul around."

"Henry seems...like a terrific kid."

"He's the best."

She smiled.

He cleared his throat. "So this ghost story, it's really important to you, huh?"

She took another sip of the coffee. "I know you think it's all a bunch of bunk." He began to protest but she waved a hand at him. "Don't pop a blood vessel, I get it." She looked at him over the top of her cup. "If you want to know the truth, I don't believe in ghosts, either."

"Then what the hell is this all about?"

She sighed in an exaggerated way that made him think she'd already had a little too much of Mimi Grant's special coffee. "I'm in competition with another journalist." Then she told him all about the magazine and her editor and some jerkoff named Chris Dougal, who wanted the same job she did.

He took it all in, sipping his laced coffee, trying not to stare at her too much. But it was getting harder by the second. She leaned back on her elbows and stretched out those legs of hers and he tried not to imagine how they'd feel wrapped around his waist.

Concentrate, Donalan.

"So tell me about this famous story of yours. Perky the Duck?"

She made a face. "Perky and I have a love-hate relationship. If you know what I mean."

Yep. Definitely too much of Mimi's coffee. Damn, but he liked talking to her. Always had. Probably always would.

She shifted around and pulled her legs together Indian style. The motion brought her closer to the mattress. Dangerous territory, for sure. He should probably move back some. But he didn't.

"The only reason I got the story is because a friend from college volunteers at a wildlife sanctuary in Tallahassee. There was this hunter who'd put a bunch of ducks he'd killed in a freezer in his garage and later that night his wife was out there and heard a noise. So she opened the freezer and found one of the ducks still alive."

Tom shook his head and laughed. "Crap."

Allie grinned. "Yeah, I'd probably have a stroke. Anyway, she grabbed the duck and called the wildlife sanctuary and the rest is history. Thanks to the miracle of modern veterinary care, Perky made a miraculous recovery."

He didn't want to offend her but he was curious. "And that's it? That's the story that was picked up by the Associated Press?"

"It's crazy, I know. But yeah, that's it. So now you know about my love-hate relationship with Perky. I love that the story got so much attention, but I hate that it's the story everyone remembers me for." She divided the rest of the coffee between them and capped the thermos. "And now I'm stuck writing about this haunted building that doesn't look like it's haunted after all."

"Why don't you find something else to write about?"

"Believe me, I'd love nothing better. But my editor is hell bent on this story. And since I'm hell bent on getting a job at *Florida*! I don't have much choice. Hence, I'm stuck here for the night." She glanced at him. "You, on the other hand, don't really have to stay, you know."

He nodded slowly. "I know."

Her brows shot up. "Does that mean you trust me with your precious building?"

"I trust that you aren't going to vandalize it, if that's what you mean. But I'm still not about to let you spend the night here alone."

She hesitated, then asked, "Tom, when you walked in on me using the ghost detector app, did you smell anything...unusual?"

"Like what?"

"Just anything that you hadn't smelled before."

The only thing he'd caught was a whiff of her perfume. Something expensive. Sexy. Elusive. Just like her. "No, nothing unusual."

She looked disappointed. He wished for her sake they had seen something. Anything. But of course, that wasn't going to happen because there was no such thing as ghosts. Too bad he couldn't make one materialize so she could write her story. He had a sudden urge to beat the shit out of this Chris Dougal guy.

He thought briefly about reaching out to kiss her. She'd either shut him down or kiss him back. Yes or no. At least it would be out in the open. Must be the whiskey making him think crazy. Because kissing Allie Grant would be a huge mistake.

Tom pulled a blanket around his shoulders. "I'm going to sleep. I have a big day tomorrow."

"Sure. I'll just...hang around."

He tried to sound innocent. Non-threatening. "You're welcome to the other side of the mattress."

She snorted. "Right."

Smart girl.

Allie walked around the building, flashlight in hand. It was dark and quiet and chilly enough that she had to rub her hands up and down her arms to warm herself. Maybe if she didn't try so hard, something would happen. Because *something* needed to happen. Otherwise, this was going to be the most boring article in the history of *Florida!* magazine. She might as well hand Chris Dougal the job on a silver platter.

She made a thorough search of the building, but this time the ghost detector app was silent. It seemed ridiculous to stay awake when nothing was happening, so she formulated a plan. Get a couple hours of sleep then try again with the ghost detector. She made her way back to the main room and settled herself on the woolen blanket.

An hour later (she knew it was an hour because she kept checking her watch), Allie was still awake. The wooden floor beneath the blanket was hard and uninviting. Something scurried past her. *Oh God.* It was those cockroaches again.

She peeked over at Tom, asleep on the queen-sized mattress. Why hadn't she thought to bring an inflatable mattress? She knew for a fact Zeke and Mimi had one. Tom had invited her to share the bed, which of course she'd scoffed at, but apparently her lower back didn't have as much pride as the rest of her. It was practically screaming at her to get off the floor. Plus, there were those roaches to think about. Allie had read an article once about a woman who had swallowed a roach in her sleep…

She was being ridiculous. She and Tom were adults. He was asleep and she was beyond tired. She laid down on the edge of the mattress, trying her hardest not to disturb him, but it was a blow-up mattress, which meant the whole thing was flimsy at best. She turned on her side and shut her eyes.

After what seemed like forever, but in reality was only twenty minutes according to her watch, Allie was still wide awake. The whiskey had made her woozy. She was exhausted. The inflatable mattress was a lot more comfortable than the floor, so why wasn't she asleep?

Despite the chill in the air, her skin broke out into a light sweat. There was one definite big con to sharing a bed with Tom Donalan. Lying inches away from him, it felt like every cell in her body had gone on full alert. No wonder she couldn't sleep. Did he feel it, too?

"I don't bite," he said.

She froze.

Okay. There were at least four or five snarky retorts she could respond with, but that would only make the situation stickier. Best to pretend she was asleep.

"I'm glad you decided to be practical and share the bed, but you're going to fall off the mattress," he continued.

Her eyes flew open. "How did you know I was still awake?"

"Really?" He shifted over, creating more room on the bed for her.

Tom was right. She was so close to the edge it was ridiculous. She shuffled more to the center, still careful to keep their bodies from touching.

He turned and casually propped his head with the back of his hand so that he looked directly down at her. She couldn't avoid him even if she wanted to. The thing was, she was beginning to think that she might not want to.

"Why aren't you with someone?" He sounded almost angry, which didn't make sense.

"Who says I'm not?"

"Are you?"

She should make something up. Tell him she had a boyfriend. Except, what did it matter? "Nope, I'm free as a bird. Not that I haven't had plenty of opportunities, but a serious relationship isn't in my life plan right now." Okay, so maybe the word *plenty* was an exaggeration. But he didn't have to know that.

"Your life plan," he repeated slowly.

"Yep. My life plan. Comprised of four parts. But I've only completed two so far." She paused, uncertain whether or not to go on.

"I'd love to hear it."

Sarcasm? Interest?

Not sarcasm. He sounded too intense.

"All right." She took a deep breath. *Surreal.* That's what this was. Talking about her life plan with Tom Donalan of all people. The guy who had screwed up her original life plan. But there was nothing better to do, so why not?

She held up a finger. "Part one, get my college degree."

He nodded.

"Part two, sow my wild oats. Which means—"

"I know what it means."

"No need to get snappy. So, part one and part two are done. Part three is a little trickier. It's get a permanent

146

job with *Florida!* magazine, which this ghost story
would help me land."

"Why that magazine? Why not some other
publication?"

"Because that's the one I want. It's a perfect mixture
of everything I like to write: ecology, travel, human
interest. Plus, its headquarters are in Orlando so it would
be an easy transition from Tampa. I'd still be an hour
from the beach, close to a major international airport,
and just a long afternoon drive from family. It's perfect,
really."

"Sounds like you got it all figured out. So what's part
four?"

She startled. Had she told him her life plan had four
parts? She must have or he wouldn't have known to ask.
It must be the whiskey making her careless. "Sorry, but
part four is private."

"Private as in, you don't tell anyone? Or you just
don't tell me?"

"I'm not discriminating here. Private as in, I don't tell
anyone. Period." Before he could respond to that, she
said, "My turn to ask a question. What made you change
your mind and stop the demolition?"

He was silent long enough that she didn't think he
was going to answer. Finally, he said, "Maybe I just
didn't want you to think I was an asshole."

"Yeah, well, maybe I think it anyway."

Okay, Allie, that was uncalled for.

"I'm sorry, I didn't mean that. As a matter of fact...I
really appreciate this. I know how much inconvenience
this has caused you, not to mention what it might mean
with your job. I guilted you into it, right? That whole big
'you owe me' speech."

"You didn't guilt me into anything."

He was telling the truth. She could see it in his eyes and hear it in his voice. But if he hadn't postponed the demolition out of some sense of outdated guilt, then why had he done it?

"Allie, have you ever wondered—"

"Nope, *never.*"

Geez!

She was such a liar because *of course* she'd thought about *it*. She was thinking about *it* now, for God's sake. How could she not? She was lying a mere six inches away from him.

But what made the whole thing worse was that she knew *he* was thinking about it, too. She wasn't some naïve eighteen-year-old virgin anymore. She was a thirty-year-old woman and she knew when a man wanted to have sex with her. And it wasn't just because they were alone and she was seemingly available.

She'd seen the way Tom looked at her when he didn't think she was watching. The way his voice went husky when she got too close. The hitch in his breath whenever they accidentally touched. It would be so easy to reach over and scratch her twelve-year itch. She was single. He was single now, too.

It would be the epilogue to a sad story. Sure. There wouldn't be a happily-ever-after, but both parties would leave with all unresolved business concluded.

The End. No chance for a sequel. *Ever.*

She was tempted. She really was. But everything inside her screamed that it would be disastrous because, despite the fact that it had been twelve long years, somehow (*unbelievably*), they were still connected. And not just on a physical level. Yes, there was that, certainly. But if it was only a physical thing then it would be easy to walk away and never think about him again.

She didn't want to know what Tom Donalan was
thinking and she didn't want him knowing what she was
thinking, either. Yet, here they were lying next to each
other, and they were doing just that. It was like they
were having some sort of weird brain sex.

"Stop it," she said.

"Stop what?"

"You know. That *thing* you do."

He didn't ask her to elaborate and she didn't
volunteer anything more. Instead, she shuffled back to
the edge of the mattress. Ghost or no ghost, Allie
couldn't wait for morning to arrive.

Chapter Fourteen

IN HER DREAM SHE was cold and it was so real she could actually feel herself shivering. Then something wrapped itself around her and the cold disappeared. She snuggled closer to the warmth. There was a hint of whiskey and something else—something familiar she hadn't tasted in ages but suddenly craved more than air itself. She opened her mouth, wanting more. A tongue, hot and aggressive, met hers in an urgent kiss. A large hand snaked beneath her T-shirt and cupped her breast, teasing her nipple into a tight bud.

Oh, so it was *that* kind of dream.

She sighed and shifted her legs, only to encounter something hard and unyielding. It took Allie a few seconds to realize what it was.

A boner—the size of Texas—pressed against her lower abdomen.

If you were going to have a fantasy, you might as well go for the gold.

She rubbed herself against the imaginary erection, eliciting a moan. Only the moan wasn't hers. It came from somewhere close, next to her ear. "*Damn*, Allie," whispered a dark voice. A voice that sounded suspiciously like...

Her eyes flew open. No, no, no! This wasn't happening. She shoved Tom off and rolled out from beneath him.

"*Hel-lo*! Can you please tell me what that was all about?" She struggled to regain some semblance of dignity.

Tom sat up and shook his head as if to clear it. He looked as disoriented as Allie felt. "All I know is that I was innocently sleeping when I woke up to find you kissing me."

"I wasn't kissing *you*. You were kissing *me*!"

He grinned, all lazy and smug looking. "I was kissing you all by myself?"

"Yes, absolutely. I didn't participate in the least." It sounded dumb, even to her. She ran a shaky hand through her hair. She probably looked a mess. Not that she should give a rat's ass what she looked like. Except she did. Dang it. "Okay, so I thought I was dreaming," she said in her defense.

"You dream about me?"

"Ha! Hardly. You were the one dreaming about me."

"You were shivering so I wrapped my arms around you to keep you warm. End of story. Can I help it if you took advantage of my chivalrous nature?"

She shook her head. "What are you so happy about?"

"The hell if I know." He stood and stretched his arms above his head. Allie tried to ignore the way his biceps bulged and how deliciously sexy he looked. He turned and caught her peeking. She quickly looked away. Pockets of sunshine streamed through the closed windows.

Wait. It was morning? She had planned to take another walk through the senior center with her ghost detector. How could she have slept through the night when her entire career hinged on this story? Maybe if she hurried, there would still be time for one last walk through.

"You want to talk about it?"

"Talk about what?" she asked. Although she knew perfectly well what he wanted to discuss. "That kiss was a freak one-time occurrence. Never to be repeated again. You have your life and I have mine. Right?"

His jaw tightened. "If you say so."

"PEOPLE, STAY OFF THE SIDEWALK!" boomed a voice from outside.

Tom and Allie stared at each other in confusion, and then he walked over to the front door and swung it open, letting in a flood of light. With a determined stride, he took off for the parking lot. Allie instinctively ran after him.

The scene in front of them was chaos.

Like yesterday morning, there were workmen and machines everywhere, but unlike yesterday morning there was a crowd gathered in the parking lot. They held signs and walked around in a circle.

"Keep the ghost alive!" yelled an elderly gentleman wearing a Gray Flamingos T-shirt. Viola, Gus, and at least a dozen other seniors marched alongside him.

There was another group, as well. A much younger, all female group, that Allie instantly recognized as Mimi's Bunco group, the Bunco Babes.

She also recognized Tom's foreman. He stood at the edge of the crowd with a bullhorn in his hands. "People! We need you to clear the premises. This building is scheduled to come down and we don't want anyone to get hurt!"

Tom took the bullhorn away from Hard Hat. "I got this, Keith."

"I did the best I could, Tom, but…" Keith raised his arm to blot the sweat dripping down his forehead. "They just keep coming!"

"What are all these people doing here?" Allie asked.

Keith turned to glare at her as if to say YOU. "I should have known it would be the Flaky Biscuit. Were you the one responsible for setting up this little protest?"

Tom's gaze flew to her face. Accusation and something else shone in his eyes. Something that looked suspiciously like hurt. Which was ridiculous. Tom Donalan didn't do hurt. He inflicted it.

"*Me*? No, I mean, I did ask the Gray Flamingos for help, but that was yesterday morning before I knew I was going to spend the night here. I had no idea they would organize anything like this."

Allie couldn't tell whether or not he believed her. "I'm going to make sure the equipment is secured before someone gets hurt." He signaled to Keith and both men took off toward one of the construction trailers.

Allie was about to follow as well when Mimi's friend Pilar stopped her. Her short dark hair was pulled back in a headband and her brown eyes were flushed with excitement. "Long time no see!" she said, wrapping Allie up into a hug. "I hear you're joining us for Bunco this week."

"Bunco? Um, yeah, maybe. What's going on here? How did all this happen?"

"Mimi initiated the Bunco phone chain and filled us in on this ghost situation," Pilar said. "As the city's attorney, I can't officially protest. Conflict of interest, and all that. But you have to admit, this is pretty exciting."

"Mimi helped organize this?"

"Along with the Gray Flamingos, of course. That's

quite an email if you ask me. You really don't know who sent it?"

"You read the anonymous email?"

"Viola forwarded it to the rest of the Gray Flamingos, my parents included, who forwarded it on to me. As you can see, word spreads fast in Whispering Bay." Pilar studied the building with renewed interest. "I knew the center had been vandalized a few times, but a *ghost* taking up residence? Do you think it's for real?"

"Oh, it's real all right," said a voice that could only come from smoking three packs of cigarettes a day.

Allie whipped around to find herself face to face with a tall, thin woman in her late sixties. It only took her a couple of seconds to realize who was standing in front of her. "You must be Phoebe Van Cleave."

"In the flesh," Phoebe croaked.

"What's going on? I figured when you didn't call me back that you weren't interested in my ghost story."

"Not interested? Are you kidding? I got sidetracked by the Dolphin Ghost, which turned out to be nothing but a big fake." Her face crinkled in disgust. "But don't worry; I plan to give this ghost one hundred percent of my full attention. My people are here now. That's what counts. And this building isn't going anywhere."

Roger Van Cleave walked up holding a homemade sign that read GIVE THE DEAD A CHANCE. "It's just like the good old days, huh?"

Allie frowned. "The good old days?"

"The sixties. Vietnam. Flower Power." Phoebe shook her fist high in the air to accentuate her point. "You're too young to understand but that's the beauty of this great country. If you don't like something, then protest the hell out of it."

"Um, yeah, okay, I read about the sixties."

"So, what happened last night? Did you make contact?" Phoebe asked.

The only contact Allie had made was the kiss-that-shouldn't-have-been. She felt her face go warm. "Honestly, Ms. Van Cleave? Not a whole lot happened." Allie briefly thought about mentioning the ghost detector app, but Phoebe was a professional and Allie didn't want to come off amateurish. But the lemons… Could it mean something? "I did smell this lemon odor. Twice now. And there was this warm fuzzy kind of feeling. But that's it."

"Lemons? This isn't a potpourri shop." Phoebe looked her over like a bug she wanted to squash. "Could be you and the ghost aren't simpatico."

"Could be there's no ghost at all and this whole thing has been some elaborate prank." She'd said it to get Phoebe's goat, but Allie had to start facing facts. She'd never really believed there was a ghost, but she'd hoped there would be *something* to write about. Something spooky or unexplained that she could milk into an article. But the whole thing was looking like nothing more than a dead end.

Phoebe planted her fists on her bony hips and glared at her. "No wonder he hasn't responded to you. You're a *non-believer*, aren't you?"

Allie sighed. She didn't need this. Not now. What she needed was… "Wait. What do you mean *him*?"

"Oh, whoever's haunting this place is definitely male. I'm getting an unusually high testosterone vibe." She raised her palm in the air like she was touching something and closed her eyes in concentration. When she opened her eyes again there was a serene, almost taunting look in them. "You really can't feel it?"

Allie couldn't feel the ghost vibe but she could

definitely feel the testosterone aura. And it wasn't friendly. She turned around to find Tom staring down at her.

"Can I speak to you? In private?" he asked.

"*Well*, I think I know where that warm and fuzzy feeling is coming from," Phoebe mocked. She waved them away. "You two lovebirds go on. I'm just going to have a word with my people."

"Oh, we aren't together," Allie said, but Phoebe had already taken off into the crowd.

Tom's expression was unreadable. "We can't do the demolition with all these people here. Can you get them to leave?"

"I'll try. But that crowd looks pretty determined. I'm not sure they'll listen to anything I have to say."

"Then try hard," he shot back.

Unbelievable. He did think this was all her fault! Which, it sort of was, she supposed, but his attitude was unfair. Just like him, she'd only been doing her job.

"Look, Donalan, I didn't go back on my word. Yes, I did contact these people to see what they knew about the ghost rumors, but I didn't ask them to show up here this morning. I really expected this building to come down today."

He studied her face like he was trying to figure something out, then slowly nodded. "If you say you didn't organize this, then I believe you."

Relief, simple and sweet, flooded her insides. It shouldn't matter what he thought, but it did. Allie didn't want to begin to think what that might mean. She took the bullhorn out of his hands. "I can't promise they'll leave, but I'll do my best."

She prepared herself to face the crowd. There were more people now than there'd been fifteen minutes ago.

Besides the Bunco Babes and the Gray Flamingos there were at least ten people wearing Sunshine Ghost Society T-shirts, as well as an assortment of onlookers.

"We've called in the troops from Panama City," Phoebe said, seeing her look of astonishment. "It's barely even eight and we already have almost forty people here. Should have another couple dozen by ten."

"Troops? As in…the military?"

"No, silly, the rest of the Sunshine Ghost Society."

"How many of you people are there?"

"A hundred, as of last count."

"A hundred!"

Phoebe nodded proudly. "Of course, not all of us are official investigators. Most are associate members and they're hoping to get their first glimpse at a real, honest-to-goodness ghost. A sighting could take them to the next level of our organization."

"What? Like a merit badge? Good luck with that because this is one shy ghost," Allie muttered.

"As I've said, the ghost is searching for a kindred spirit. Someone who'll be open to listening to whatever it is he needs to tell us. Obviously, that person isn't you."

Be polite, mi amor, Buela's voice whispered in her ear. Allie suppressed a shiver. Her grandmother's voice was always somewhere in the back of her head, but that bit of advice had sounded eerily real. As if Buela really were standing next to her.

"Well, here's the thing, Ms. Van Cleave, I truly do appreciate the effort you've made. Coming out here like this and all. But the building has to come down today, so I'm going to have to ask you and your group to clear the premises."

Phoebe searched Tom out with her gaze. "Gone over

to the other side, have you? Not that I blame you. Your boyfriend's mighty nice to look at but I can't be swayed by a pair of pretty blue eyes and a tight set of buns. No, ma'am, this is serious work we're looking at."

"I already told you, he's not my boyfriend." But her protest only seemed to amuse Phoebe. Allie wished she could wipe the obnoxious grin off the woman's face. "Maybe the ghost's spirit will be dislodged during the demolition," Allie said, grasping at straws. "I've been in this building two nights now and pretty much nothing has happened. Maybe the ghost just needs a push in the right direction to make himself known."

"You think *destroying* his home will get the ghost to cooperate?" She cackled, causing an eerie tingle to run down Allie's spine. "You have a lot to learn about the ghost business, missy. We're not trying to start Armageddon here. Destroying his home could cause all sorts of nastiness that, personally, I don't think this backwater town is ready for." Phoebe picked up her sign. "Now, out of my way, I have a protest to get on with."

Great. She'd summoned Attila the Ghost Hunter.

Allie raised the bullhorn to her mouth. "May I have your attention," she said to the crowd.

"It's the reporter!" shouted one of the Gray Flamingos.

"Hello, everyone," Allie said, trying to sound authoritative, in a friendly kind of way. "I'm Allison Grant and I'm a journalist representing *Florida!* magazine. I circulated the letter from my anonymous source that many of you have read, and while I do appreciate the support you've shown this morning, I'm sorry to say that I've spent enough time in the building to conclude that I just don't think there's a ghost in there. Or...at least not one who wants to make itself known."

The crowd began fidgeting.

"And, so, here's the thing. This protest is getting in the way of people's jobs—"

"You're giving up?" someone yelled. "Just like that?"

"Just because the ghost doesn't like you doesn't mean he's not here!" came another voice.

"Look," Allie said, "I'll be more than happy to embrace this ghost, but without some kind of proof I can't support another delay in taking down the building."

"You want proof?" yelled a familiar voice. Allie searched the crowd. It was Roger Van Cleave. "I'll give you proof. I've seen the ghost!"

Everyone turned to stare at Roger.

Allie lowered the bullhorn. "What do you mean, you've seen the ghost?"

"I confess. I wrote the anonymous letter." He reached into his shirt pocket to produce a folded sheet of paper and waved it in the air. "I'm Concerned Citizen!"

Chapter Fifteen

THE CROWD BEGAN TO cheer. *Roger Van Cleave was Concerned Citizen*? Why didn't he tell her that yesterday? Why all the secrecy? Especially if he planned to blurt it out in front of half the town. The protestors began deluging him with questions.

"I've seen the ghost, too!" said a woman with a Sunshine Ghost Society T-shirt. "He's here right now!" She pointed to the building. "He's on the roof!"

Shouts filled the air.

"There he is!" someone cried.

Allie whipped around to look where everyone was pointing, but all she saw was a big fat *nothing*.

Tom came up to stand beside her. "It's like the damn Salem witch hunts."

"You don't see anything, either?"

He shook his head in disgust.

The wail of a police siren drowned out Allie's next thoughts.

"It's the pigs!" Phoebe yelled.

Allie almost expected her to take off running, but Phoebe, like the rest of the protestors, stood their ground as the Whispering Bay police cruiser cautiously made its way through the parking lot.

The door opened and Zeke emerged.

Allie had to admit, she was both happy and a little anxious to see her big brother. Happy, because surely he was going to take care of this mess and anxious because he had his Allie-what-have-you-done-now face. Rusty had come along as well. He attempted to clear the crowd, but from what Allie could see, no one was bothering to listen to his orders.

Zeke came up and touched her arm in brotherly affection, a far cry from their usual kiss and hug, but there was a crowd present and he was here on official business so she didn't take it personally. He whipped off his cop sunglasses. "Got a call there was a disturbance going on. What are all these people doing here?"

"They're protesting the senior center demolition," Allie said, "but I swear to you, Zeke, I had nothing to do with this. We woke up a few minutes ago to find…all this"—she waved her arm through the air—"in the parking lot."

Zeke scratched his chin in a deceptively pensive move that Allie swore he must have learned from some cop movie. "We?" His gaze zeroed in on Tom.

"Tom and I spent the night in the senior center hoping to make contact with the ghost. My idea. Not his," she added quickly.

"The *ghost*?" Zeke laughed incredulously. "Let me get this straight, Donalan. My sister bamboozled you into spending the night here in the hopes of catching a ghost?"

"We weren't trying to catch it; we were trying to make contact. I'm writing a story about it for *Florida!* magazine. Hasn't Mimi told you any of this?"

To Allie's surprise, Tom backed her up. "Allie's just following up on a lead. It's what any journalist would do. The building's been vandalized a couple of times in the past month so I couldn't let her stay here alone."

"Not to throw kerosene on the fire," Rusty interrupted, his face pale. "But I could have sworn I just saw something on top of that building."

The three of them turned in unison. "Like what?" Zeke demanded.

"Like a vapor," Rusty said. "A dancing vapor!"

Zeke shook his head like what the hell, but it was Rusty, right?

Phoebe Van Cleave, who was close enough to hear Rusty's words, didn't waste time capitalizing on them. "See!" she cried. "Even the fuzz sees the ghost!"

Excitement hummed through the parking lot as word spread. Was it possible there was really a ghost on top of the building and Allie just couldn't see it? Or was the power of suggestion causing some kind of mass hysteria?

Zeke ignored the pumped-up crowd and walked inside the building. Tom and Allie followed. It took her brother exactly two seconds to hone in on the lone mattress.

"Looks pretty damn cozy here." Zeke turned his scary cop stare on Tom. "Do I need to ask what your intentions are toward my sister? Or should I save time and just beat the shit out of you instead?"

Allie punched her brother on the shoulder. Just enough to get his attention. "Oh for the love of—nothing happened, Zeke."

Tom nudged her out of the way until both men stood eye to eye. "Look, Grant, whatever happened between Allie and me is none of your business. I need the premises cleared. So, I'd appreciate it if you did your job so I can do mine."

It was like watching one of those old time westerns where the two gunslingers faced each other in the final showdown. Each of them waiting for the other to draw first.

Rusty came running in from the parking lot, his face flushed and his forehead covered in sweat. "Those Gray Flamingos say they ain't leavin' till the ghost tells them what they want to know. Something about the world coming to an end."

Allie moaned.

Rusty took a handkerchief from his back pocket and mopped his brow. "Yeah, and that Van Cleave woman? Piece of work, that one. Says she's gonna call a judge friend of hers from Panama City to keep the building from coming down until her Friendly Ghost Society can do a proper investigation."

"That's Sunshine Ghost Society," Allie corrected.

Zeke broke out of his badass sheriff routine to deal with this newest development. "Rusty, get Bruce Bailey on the line." Bruce Bailey was Whispering Bay's mayor and the way Zeke said his name didn't bode well.

"I'm on it, Chief." Rusty exited the building like he was on a mission.

"That's my cue to give Steve Pappas an update," Tom said. He glanced between Allie and Zeke, then left to make his call.

"What's going on between you and that guy?" Zeke asked once they were alone.

"I already told you. Nothing's going on."

"Don't bullshit me. I saw the way he looked at you."

"Oh yeah? Like what?"

"Like you were breakfast and he hadn't eaten in days."

That certainly described what she'd woken up to this

morning. Only to be fair, she'd been just as hungry as Tom. She tried for a blank expression. "French toast or scrambled eggs?"

"Allie," Zeke said in a warning tone.

"No worries, big brother. It's all good. Tom has actually been…kind of cooperative here."

"I don't care if he did a rain dance trying to call this ghost of yours out." Zeke ran an agitated hand through his cropped dark hair. "Are you getting back together with that guy?"

"What? No!"

"Good, because that asshole broke your heart. You cried for days, hell, it was more like weeks. Think I've forgotten about that?"

That asshole, as Zeke put it, walked back into the building the exact moment her brother uttered those words. No sense hoping he hadn't heard it. It was clear from the look on Tom's face that he'd caught Zeke's entire tirade.

Captain Crunch. Leave it to Zeke's big mouth to make things even worse than they were before. Now Tom Donalan felt *sorry* for her. This was totally unacceptable. It had been twelve years. She got why *she* might feel bitter, but why did Zeke still harbor so much animosity toward Tom?

"For the record, no one broke my heart. Okay?" she announced. "And while I appreciate the big brother routine," she said to Zeke, "I'm thirty years-old and I can take care of myself, thank you very much."

Neither of them said anything and somehow that made it all worse. Like they didn't believe her. She could barely look Tom in the eye. If her license wasn't suspended, she'd get in her car and drive back to Tampa this instant.

Rusty walked back in the building with a long face. "Bad news, Chief. Mayor Bailey says he can't interfere with what's going on here. Something about not wanting to take sides."

"More like not wanting to lose votes," Zeke muttered.

Allie glanced over to find Tom staring at her hard. "I think I have a solution," he said. "Follow me."

They all marched outside. Allie was curious to discover what sort of solution Tom had come up with. He positioned himself at the edge of the crowd. The protestors, sensing something was up, quieted down to listen. "I've just spoken to my boss at Pappas-Hernandez Construction. We don't want anyone to get hurt here, so the company is willing to compromise."

The crowd began chanting, "Séance! Séance! Séance!"

"You have forty-eight hours. And that's it," Tom said sternly. "Forty-eight hours and this building comes down. No matter what."

A cheer went up among the protestors.

Forty-eight hours? Steve Pappas was willing to give them another forty-eight hours! Only this time, Allie wouldn't be going solo. She'd have Phoebe and the rest of the Sunshine Ghost Society to back her up.

"That doesn't sound like Steve Pappas," Zeke muttered.

"What do you mean?" she asked.

"Pappas is all about the bottom line. He's a nice guy, but he's a businessman first and he's doing this project pro bono, so he doesn't need any more PR. Bruce Bailey already wants to give him the key to the city."

Allie used her hand to shield her eyes from the sun and searched Tom out. He appeared busy talking to a group of his workmen. She thought about what Zeke had just said, but what reason would Tom have to lie about the demolition extension?

Allie's thoughts were interrupted by a familiar gravelly voice that she was beginning to dread. "Forty-eight hours isn't nearly enough time to prepare for a proper séance, but I suppose we'll just have to make do."

Phoebe kept popping back up like some evil jack-in-the-box. Still, if she could get this séance off the ground, Allie would personally buy her a year's supply of her favorite cigarettes. Allie frowned. That seemed a little...uncharitable of her. She'd get Phoebe a year's supply of nicotine patches, instead.

"Do you really think you can make contact with the ghost through a séance?" Allie asked. "I mean, are those for real?"

"Of course they're for real. This being, whoever he may have been in life, has made contact for a reason and we need to get to the bottom of it. From what my brother tells me the ghost has only recently made himself known, which means something's got his tighty whities twisted in a wad." Phoebe glared at the large Demolition in Progress sign in front of the senior center door. "Doesn't take a genius to figure out what that something is."

"Can I ask you a question?"

"That's what I'm here for," Phoebe said. "In case you weren't aware, *I am* the area's leading ghost expert."

"Then why didn't your brother go to you directly with this? Why send me an anonymous email signed Concerned Citizen?"

Phoebe's face clouded over. "Who knows why Roger does anything these days? Maybe he's off his meds."

Allie wasn't sure what that meant, but despite her

mixed emotions at the morning's events, she began to feel hopeful. A séance. An honest to God séance. Whatever else happened, ghost or no ghost, *this* was a story she could run with.

The crowd had thinned down by the time Allie made it back inside the senior center. She watched as Tom deflated the air mattress, folded it into a square, then punched it back inside the bag to make it fit. He glanced up to see Allie standing over him.

"What made Steve Pappas give us the extension? I mean, is everything going to be okay with your job?"

"Sure, everything's fine." He shrugged. "It doesn't make sense to go ahead with the demolition if we're going to have to fight half the town to do it. Steve Pappas knows it's good PR to hold off for a couple days. That way, everyone ends up happy." He sounded convincing enough, but there was that twitchy thing he did with his mouth that made Allie think he wasn't being one hundred percent honest with her.

"Look, I want you to know I appreciate everything you've done trying to help me with this ghost story, even though you're not a believer and you have your own agenda here. So I was thinking, maybe we can start over? If this ghost exists, then I want to flush him out so I can write my story. And obviously, that's in your best interest, too, because once we do that then there can't be any more objections to the building coming down."

"What are you saying?"

"I'm saying I don't see why we can't be on friendlier terms."

"Friendlier?"

"Not like this morning friendly, which for the record, I did *not* initiate. I just think we should be partners."

"So now we're the two musketeers? Did you really buy that little show out there? A ghost on top of the building? C'mon, Allie, you're smarter than that."

"Just because I didn't see what everyone else saw doesn't mean there wasn't something there." She bit her bottom lip. "I admit I'm not sure what to think about Concerned Citizen."

"Roger Van Cleave? You know his wife died last year."

"What does that have to do with anything?"

"Roger doesn't know what to do with himself and now this ghost thing has fallen right into his lap. I'm sure he thinks he saw a ghost. He probably even believes he wrote that letter, and maybe he did, but this is all just something to tick away the hours for a lonely old man."

"How do you know all this?"

"He's a member of Dad's parish. Calls him three, four times a week with some suggestion or other for Sunday's sermon. I helped patch his roof a few weeks ago. Kept me there all day plying me with iced tea and stories about the good old days."

"That's…that was really nice of you."

"Don't look at me like that," he said. "I'm not that nice. You should know that better than anyone."

"What exactly are we talking about here—" *Argh.* She knew *exactly* what he was talking about. She was going to kill Zeke with her bare hands. "How many times do I have to tell you? *You. Did. Not. Break. My. Heart.* Got it?"

"Got it. No one broke anyone's heart." He paused and lowered his voice. "But I owe you an apology anyway."

169

"If it makes you feel better, than by all means, go ahead. Add in some sack cloth and ashes while you're at it."

"Can you cut me a little slack here, Allie? This isn't easy for me. Because the truth is, whenever I look at you it reminds me of a time in my life that I'm not so proud of. And then, there's that other thing."

"What other thing?"

"The fact that we both want to screw each other's brains out."

Her jaw dropped.

Phoebe Van Cleave appeared in the open doorway. "May I enter?" she asked in a loud dramatic voice.

"Sure, why not? Come on in," Tom said.

Phoebe glared at him. "I wasn't speaking to you. I'm asking the ghost for permission."

Tom laughed in that not nice way of his. "In that case, the ghost says wipe your feet before you come inside."

Despite the tension between them, Allie couldn't help but smile. Just a little.

"Make fun all you want," Phoebe said. "I guarantee tomorrow night you won't be so cocky."

"Is that when you've arranged for the séance?" Allie tried to appear contrite. Sharing a joke with Tom at Phoebe's expense wasn't going to win Phoebe over to her side. And like it or not, that was exactly what Allie was going to have to do if she wanted an exclusive on this séance.

Phoebe cautiously stepped inside the building, like any second now she'd trip on a land mine. "I just heard from Madame Gloria. She's available to host a séance tomorrow night. I tried for this evening but she's booked. We're lucky she's available on such short notice."

Tom crossed his arms over his chest. "I almost hate to ask, but who's Madame Gloria?"

"Just the best medium in north Florida, probably even in the whole southeast," Phoebe declared proudly. "If there's a ghost haunting this building, which of course there is since we've all seen him, she'll tap into him. Yep, tomorrow night *all* will be revealed."

Allie pulled her cell phone out of her backpack. "This is great, Phoebe. I really appreciate this. Does Madame Gloria have a website? Or maybe a bio I can look up? Do you think she'll let me tape the séance?"

"Oh, you won't be there," Phoebe said. "This will be a closed event. Open to only a few selected individuals. Madame Gloria usually only allows four witnesses of her choice, tops."

"Make that six," Tom said.

Phoebe scowled. "How did you come up with that number?"

"Her four, plus Allie and me make six."

"I'm afraid that's not possible. Only true believers allowed."

"But I'm a true believer," Allie said. No need to mention what she believed in was that she needed this story. "And I'm the one who got this whole thing started!"

"Nevertheless, the ghost gets to pick. And he doesn't pick you," Phoebe said.

The front door to the senior center slammed shut, startling all three of them.

"That's weird," Allie said. "Must have been a breeze."

"Probably." Tom opened the door again and poked his head out.

Allie came up behind him. There was no breeze.

Nothing but warm, humid air. Now that the cooler weather brought by the rain had passed it was already climbing back into the eighties, typical Florida fall weather. She scanned the parking lot. Most of the protestors and the construction crew had cleared out. Zeke and Rusty were chatting it up with some of Mimi's Bunco group and the Gray Flamingos were packing up their signs.

Roger Van Cleave caught her looking, then quickly cut his gaze away. She remembered what Tom said, about Roger's wife passing and how he didn't think Roger was Concerned Citizen. The more Allie thought about it, she had to agree. She watched as he stashed his sign in the backseat of his car. Poor old guy. You'd have to be pretty lonely to make up stuff just for attention.

Phoebe cleared her throat. "As I was saying, six is impossible. No, I'm afraid the two of you will have to sit this one out."

"Phoebe," Allie began, "I don't think it's fair to not include me when—"

"Here's the bottom line," Tom said. "This is my building. If the ghost doesn't pick me and Allie, then I say to hell with the ghost. Go have your séance somewhere else."

"What's that supposed to mean?" Phoebe demanded.

"It means I'm responsible for whatever happens in this building so unless you agree to our presence, you can kiss your séance good-bye."

"You're not serious," Phoebe sputtered.

"Oh believe me, he's serious," Allie said. "Insurance complications, and all that."

Phoebe looked ready to spit. "It's simply not possible. The ghost will never manifest himself if he doesn't feel that everyone here is on his side."

The door slammed shut again. A clean lemon smell crept through the air, jolting Allie into a heightened sense of awareness. And then it hit her. It wasn't lemons at all. It was something else. Something comforting and warmly familiar. It was the smell of Jean Nate, the only cologne Buela had ever worn. Allie closed her eyes and tried to concentrate, but the smell was now gone.

"Did you smell that?" she asked.

"Smell what?" Phoebe stared at the closed door in disbelief.

"Lemons."

"What is it with you and lemons? We have a ghost to concentrate on here." Phoebe walked over to the door and placed her palm against the old wood then swayed back and forth like she was in a trance. After about a minute, she turned to face them with a wide smile on her face. "He's here! He's really here. And...for some reason, he doesn't object to your presence at the séance."

"How convenient," Tom said.

"The ghost *told you* he didn't object to us?" Allie said.

"Not in so many words, but I was able to feel it. Because as I've said, the ghost and I are—"

"Simpatico," Allie finished.

"*Exactly.*"

Allie itched to wipe the smug expression off Phoebe's face but she needed to be in the old bat's good graces. Phoebe began to list off all the supplies they'd need for the séance.

"And of course we'll tape it," Phoebe finished. "I'll put Roger in charge. He's good at that sort of thing. Oh, and it's imperative the table be sturdy. We can't have one of those flimsy card tables with the wobbly legs."

"No wobbly legs," Allie said. "Anything else?"

"Just one more thing. After I leave here the building must be closed for the twenty-four hour period before the séance. Absolutely *no one* must enter. The atmosphere must be as pure as possible. Any lingering negative vibrations and the ghost might not respond to Madame Gloria." She seared them both one last time with her bug eyes before making a grand exit from the building.

"I don't get it," Allie said. "Why doesn't she like me?"

"She's a kook. And she's threatened by you."

"By me?"

"Sure, you honed in on her little ghost business."

"You have to admit the door thing was creepy. And the smell—"

"A random burst of air shut the door. The windows are all boarded up, so any lingering smells are going to be exaggerated. That's all it was, Allie."

"You really believe that?"

"Yeah, I do."

She sighed. "Well, thanks for getting Phoebe to agree to let us take part in the séance."

"Did you really think I was going to let her do her thing in here without us?"

"Poor Phoebe has no idea what's she up against," Allie said. "Insurance regulations, demolition deadlines, *and* a budget."

She hoped he might smile at that but he didn't. "So, are we going to pretend our previous conversation never happened?"

Yes, please. "I don't want to fight with you, Tom."

"I don't want to fight with you, either."

"Then, yeah, can we pretend it never happened? Can we start over as just…friends?"

He stared at her a moment, then shrugged. "Sure, we can be great pals." Before she could say anything to that, he added, "It's been a long morning, let's get out of here." He made a quick inspection, going room to room, making sure they didn't leave anything behind. He was securing the padlock to the front door when Allie stopped him by placing her hand on his arm.

"You really didn't feel anything? Or smell anything unusual? Because if we're going to be friends then we have to be honest with one another."

"I'm sorry, Allie, but all I smell is musty old building."

She wished she could say he was lying. But unlike before, this time Tom was telling the truth.

Chapter Sixteen

MIMI WAS FASCINATED BY this latest development. "So, you were the only one who smelled the lemons? I mean, if this Phoebe Van Cleave expert person didn't smell it... Do you think she smelled it, too, and just didn't want to say?" She passed the meatloaf in Allie's direction, which Allie eagerly took. All this ghost hunting could leave a girl hungry.

"I don't know. I wouldn't put anything past that woman. She definitely has her own agenda." She should fess up and tell them it wasn't lemons she'd smelled, but Buela's cologne. Wouldn't her brother just love that one?

"All the kids at school are talking about what happened," Cameron said. "Josh Bellamy said the ghost put some kind of force field around the senior center and if anyone tries to get inside they'll be vaporized."

Claire snorted. "Yeah, right."

"I didn't say I believed it," Cameron said defensively. "I just said he said it."

Allie winked at her nephew. "No one is getting vaporized. But there's definitely something strange going on in that building."

Zeke calmly took a bite of his scalloped potatoes.

"Personally, I think the whole thing is a bunch of bunk."

Her brother was out of his cop uniform and dressed in khaki slacks and a red polo shirt. Unlike Mimi, Zeke showed no signs of gray in his dark hair, which he kept military short. Allie had to admit upon occasion to being somewhat envious of her brother. The two of them looked enough alike that everyone who saw them together instantly recognized they were brother and sister, but Zeke had inherited the pretty gene. Not that Allie felt unattractive, but as a guy, Zeke was definitely in a different league.

Back in his single days, girls had phoned the house at all hours. It had driven Buela crazy. "That boy is going to end up getting some poor girl in the family way," she'd predicted. Which of course, was exactly what had happened. Allie was just glad that it had happened with Mimi. She didn't think Zeke would have straightened out his life for anyone but her.

"Don't listen to Zeke. He thinks everything's bunk," Mimi said.

Her brother kept on eating.

"Zeke," Allie said, trying to sound casual. "Do you remember the cologne Buela used to wear?"

He laid down his fork. "Where did that come from?"

"I was talking to one of those Gray Flamingos this morning at the protest and I could have sworn I smelled Buela's cologne. It got me thinking, is all," she lied. "What was it called again?"

"Jean Nate," he said, reaching for a second helping of potatoes.

Bin-go! She tried to keep her expression neutral. "Wow. You have a good memory."

He shrugged. "We used to buy it for her every Christmas, don't you remember? I don't know if she really liked it as much as she let on, but it was all we could afford. We'd go to the mall in Panama City and get the big gift pack. Cologne, powder, after-bath stuff. I think it lasted her all year, then Christmas would roll around and we'd get her another one."

Of course she remembered.

If the lemon smell was really Jean Nate, could it be Buela's spirit haunting the old senior center? Allie's pulse began dancing a jig. This was crazy! Even if she did believe in ghosts, and even if somehow, that ghost was Buela, why show up now? She'd been gone for over twelve years. Plus, there was the fact that Phoebe thought the ghost was male. Of course, Allie was beginning to think Tom was right and Phoebe wasn't quite the ghost authority she made herself out to be.

"My grandmother used to wear Jean Nate," Mimi said wistfully. "I really miss her."

Allie's pulse tripped on a step, then sputtered. Mimi was right. Every grandmother in the country probably wore Jean Nate at some time or another. Even if the lemon smell was real, and not just some figment of Allie's imagination, it could mean anything. More than likely one of the protestors had worn the perfume and Allie, being Allie and having that nose of hers, had picked up the scent.

"I hope you don't mind eating dinner this early," Mimi said. "I know it's barely five-thirty but Cameron has soccer practice at seven."

"No problem. I'm just happy to have a homemade meal. Especially yours."

"It's rare that we all sit down to dinner these days as a family. So I aim for whatever time I can get."

Allie noticed that Mimi barely ate anything herself. Was her sister-in-law watching her weight? Mimi didn't look like she needed to drop any pounds. Just the opposite. She was thinner than Allie had ever seen her. Still, she looked good tonight. She wore a lime green shift that picked up the blue in her eyes and her shoulder-length brown hair was freshly blow dried and straightened. She even had on make-up.

"Pilar told me you helped organize the protest," Allie said. "So I guess I owe you a big thanks."

Zeke put down his fork and eyed Mimi.

Oops. Maybe Allie shouldn't have mentioned that.

"Oh, I didn't do much. I just initiated the Bunco phone chain. I wanted to make sure the rest of the Babes knew about that letter. If I hadn't had a PTA meeting this morning, believe me, I would have been there, too."

"Well, thanks to you the whole town knows now," Zeke said. He picked up his fork and resumed eating.

"Good," Mimi said. "The whole town should know what's going on."

Allie coughed. "Um, I'm surprised Bruce Bailey didn't show up this morning. Seeing as how he's the mayor and all."

Zeke made a disgusted face. "Bruce Bailey is worthless."

"I agree," Mimi said. "As a matter of fact, I'm thinking of running against him in the coming election."

Everyone except Mimi stopped eating.

"The coming election," Zeke said slowly. "As in, six months from now?"

"Sure, why not?"

Zeke laughed. "I thought you were serious."

"I am serious."

He gave Mimi a long look, then laid down his napkin. "Bruce Bailey might be worthless but he's vice president of a bank. He knows just a little bit about how to balance a city budget."

"And I know just a *little bit* about how to balance a family budget," Mimi responded. "They're probably not that much different."

Allie stuffed her mouth full of meatloaf. What in holy heck was going on here?

Zeke eyed Cameron's empty plate. "You done there, champ?"

Cameron nodded, wide-eyed.

"Then finish your homework and get ready for practice. We need to drop you off early."

"Now?" Cameron whined. "But I want to hear how mom is going to be mayor."

"Your mom and I have to be in Panama City by seven, so yeah, *now*," said Zeke, the hard-ass, in a tone that encouraged no back talk.

Allie almost felt sorry for Cameron, but then, she didn't. Their own dad had been a total slouch. Zeke might be a strict disciplinarian but he was a good provider and a steady influence. Considering the role model he'd had, it was amazing he'd turned out to be such a good dad.

Cameron took his plate and laid it in the sink.

"What's going on in Panama City?" Allie asked.

Before either Mimi or Zeke could answer, Claire said, "I can take Cameron to practice."

"And what? Drive by yourself?" Mimi said.

Claire made a disgruntled teenage noise. "I'm sixteen. I've had my license for three whole weeks now but you still think I'm a baby. Everyone else at school already drives alone and half my class has their own car."

"Good for half your class," Zeke said.

Maria Geraci

"If you're nervous about Claire driving Cameron to soccer, I can go with them," Allie volunteered.

Claire brightened up. "Would you?"

"Sure," Allie said.

"I don't know. Technically, your aunt can't drive right now," said her not-so-helpful brother.

"What's the use of having a driver's license if you never let me use it?" Claire left the table in a huff with her plate barely touched.

Mimi pursed her lips.

Before Zeke could say anything about Claire's behavior, Allie said, "I wouldn't be driving. I'd be sitting in the front seat supervising her. There's no law against that, is there?"

"She's right, Zeke," Mimi said. "If Allie wants to help out, then I say let her." She glanced at her watch for the third time since they'd sat down for dinner.

"I get it," Allie said, grinning at her brother. "It's date night." No wonder Mimi and Zeke seemed on edge. After Zeke's out-of-town trip, they were probably chomping at the bit for some alone time. Not that Allie blamed them. Between Zeke's job and the kids' activities, they hardly ever saw each other.

"Date night. Right," Zeke said without much enthusiasm.

"Don't forget we have to pick up Henry," Mimi said. "It's our turn for carpool."

"I'll call Tom and see if he can drive the boys." Zeke excused himself and went to the other room.

Allie waited until Cameron left to get dressed for soccer before saying, "Speaking of the boys, why didn't you warn me that Henry was coming over last night?"

"I didn't tell you?" Mimi asked innocently.

"You know you didn't."

"He's a cute kid, huh?"

"Very cute."

"Just like his dad."

"Yeah, just like his dad, who as I said before, I have no interest in, so if you're thinking of playing matchmaker, I already told you, that's never going to happen."

"Never is a long time."

"True, but in this case it's an eternity. We're partners, nothing more."

"Partners?" Mimi said, perking with interest.

"As in, we both have a common goal. As soon as I get this ghost story, I'm out of Tom Donalan's hair for good. Other than an occasional rare sighting, I predict with my biannual visit back home, odds are I'll only run into him every fourth or fifth year, at best."

"Already figured out the odds, have you?"

"In the interest of ruining your *Fiddler on the Roof* moment here, can I change the subject? Did you hear Roger Van Cleave admitted to being Concerned Citizen?"

"Yeah, pretty dramatic timing, huh?" Allie didn't say anything. "What? You think he's lying?" Mimi asked.

"Let's just say, I wouldn't be surprised to find out he made it up. Plus, it makes no sense really. Why write me an anonymous letter when he could have gotten his sister, the ghost hunter, to investigate?"

Allie couldn't put her finger on it, but there was something decidedly *feminine* about that letter. She'd wanted to ask Roger about it this morning, but by the time she and Tom had locked up the senior center, Roger had disappeared. She tried calling him, but there was no answer, so she left a message on his machine, but he still hadn't returned her call. It didn't take a genius to figure out Roger Van Cleave was avoiding her.

"Well, eventually, the truth will come out."

"It usually does," Allie agreed. She just wished it would come out sooner than later. She watched as her sister-in-law made a pot of coffee. It occurred to Allie that she'd never really questioned what Mimi did or didn't know about the ghost. "You sure you never heard the ghost rumors before? I mean, before I came to town to investigate?"

"I think I would have remembered anything about a ghost," Mimi said. She narrowed her eyes at Allie. "What are you thinking?"

"I just find it strange that I get this anonymous letter but there isn't one person who's come forward to say that they've seen anything, before today's sighting, that is. Even Phoebe, who's supposedly on top of all the paranormal activity in the area, was surprised to hear about this ghost."

"And?"

"And I have no idea what I'm doing. I just hope this séance makes a good enough story to trump a piece on illegal immigration."

"I'm just bummed that the séance has to be on the same night as Bunco. I would have loved to have you come play with us." Mimi poured herself a cup of coffee. "So who's going to be there tomorrow night?"

"Whoever Phoebe and Madame Gloria think the ghost will approve of."

Mimi giggled. "But you and Tom will be there, right?"

"Oh, yeah, he made sure of that."

"He's a good man to have around."

"If you say so." Which, in this case, Allie had to silently agree with, but she didn't want Mimi thinking she was jumping on Team Tom. "Phoebe says there can only be six people at the séance, tops."

"I know of at least a dozen people who want to be there," Mimi continued. "As head of the Gray Flamingos, Viola Pantini should be considered."

Allie nodded. "Definitely." *Pause.* "Were you serious earlier? About running for mayor?"

Before Mimi could answer, Zeke came back in the room. "Tom can't drive tonight. And Lauren and her parents are still driving back from seeing the doctor in Pensacola. They won't be back home till after practice starts."

Mimi's forehead scrunched in worry. "Is Dan all right?" She turned to Allie to explain. "Lauren's daddy hasn't been himself lately."

"He's what, a cousin of your mother's?"

"Something like that."

"He doesn't see Dr. Morrison here in town?" Allie asked.

"I believe he does, but they wanted a second opinion."

Allie thought about Lauren and her quirky little sixties shop and of course, how darn *nice* she was. "I hope everything's okay."

"The bottom line is we're responsible for getting the boys to soccer," Zeke said, getting them back to the dilemma at hand.

"Really, guys, I think you two are making a bigger production of this than you need to."

"Allie's right. If she goes, then it will be fine if Claire drives," Mimi said.

"It's up to you," Zeke said. "You're the one who's been supervising her driving."

"Fine." Mimi began loading the dishwasher. "Let's give Claire a chance. And if after next week she hasn't crashed the car, I say we let her go solo."

Chapter Seventeen

"**THANKS, AUNT ALLIE,**" **CLAIRE** said, getting behind the minivan's wheel. "You're the best."

"Just drive safely." Allie watched as her niece went through the routine of adjusting the mirrors.

Claire drove the short distance to Tom's house perfectly. No speeding, no wobbling, no slamming on the brakes. Allie leaned back in her seat and relaxed. Mimi and Zeke were too overprotective. If she ever had kids, she hoped she wouldn't be as anal as her brother and sister-in-law.

Claire cruised the minivan up a paved driveway leading to a cream-colored stucco house directly across from the beach. Allie had to admit to being curious about Tom's place of residence. From the outside the house looked small, but cozy. Nice location. A perfect bachelor pad. She'd love an excuse to take a look inside, but Henry was out the door the instant they pulled up.

A few seconds later, Tom emerged from the house. He walked over to the minivan and propped his arm on the car's roof, then leaned his head in through the open window. His gaze quickly took everything in. "Hey, Cameron, how's it going?"

"Doing good, Mr. Donalan," Cameron answered from the back seat.

"You boys have a good practice." He glanced over at Claire, then back at Allie. "So, Claire's driving, huh?"

Claire was busy messing with the car's radio dials, clueless to their conversation.

"With my supervision, of course," Allie said.

"Of course." After a few seconds, he stepped back and tapped his hand on the car's roof, as if giving the go ahead for take-off. "See you later," he said to his son. "Don't forget, after practice you're going to your mom's tonight."

"We're dropping Cameron off at Lauren's?" she asked.

"Is that a problem?"

"No, of course not. I just thought it was probably your night...you know, to have him over." Allie didn't know much about the way divorced couples split their child custody arrangements, but since they'd picked Henry up at Tom's, Allie had naturally assumed Henry would be spending the night with his dad.

"I pick Henry up at school most afternoons while Lauren is at the shop. It gives me a chance to spend more time with him and it helps her out, too. But he doesn't always stay over."

The way Tom talked about his son made Allie pause. He sounded so...proud and protective. She had never found fatherhood sexy. Until now.

"You could join us, you know, at soccer practice," Allie blurted. "I plan to stay and watch."

His face went blank. "Thanks, but I have something important to do."

"Like what? A hot date?" she joked.

"Something like that." Before Allie could respond, he told Claire to drive safely, then stepped away from the minivan, clicked open the door to his pickup truck and got inside.

Claire backed the minivan down the driveway and they were off.

A hot date? Argh! Why had she said that? And then of course, there was that evasive response of his. *Something like that.*

Was he serious? Normally, she could tell when he was joking. At least, she used to be able to. He didn't look like he was kidding around, but he did look taken aback by her invitation to join them at soccer practice. As if he wanted to join them, but couldn't.

They drove the rest of the way to the soccer field without any incident, which was good, considering Allie was having a hard time concentrating on the road. So what if Tom had a date? Bully for him! He was a divorced man and Allie had made it abundantly clear after this morning's kiss that she wasn't interested in a romantic relationship.

"Good job driving," Allie said, ignoring how Claire parked the minivan halfway into the adjacent space. The boys ran toward the grass where the rest of the team was already warming up. Allie unloaded a couple of folding chairs from the back of the van and offered one to her niece.

"You're really going to stay and watch?" Claire asked.

"Of course I am."

"I thought that was just a pretext." Claire shrugged. "You know, to spend more time with Mr. Donalan."

"Why would I want to do that?"

"Why *wouldn't* you want to do that? It's okay. Your secret is safe with me. So you have a crush on Henry's dad. Big deal. He likes you, too, by the way."

"I think you've been watching too much cable TV."

Claire made a face that made Allie feel like she was a hundred years old. "I'm not a child, Aunt Allie. And by the way, he wasn't going on some hot date."

Allie narrowed her eyes at her niece. "I thought you were messing with the radio."

"That doesn't mean my ears have fallen off."

There was something semi-pathetic about talking to one's niece concerning your love life. But Allie couldn't seem to help herself. "Okay, Miss-Sixteen-Going-On-Thirty, how do you know he wasn't going on a date?"

"Because he was wearing faded jeans and a T-shirt, and a guy like him doesn't wear that on a date."

"Oh? What does a guy like *him* wear on a date?"

"Hot guy stuff." Claire batted her eyelashes. "Nicer jeans, black turtleneck, and cowboy boots." She was describing what Tom had worn last night for their senior center slumber party. Which had certainly *not* been a date.

Allie tried to shrug it off. "Maybe he was taking some poor girl...fishing or something. Let's change the subject, please."

"Whatever you say." Claire moistened her lips. "I was thinking of driving by my friend Jordan's house. She only lives two blocks away."

"Not a good idea. I think we pretty much promised your parents I'd supervise your driving tonight."

"Parents!" Claire said with a conspiratorial smile. "Can't live with them, can't live without them."

"Yeah, well, I think my brother would pretty much have my head if I disobeyed his orders."

"Dad can be pretty intense," Claire agreed. "Okay, so you can watch me drive to Jordan's house and then you can drive back here to the soccer field. Just pick me up on the way back home."

"No can do, kiddo. My license is suspended. You know that."

"You're kidding, right? It's like three blocks away. What's going to happen in three blocks?"

"I thought you said it was two blocks."

"Two blocks, three blocks. What does it matter? It's not like you're going to be on a major road or anything. The most that can happen is you might hit a squirrel. Big deal."

"Aw, don't say that. I love squirrels."

But Claire didn't smile. Instead, she rolled her eyes.

Allie had seen her niece pull the eye roll plenty of times, but never with her.

Claire was right. Three blocks didn't sound like a big deal, but Allie was in a precarious situation with her license. If anything happened (and with Allie's luck lately, *something* would happen), she'd never be able to talk her way out of this one with Zeke. "Sorry, hon, but I can't chance it. I don't want to put your dad in a bad position."

"Then you don't mind if I walk there, do you?" She placed her hands on her hips. That's when Allie noticed Claire had on the short skirt from the other morning. The one Mimi had banned her from wearing to school. How had Claire gotten out of the house without anyone noticing? How hadn't Allie herself noticed?

"Just how far away is this house?"

Claire sighed the sigh of the long suffering. "Forget it. I'll call Jordan. She'll come pick me up."

That sounded reasonable enough. Despite Claire's teenage attitude, she was trying to compromise, so Allie should, too. Kids respected that. "Are you sure that's okay with your mom and dad?"

"Sure, it's cool."

191

"I'll just check with them first." Allie took out her cell phone and dialed Mimi but it went directly to voice mail. Next, she called her brother but he didn't pick up either. "That's weird. Maybe they're at a movie and had to silence their phones."

"Yeah, right."

"What does that mean?"

"Nothing." Claire squeezed her cell phone out of the back pocket of the tight little skirt (a magician's trick if ever Allie saw one) and made a short call. "Jordan's picking me up," she informed Allie. "We're cool now, right?"

Allie thought about it a second. Claire was right. What could it hurt for her to visit her friend? And it wasn't as if Allie hadn't tried to get in touch with Mimi and Zeke. They'd placed her in charge of the kids and it was up to Allie to use her own common sense.

"Sure, it's fine." She set up her chair to watch the practice, which turned out to be a scrimmage. Cameron dribbled the ball, zigzagging around his opponents. Henry, who was playing goalie, was no slouch either. He blocked the ball every time it came near him, except the one time Cameron managed to score a goal.

Allie couldn't help but cheer, which garnered her a few friendly smiles from the other adults present. After about fifteen minutes, a red Mustang convertible driven by a girl who appeared to be Claire's age, pulled into the parking lot. Claire practically flew into the front seat. Allie stood to go talk to the girls but before she could get to the car, they were already halfway down the block.

Claire turned and waved good-bye. "See you in about an hour!" she cried cheerfully, all evidence of her prior sulking gone. *Teenagers.* Allie shook her head. It seemed like a lifetime ago that she'd been one herself.

The rest of the practice went by quickly. Daylight Saving Time was still in effect but even that wasn't enough to keep it from getting dark by eight-thirty. The coach blew a whistle, signaling the end of the scrimmage. He spoke to the boys, going over a few points, then dismissed them. The boys all grabbed a water bottle from a cooler and soon everyone had taken off, leaving Cameron, Henry, and Allie the only ones on the field.

"Where's Claire?" Cameron asked.

Allie glanced at her watch. "She went to her friend Jordan's house but she promised she'd be back by now." She dialed Claire's number but there was no answer. Allie texted her and waited for a return message. "Do you know Jordan's number by any chance?" she asked her nephew.

"Jordan who? I don't know any of Claire's friends with that name."

Henry pulled out a smartphone from his backpack and he and Cameron entertained themselves by playing Tetris. Allie began to pace the parking lot.

Fifteen minutes went by and it was now completely dark. Why hadn't she gotten Jordan's last name? She felt like the ditzy spinster aunt who was easily bamboozled. She hated calling Mimi and Zeke but there was no choice. She dialed both their numbers, but once again, neither of them answered.

"I must be in a dead zone." Allie shook her phone. What that would do she didn't know, but it felt like a good substitute for Claire right about now.

"My cell phone works fine," Henry said. "I just called my friend Pete to check on our math homework."

"I'm hungry," Cameron said.

"Again? Didn't you eat less than four hours ago?"

193

"That was first dinner. I eat light whenever I have soccer practice then I eat again when I get home."

"Me, too," Henry chimed in.

"Oh. Well, maybe there are some snacks in the van."

There were no snacks, but the key was still in the ignition. All this time they'd been on the soccer field the minivan was sitting in the parking lot just waiting for someone to come along and steal it. Not that Whispering Bay was any sort of crime hub, but still. Claire had been in such a rush to leave that she'd foolishly left behind the keys. Why hadn't Allie thought to ask her for them?

Allie was torn between being angry at herself, angry at Claire, and worried sick that something had happened to her. Maybe this Jordan had gotten in a car accident. Or maybe they hadn't even gone to Jordan's house at all.

A vision of Claire in her tight little skirt smoking pot, shooting up drugs, and having unprotected sex with the sleaziest boy in the high school (who even now was giving her an STD) flashed through Allie's brain in a panoramic nightmare.

Oh God. She was too young to be a great aunt. Or dead. Because Zeke was surely going to kill her when he discovered that she'd lost his daughter.

It was a miracle Mimi's hair wasn't entirely gray.

There was no choice. She was going to have to find Claire. *Now.* She wasn't supposed to drive, but this was an emergency.

She'd just cruise around the adjoining neighborhoods, very slowly, going at least five miles under the speed limit. There was no way she could get in trouble if she didn't call any attention to herself.

"Boys, buckle up your seatbelts and be on the lookout for a red Mustang parked somewhere nearby." Allie clutched the steering wheel and glanced at the dashboard clock. It was almost nine p.m. It had been over two hours since Claire had taken off. When she found her, Allie was going to wring her neck. Or throw her over her lap and spank her. Or grab her and hug the hell out of her. Probably all three.

Cameron and Henry each manned a window and Allie began to slowly drive up and down the streets. Within a few minutes, she was certain she spotted Jordan's car but after pulling into the driveway of a modest, red brick ranch, Allie could see that it wasn't a Mustang after all, but some foreign model. The front door to the house opened and a man poked his head out, probably to see what the heck a strange car was doing in his driveway.

Allie waved to him. "Sorry! Wrong house!"

He waited until she backed the van out, then scowled and slammed his door shut. Boy, what a grouch.

She drove around the rest of the neighborhood but there was no sign of a red Mustang. The only other residential area close by the soccer field was across Beach Street, a main thoroughfare in Whispering Bay. Claire said that Jordan's house was close enough that they wouldn't have to go through any main roads to get there, but of course, Allie now realized that was probably a lie.

When had Claire become so duplicitous? Allie felt like crying. Instead, she tried calling Zeke and Mimi again, but it was like their cell phones had been abducted by aliens.

"Maybe we should stop and ask for directions," Henry suggested.

"Good idea. If I had an address, that is."

"I have to go to the bathroom," Cameron said.

"Of course you do. Do you think you can hold it, big

guy? Just for a few minutes? I'm going to go through this neighborhood one more time."

And then what? Give up? Drive the boys back home?

Allie was about to call Claire one last time when she glanced into the rearview mirror to see a patrol car behind the van, its blue lights flashing obnoxiously.

Chapter Eighteen

THE PATROL CAR WASN'T after her, was it? She hadn't been speeding and she'd stopped at every stop sign. She even used her turn signal even though the van was the only vehicle out in the neighborhood. She stuck her arm outside the car window and waved the police car by. But instead of passing her, the cruiser turned on its siren. Allie's palms broke out into a sweat.

Cameron and Henry began whispering in excited tones.

"Uh-oh," Cameron said. "Are you going to jail?"

"Jail!" Allie faked a laugh. "Don't be silly. It's okay, boys, I got this." She only wished she felt as confident as she was trying to sound. She pulled the minivan over to the side of the road. To her relief, it was Rusty who got out of the cruiser.

Allie practically leaped out of the car and hugged him. "Rusty! Thank God, it's you. You have to help me find Claire."

Rusty disentangled himself from the hug. "Allie, what in tarnation are you doing driving?"

"I know this looks bad, but it's an emergency." She went on to explain how Claire had tricked her. "And believe me, I now know what people mean when they say *teenagers* in that tone of voice. So, do you know this Jordan person? Has Zeke ever mentioned her to you?"

"Can't say that I recall the chief ever mentioning a friend of Claire's named Jordan." He peered inside the van. "Is that Cameron in there?"

"And Henry Donalan. I was supposed to supervise Claire's driving. From a purely theoretical standpoint, of course, because I know my license is still suspended, and I *certainly* knew it was wrong of me to drive, but I didn't know what else to do. Neither Zeke nor Mimi are answering their cell phones right now."

Rusty's face scrunched up like he was constipated. "You know, Allie, I cut you a break and gave you a warning the other night. Breaking and entering is bad enough. But this second infraction? I can't overlook it. No matter who you're related to. Zeke would be the first one to tell me that I gotta do the right thing here."

"You're *kidding.* Claire could be God knows where and you're worried about something as stupid as a suspended license?"

"Now, Allie," Rusty said like she was some skittish poodle about to be put down. "I'm going to have to ask you to lower your voice."

"Lower my voice? Lower my voice!" She sounded hysterical but she couldn't help herself.

The man from the red brick house, who'd poked his head out the door earlier, joined them on the street. "That's her," he said, pointing to Allie. "She's been driving up and down the street real suspicious like. Probably casing out the neighborhood."

Allie stared at him in disbelief. "You called the cops on me? Is this a joke? I'm driving a minivan with two eleven-year-olds in the back seat! Does that sound like the modus operandi of a cat burglar?"

Rusty scratched his head and began mumbling to himself. Then he grinned, like a light inside his brain had just been turned on. "This is a test, ain't it?"

"A what?"

"Zeke put you up to this, to see how I'd react." Rusty opened the driver door to the minivan and stuck his head inside. "Is there a hidden camera in there?"

A hidden camera?

"Rusty, are you high?"

"Oh, no worries. I've already passed my drug test for this quarter." He put a hand up in a peaceful gesture to the idiot who'd called the cops on her. "Don't worry, sir, the Whispering Bay Police Department has this all under control." He unclipped a set of handcuffs from his belt. "Allie, can I get you to turn around?"

"You're going to *handcuff* me?"

Rusty leaned forward to whisper in her ear, "It's just for the cameras."

"There are no cameras!"

Car lights caught their attention. Allie turned to see a familiar black pickup truck. *Great.* Just what she needed. Tom Donalan witnessing this latest humiliation of hers.

Tom parked his truck behind the police cruiser and calmly walked toward them. "Hey, Rusty, what's going on?"

"Where did you come from?" Allie asked.

"Henry phoned and said you were in trouble. I was just a few blocks away." He eyed the handcuffs. "Looks like he was right."

"Hey, Tom," Rusty said amiably like they were all on a picnic. "Allie's giving me a hard time about these handcuffs."

"Yeah, I don't think Allie is a handcuffs kind of girl,

Rusty. Of course, I wouldn't know that firsthand, if you know what I mean."

Even under the dim streetlights, she could see Rusty's face turn the color of a splotched tomato. "Uh, the thing is, I don't have a choice here, Tom. Caught her red-handed breakin' the law."

"Wait a minute." Tom glanced between her and Rusty in mock disbelief. "Don't tell me Allie was driving."

"That she was, Tom. And I have to tell you, she's put me in an awful pickle here."

"I can see that, Rusty."

"Stop talking about me in the third person," she said, waving her hands in the air. "I'm right here."

Cameron and Henry got out of the minivan and joined them on the street. The relieved looks on their faces when they saw Tom made Allie feel like the world's most irresponsible adult.

"Boys," Tom said, "would you mind getting back in the car? We'll be done here in a few minutes."

Both boys instantly obeyed him, for which Allie was grateful. She didn't want her nephew (or Tom's son, for that matter) witnessing her trying to argue her way out of being arrested. She'd already lost her cool aunt status (and frankly, she didn't care anymore) but she'd really like to maintain some sort of credibility. At least with the eleven-year-old crowd.

"I'm curious," Tom said to Rusty. "How did you happen to catch her in the act?"

"Got a call saying there was a car driving up and down the neighborhood. Been a few burglaries here in the past couple of months so I drove over to check it out."

"I think you should check out the back of that van,"

Neighborhood Guy said. Allie had almost forgotten about him. "Just to make sure there's no stolen property stashed in there."

Rusty's jaw dropped. It didn't take a genius to figure out what he was thinking. The minivan he was being pressured to "check out" was registered to none other than his boss, Ezequiel James Grant, Whispering Bay's police chief. Rusty was in way more than just a pickle. More like an entire onion.

Allie almost felt sorry for Rusty, except he could have handled this whole thing a bit differently. Of course, *she* could have handled the whole thing a whole lot differently (as in, she could have adhered strictly to the rules).

Tom smiled at Neighborhood Guy. "Matt Connelly, is that you? Remember me? Reverend Donalan's son?"

"Tommy? What are you doing back in Whispering Bay? Thought you lived in Atlanta." His expression grew somber. "Heard a rumor that your wife left you. Guess it's true, huh?"

Allie cringed, but Tom shrugged good-naturedly. "True enough."

Neighborhood Guy shook his head sympathetically. "Tough break, man."

"Yeah." Tom glanced at Rusty, then back at Neighborhood Guy. "Say, Matt, I think there's been a misunderstanding. This young lady here is a personal friend of mine. As a matter of fact, she's got my son, Henry, in the car. Giving him a ride home after soccer practice. I think she got confused by the neighborhood." Tom slapped him on the back. "By the way, I haven't see you in church lately."

"Oh, well, been doing a lot of fishing and Sundays are usually the best day for that," he mumbled.

"I bet Dad would love to see you back. You being such an upstanding member of the parish and all."

Neighborhood Guy nodded slowly. "Yeah, I should go back to church," he said as though the idea were his to begin with.

"So, no problems here?" Tom asked.

"Sure. If you vouch for her then everything's good here, Tommy."

"Then I say we all get back to our lives. I'll take care of the car situation, Rusty, so you can get back to more important things, like patrolling the city."

Rusty looked equal parts confused and relieved. "Thanks, Tom. About Allie—"

"I'll make sure she doesn't drive anymore."

"So, no hidden cameras?" Rusty said, clearly disappointed.

"I can guarantee you there are *no* hidden cameras anywhere," Allie said.

"And Rusty," Tom said, "there's no need to involve Zeke in this, is there?"

"I won't tell if you won't," Allie quickly added.

Rusty scratched his chin. "Well... I guess you're right, there's no need to involve the chief. Especially not if I got Tom's word that you won't be driving." He turned to Tom. "And I can count on you getting Allie and the boys home?"

"You have my word. She's not getting behind the wheel of a car until she can legally drive again. Even if I have to handcuff her myself."

"Gee, thanks!" Rusty tipped his hat at Allie then drove away in his police car.

Neighborhood Guy shook Tom's hand then headed back to his house and, before Allie knew it, she was standing alone in the middle of the street with Tom.

"Handcuff me yourself? Really?"

"Don't say another word," he said in a quiet voice that should have been reassuring, but wasn't. "Because I'm pretty close to wringing your neck. You can do whatever you want on your own time, but that's my son you've got in that car. If you'd gotten arrested, what would have happened to him? And to Cameron? Did you think about that?"

Allie blinked to keep the tears from falling. Of all people, she didn't want to cry in front of Tom, but she was perilously close to doing just that. Not because he'd just berated her for her stupid behavior, though.

"Tom... I'm... I can't find Claire." She blurted out the whole story. "I know it was incredibly naive of me to let her go off like that. And now I can't get ahold of Zeke or Mimi and I don't know what to do. What if someone's kidnapped her?"

His expression softened. "Nobody's kidnapped her." He pulled out his cell phone. "What's this girl's name again? The one in the red Mustang?"

"Jordan. I don't know her last name."

He punched in some numbers then waited. Allie wanted to ask who he'd called but she didn't want to interrupt him. And frankly, she was more than just a little relieved that he seemed to have some sort of plan. Especially since she'd been batting zero.

"Keith? It's Donalan. Sorry to call you at home but I need some information. Tyler's a junior over at the high school, isn't she? Does she know a girl named Jordan? Don't know the last name. Drives a red Mustang. Maybe friends with Claire Grant?" *Pause.* "Sure, I'll hold." Tom glanced her way, then nodded toward the minivan. "Go check on the boys."

Something that Allie was more than happy to do,

partly because it gave her *something* to do. Plus, she wanted to make sure they hadn't been traumatized by her near arrest.

Both boys were immersed in a video game on Henry's phone. Okay, good. No trauma here that Allie could see.

She went back to check on Tom's progress. "Her name's Jordan Young and she lives near Grayton Beach," he said.

"Grayton Beach! That's not a couple of blocks from here."

"Yeah, more like ten miles. Get in the car," he said. Then he plucked the minivan keys out of her hand. "Obviously, I'm driving."

Chapter Nineteen

THEY PULLED UP TO a swanky beach house. Lights, music, *lots* of parked cars. Cameron stuck his nose to the car window. "Wow. I'd like to live there!"

"Who wouldn't?" Allie muttered. *A party*! She should feel relieved that it was nothing worse than a case of Claire lying to her, but at the moment all she felt was too stupid to live.

Tom unbuckled his seat beat. "Need me to come inside?"

Allie knew this was probably something she should do on her own but she'd never played the role of angry, disappointed guardian before. She was pretty sure Claire would come willingly, but she had no idea what kind of scene to expect. Having Tom by her side seemed smart. Or cowardly. She didn't really care which it seemed to him. She only knew she wanted Claire safely home as soon as possible. So that she could strangle her.

"If you wouldn't mind?"

Tom twisted around in his seat to address the boys. "Stay here. We'll be back in a few minutes."

"But I have to go to the bathroom," Cameron said.

Henry jumped on the bandwagon. "Me, too."

Tom tossed Allie a look that said they were probably being played, but what choice did they have? "I guess we're all going in, then."

The boys smiled at each other but were smart enough not to say anything else. The four of them walked to the front of the house. Somewhere upstairs Fergie and Will.I.Am's version of "True" played loud enough that Allie could hear it through the closed door. Twelve years ago she and Tom had slow danced to the classic original by Spandau Ballet. To this day she couldn't hear it without thinking of him. Or of the kiss he'd given her afterward…

Flash forward, Allie.

What was she going to say to Claire? Better yet, how was she going to explain this to Mimi and Zeke?

Allie rang the doorbell but the music was so loud that they couldn't hear whether the ringer worked or not. A couple of minutes went by but no one answered. Tom raised his fist and pounded on the door.

A teenage boy holding a red plastic cup finally answered. "Yeah?"

Tom's gaze zeroed in on the cup. "You live here?"

"Who wants to know?"

"How about you answer my question first," Tom said in a far more neutral tone than Allie would have used.

The kid must have decided they didn't look old enough to be the parents of anyone inside because after a few moments he visibly relaxed. "Nah, this is Jordan's house."

"We're looking for Claire Grant," Allie said.

"And Jordan's parents," Tom added.

"Claire… Yeah, I think I know her. Hold on."

The kid attempted to close the door, but Tom was too

fast for him. He propped the door open with his shoulder, grabbed Allie's hand, and whisked all four of them into the foyer.

The house was a large, two-story Mediterranean with tiled floors and plush leather furniture. All the noise seemed to be coming from upstairs. Still holding on to her hand, Tom headed toward the party. "Everyone stay together," he instructed the boys.

"Hey! You can't go up there," the kid shouted.

"Watch us!" Allie said, scrambling to keep up with Tom.

They took the stairs two at a time and found themselves in a rec room, complete with a wet bar and a huge flat screen TV. The scene in front of them seemed typical of most teenage parties but Allie couldn't help but feel a bit shook up. She still thought of Claire as playing with her American Girl dolls. Not being a typical American girl herself. A typical *teenage* American girl, that is. But there she was, a beer in one hand, giggling away at something some pimply faced, skinny hipster kid was saying to her.

Allie marched over to confront her niece. "Do you have any idea how worried I've been?" she heard herself screech.

Claire whipped around. The look on her face was almost comical. "Aunt Allie! What...what are you doing here?"

"What am *I* doing here? I thought someone kidnapped you, for God's sake!"

"I know this looks bad," Claire began.

"Looks bad? Claire! You lied to me."

Some of the kids began looking their way. "Can we talk about this outside?" Claire whispered.

"She's right. Save the reunion for later," Tom said.

He took the beer out of Claire's hand and dumped the contents down the wet bar sink.

"Where's your friend Jordan?" Allie demanded.

Claire's nervous gaze darted through the room. "She's here somewhere."

"And her parents?"

"I think…her mom's outside by the pool."

"Wonderful," Allie said. "Let's go meet her."

"No, Aunt Allie, *please*, don't make a scene."

"You're just lucky your dad's not here."

At the mention of Zeke, Claire's eyes widened. Allie gave Hipster Boy a steely glare before they headed down to the pool area, where they found a slim blonde woman in her forties lying on a recliner, reading a magazine and sipping what looked like a margarita, complete with salt around the glass rim. Allie fought the urge to snatch the drink from the woman's perfectly manicured hands and either toss it into the pool or gulp it down herself.

"You know you got kids drinking inside the house?" Tom said.

The woman slowly folded herself out of the lounge chair. She wore a tight white tank top emphasizing a set of knockers that probably cost the equivalent of six months' worth of tips at The Blue Monkey. Her denim skirt was almost as short as Claire's. "Who are you?" she demanded.

"I'm her aunt," Allie said, pointing a finger at Claire. "And she's barely sixteen."

The woman didn't even blink. "Are you her guardian?"

"No, that would be her father, the police chief of Whispering Bay."

"Police?" The woman made a frowning motion but her brow remained frozen in an obvious case of plastic surgery overdose. "I think there's been a misunderstanding."

"Yeah, well, you have about ten minutes to clear it up before he gets here," Allie said. Tom raised a brow. Okay, so she was bluffing. But Jordan's mom didn't have to know that.

"I suggest you round up the kids and have them call their parents. Underage drinking in your home is one thing. But letting these kids drive while under the influence is asking for trouble. Not to mention all the lawsuits that could come out of it." Tom gazed around the ritzy pool area. "Of course, seems to me you could probably afford it."

Jordan's mother appeared shock. "You mean the kids are drinking *liquor*?"

"No, they're having milk and cookies upstairs," Allie said.

The woman barely glanced at Allie but she gave Tom a more generous perusal. "Good idea about getting the kids to go home. Ever since my divorce, it's just been me and Jordan and I'm afraid I've let her get away with too much. Maybe you could stay to help me?" she asked Tom, batting a set of eyelashes that had be extensions. As if she was fooling anyone! Was there any part of her that was real?

"Sorry, but my husband's busy," Allie said. Maybe a shove in the pool would bring this woman back to reality. Except Allie had a feeling Jordan's mother wouldn't mind a little wet T-shirt action. Especially not if Tom was around to witness it.

The woman's gaze honed in on Allie's left hand. "The two of you are married?"

"It's a modern marriage. We don't believe in rings." Allie grabbed Tom's hand and led him back through the house and out the front door. She glanced back briefly to make sure Claire was following, which thankfully, she was.

Claire meekly took a seat in the mid row of the minivan and buckled herself in.

"Can you believe that woman?" Allie said to Tom. "And by the way, you can thank me later for saving you from that…Botoxed barracuda back there."

The corner of his mouth twitched up into a half grin. Then he glanced around and the grin disappeared. "I think we lost the boys."

"What?" She whipped around. Tom was right. The boys were MIA. It was official. She was the world's worst adult. "*Captain Crunch*," Allie muttered.

"In this case I think I would have gone with something a little stronger."

She shrugged. "If I could, I would."

"Right. You stay here with Claire and I'll go back in the house and find them."

As she watched Tom walk away she couldn't help but yell, "Watch out for the water!"

He didn't turn around but he put a hand up in the air acknowledging her remark. Allie gritted her teeth, instantly regretting her little outburst. He probably thought she was jealous. Which she most certainly wasn't. As a fellow member of the female species, she was simply embarrassed for Jordan's mother, that's all.

Speaking of the female species.

She climbed into the front seat of the minivan, took a deep breath, and turned to face her niece. Somehow, Claire managed to make herself appear small and pitiful. Before Allie could think of what to say, Tom and the boys were back in the car. Henry's eyes were bright were excitement and Cameron was beyond giddy.

"That was awesome!" Cameron said. He nudged his sister in the shoulder. "Boy, I bet Dad is going to ground you for a year."

Claire had enough sense to keep her mouth shut.

The boys began interrogating her for party details but Tom quickly put an end to it with the same kind of look she'd seen Zeke use. Allie leaned back in her seat and closed her eyes. Every synapse in her body raged on full alert. She tried to will herself to relax, but with each minute, it only seemed to get worse.

What if Tom hadn't come along tonight? What if he hadn't known to call Hard Hat and get Jordan's address? What if... Her brain spun with a hundred different *what ifs*. Each one worse than the last.

Allie turned around to make sure the kids were settled in their seats. And to assure herself once again that Claire was still really there. Claire glanced up and caught Allie's eye. "I'm sorry," she mouthed.

Allie nodded, acknowledging Claire's apology, but she didn't think she was ready to talk to her yet. For one thing, what would she say? A part of Allie was still angry at her niece. But mostly, she was angry at herself. Yes, Claire had played her, but Allie had naively let herself be played.

Is this what being the parent to a teenager was like? A constant struggle just to make sure they didn't do anything stupid? No wonder Mimi and Zeke didn't want Claire driving on her own. If it were up to Allie, Claire would be locked up in the proverbial dungeon with the key thrown away. Tonight had been a real eye-opener. On all counts.

She took a moment to take a good look at Tom, discreetly, of course, because she didn't want him to catch her staring at him. All these years, she'd always pictured him as the same eighteen-year-old boy who'd carelessly played with her heart. But there was little resemblance between that Tom and the thirty-year-old man she'd gotten to know in the past few days. For one thing, he was such a...*dad*. His whole world revolved around Henry, and yes, it was sexy but it was also so...grown up.

She wasn't the same Allie she'd been at eighteen, either. But while Tom had experienced marriage and a son and *responsibilities*, she was still paying for all the fun she'd had in Part Two of her Life Plan. She'd frivolously squandered her share of the life insurance money that Buela had left her. It wasn't a fortune, by any means, and although a part of Allie didn't regret that she'd used the money to travel, she did regret that she hadn't thought to hold some back. A nest egg. Security. Those were the things she now craved.

The things she could have if she got the job at the magazine.

Correction: *when* she got the job at the magazine.

They drove the rest of the way back to Mimi and Zeke's in silence. Thankfully, Zeke's car was parked in the driveway.

"Henry, stay in the car," Tom said to his son. He turned to her. "If you wouldn't mind. I need Mimi or Zeke to tag along so they can drive us back to pick up my truck."

He didn't seem mad. Or upset. Or even put out. He didn't seem...anything, actually. Which was almost worse because Allie knew what it meant. It meant he felt bad for her. And he didn't want to add to it by giving her any grief. She supposed she should feel grateful but she almost preferred he'd yell at her because the fact was she was as much to blame for tonight's fiasco as Claire.

More so, because Allie was supposed to be the adult here. She'd been irresponsible and foolish. She tried to view herself through Tom's eyes. The image she came up with made her cringe.

Claire dashed out of the car and into the house with Cameron hot on her heels.

Allie swallowed hard. "It seems like all I do these days is thank you for something or other."

"You're going to tell Mimi and Zeke what went on tonight, right?"

"Of course. But... I was hoping Claire might come clean first."

Tom glanced in the minivan's rearview mirror to make sure Henry wasn't listening. He lowered his voice. "You mean, like I told my parents and you told your grandmother about the time we spent the night on the beach?"

"Nothing really happened that night. I mean, not *much*." She was hoping that would elicit a smile from him, but it didn't. She sighed. "Okay, I get it. Claire probably isn't going to tell."

"Put yourself in her parents' place. Would you want to know if your sixteen-year-old was at a party where there was underage drinking involved?"

Put that way, she had no choice. Tom was right. She was going to have to tell Mimi and Zeke. But she still wanted to give Claire a chance to do the right thing. Oh, boy. Allie had a terrible feeling that tonight would not end well.

Chapter Twenty

MIMI MET HER BY the front door. "I thought you'd be home by now." She looked out into the driveway. "Is that Tom inside the van?"

"It's a long story, but basically, he needs a ride back to his truck."

Mimi's breath caught. "Did Claire get in an accident?"

"No, everyone's all right," Allie rushed to reassure her. "There was just… Well, like I said, it's a long story."

Mimi frowned. "Okay, you can tell me all about it when I get back. I'll go grab my purse so I can drive Tom to his car."

Allie took in the quiet house. "Where's Zeke?"

"He went for a run on the beach."

"At this time of night?"

"He says it helps him clear his head after a long day."

Allie was dying to ask Mimi where the heck she and Zeke had been all night, but this wasn't the right moment. She found Claire lying on top of her bed, her cheeks wet with tears. Crocodile tears or the real thing? Either way, Allie steeled herself. She wasn't about to be sucked in by anymore teenage theatrics.

Claire sat up and swiped her cheeks clean. "I'm so sorry."

"Do you have any idea how frantic I was? Not to mention the fact I could have been arrested for driving with a suspended license?" Allie tried to keep her voice calm. What would Mr. Rogers do? He'd probably strangle Claire with one of his argyle sweaters.

"You were driving? But I thought Mr. Donalan drove the van."

"That was after one of your father's deputies nearly handcuffed me with plans to drag me off to jail."

"Oh God. Do you think Daddy will find out?"

"Of course he's going to find out. But not from me."

"Really? Oh, Aunt Allie, you're the best!"

"I don't think you understand, Claire. I don't plan to tell him, because *you're* going to tell him."

"You're kidding, right?"

"Do I look like I'm kidding?"

"But nothing happened! I didn't even have any of that beer. I was just holding it and pretending to take sips."

Allie sat down on the edge of the bed. "Why would you do that?"

Claire's face scrunched up in adolescent embarrassment. "You know, so no one would think I was a prude. You don't know what it's like having your father be the chief of police. Everyone already thinks you're some kind of goody-goody. And I really did plan on only being there an hour. I just lost track of time, is all."

"Claire." Allie shook her head. "Do you know how childish all that sounds?"

"Fine. I'll go tell Daddy and then he and Mom can get in a big fight about it. They're already in couples

216

counseling. This will probably drive them over the edge."

Allie stilled. "Couples counseling? How do you know that?"

"They think they're fooling everyone with their big date night story, but I had to use Mom's phone one day and I listened to a message from their counselor changing their appointment time. That's where they were tonight, you know. Maybe I did lie about where I was going, but they lie all the time."

Allie took a few seconds to absorb this. "I'm sure a lot of married couples probably go to counseling."

"Yeah, and a lot of couples are on the brink of divorce, too."

"Don't be ridiculous. Your parents are *not* on the brink of divorce. Are...they fighting a lot?"

"You have to talk to someone to fight with them. They're probably the most polite parents on the planet."

"Polite is good, isn't it?"

"If you say so." She put on her little girl face, the one Allie found so hard to resist. "I'll tell Daddy, I swear I will. Just not tonight."

"Claire—"

"*Please*, Aunt Allie. I promise, I'll tell them. The thing is, Friday night is a big home football game, and I *really, really* want to go."

"A football game? What does that have to do with anything?"

"When Daddy finds out about the party he'll ground me, which means no football game, which means they'll kick me off the cheerleading squad."

"For missing one game?"

"He'll ground me for the entire season!"

"Don't be ridiculous." *Pause.* "What about your

mom? Doesn't she have any say in your punishment?"

"That's the thing. She's a lot softer than he is. More reasonable, really. And after he pronounces sentence, she'll get upset and the two of them will lock themselves in their room and when they come out they won't be talking." Claire squeezed out a couple more tears. "I hate to be the reason for another fight between them."

"Then maybe you shouldn't have snuck out to that party in the first place."

"I know what I did was wrong. But didn't you ever do anything you weren't supposed to? Do you know how *hard* I worked to get on the cheerleading squad? I had to take gymnastics lessons just to learn to do a back flip, which you have to do to make the squad and the lessons were expensive. Mom had to talk Daddy into them and if I get kicked off the squad the whole thing will have been for nothing."

"I don't know, Claire—"

"*Please, please, please*, Aunt Allie." It was like the tears faucet had been turned on full force. Claire's eyes were puffy and mascara ran down her cheeks.

Allie shouldn't give in to the drama. But would Zeke really punish Claire to the point that she got kicked off the cheerleading squad? It didn't seem a fair punishment for what was undoubtedly a typical teenage indiscretion.

Instinctively, Allie knew the answer to that question was a resounding *yes*. Zeke was more than capable of grounding his daughter for the entire football season.

Good Grief. Her brother had turned into the Gestapo.

But more than that... Allie had to admit what Claire said was beginning to make sense. Mimi wasn't the old Mimi. She and Zeke walked on eggshells around one another. And Zeke... Had Allie seen her brother smile once this visit? He was like a grenade, ready to explode.

218

Oh God. Claire was right. Zeke and Mimi were on the brink of divorce.

It was against her better judgment, but nothing could be served by telling Mimi and Zeke what had gone down tonight. At least, not until Allie had a chance to think about it some more.

"What about Cameron? He witnessed the whole thing and—"

"Don't worry about Cameron," Claire said, her voice filled with hope. "If I tell him not to say anything, then he won't."

Allie hated to think what methods Claire might use to extract a promise like that from her younger brother. Bullying? Blackmail? Bribes? None of those options sounded good.

"You have to promise me you'll *never* do anything like this again. And you have to stop fighting with Cameron. No bullying him into getting your way. In other words, you have to be a complete angel."

Claire grabbed her into a hug. "I promise! I swear, no more sneaking off. And I'll stop whining about my own car and everything. You'll see; I'll be perfect." She swiped her tears, taking most of the mascara along with it. She almost looked like Claire Bear again.

Why couldn't her niece go back to being eight years old? When life had been uncomplicated?

"This is just a reprieve," Allie warned. "Just till after the game Friday night. Then you and I are going to sit down with your parents and tell them everything. Got it?"

Claire nodded eagerly. "Got it."

"Let me get this straight," Mimi said. "Tom just

happened to be driving by when the van wouldn't start up? And now it's miraculously running just fine?"

"Weird, huh?" Allie faked a laugh. "He insisted on driving us back to make sure it didn't happen again."

"Why didn't he just follow you in his truck?"

"Can you believe no one thought of that?"

It was obvious from the look on Mimi's face that, no, she didn't believe it.

Allie hated lying to her sister-in-law, but if she told her the whole story then Mimi would be forced to tell Zeke and then Allie would have betrayed Claire's trust. Or worse, Mimi would keep the truth from Zeke and the lie might cause their marriage to crumble. Was she doing the right thing? Or was she just making everything worse? Maybe it was best to get everything out in the open. Allie decided to test the waters.

"Claire told me you and Zeke are going to counseling."

Mimi looked taken aback. "She said that? I had no idea—that is, I didn't know Claire was aware."

"She found out accidentally by listening to a voice mail from your counselor." Before Mimi could ask, Allie said, "And no, I'm pretty sure Cameron doesn't know anything."

Mimi smiled but her eyes looked blank. "It's more like couples communication. No big deal. It's been great for our marriage."

Allie nodded. She desperately wanted to believe Mimi, but the sour feeling in her gut told her Claire was right. Mimi and Zeke were having major marital problems. They would have to be told about Claire's extracurricular activities, of course, but delaying the bad news for two days would give Allie a chance to gauge just how serious those problems were. Despite feeling guilty, Allie was convinced more than ever that she was doing the right thing.

Allie punched her pillow, for what, she didn't know, but it felt good doing it. She turned to her side and glanced at the bedside clock. It was nearly one a.m. and she hadn't gotten a wink of sleep.

Heard a rumor that your wife left you.

At least, that's what Neighborhood Guy *aka* Mr. Nosy Pants had said. It had felt like such an invasion of Tom's privacy, hearing it the way she had. But Tom hadn't appeared the least bit ruffled having his personal failings put out there for everyone to see. He had handled it all with the grace of a man who was...*a man.* Like he didn't have anything to be ashamed of or owe anyone any explanations.

Still. Allie had wanted to knock Mr. Nosy Pants down a peg or two.

Did Lauren really leave Tom? Did Tom still love her? According to Mimi, Henry had been a large part of Tom's motivation in returning home, but could there be more to it? Did he hope to win Lauren back?

Then there was Jordan's mother, Cougar Extraordinaire. Now, lying alone in her bed, Allie could admit she'd been jealous. Not of Jordan's mother. She didn't think she was Tom's type. But the incident had her wondering about Tom's love life. He'd been divorced a year now.

He'd asked her why she wasn't with someone, but Allie hadn't asked him the same question in return. Why wasn't *he* with someone?

Or maybe he was. Despite what Claire thought, there

was a very real chance that he'd been out on a date tonight. But then, there was *that kiss* they'd shared. He couldn't have kissed her like that if he had a girlfriend. Could he?

Allie punched her pillow again. *Men.* Of course, he could have kissed her *like that* and still been in a relationship with someone else.

Confusion and insecurity and…something else roiled through her. She didn't hate Tom. But she didn't want to like him. And she certainly didn't want to *want him.* Not again. But she did. On both counts. There was no use denying it any longer. But did she have the guts to do anything about it? Probably not.

Compared to Tom, she was a fraud. Running around town masquerading as this hot-shot journalist, when the truth was all she had to show for her career was a near empty bank account and one good article under her belt. That, and the slim promise of a maybe job that in all probability depended on Phoebe Van Quack and her mysterious Madame Gloria.

Then there was the matter of her personal life.

What a joke that was.

She told Tom she'd sowed her wild oats. Sure, she'd gotten to do a lot of traveling, (which, if he'd let her explain the other night, was what she had meant by the expression). She'd surfed in Australia, backpacked throughout Europe, and even gone on safari in Africa. But her love life had been nothing more than a couple of semi-serious relationships, neither of which had been more inspiring than an *I really like him a lot.* And the sex? She didn't have much to compare it to, but even she knew it hadn't been much more than a mediocre episode of *Sex and the City* or worse, it's more modern-day counterpart, *Girls.*

Maybe that was the problem. She'd watched too much TV. Her expectations were too high. Or maybe nothing ever compared to the way Tom had made her feel at eighteen.

Maybe all these years she'd been waiting for Tom Donalan to *just do her* so she could get on with the rest of her life. Allie rolled onto her back and stared up at the ceiling.

Big Girls Don't Cry

Wait. Where had that thought come from?

Frankie Valli began wailing in her ear in his falsetto voice.

Strange. Her room was adjacent to Claire's. Had her niece turned on the radio? The music suddenly got louder.

BIG. GIRLS. DON'T. CRY...

Allie sighed. Maybe Claire had been messing with the alarm on her clock radio and accidentally hit an oldies station. But you'd think she'd have hit the off button by now.

After tonight's teenage drama, she couldn't believe how inconsiderate Claire was being. How was anyone supposed to sleep with all that racket going on?

She sat up and grabbed a sweatshirt to pull over her camisole top. Then the music stopped. Good! But she needed to make sure it didn't happen again, so Allie padded her way to Claire's room and opened the door. It was quiet and dark.

Claire sat up in her bed and rubbed her eyes. "What's wrong?"

"I just want to make sure we don't have a repeat with the clock radio."

"What clock radio?" Claire asked, still sounding sleepy.

"The sixties station you were listening to. You know, 'Big Girls Don't Cry'?"

Claire flopped back in her bed. "I don't have a clock radio. Will you close the door, Aunt Allie? I have to get up really early in the morning."

Allie stood there a moment, frozen. If the music hadn't come from Claire's room, then where had it come from? Maybe she'd imagined it. Maybe the stress of lying to Mimi and Zeke was causing her to hallucinate. Maybe her brother and sister-in-law weren't the only ones who needed counseling. Allie wondered briefly if the medical benefits at *Florida!* magazine included mental health screening.

Argh! There was certainly no use trying to get any sleep. Not now. Not with all the crazy, *woops*—strike that word from her vocabulary—not with all the *unusual* things swirling through her brain. Maybe Zeke was on to something and a run along the beach would clear her head. Allie slipped on her sneakers and quietly made her way out the back door.

Chapter Twenty-One

TOM REPOSITIONED THE PILLOW behind his neck and settled back for a long night spent sleeping inside his truck. *Damn kids*. He'd caught a couple of teenagers, probably stragglers from the Grayton Beach party, sneaking around behind the building. A few stern words had scared them off, but he couldn't count on that keeping them away all night. An abandoned building was too much of a temptation. Especially one that was rumored to have a ghost dancing on the roof.

Not that he was concerned about damage to the building. In two days it would be gone. But he was concerned about someone getting hurt. One dumb kid breaking their leg on the premises. One dumb mistake and everything he'd worked for in the past couple of months could go up in smoke.

Two more nights and his problem would be solved. Like it should have been a couple of days ago. Then he could get on with what he'd been hired to do—build a new state-of-the art recreation center.

He'd always liked watching things go up. Creating something new out of nothing. When he was a kid he thought he'd become an architect, but like he'd told Allie the other night, things hadn't turned out the way he'd planned, so he'd majored in Construction Management, and it had served him well. His career had taken off. He'd been successful at something he genuinely liked. Not many people could say that.

But his personal life? That had been another story. Married at eighteen with a pregnant wife wasn't the way he'd envisioned college. He'd planned to live in a dorm, probably even join a frat. Instead, he'd lived in married student housing and worked construction full time while going to school. Despite having a new baby, Lauren managed to get a degree in education, something her mother had called "practical." After graduation, they'd moved to Atlanta where Tom had signed on with a major contractor and Lauren got a job teaching first grade. After just a couple of years, Tom's income was more than enough to allow Lauren to be a stay-at-home mom.

They were healthy, young, and making more money than most of their peers.

But Lauren was right. They hadn't been happy. Not the way they should have been. Something had been missing from the start. That elusive thing that not only drew two people to one another, but kept them together, as well. The fact was they'd gotten married because of Henry. End of story. Not that Tom regretted it for a minute.

All in all, he had no right to complain. He had a job. He had a son he loved more than life itself and an ex-wife he genuinely liked. Even his parents, who were getting on in years, were still doing well. His paycheck might not be anything like it used to be, but one day he'd be on top again. It would just take time and hard work. Nothing he hadn't been through before.

The night air felt brisk. It would probably drop into the fifties again like it had last night. He went to roll up his window when he spied a shadow near the edge of the building.

God damn kids.

He opened the door to his truck and walked stealthily through the parking lot. There was a full moon, more than enough light to make out the lone figure standing by the window. He'd recognize those legs anywhere. What in all that was holy was she doing here?

Allie leaned over to catch her breath. She spotted him and placed a hand in the air. "Before you say anything I was *not* about to break into the building. Been there. Done that. Learned my lesson."

"Why are you wheezing?"

"Because I just ran two miles in under fifteen minutes." Her long brown hair was pulled in a high ponytail and her face was covered in a light sheen of perspiration. She straightened and stretched out her back, causing her sweatshirt to tighten across her breasts. Most guys would have been mesmerized by the sight. But he was a leg man, and those tiny nylon shorts of hers should have been outlawed.

"You run at night? By yourself?"

"Only when I can't sleep. And this is Whispering Bay, not Tampa. What are you doing here?" She glanced around the parking lot. "Wait. Don't tell me. You're patrolling the premises. Does your boss know how dedicated you are? What's with you and this place, anyway?"

"I've already told you. This place is my responsibility."

It was true. The senior center project was his baby, but she was right. He'd gone above and beyond anything Steve Pappas expected of him. Usually, he'd just drive by a few times a night to make sure the building appeared secure. But spending the night in the parking lot? In his pickup truck? He'd never done that before. So why tonight?

The answer made the muscles in his neck spasm.

Admit it, Donalan, you were hoping she'd show up.

He placed his palm on the back of his neck and tried to rub away some of the tension.

Allie frowned. "Someone's in a bad mood."

"Lack of sleep usually does that to a person."

"You didn't sleep last night?"

Was she serious? He'd slept six inches away from her. With a hard-on that could have cut through the Hope diamond.

"I caught a few winks here and there."

"Funny, I slept like the dead." She pointed to the rooftop. "What do you think was up there today that made everyone think it was a ghost?"

"I thought we already went over that. There was nothing there. How did Mimi and Zeke take the news on Claire?"

She looked uncomfortable by his change of topic. "I'd rather not talk about that right now."

He wanted to challenge her, but decided against it. Avoidance had always been Allie's way of coping. Who was he to try to change her? Not that he'd want to. As infuriating as she could be sometimes, she was damn near perfect in every way. He'd forgotten that about her.

"What do you want to talk about instead?" he asked.

She began rolling a pebble with the toe of her sneaker. Back and forth. Like she was nervous. "How about you tell me what was so important that you couldn't go to your son's soccer practice?"

"What if I told you I was on a date? Would you be jealous?"

Her gaze collided with his. Bright and hot. "Absolutely not."

"Liar."

Her face fell. He watched in fascination as she tried to regroup her emotions. "You're right," she admitted. "I was jealous. Happy now?"

Fuck, yeah, he was happy. Happy enough that maybe he'd take a chance on telling her where he'd really gone. On the other hand, she'd probably think he was pathetic. "You want to know where I was tonight? I drove over to Panama City."

"Is this where you tell me all about your big date? Cause that might be kind of weird." She laughed, but it sounded hollow.

He didn't want to play games with her. He wanted to tell her everything. That ever since she hit town he hadn't been able to stop thinking about her. That seeing her again was like ripping open an old scab and that he was slowly bleeding to death and she was the only one who could staunch the flow.

"I had to go to Panama City to get some supplies to patch up a window for the parish hall in Dad's church." It wasn't a lie. But it wasn't the entire truth, either.

Hold on. That made absolutely no sense. "What's wrong with the Ace Hardware here in town?" she said.

"Absolutely nothing." He smiled. Slow and lazy, as if he knew her better than anyone else. And in some ways, that was probably true.

Her skin felt tight, like it was ready to explode.

She didn't love him. But she did want him. Even more than she had at eighteen. Enough with the sly flirtation and the innuendos and all the other bull. It was time to get down to the nitty gritty.

"You know what? I don't care where you went tonight. Here's the thing. I was thinking maybe we should have sex. Just once. To get it over with."

His smile disappeared. *Weren't expecting that, were you, Tom Donalan?*

"Because I think there's a little bit of sexual tension going on that's probably interfering with our partnership and—"

"Good idea." He grabbed her hand and began pulling her toward the front door of the building. She dug in her heels but he was like a freight train, full steam ahead with no stopping him.

"Wait! I didn't mean right *now*, this instant."

He let go of her hand and reached inside his jeans to produce a key that he slid inside the padlock. "What's wrong with now?"

She glanced down at her oversized sweatshirt. This wasn't how she wanted to look the first (and most definitely the only) time she and Tom made love. There was that Ben and Jerry's fantasy, after all—the one where she looked unbelievably gorgeous and was utterly in control. Nothing could be further from that right now. "Because I'm a hot mess!"

"Is that a description? Or a promise?" Before she could answer, he scooped her up and carried her over the proverbial threshold.

She should demand he let go of her this instant. What was he thinking? What was *she* thinking? Letting him manhandle her like some Neanderthal claiming his woman? Trouble was, she couldn't think at all right now.

He set her down in the middle of the room. "I'll be

right back." Then he walked out the front door, leaving her standing there, still too stunned to speak. She thought she'd put the sex idea out there, then they'd discuss the pros and cons. Like rational adults. Not lunge at each other like a couple of love-starved teenagers.

He returned with the inflatable mattress and his backpack.

Allie could hear herself breathe. Raspy, like she was on the verge of an asthma attack. Only she didn't suffer from any breathing problems. Nope. The only problem she had was standing in front of her. She could hear Tom breathing, too. Good to know she wasn't the only one having trouble getting air in and out of her lungs.

Then she remembered that they weren't supposed to be inside the building.

"What about Madame Gloria? Phoebe said the building's aura had to remain pure, as in no trespassing and certainly no—"

"Fuck Madame Gloria. It's here, against the side of the building, or my truck. Take your pick."

Against the side of the building?

Maybe it was the tone of his voice. Or the way he was looking at her. What had Zeke said? Like she was breakfast and Tom was starving. So maybe this wasn't the way she'd always envisioned this scene. But this was the way it was going to happen. It was probably best not to think too much at this point. Action. That's what was required here.

She grabbed the hem of his T-shirt and tugged it over his head.

God he was beautiful. A combination of smooth muscle and hard edges that nearly had her drooling. It only took them a minute to get each other naked. Flat on her back on that mattress with Tom Donalan on top of her. Like *déjà vu*. Only not from last night. It was like the two of them had been whirling around in some weird time machine and they'd gone back twelve years and were eighteen again. Maybe not in body, but in spirit they *were* a couple of horny teenagers getting down to the business of doing what they'd set out to do all those years ago.

He stroked his thumbs over her nipples. "I remember these." Then he latched onto one breast and suckled it, slow and thorough, like he had all the time in the world. The first time he'd touched her breast was at the beach, late one night after their fourth date. She'd been shocked to discover how something so simple could feel so unbelievably good.

"They remember you, too," she rasped.

He chuckled and changed breasts.

She rubbed the soles of her bare feet up and down the back of his calves. He must have taken that as a signal because then he began doing *that thing* with his hands, touching her everywhere. Sliding his palms over her hot, itchy skin until she couldn't take it anymore.

She wanted to tell him she didn't need any more foreplay. That she was ready now. That'd she'd spent the past twelve years *ready*. But there was something she needed to say first.

"Remember…last night when I told you about my life plan?"

"Uh-huh," he murmured, his mouth still on her nipple.

"About part two…sowing my wild oats. I didn't mean it the way you probably think I did."

He glanced up.

It was the twenty-first century. She shouldn't care what he thought, but she couldn't help herself. "That is, I don't want you to think that I've been—"

"I know what you meant."

"But how—"

"Allie, I know." He shook his head. "You're…not the kind of girl who sleeps around."

Their eyes locked and suddenly she didn't trust herself to speak, because who knew what kind of garble would come out of her mouth? So she grabbed his hand and placed it between her thighs where it was so wet that she should have been embarrassed, except she wasn't.

Balancing himself with one hand, he reached into his backpack to produce a small foil packet.

Bring a condom. On second thought, bring two.

Allie swallowed hard. "So that's where you keep the protection, huh?"

Her voice sounded thin and far away, like it was somebody else speaking. She mentally shook her head. Of course she wanted him to use a condom. She willed herself to relax again. To be in the moment because whatever else might have happened between them in the past, the present was shaping up to be pretty friggin' fantastic.

He slid inside her, hot and hard, filling her so completely that it took everything she had not to scream because it felt so good.

"Just for the record," he said. "I bought those condoms yesterday."

"Because…you knew this would happen?"

"Because I hoped it would happen. Prayed, even," he said on a strained laugh. "Sorry, I don't… I don't think I can wait any longer." Then he began to move.

Allie wrapped her legs around his waist.

"*Yeah*, just like that," he urged. From somewhere in the deliciously foggy haze that was her brain, she realized Tom was whispering in her ear. Telling her how beautiful she was. How much he'd missed hearing her laugh. How much he wanted her. How much he'd *always* wanted her.

If he had to talk during sex, why couldn't he just talk dirty? Why did he have to be so darn…sweet?

She didn't love him. And he certainly didn't love her. But something was happening here. Besides the sex.

And it was in that moment that she realized what that something was. It was like all these years her heart had been in some kind of deep freeze. Stored away neatly in a big ziplock bag, just waiting for Tom Donalan to come along and thaw it out.

She slapped her palm against his mouth, causing his entire body to go still.

"Shut up. This isn't… It's just sex. And for the record, you're wrong. I've had *lots* of sex. With *lots* of guys. So this doesn't mean anything."

The instant she said it she wanted to take it back. But she couldn't and a part of her didn't want to anyway. Damn him. Why did he have to make this all so *personal*?

The corners of her eyes dampened. She squeezed her eyelids shut. It was one thing to let him see her cry because she'd been worried about Claire. She'd forgiven him for what had happened twelve years ago, but she'd never forgive him if he made her cry now.

He didn't move or try to remove her hand. He was waiting, she knew, for her to open her eyes again. When she finally did, he was staring down at her with a gaze as hard as the rest of him.

She eased her hand off his mouth. Now it was his turn to say something. But he didn't say a word. Instead, he began to move again. Long, slow, delicious strokes that seemed to go on forever. And it was Allie who began to talk, like a patient in the middle of a delirious fever, spouting off whatever nonsense popped into her head.

Afterward, they both lay completely still. Tom carefully rolled off to the side and began pulling his clothes back on. It was the most awkward moment of Allie's life. She didn't know whether to apologize for telling him to shut up, or thank him for giving her the mother of all orgasms. Thankfully, she was too winded to say anything at the moment so she didn't have to make a decision.

It was Tom who spoke first. "Big girls don't cry?"

"*What*?" Allie finally managed to say.

"That's what you said when you came. Big girls don't cry. Not sure if that was a compliment. Although, by the way you were heaving around I'd say—"

"It's a song. You know, from the sixties?"

It occurred to her that he was now fully clothed, while she on the other hand... So she started pulling her clothes on, too. "I got that old Frankie Valli song stuck in my head." She glanced up at him. "That ever happen to you?"

"I can honestly say I've never had 'Big Girls Don't Cry' stuck in my head."

"Okay, so maybe not that song in particular," Allie said. "But you know? Something else. A song you just can't seem to shake no matter what."

An odd expression flicked across his face.

"What?"

"Nothing."

"Oh, it's definitely something."

"How do you know it's something?" he challenged.

"Because I just know. So you might as well tell me because I'm not going to let it go until you do."

He contemplated this over a few seconds. "You wanted to know why I halted the demolition that first day?"

Allie nodded.

"The truth is," he said sheepishly, "I had that old Beatles song 'Help' stuck inside my head. It was driving me crazy. Then I said I'd stop the demolition and the song stopped, too."

Allie stilled. "You're kidding."

"You think I could make that up?"

"That's crazy! I had an old Beatles song in my head the other day, too." She glanced around the empty room and took a deep breath. No warm smell. No lemons. Just musty old building.

"You think your ghost is some demented Beatles fan who gets a kick out of taking over people's heads?"

"Technically, not just a Beatles fan, since it was a Frankie Valli song I had in my head tonight."

He offered her his hand, just like he'd done a couple of nights ago. This time she took it. He was right. Her "theory" sounded crazy, even to her. She'd been at Mimi and Zeke's both times she'd experienced the music in her head phenomena, and according to Tom he'd heard "Help" during their conversation in the parking lot, which was technically part of the senior center, but not *in* the building itself.

Her face must have showed her frustration because Tom shrugged, then said, "Hey, there's still tomorrow night's séance."

"Speaking of which, we can't let Phoebe or this Madame Gloria know we *um*...you know, broke their rules by entering the building."

"Right. I won't tell if you don't," he said with a straight face. There was no smile at her lame attempt to make a joke. Or any hint of warmth behind his words. He deflated the mattress, picked up the backpack and headed for the door. "I need to lock up now. Get in the truck and I'll give you a ride to your brother's."

She thought about telling him that she could jog back, but something told her not to.

Neither of them said a word the entire way home.

She was afraid Tom would be angry or standoffish (she didn't think most men would appreciate being told to shut up in the middle of sex), but he appeared more pensive than anything else.

And that was good, right? After all, he'd given her exactly what she'd asked for. Straight sex with no emotions. It was a relief really, not to have to pretend to feel something they didn't. Allie turned to stare out the truck window. The weird thing was she felt more like crying now than she had earlier. Which made absolutely no sense at all.

Chapter Twenty-Two

TOM WALKED INTO THE offices of Pappas-Hernandez Construction. Stacey, the receptionist, sat at her desk, cradling a phone in one hand and a cup of coffee in the other. She was in her mid-twenties. Cute. Good sense of humor. Killer ass. She'd asked him out once but he'd gently put her off. Not that he hadn't been tempted, but generally it wasn't a good idea to date someone from work. Too much potential for disaster.

She quickly ended her phone call. "Well, if it isn't the prodigal son."

"I'm in that much trouble?"

"Mister, that building was supposed to come down three days ago." She pointed to a stack of papers on her cluttered desk. "See those? Those are all the schedule changes I've had to make to keep everyone working."

Tom winced.

She leaned forward. "Can I ask you a question? What are you doing? I mean, I know it's none of my business but isn't your bonus tied into the timeline on this project?"

Well I ran into this girl I used to know…

"Long story." He nodded toward Steve's office. "He busy?"

"Not for you he isn't. Go on in." She smiled in a way

that made Tom think she might still be open to going out with him. The trouble was there was only one woman on his mind right now.

He opened the door to his boss's office. Steve Pappas was a big guy, in his late thirties with an even kind of temper that suited Tom just fine. Steve glanced up from his laptop. "What's up?"

"Just wanted to keep you updated on the situation at the senior center."

"I hear there's going to be a séance tonight."

"Word spreads fast," Tom said. He'd come to tell his boss the details himself but it looked like someone had already beaten him to the punch. He didn't know whether to be relieved or irritated.

"You're going to be there, right?" Steve asked.

"Wouldn't miss it for the world."

"I hope she's worth it."

Tom raised a brow. "She?"

Steve leaned back in his chair and crossed his hands behind his head. He smiled like he was enjoying himself. "I'm a married man. Which means I pretty much hear everything that goes on in this town."

"Your wife's been talking about me?"

"Not just my wife. Her whole Bunco group. Something about you and your old girlfriend getting back together. How romantic the whole thing is and how I'm supposed to help with the cause."

"I'm a cause?"

"Brother, we're all causes to them."

"Yeah, well, this cause doesn't need any help."

"I didn't think so." Steve's gaze turned serious. "I get the initial delay on the demolition. One day isn't a big deal. But another two days after that? Are you out of your fucking mind?"

Probably.

"I didn't think it was a good idea to continue. Not with the crowd we had. Delaying the demolition makes us look like the good guys. It's solid PR for the company."

But he hadn't done it for the company. The first time he'd agreed to delay the demolition was because he hadn't been himself. Like he'd told Allie last night, he'd had that song in his head and it literally compelled him to put a halt to things. But this second delay? It had been easy to let Allie think it was courtesy of Steve Pappas, but the truth was it was more likely courtesy of Tom's bonus. He'd hated seeing the disappointment on her face when she realized her story was going nowhere. If this séance helped her land her dream job, then it would be worth putting his bonus in jeopardy. There would always be other projects. Other bonuses. But most likely, this was the only time he'd ever have with Allie Grant.

Steve looked like he wasn't buying the PR bullshit. "Just so you know, there's no overtime for this project."

"Understood."

"So there's no problem with the building coming down tomorrow morning?"

"Absolutely not."

"Good. That's all I needed to hear." He nodded toward a chair. "Have a seat. Now that we've cleared that up I want to talk to you about something."

Tom settled himself into a chair but didn't make himself too comfortable. Steve Pappas was a man of few words so Tom didn't picture himself staying long.

"You know my partner, Dave Hernandez, is growing the Tampa office. New construction is on the rise in the Bay area and now's a good time to get an in there. You interested?"

Tom shifted in his chair. "In moving to Tampa?"

"Once the new rec center gets built. I envision that's about the time we'll be ready to expand our operation. I know you have an ex and a son here in town, but the money could be substantial. Hell, you could keep a place here and live on the cheap in Tampa. Come back home every weekend if you wanted. Have the best of both worlds."

It was a similar deal he'd thought he could make work when he'd stayed behind in Atlanta, and Lauren and Henry had moved back to Whispering Bay. But the weekend visits hadn't always been regular, and even when they were they never seemed to be enough. He'd missed soccer games, a birthday, school teacher conferences, the everyday stuff that came with being a parent. The little stuff that added up to a life. A life he didn't want to give up. On the other hand, that life was definitely missing something. The last few days had taught him that.

Allie lived in Tampa. Plus or minus?

Yesterday it would have been a plus. But today? Last night she'd made her feelings crystal clear. She'd slapped her hand over his mouth and told him to shut up.

This doesn't mean anything. It's just sex.

Golden words to most guys. But he wasn't most guys. Those words had registered somewhere in that tiny portion of his brain that had still been getting some kind of blood flow. If he could have stopped, he would have. He would have rolled right off her and told her to go straight to hell.

Those words had served another kind of purpose, though. Before she'd spoken, he'd been full steam ahead. He'd have lasted a few minutes, max; he'd been so hot for her.

This doesn't mean anything.

It had been almost as effective as a cold shower. In retrospect, he should have thanked her. It had enabled him to gain enough control to slow things down. To draw it out. He'd wanted to make her scream. He'd wanted to make her want him as much as he wanted her. She'd screamed all right. There'd been a hell of a lot of satisfaction in that.

The crick that had begun in his neck last night seemed to have settled there permanently. He rolled his head from side to side trying to loosen it up. Did he want to move to Tampa? Not particularly. If he'd wanted a big job with big bucks, he could have stayed in Atlanta. He'd moved to Whispering Bay to take charge of his personal life. Moving to Tampa seemed like a step backward.

On the other hand, Tampa had something Atlanta and Whispering Bay didn't. It had Allie Grant. Of course, if she got the job she wanted at *Florida*! magazine, chances were she wouldn't be in Tampa anyway. She'd move on with her life. Just like he needed to.

I've had lots of sex. With lots of guys.

He'd wanted to call her out on that spectacular piece of bullshit, but what would have been the point? He needed to get that out of his head. Get *her* out of his head.

"Thanks, Steve; I appreciate your confidence in me."

"But you aren't interested?"

"Didn't say that," he said, not wanting to burn any bridges. "But it's definitely something I'd have to think long and hard on."

Allie decided to consult Jen on séance protocol. She'd spent most of the day on the Internet without any success. There was simply too much conflicting information out there, and Jen always seemed to know something about everything.

Jen answered on the first ring. "What's up? You didn't forget to the pay the electric bill, did you?"

"Is the electricity shut off?"

"No."

"Then I didn't forget to pay," Allie said.

"True. So, why did you call? Make it quick cause I don't have much time to talk. Sean and I are kind of in the middle of something."

Yikes. She had no intention of asking what that something might be. "I'll call back later."

"Not *that* kind of something, silly! I wouldn't have answered my phone if we were having sex."

"Who's having sex?" Sean yelled in the background.

"Allie thinks she interrupted us having sex," she heard Jen explain to Sean. He gave a loud Tarzan yodel that made Allie momentarily forget why she'd called.

Jen giggled into the phone. "We're playing strip poker and we're both down to our socks."

"And...that's it?"

"That's it." More giggling. This time, from Sean.

"Okay, I'll make this quick. There's going to be a séance in the building tonight and I want to know what I should look out for."

"Ooh! I'm jealous! I've never been to a séance, but I've used a Ouija board. Same concept. There's going to be a professional there, right? Like a medium?"

"Her name's Madame Gloria, and yeah, I've been told she's the area's premier expert."

"Cool. Don't worry. You don't have to do anything, doll. Just take your cues from her."

"All right. Um, there's one other thing. We were told

that the building was supposed to remain empty until the
actual séance, to keep it pure, or something like that, but
someone did kind of accidentally go inside."

"You didn't break in through a window again, did
you? Who *are* you and what have you done with Allie
Grant?" Jen asked playfully.

"I was kind of dragged inside. Well, picked up and
carried in, really. By this guy I used to know."

"Guy you used to— This isn't the guy in your high
school prom picture, is it? The one you keep hidden in
the bottom drawer of your nightstand. What's his name,
Tim?"

"Tom."

Jen barked with laughter. "Allison Grant, did you
hook up with an old boyfriend?"

"I really hate that expression. And how do you know
what I keep in my nightstand?"

"Oh my God. Sean! Allie had sex. With a real live
guy!" Allie could hear the two of them whooping it up.
What? Did they think she was a nun or something?

"All right, so…I guess I really didn't call to ask about
the séance. I mean, I did, but I need some advice on
something more personal."

Jen cleared her throat. "Ask away," she said in a
serious tone.

"First off, is Sean still listening in?"

"Well—"

"Never mind, it's okay. Maybe he can offer me some
advice here, too. From a guy's point of view." *Pause.*
"You were right. I did have a close encounter with my
ex. But it was strictly a onetime thing."

"So, what's the problem?"

"I have to see him tonight at this séance, and we left
things a bit…awkward between us."

Sean must have grabbed the phone away from Jen. "Hey, Allie, no worries! The dude isn't going to bring it up or anything."

"Oh, hey, Sean. How do you know he's not going to bring it up?"

He laughed. "Trust me. His number one objective is to make you feel comfortable around him. So he can get in your pants again."

"That's not happening."

"That bad, huh?"

"*No*—never mind. Can you put Jen back on please?"

Jean came back on the line. "Okay, so here's my advice. If you want this guy to know there's no way it's ever going to happen again, then just tell him up front. And then you end it by saying the sex was *nice* and that you just want to stay friends. Believe me, he'll practically run away."

"Cold, man, really cold!" Allie heard Sean shout.

"*Nice*. Okay. Got it." Allie felt strange taking this kind of advice from Jen, but who else could she ask? Certainly not Mimi. Her sister-in-law would throw a parade if she found out Allie and Tom had slept together.

"By the way, I'm glad you called. Sean moved a few things into the apartment. You don't mind, do you?"

"What kind of things?"

"Just a change of clothes, that kind of stuff."

"Oh, sure, that sounds okay."

"Listen," Jen said, trying unsuccessfully to muffle a giggle. "I'm down to one sock. Gotta go! And good luck tonight!"

Allie glanced at her wristwatch. Tom was two

minutes late. Not that she was worried about him not showing up. Responsibility was his middle name, after all. Plus, he had as much to gain from being at this séance as she did. Two minutes was nothing in the scheme of things. Heck, her watch might even be off.

Zeke caught her staring at the kitchen clock. "I could drive you, you know. You don't have to go anywhere with that guy." He sat at the kitchen table pretending he was reading the paper, but Allie wasn't buying it. Zeke had already read the paper that morning while drinking his coffee.

Here's the thing, big brother, Tom and I had sex, so not much else to worry about there…

Wouldn't Zeke just love that reply?

She probably shouldn't ask, but she couldn't help herself. "Why don't you like Tom?"

"I already told you. That son-of-a-bitch broke your heart."

"And I already told *you* no one broke my heart. Besides, I'm over it, so why aren't you?"

"People don't change, Allie. Once a cheater, always a cheater."

She wanted to say that Tom had never cheated on her. That he and Lauren had gotten pregnant before Allie and Tom had ever gone out. She *wanted* to say that. But she couldn't. Not with any certainty because she'd never asked. *Because she'd never wanted to know.* After all this time, did it even make a difference?

"You changed," she pointed out.

"I was never a cheater."

Now it was Allie's turn to glare at her brother.

"Okay, so maybe I slept around, but that's when I was young and stupid. Once I laid eyes on Mimi there was never anyone else."

The way Zeke said that made Allie's shoulders relax. She was tempted to ask her brother about the couples counseling, but since he didn't seem likely to bring it up himself, she was hesitant to break Mimi's confidence. Not that Allie had suspected her brother of being unfaithful, but it was good to know that cheating wasn't one of the issues her brother and his wife needed to work through.

"I don't know how or what I can do to make you stop hating on Tom, except to tell you I'm not getting together with him. Now or ever. Once I have this story, I'm out of here."

"You mean, once you get your license back."

"That, too."

They both heard the truck pull up into the driveway. No sense in making Tom get out of his truck to knock on the door. Especially when it would mean running into Zeke. The last thing Allie wanted was another confrontation between them. She grabbed her jean jacket.

"See you later," she said. "I'm off to my first séance."

"Hold on." Zeke laid the paper down on the table. "I know I don't say it enough, but, you do know I love you, right?"

"Aw, I love you, too."

She thought he might grin at that, but instead he looked troubled. Like he had something big on his mind. "Just don't…Donalan's not a bad guy. But he's not the right guy for you. You deserve someone who's going to put you first, and he's already proven that he's not going to do that."

Chapter Twenty-Three

THE DRIVE OVER WAS chillingly polite. On both their parts. Tom hadn't said more than two sentences combined when they pulled into the senior center's empty parking lot. Best to clear the air between them now, in private, before Phoebe and Madame Gloria and the rest of her gang got here.

"So...about last night," she began.

He gave her a look that said he'd been expecting this and wasn't looking forward to it. "Why do women always want to talk about sex?"

"What? And men don't?"

"Men want to have sex. Not analyze it," he snapped.

"Boy, someone woke up on the wrong side of the inflatable mattress this morning." She thought he might smile at that, but he didn't. "I just wanted to say that last night was...nice, but obviously it's never going to happen again, and I'm glad we're able to move past it like rational adults."

"Nice, huh?"

"Well, yes, it was...*very nice*."

He snorted. "Admit it. It was the best damn sex of your life."

Allie felt herself flush. He wasn't supposed to

challenge her on this. He was supposed to slink his tail between his legs and go off like a good puppy dog.

"*Wow*. Someone has a big ego. Is that why you're pouting? You're upset because afterward I didn't fall on my knees and profess my undying love to the great Tom Donalan?"

He turned to face her. "Let me rephrase that. It started out to be the best damn sex of *my* life. So whatever you want to tell yourself, however you need to rationalize it, go right ahead, but I'm not going to trivialize it. Last night was important to me." He shook his head. "I'm old enough to know that the reality shouldn't have been as good as the fantasy. But you know what? It was a thousand times better. So for me, last night was pretty fucking fantastic. Well, except for the part when you told me to shut up and that it didn't mean anything to you. But otherwise? It was A plus. And if it wasn't that way for you, I don't want to hear it."

He'd fantasized about her? She tried to think of something to say, but her throat felt like the Gobi desert.

"So you want to move past last night?" he continued.

"Of course," she squeaked.

"Right. Just like we've gotten past what happened twelve years ago?"

"I thought we already had this conversation three nights ago."

"No, you had this conversation. I listened."

It was true. She'd hadn't let him get much in. But what was the point of hashing out the events of twelve years ago? "Why are you bringing this up now?"

"You're the one who brought up last night. I figured now was as good a time to bring it all up." His voice went quiet. "No matter what I do, I don't stand a chance with you, do I?"

The glaring lights of a car turning into the parking lot made them both look away. It was quickly followed by another car that parked alongside it. Phoebe and Roger Van Cleave got out of the first car. Roger spotted them and waved.

A reprieve!

"Looks like the gang's all here." Allie reached for the truck door but before she could make her escape, Tom leaned over and blocked her from opening it.

"We're not done yet."

"But we can't keep everyone waiting." She hated the shakiness in her voice.

"As long as you know that before you leave town, you and I are finishing this conversation. My way."

Allie had never seen a medium before, but Madame Gloria was nothing like she expected. She had to admit, a Whoopi look-alike would have been comforting, but she would have settled for someone with white hair and a turban. And a Russian accent. Yes, a foreign accent would have been impressive. Instead, Madame Gloria was maybe mid-thirties with long blonde hair and a skull and crossbones tattooed over her right bicep. Despite the chill in the air, she wore a flowery skirt with a tank top and Birkenstocks. At least a dozen thin gold bracelets dangled from each of her wrists.

Besides Allie and Tom and Phoebe and Roger, Viola Pantini and Gus Pappas were also present. Allie was glad to see Viola and Gus. If anyone deserved to be at tonight's séance, they did, considering that they'd spent so much time in the senior center. Allie wondered what they'd had to do to get on Phoebe's illustrious guest list.

251

More than likely Roger (who Allie was still ninety-nine percent certain *wasn't* Concerned Citizen) had talked his sister into including them.

Madame Gloria clapped her hands to get their attentions. "Before we begin. I need to make sure that everyone present is a true believer. Any negative vibrations will only frighten our spiritual visitor. We want to create a loving, positive environment conducive to free-flow communication."

Everyone began mumbling at once. Even Tom nodded his "belief" although Allie knew he was just faking it to get things going.

"Sure, sure," Gus said. "I believe in the dead coming back."

Madame Gloria's face twisted. "I've found the word 'dead' has a negative connation. I prefer the term 'non-living.'"

Non-living sounded pretty negative to Allie, too, but she wasn't about to disagree with a professional like Madame Gloria. Not when she wanted to get on her good side. After the séance, she was hoping Gloria would agree to an interview.

Allie gave a thumbs-up. "Non-living. Got it."

"Excellent." Madame Gloria waved a hand in the air with a flourish, exposing a small tuft of hair beneath her underarm. "Now, if everyone will kindly turn off any unnecessary electronic devices, we can all take a seat."

A sturdy-looking card table (as previously specified by Phoebe) had been set up in the middle of the room surrounded by seven folding chairs. No flowing tablecloth to hide anything under or burning candles to provide the expected ambiance. A trio of kerosene lamps stationed on the floor around the table provided the room's only illumination. Roger set up his video camera, then took the seat next to Allie. Phoebe sat to her other side with Tom directly across the table.

Madame Gloria made a point of making eye contact with each of them. "Shall we all hold hands?" Allie reached out to Roger and Phoebe. Roger's hand felt warm and secure in her grasp, as opposed to Phoebe's clammy grip. For several long minutes nothing happened. Allie waited for Madame Gloria to begin chanting or to say something, but she didn't.

She glanced over to find Madame Gloria frowning. "Someone has been inside this building. And he or she has left a very disturbing aura behind."

Allie's gaze immediately darted to Tom. Could Madame Gloria "see" what they'd done last night? The thought of it nearly gave Allie a heart attack. But Tom looked more amused than worried, which helped her relax. Of course Madame Gloria couldn't know about last night! She was a medium, not a psychic. Although...they weren't the same thing, were they? Allie was still confused about that.

Gloria narrowed her eyes at Phoebe. "I thought you'd know that the building's integrity was to be maintained."

"I can assure you; I left explicit instructions that the building was to be left empty for twenty-four hours. I'm not an amateur, you know."

"Nevertheless, I know what I feel."

"Maybe this disturbing aura you're feeling is just the ghost," Tom said mildly.

Allie forced herself not to look at him.

"Perhaps." Madame Gloria puckered her lips in distaste. "Or perhaps not."

"Maybe if you describe this feeling, we can help." Viola nodded toward Gus. "We spent a lot of time inside this building."

"Very well. I'll try to articulate what I'm sensing." Madame Gloria closed her eyes and began swaying.

This was more like it. Allie closed her eyes as well and tried to concentrate. A vision of Tom staring down at her as he slowly rocked inside her popped into her head. *Oops.* Nope. Don't concentrate on that.

Last night was important to me.

"Yeah, right," she muttered. What a line!

Phoebe's grip on her hand tightened. "Hush!" she admonished Allie.

"Sorry," Allie whispered.

Okay, concentrate. She'd think about the dead—*no*—the non-living entity they were trying to communicate with.

"I sense a great disturbance in the force," Gloria announced.

Oh, Madame Gloria did not just go there. Allie steeled herself to keep from giggling.

"It's passion," Madame Gloria said. "The disturbance involves a great deal of passion."

"Like a murder?" Phoebe sounded as excited as a Chihuahua on crack.

"Perhaps. But…no, I don't think so."

Allie could have told them there hadn't been a murder in the senior center. But she kept her mouth shut.

As long as you know that before you leave town, you and I are finishing this conversation. My way.

What did that mean anyway? *His way*? Who did he think he was? Frank Sinatra?

Madame Gloria made a tsking sound. "This is a different sort of passion. One that had been long denied. And only very *recently* satisfied."

Allie's eyes flew open to find Tom staring at her. She

shut her eyes again. *Coincidence.* Madame Gloria's choice of words were just a coincidence.

"I sense a huge range of emotions here," Madame Gloria continued, her voice rising with enthusiasm. "Betrayal, sadness, anger and…something else."

"Like what?" Gus asked.

Roger leaned forward in his chair. "Yeah, like what?"

"A release. A *very great* release. Right here in this exact same spot."

Okay, this was getting voyeuristically creepy. The table had been set up in the same location where the air mattress had been last night. Allie peeked around the room. No one was looking at her, except Tom, but Allie refused to make eye contact with him. Her palms began to dampen. She tried to pull her hand out of Phoebe's to wipe off some of the moisture, but Phoebe's bony fingers had her in a death grip.

Madame Gloria shifted in her chair, causing her bracelets to jangle against one another. It wasn't a particularly scary noise, but Allie still shuddered.

"Perhaps if I concentrate a bit more. Let's start again. Everyone must clear their minds and focus. The more communal energy we create the harder it will be for the spirit to resist us. And this time, no talking," Madame Gloria instructed. "All this input is only confusing the spirit. My voice must be the only one he or she hears."

Once again the room went silent. Allie could hear the wind rustling over the building and the occasional sound of a car engine in the distance. She tried her hardest to focus like Madame Gloria urged.

Do you know how long I've wanted to do this? Tom's silky voice whispered in her ear. Allie's eyes flew open. No one had spoken. It was just her imagination. She tried to swat the memory of last night from her mind the way she'd do with some pesky fly.

Concentrate, Allie. Think of...the warm smell. Only that made her think of Jean Nate, which led her back to Buela.

"Maybe if you ask the ghost a question, he'll answer," Phoebe said.

"Who's the medium here?" Madame Gloria demanded.

Phoebe looked as if she'd just been struck. "Why, you of course."

"Then kindly allow me to direct this séance in the proper fashion. Which means no talking."

Phoebe lowered her eyes and nodded.

Allie almost felt sorry for Phoebe, except wasn't she the one who had bragged how Madame Gloria was the best medium in the business?

A few more minutes went by. No one dared utter a peep.

"I'm getting something," Madame Gloria said. "It's coming back. The same feeling I had before. Great emotion. In this very spot."

Allie tried to ignore everything else and concentrate as hard as she could. *Lemons.* Could she smell them? She inhaled deeply. No. No lemons. No Jean Nate. No nothing.

A faint sound interrupted Allie's thoughts. She recognized it instantly because she'd heard it just a few nights ago. It was the sound of crunching gravel. Ghosts didn't walk on gravel. Only something alive could make that noise.

More gravel crunching. Followed by what sounded suspiciously like giggling. Allie began to get a very bad vibe.

"I'm sensing conflict," Madame Gloria announced, oblivious to the noise. "Conflict of a very dark nature."

That's when the music began. Softly at first. And then the melody rose and before Allie knew it, a full-blown version of Jim Morrison and The Doors singing "Light My Fire" was blasting away in her eardrum.

Oh no. Not again.

It had to be a hallucination. Like thinking just a few minutes ago that she'd heard Tom whisper in her ear.

She scanned the table. Madame Gloria had her eyes closed and was swaying slightly from side to side as if she were in a trance. Viola and Gus seemed fascinated by Gloria's movements. Phoebe's eyes were shut tight and Roger looked as if he'd won the lottery. Tom, on the other hand, was still staring at her. Only now he was frowning, as if he found something suddenly strange. Could he hear the music, too?

Do you hear that? She silently mouthed to him.

He paused long enough to make her wonder if she truly was going crazy. *Hear what?* He mouthed back. But there was a momentary flicker in his eyes that gave him away.

Liar! He could hear it, too!

"You know what," she said to Tom.

The rest of the table turned to look at her. *Woops.* She hadn't meant to say that out loud.

"Please, Ms. Grant!" Madame Gloria said. "You're breaking my concentration. I am the only one allowed to speak here."

Come on baby, light my—

"I know, and I'm sorry, but don't you hear that?" Allie asked. She glanced around the table but all she saw was confusion on their faces. Except for Tom, who shook his head at her as if to tell her *no*. But no what?

257

No, he couldn't hear that (although she knew perfectly well that he could) or no, she shouldn't say anything to anyone else about it?

"Hear what?" Gloria demanded. "The only thing I hear is you talking."

"You don't hear the music?"

"What music?" Phoebe asked.

"Sorry," Allie muttered. Oh lord, the music was actually getting louder now.

Come on baby, light my fire.

"Now, where was I before this latest interruption? Oh my. I'm sensing two spiritual entities, not just one! Two entities in *great* conflict. A struggle, you might say. A struggle going back and forth, a great flow of energy going in and out, in and out, as if...*hmmm*...well, *that* can't be right." Madame Gloria cleared her throat.

"Two entities, huh? In and out?" Gus said.

Madame Gloria let out a long-suffering sigh. "I should have brought a muzzle for you people."

This was apparently all the permission Phoebe needed to speak again. "Two entities? Are you quite certain? I only picked up a masculine spirit."

"*Two* entities," Gloria repeated. "One male and one female."

Gus began chuckling.

Somewhere in the back of Allie's mind she registered the sound of more gravel crunching but the music was beginning to drown out everything. Louder and louder until she thought her head might explode.

COME ON BABY, LIGHT MY FIRE.

Oh, Lord, maybe she had a brain tumor. Or maybe Martians were invading the planet and using her as a conduit to get to other earthlings or maybe—

COME ON BABY, LIGHT MY FIRE.

She had to stop it. She had to. Or she'd go crazy. But how? It was as if whatever was making the music in her head was urging her to do something. Or say something. Like when Tom admitted he'd heard the song "Help" in his mind and it had only ceased when he'd told her he'd stop the demolition.

Impulsively, she pushed herself up from the table. "Okay! I admit it! Tom and I had sex last night."

The music came to a screeching halt.

"Oh, thank God!" She placed her hands against the sides of her head. Beautiful, blissful peace! Her head belonged to her again.

"I knew it," Gus said. He grinned and gave Tom a big thumbs-up.

Madame Gloria pointed a finger at Phoebe. "How can I be expected to commune with the non-living when my instructions to keep the building pure were deliberately disobeyed? I *thought* you were a professional."

Phoebe kicked back her chair and stood. "I am a professional! And I can vouch that no one has stepped foot inside this building for over twenty-four hours." She waved her hand at Tom. "Isn't that right?"

Tom didn't say anything.

"Right?" Phoebe persisted.

"Go ahead," Gloria said smugly. "Tell them."

"It was an accident," Allie blurted. "We didn't mean to have sex. It just sort of happened."

Phoebe looked incredulous. "You had sex *here*? Inside this building? When?"

"Um, last night," Allie admitted.

Viola reached out to pat her on the arm. "Isn't that lovely? Er, at least, I assume it was lovely. Was it?"

Everyone at the table turned to look at Allie.

"It was…you know, nice."

Tom muttered something under his breath that Allie didn't catch.

Phoebe looked incredulous. "I specifically told you that the atmosphere was to be kept pure for tonight's séance! What are you people, *animals*?"

More gravel crunching. More giggling.

Madame Gloria threw her hands in the air. "Does anyone besides me hear that?" she demanded.

"I hear it," Gus said.

"Me too," Roger chimed in.

"I think I know where it's coming from." Tom walked across the room and threw open the front door. Mimi, Pilar and the rest of the Bunco Babes stood huddled at the threshold. They looked a mixture of both surprised and elated at being caught eavesdropping on the séance.

"*Oops.*" Mimi said. She looked at Allie and shrugged. "Sorry, I tried to talk them out of it but a séance was just too hard to resist."

The women began filing into the building, talking at once and snapping pictures with their cell phones as if they had every perfect right to be there. Frida Hampton, the owner of The Bistro by the Beach held an empty margarita glass in her hand. "What have we missed?"

Kitty Pappas took the glass from Frida's hand and smiled apologetically. "Don't worry, we have designated drivers."

"This is a mockery!" Madame Gloria cried. "First the aura is desecrated by...by these two"—she pointed to Allie and Tom—"and their sexual shenanigans, and now we have séance crashers. I cannot be expected to work in this kind of environment!"

Allie felt a dozen pairs of eyes on her, including Tom's ex. What in all that was holy was Lauren Donalan doing here? "I can explain," she said.

260

"Oh, no need to explain," Lauren said. "We all know what sexual shenanigans are." She didn't seem upset. On the contrary. She seemed almost giddy. Must be the work of those super-secret margaritas Mimi was always bragging about.

Kitty glanced nervously around the room. "So, how's it going? Has the ghost showed up yet?"

"Not yet," Allie muttered.

"Okay, ladies, show's over," Tom said, nodding his head toward the still-open door.

"You're kicking us out?" a short redhead asked, slurring her words. Hopefully not one of the designated drivers.

"You got it," he said with the sort of smile any woman would find hard to resist. Especially a slightly inebriated Bunco Babe.

"Party pooper," Frida said, playfully sticking her tongue out at Tom.

"C'mon, girls," Mimi said. "I think we should leave." She threw Allie a meaningful look on her way out the door. A look that said, *We'll talk later.*

Tom waited till the last woman had exited the room, then he firmly closed the door behind them. "All right, let's start over."

"Absolutely not," Madame Gloria said. "The conditions under which I'm expected to work have been ruined."

Tom crossed his arms over his chest. "The conditions are not ruined. You claim to be a medium, so go ahead. Do your thing. Make me a believer."

The second the words were out of his mouth, Allie cringed. Madame Gloria's eyes glittered in triumph. "I knew you didn't believe. No wonder I haven't been able to make contact with this ghost."

"I thought you preferred the term non-living," Tom said.

Madame Gloria shook her head as if she felt sorry for him. She pulled her bangles up her arms and made a grand departure, slamming the door on her way out.

Gus stood. "Well, I guess that's it."

"Do you have any idea how hard it was to get Madame Gloria?" Phoebe screeched at Tom. "And *you*." She turned to Allie. "Don't ever call the Sunshine Ghost Society again. You're officially on our blackball list." She ran after Madame Gloria. "Wait! Come back! I had nothing to do with this!"

Viola shrugged. "I think we should go," she said to Gus.

"Right," Gus said, looking disappointed. Then he winked. "At least we can report to Betty that the world isn't coming to an end."

"I'll go make sure Phoebe doesn't hang herself," Roger said, trying to follow Viola and Gus out the door.

"Hold on, mister," Allie said.

Roger froze.

"Why did you lie about being Concerned Citizen?"

Those bushy eyebrows Allie had initially found distracting went up a notch. "Who says I'm lying?"

"Tell me exactly what you love about my Perky the Duck story," Allie said.

He put his hands up. "What's not to love about it?"

"You've never read it, have you?"

Roger had the good manners to look shame-faced. "What gave me away?"

"Let's just say you seem like the type of man who wouldn't hide behind an anonymous letter. Plus, if you really had seen a ghost why not go to your sister the ghost hunter in the first place? Why write a letter to a journalist you've never met? It didn't make sense."

"I'm sorry," he said. "I never meant to mess with your story. It's just... I wanted to be a part of it, I guess." He glanced away. She could hear the confusion and regret in his voice and Allie had to fight the urge to reach out and hug him. Tom was right. Roger was lonely. This whole ghost thing had been nothing more than an adventure for him.

Tom cleared his throat. "Maybe there's something on the video that could help," he suggested.

The three of them watched the replay of the tape on the small camera screen. Allie kept her eye on the lookout for any of those white blobs, but all she saw was the seven of them holding hands while Madame Gloria tried to channel the ghost, and of course, her big "confession" (oh, God, she needed to make sure Roger erased this *pronto*). Then there was the part where Mimi's drunken Bunco group had come crashing through the door.

"Looks like something you'd see on that *America's Funniest Videos* show," Roger said, placing the camera equipment back into a bag. "Sorry that wasn't more helpful."

Allie tried to squelch her disappointment, but it was impossible to not feel defeated. This was it. No ghost story. No creepy séance to write about. Nothing to impress Ben or anyone else at *Florida!* magazine. Chris Dougal was going to win. And it was back to waiting tables at The Blue Monkey for Allison Grant.

Chapter Twenty-Four

WITHOUT THE REST OF the group, the building once again seemed dark and lonely. It was like Allie had come back full circle to find herself exactly where she'd been three nights ago.

"I'm sorry things didn't work out the way you wanted," Tom said.

"Are you?"

"You know I am. I wanted this ghost thing cleared up almost as much as you did."

He was right. Allie couldn't blame him for tonight's epic failure. Or Mimi's Bunco group, either. She couldn't blame anyone really, except herself. If only she'd kept her mouth shut, maybe Madame Gloria wouldn't have stalked out. But Allie hadn't been able to help herself. It was either admit to the sex or go crazy listening to that music. It had to mean something, didn't it?

"The thing is," Allie said, "I think Madame Gloria could have helped."

"You're kidding, right?"

"Tom! She knew we'd had, you know, *sex*. Right here in this building. If she isn't a medium, then she sure as heck is psychic. It's like…she was reading my mind the entire time."

"Allie, it's not too hard to figure out that we've been together. I bet everyone else here knew, too."

"How?"

"They've got eyes, don't they?"

"What's that supposed to mean?"

"The way you've been looking at me all night? It's a miracle you didn't leap over the table."

"Looking at you? I had my eyes closed most of the time!"

"Okay. So maybe it was the way I was looking at you." He sounded absolutely serious. And sexy as hell.

"That sounds...painful. Maybe you should get that looked at."

He stepped toward her, close enough that she could reach out and touch him. If she wanted to. "It's excruciating," he said. "Got any suggestions?"

Flirting with Tom Donalan was dangerous. If she didn't want a repeat of last night then she'd better put a stop to it now. The problem was, despite what she'd told Jen earlier, she was beginning to think a repeat of last night was exactly what she needed. "Nope. No suggestions. So, what about the music?"

He took the change of topic gracefully. "What music?"

"Don't play games with me, Tom. You know what I'm talking about."

He blinked. "'Light My Fire.'"

"Yes! You heard it, too?"

He took another step. He was close enough now that she could smell his aftershave. It was different from his regular scent. This one was darker...spicier. Or was she simply smelling *him*?

"Not exactly. The song just kind of popped into my

head." He looked at her strangely. "You heard actual music?"

She nodded. "That's why I went all Jerry Springer on Madame Gloria. It's like the music compelled me to admit to everyone what we'd done. Kind of like when you heard the Beatles' 'Help' in your head and it didn't go away until you cancelled the demolition. Don't you see? It's the ghost. It's trying to communicate with us."

"Allie," he said gently. "We've already gone through this. Do you know how crazy that sounds? Besides, I thought you didn't believe in ghosts."

"How else can you explain it?" She sighed. "I'm one step away from Chattahoochee, aren't I?"

"What? The psych hospital? Nah, more like a couple of steps."

She grinned. This story might be turning her into a nut job, but at least she could still laugh at herself. That had to mean she wasn't really going crazy, right?

"You want to know what I think?" Tom said. "I think for some reason you got that song stuck in your head and somehow, you made me think of it, too. Not because of some ghost or some non-living spirit, but because, hell, I don't know. Maybe we just think alike. Or maybe we just really get each other." He shoved a hand roughly through his hair, like that last omission had left him vulnerable, and he'd needed to do something physical to shake it off.

"Well, we certainly used to. Get each other, I mean."

His gaze darted straight to hers. Dark and intense and probing. Was he about to bring up the past again? He seemed intent on hashing out the events of twelve years ago, but right now Allie felt too emotionally worn out for a walk down memory lane. What she needed was some time away from this story. Away from this building. Away from thinking about Mimi and Zeke and their marital problems. What she needed was…standing right in front of her.

"If you want we can stay the night here again. Just in case anything happens," he offered.

"Why are you being so nice to me? I've done nothing but wreak havoc on your life since I've hit town."

"Don't you know why?" He placed his hands on her shoulders and leaned down to whisper in her ear. "I could be a lot nicer, Allie. If you let me."

Her heart nearly catapulted out of her chest. She didn't have to ask what that meant. God, she was weak. Because, yes, despite the fact that it was probably a terrible idea, she was going to let him be *very nice* to her.

Tom opened the front door to his house and stepped aside to let Allie enter. It was unnerving having her here. He wasn't worried what she'd think of the place. It wasn't fancy, but he was a stickler for keeping things clean. It just felt like a lot was riding on tonight. Like he'd placed all his chips into a single pot. All it would take was the one wrong draw of the cards and he'd be out of the game permanently.

"You sure you don't want to stay the night at the senior center?" he asked. *Again.*

"Positive," she said. *Again.* "You sure you want to invite me inside?"

"More than positive. I just don't want you to regret anything."

She gave him a shaky smile. "Ask me that in the morning."

Come tomorrow morning he'd make sure neither of them had any regrets, or any doubts about where this relationship was headed. Somehow, the fates had seen clear to giving him a second chance with this woman and he wasn't about to screw it up.

He flipped on the living room light, then made his way to the tiny kitchen in the back of the house. "Want a drink?"

"Just some water, thanks." She looked like she needed something a lot stronger but he filled two glasses with ice water and handed her one. She gulped it down then laid her empty glass on the counter.

"How about you show me your place?" she said in an overly bright voice.

He led her back out to the living room, and then he showed her his den, the room where he spent most of his waking time. She looked around the walls, at his diploma from the University of Florida nestled in the brown frame with the orange and blue trim, at the photos of the projects he'd worked on. She seemed impressed, but he hadn't shown her his work to impress her. He wanted to take her mind off that damn story. She was brilliant. Couldn't she see that?

Next stop was Henry's room. It probably wasn't much different from Cameron's. Dark beige walls, a double bed, chest of drawers, and a desk. The walls were covered in sports posters. Mainly football and soccer, since those were the sports he was into. Tom had tried to steer Henry toward baseball, but he wasn't interested.

"Does Henry spend a lot of time here?" she asked.

"As much time as I can get with him."

She smiled again, only this time the smile came easier. "Can I just say how weird all this is? In a good way, though."

He didn't respond, but he knew what she meant. Having her in his home was like opening up his life to her. Showing him all those parts of himself that she hadn't been there for.

They came to the end of the hallway, to his bedroom, and Tom was grateful that he'd taken the time to make his bed this morning.

She looked nervous again. Hell. He was nervous, too. He didn't want this to seem forced. Or unnatural. He took her hand and led her to the bed. "It's been a long day. Let's get some sleep."

"Honest?"

"What? You think I can't sleep next to you without mauling you?"

She yawned. "I wouldn't mind a good mauling, but..." She shrugged. "Maybe later? It's been a strange night."

He could wait till later. He could wait a long time. Maybe even forever. Just as long as she stayed right here next to him.

Still keeping his jeans on, he toed off his shoes then drew back the comforter and slid in between the sheets. Allie wasn't as thoughtful. She took off her boots and unbuttoned her jeans, letting them drop to the floor. Which left her in nothing but a tank top and a piece of black string that must have been her idea of underwear.

He was a prince, no doubt about it.

Might as well go all the way and aim for sainthood.

He put his arm around her and drew her close, letting her snuggle up against him. If she needed warm and cuddly then that's what he'd give her. She sighed and for the first time tonight, he could feel her relax.

He tucked the top of her head beneath his chin,

bringing them closer. Her hair smelled like some kind of fruity shampoo and her skin…it was both soft and firm at the same time and all he could think about was how good it would feel to slide inside her.

Just a few well-placed kisses and she'd let him. He knew that. But he wasn't going to blow whatever it was they had going. Right now, despite the fact that he was so hard it hurt, there wasn't anything on earth he'd rather do than hold Allie in his arms.

The room was dark and unfamiliar. How long had she been asleep? She glanced at the soft green glow of a bedside clock. It was three in the morning. She shifted slightly and felt Tom's arms tighten around her. She'd fallen asleep in his bed, wearing nothing but a top and her raunchiest panties. And he hadn't made a move. He'd wanted to. She knew that. Just like he had to know that she would have made a move right back. But she appreciated his restraint.

The night had started off terrible, that scene in the parking lot, sitting inside his truck. He'd been angry with her, but during the séance something had shifted. He'd put aside his own feelings to be there for her when she'd needed him most. He'd argued with Madame Gloria for her sake. Not because he believed the séance would actually work, but because he wanted her to get her story.

As incredible as it seemed, they were right back to where they were twelve years ago. Somehow, in the short span of just four days he'd become her best friend all over again. A best friend she wanted to have sex with, that is.

271

She pressed her thigh against his jean-clad leg.

"If you're trying to kill me, you're doing a damn good job," Tom muttered.

She leaned up on her elbow. "Oh, did I wake you up?" she asked, trying to sound innocent.

He laughed. "Are you kidding? I haven't slept a wink since you've hit town."

"Aren't you exaggerating a little?"

"I wish."

"Then...maybe I can help you with that." She bent down and kissed him on the mouth, slow and soft. He didn't deepen the kiss although she sensed that was exactly what he wanted. She broke it off and straddled his waist, then drew off her tank top and bra, leaving her in nothing but the black lace panties.

He looked at her as if she were the most beautiful thing on earth. "It's not enough that I can't sleep; now you want me to have a heart attack."

She smiled. Tom was hers. To do with whatever she wanted. It was like all the walls between them came crashing down and just for tonight she was the old Allie and he was the old Tom and the Night of the Great Humiliation had never happened.

She leaned down to kiss him on the chest, causing him to suck in his breath. "Maybe just a little heart attack," she joked. She slid down his body, positioning herself to place a kiss near the top of his belly button. His hands clamped down on her shoulders, but whether it was to urge her on or stop her, she wasn't sure. After a few seconds he let his arms drop. "I give up. Go ahead, kill me. But make it fast."

"Sorry," she teased. "But I think you should know that I intend to go very slow."

He closed his eyes and groaned and Allie didn't

know whether she was more turned on, or just simply…happy. Or maybe both.

She unbuttoned his jeans, freeing his erection. He raised his hips and pushed both his jeans and boxer shorts off in one frenzied motion. She took him into her mouth then proceeded to lick and suck like she had all the time in the world, and he took it like a champ. Until he couldn't anymore.

"My turn," he said. Then he flipped her over and now she was the one in the vulnerable position. Only she didn't feel vulnerable. She felt the exact opposite. A power she'd never imagined before surged through her veins, making her bold. She laughed and stretched her arms over her head. "Go ahead. But I bet I can last longer than you did."

He chuckled softly. "You're on." His warm breath left goose bumps over her skin. He hooked his thumbs in the side of her panties and slid them down, studied them with a look of sheer appreciation, then tossed them somewhere over his shoulder. Then he lowered his mouth between her thighs.

Oh. My. God.

The bastard. She should have known he'd try to show her up. If she'd gone slow, then he was going slower. And in between that delicious thing he was doing with his tongue, she could hear him whisper against her skin. All the things he'd begun to say to her last night that she hadn't wanted to hear. How beautiful she was. How much he'd always wanted her.

After what seemed like both forever and not long enough, he paused to pull a condom from the nightstand. They laughed as he struggled to get it on. "Let me do that," she said, taking over the job. She pushed him onto his back. He watched from beneath hooded lids, and her mind couldn't help but flash back to last night. But this wasn't anything like that other encounter.

Last night had been hot and furious and incredibly exciting. This was hot and exciting, too. But in a different way. She straddled him once again and took him deep inside and began to move. After a minute or so, he gripped her hips, guiding her with his hands to slow down the pace, their gazes locked. Neither of them said anything. But they didn't look away, either. Not until the very end, when Allie had to close her eyes as she shattered into a thousand tiny pieces. He owned her body, no doubt about that. But that was all she was willing to give him.

Chapter Twenty-Five

ALLIE SEARCHED THE FLOOR for her panties. They had to be here somewhere. Underwear didn't just get up and fly away on its own. Tom lay on the bed, naked, with his arms crossed behind his head, looking more than a little pleased with himself. "So I was thinking of going up to Tampa next weekend."

She froze for a second. "Yeah?"

"I'm taking you out."

"Like on a date?"

"That's usually what taking you out means."

"Well, it could also mean putting a hit on someone." *Oh no.* She was going to start babbling. She found her panties beneath one of her cowboy boots and quickly began to dress.

He frowned. "What's wrong?"

"Wrong? Nothing's wrong. Everything was perfect. Better than perfect."

He sat up. "Then come back to bed."

She carefully sat next to him and pulled her knees up to her chest. He didn't try to pull her into his arms and for that she was grateful. Last night had been epic. But she hadn't anticipated what they'd say to one another this morning.

"I owe you an apology. For the other night. I…" She shook her head. "I don't know what got into me. I should never have told you to shut up."

"I get it."

This nice guy routine of his was well and fine but no one was *this* nice. There was a chink in his armor. She just hadn't found it yet.

"The other night, when we picked Henry up for soccer and you went to Panama City. You said you went to the hardware store."

He slowly nodded. "Yeah."

"But that's not the whole story. I mean, I know it's none of my business and you don't have to tell me—"

"I went to the library," he said. "To check out the periodical section where they keep old copies of *Florida!* magazine. I wanted to read your Perky the Duck article."

He'd driven all the way to Panama City to read her article? "That's…the sexiest thing anyone has ever said to me," she blurted.

He grinned. "Yeah? Because I thought last night—"

She threw a pillow at him. "I said it's the sexiest thing anyone has ever said, not *done*."

He relaxed back on the bed. "So about next weekend—"

"What did you think of it? My Perky the Duck article?"

She felt him stiffen. Because she'd redirected the conversation, or because he was about to tell her something she didn't want to hear? "The truth?" he asked.

"Of course I want the truth."

He hesitated long enough that she almost thought he wasn't going to answer. "I hated it," he said quietly.

Her whole body ricocheted like she'd just been shot. Did he just say he *hated it*? No one hated that story! Even cold-hearted publisher Ben Gallagher had tried to hide a watery eye after reading it.

"Excuse me?"

"I hated it because it was warm and funny and real, and reading it made me feel like you were talking to me. Only I couldn't talk back. It was like looking into a two-way mirror and seeing everything you'd become, but I wasn't a part of it." He let out a slow breath. "The truth is, I haven't thought about you in twelve years. Not really. And now, the crazy part is that I can't stop thinking about you at all."

He couldn't stop thinking about her?

"Wait. Did you just say you haven't thought about me in twelve years? Not even *once*?"

He rubbed a hand down his face. "I don't know if this is a good time to talk about this."

"You're the one who said I wasn't leaving town until we had this conversation. Well, it's now or never, Tom. Because believe me, as soon as I get my license back I'm out of here."

A muscle twitched on the side of his cheek. "Remember the night of the senior awards banquet?"

"What has that to do with anything?"

"That night…" He shook his head. "Man, I was on fire. I won almost every award they gave out. Even that cushy scholarship from the Rotary Club."

The memory of a packed high school gymnasium, Buela sitting on one side of her, Zeke, Mimi, and baby Claire on her other side, came flooding back. Allie had worn a purple dress and a new pair of sandals Mimi had helped her pick out at the outlet mall in Destin. She'd felt pretty and excited and full of senioritis energy—

277

ready to leave one chapter in her life and begin another.

She had won the English award, and Nate Miller had won the science award, but Tom's memory served him right. He'd scooped up every other academic award and had even been named top athlete. He'd looked so handsome in his navy blue blazer with the orange-and-blue-striped University of Florida tie. She hadn't been able to keep her eyes off him. Neither had anyone else. It was his night, all right. A tribute to Whispering Bay High's star of the year.

"Of course I remember that night," she said.

"Afterward, a bunch of us went to the beach. I'd swiped a bottle of rum from my dad's liquor cabinet and we got pretty wasted on rum and Cokes."

"Buela and I went to the Denny's in Panama City," she said in contrast. "She used to love how they served breakfast even at night. She'd get the Grand Slam, although she could never eat even half of it, and I'd get the short stack with the strawberry syrup, bacon on the side. Which I definitely finished."

He smiled. "You were always a good girl, Allie."

"Getting drunk on the beach isn't exactly bad ass. Every kid I know has done that."

"Yeah, but not everybody gets their girlfriend pregnant."

Bam! And there it was. The conversation she'd been dreading for over twelve years. But at the same time, she needed to hear it. She took a deep breath and forced herself to relax. She could handle whatever it was he had to say.

"You weren't alone in that, Tom."

He shook his head. "I'd just had the night of my life and I was dating the most popular girl in school. I didn't have a condom with me, but hey, I was king of the

278

fucking world. Lauren and I had had sex a few times, but never without protection. She didn't want to do it, but I told her one time wasn't going to get us in any trouble. She only went along with it because I talked her into it."

Allie gulped. She didn't have to imagine how persuasive Tom had been. Nor could she blame Lauren. Not when Allie herself had uttered those famous words of hers. *Just do me* took on a whole new meaning. If Allie had been in Lauren's place, she wouldn't have waited for a condom either. Stupid, but true.

"The next day Lauren broke up with me. Said she thought our relationship was moving too fast. And here's the kicker. I was relieved because I was planning to break up with her before we left for college anyway, so she saved me the drama. I was a real prince, huh?"

Allie looked away from his gaze. There was something in his eyes that made it hard to maintain eye contact.

"So that afternoon I asked you to prom because I needed a date, and because I thought you were hot and we were friends and I knew we'd have a good time. But it wasn't supposed to go any further than that."

She nodded. Their relationship had surprised her, too.

"And the more we hung out, the more I liked you. The thing is… I want you to know, even though we were planning on going to different schools, I wouldn't have broken up with you at the end of summer."

She felt her breath hitch. "But you did anyway."

"That morning after you told me…" He shrugged, like he was too embarrassed to go on.

"After I told you I loved you?"

"Lauren came to see me. She hadn't had her period in over three months and she'd finally broken down and told her mom. The rest… Well, you can figure it out. I could tell you that my dad put a lot of pressure on me to do the right thing, but that's not why we got married. The way I saw it I had a couple of choices. I could let Lauren figure it out for herself. Go on to school like nothing had ever happened. Or I could be a part of my child's life. Try to build a family. Try to make things work between the two of us. But to do that I had to completely cut you out of my life. So I made a decision and I stuck to it. I gave it everything I had. And the thing is I don't regret it. Not a minute of it. I'd only have regretted if I hadn't tried."

What could she say to that? There was nothing she could say to that. He was who he was. He couldn't help that. Just like she couldn't help who she was, or the decisions she'd made along the way to this moment.

"You want to know what's craziest about this whole thing?" he said. "I left Atlanta to move back here to be close to Henry. And now I'm thinking of moving to Tampa so I can be close to you."

"*What?*"

"Steve Pappas offered me a job in Tampa. I don't want to take it. But I don't know if I can *not* take it either. Not if it means you and I might really have a shot at making this work."

It felt like all the air had been sucked right out of her. "You want to move to Tampa? So you can be with me?"

"I loved Lauren. We had a good marriage but not a great one, I guess. I threw myself into my work and Henry, because, hell, that kid is worth anything. I would have kept going on if she hadn't called it quits. For a while there, I was even pissed at her. What the hell did she want from me? But then, I got it. She wanted something better. She said I should wait for it, too. So I dated a little. And it was great at first, being single again.

Having all this freedom. But I missed Henry too much, so I came back to Whispering Bay, and then you came along. Back into my life and it was like all those feelings I had for you that summer had never gone away. They just came rushing back. And I get it. I get what Lauren means about waiting for something better."

"And you think that *I'm* that something better? Tom…you haven't seen me or thought about me in twelve years, but after four days, now you suddenly think I'm, what? The love of your life? We don't even know each other for God's sake! Not really."

He held her gaze with a fierceness that this time Allie couldn't look away from. "I know you're loyal to the people you love. That you hate confrontation and when you're nervous, you talk too much. But it's so damn cute I could let you go on talking for days even if you just said the same things over and over. I know you have no clue how beautiful you are, or what kind of effect you have on me, because if you did I'd be in a hell of a lot of trouble." He shook his head and laughed. "Shit. Look at me. I'm in trouble now, aren't I?"

He took her hands in his and lightly squeezed them. "I know you can't cuss to save your life and that no one but you could have written a story about a half-dead frozen duck that made most of the south want to give up hunting." He paused. "Want me to go on?"

She was flabbergasted. Speechless in a way that she'd never been before. Tom Donalan had just exposed his jugular. He'd basically told her he loved her. Without saying it, of course. But that's what he was leading up to. It was her Ben and Jerry's Chunky Monkey fantasy come to life. She should jump up and pump her fist in the air. Or do a happy dance. Or feel something. Shouldn't she? But all she felt was sad.

"What do you want me to say to all that, Tom?"

"You know what I want." He bent down to kiss her.

She turned her head to avoid his touch and the sadness quickly turned to anger. It was all she could do to not punch him in the nose. *How dare he do this to her twice in a lifetime*? She snatched her hands away.

He reached out for her again. "Baby, I—"

"*No.* It's my turn now." She jumped up from the bed and began to pace the room. "That day I told you I loved you? It didn't matter that you didn't say it back. I mean, yeah, I wanted to hear you tell me you loved me, too. I wanted to hear it so bad, but I knew you weren't ready. And that was okay, because...my love wasn't some conditional thing. But then when you told me you and Lauren were getting married? I wanted to *puke.* I wanted to hate you, but I—" She swiped a tear from her eye. *How had that gotten there?*

"I admit it. Okay? You broke my heart, Tom. You spent an entire summer making me fall in love with you and then you looked me straight in the eye and told me you *thought* you loved someone else. That you had this big *responsibility* to take care of your mistakes. Well, what about me?" she asked, her voice rising with each word. "Where was your responsibility to *me*?"

He looked stunned by her outburst. Like he'd never considered her side in all this before.

"So I went home and I locked myself in my room and I cried because all I could think of was myself. And how *I felt.* And Buela was banging on the door, trying to get inside because she could hear me crying. And she kept begging me to tell her what was wrong. But I told her to go away. And after a while, she did. And she must have gotten Zeke...because then he started banging on the door, too."

Allie stopped her pacing. She'd forgotten all about Zeke trying to coax her out of her room. It was like she'd buried that memory along with a bunch of other stuff from that night. Obviously, Zeke hadn't forgotten a thing. His animosity toward Tom made perfect sense now.

"But I wouldn't let Zeke in, either," she continued. "So I cried myself to sleep that night. And the whole next day I acted like nothing was wrong, even though she knew that was bullshit. All she wanted was to comfort me. And I...I wouldn't let her. And then two days later, she was gone."

"Allie, you didn't cause your grandmother's heart attack." He stood and tried to pull her in his arms but she placed a hand up, warning him to back off.

"Don't you think I know that? But the last two days she had on this earth...all she wanted was... After Mom died, she gave up her whole life to come take care of me and Zeke. If it wasn't for her, who knows where we would have ended up? And the one little thing she wanted from me I couldn't give her because I was so *fucking* selfish. All I could think about was myself."

His voice cracked. "We were kids, Allie. You couldn't have known what was going to happen. You thought you'd have more time with her."

"Yeah, well, life *sucks*. Tell me something I don't know."

"You blame me, don't you?" he said quietly.

"No, Tom, I don't blame you. I blame *me*. But, somehow you're tied into it. At least...into that version of me. So, yeah, you've been terrific these past few days, and yeah, the sex was fantastic. I admit it. It was best sex of my life, too. But you and I are never going to be

283

together because you're always going to be a reminder of the biggest regret of my life."

He flinched. But she wasn't trying to hurt him. She was only trying to be honest.

"So that's it. No second chances. No nothing? Is that what you want?" He sounded bitter, and a part of her wanted to tell him…what? That they could start over? Zeke was right. Tom wasn't the guy for her.

"What I want is for you to take me home."

Chapter Twenty-Six

ALLIE CREPT THROUGH THE kitchen door. She was surprised to find Mimi sitting at the table, drinking what looked like a cup of hot cocoa. Mimi put her hands up as if to surrender. "I tried to stop the girls, I really did. But you know the Babes. Toss in some margaritas and the instant they heard about the séance there was no stopping them."

"Don't worry about the séance. It's not your fault." Allie glanced at the clock above the stove. It was a little after six. "Why are you up so early? Or haven't you gone to bed yet?"

"I've been waiting up for you."

"Sorry."

"Don't be sorry. I want to hear all about it. Including where you've been all night." She made a smirky face, then paused. "What's wrong?"

"The right question would be what isn't wrong."

Allie sank into the chair next to her sister-in-law. Mimi slid the cocoa across the table in silent offering. Allie picked up the mug and took a deep sip. Marshmallows with a hint of cinnamon. It would figure that Mimi made the best cocoa, too. Too bad chocolate couldn't cure her messy life.

Mimi fidgeted with the edge of a napkin. "So I take it the ghost didn't show up?"

"The only thing that showed up was your Bunco group."

"Ouch." Mimi reached to get her cocoa back but Allie held onto the mug.

"I need this more than you do. As a matter of fact," Allie said, glancing around the kitchen counter, "do you have some more of that stuff you laced my coffee with the other night?"

"That bad, huh?" Mimi took a bottle of whiskey from the pantry and sloshed a little into the cocoa.

"Let's just say the night was a disaster, all the way around."

Mimi looked like she wanted a detailed explanation, but she must have sensed Allie's weariness because she didn't press her. "So what happens next?"

"The senior center comes down in a couple of hours."

"Will you be there?"

"I almost feel like I should be. Who knows? Maybe something will still happen." *Ever the optimist, Allie.* Maybe it was the pessimists of the world who won at the end. At least they didn't get their hopes up. "But I'm not fighting it any more. I can't justify trying to keep the building intact when it seems pretty obvious that there's no ghost. Or at least, not one that makes sense."

She told Mimi all about the music she and Tom had been hearing in their heads, starting with the Beatles "Ob-La-Di, Ob-La-Da" and finishing with last night's "Light My Fire." The only part she omitted was the crazy feeling that somehow Buela was tied into all this. She wanted to share it with Mimi but it all seemed so—

"Do you think I'm crazy? Oh, God. This is like the

286

eighteenth time I've asked myself that same question, which means that yes, I probably am."

Mimi smiled patiently. "And Tom heard it, too? If he heard it, then no, you can't be crazy, unless the two of you are doing some kind of special drugs together?"

"He only experienced it the one time, although he knew the song in my head last night."

"Weird. And…you still don't know who wrote the anonymous letter?"

"Well, it wasn't Roger Van Cleave. He finally admitted it to me last night. Honestly? If I didn't have a copy of that email I'd think the whole thing was a figment of my imagination." She downed the rest of the cocoa. "The good news is I get paid today. So I can pay my fine and get my license reinstated."

"You're leaving town?" Mimi asked as if that wasn't a foregone conclusion.

"I'll stick around for the football game. Watch my niece cheer. Then head out tomorrow morning." *After I make sure Claire tells you and Zeke about her extracurricular activities…*

"I'm sorry, Allie. I was really hoping something big would happen for you."

"Thanks. But I'll think of something else to send in to the magazine. Either they'll hire me or they won't. Not much I can do about that." She glanced down at the empty mug. "I think… Tom thinks he's in love with me," she blurted.

"What the hell, woman! Why didn't you say so earlier? Does this have something to do with the fact that you announced to everyone at the séance that you and Tom had sex?" Mimi leaned forward in her chair, her blue eyes glittering with excitement. "I wasn't going to say anything because you seemed so down, but… Was it completely and totally *awesome*? You don't have to tell me the details, but then, I might have to kill you if you don't."

Despite herself, Allie managed a laugh. "It was all right."

"You're kidding? Just all right? Cause he looks like he'd be—"

"It was fine," Allie said, hoping that would be enough to satisfy Mimi's curiosity. If she told Mimi exactly how all right it was, she'd never hear the end of it. "I thought it would make things easier between us. You know, cut out some of the sexual tension? But I think it just made everything worse."

"Because now he thinks he's in love with you? Just exactly how is that making everything worse?"

"He didn't actually say the words, but, basically, yeah. I think he's got love confused with some nice sex. And of course, I don't feel the same way. Not at all."

Mimi raised an incredulous brow.

"Promise you won't tell Zeke. He'll blow a kidney. He already hates Tom enough as it is. If he finds out we had sex and that half the town knows he'll have to go on dialysis."

Mimi made a face. "I can't promise Zeke won't find out, but he won't find out from me."

It occurred to Allie that she was putting Mimi in a bad position with her husband and she didn't want to be responsible for adding any more tension between them. "I changed my mind, please do tell Zeke. Just wait till I leave town." *Pause.* "By the way, when did Lauren Donalan join your Bunco group?"

"She was subbing last night."

"Talk about awkward," Allie muttered.

"Oh, I don't know, she seemed kind of pleased, really, to find out you and Tom had been together."

"Just what kind of relationship do those two have?"

"Not the typical divorced couple, that's for sure," Mimi said. "It's kind of refreshing, actually. I really think she wants Tom to be happy."

"Sorry to disappoint her, but he's not about to be happy with me, that's for sure."

Mimi looked as if she'd just opened up a box of Oreos only to find the luscious cream filling missing from each cookie. "You don't think he was sincere when he told you he had feelings for you?"

"We were together for a few months twelve years ago and a few days now. How can anyone be in love after that?"

"Oh, sweetie, I fell in love with Zeke in ten minutes. I didn't want to. I knew his reputation, but when your brother decides to lay on the charm..." Mimi shrugged.

"That's different."

"How?"

"It just is, is all."

Mimi stood and placed the dirty mug in the kitchen sink. "You can tell yourself whatever you want, Allie, but the truth is, if we got to pick who we fell in love with, the world might be a tidier place. But a lot more boring, too."

Allie took a quick shower, then caught a ride with Zeke on his way to work. He pulled into the senior center parking lot. "You sure you want to be here?" he asked.

She didn't expect the ghost to suddenly materialize, but after all that had happened this past week, it seemed fitting that she be here for the big teardown. "Yep, I'm positive." She opened the door to the police cruiser and hopped out.

Zeke stuck his head out the window. "How are you getting home?"

"I can walk. It's a beautiful day and I could use the exercise." *Pause.* "I checked my bank account online and I have enough money to pay the suspension. Do you think you can give me a ride to the courthouse later?"

"Not a problem." There was relief in his dark eyes and Allie realized, not for the first time this visit, how much stress Zeke must have in his life. To him, she must be one more person to take care of. She hated that she was a source of worry for him. Especially now that she knew he had more important things to worry about. They made plans to meet back at the house at noon.

The scene in the parking lot was similar to what it had been the past few mornings. Lots of men. Lots of machines. She spotted Tom speaking to Hard Hat, *aka* Keith and waved to him. Tom made his way over to her. He looked surprised to see her and Allie realized what he must be thinking.

"Before you say anything I'm not here to ask you to stop the demolition. No tricks. No last-minute appeals. I concede defeat."

"Then why are you here?"

"I couldn't help myself."

He glanced around the parking lot and turned back to her as if he was going to say something but then changed his mind.

"I'm leaving town tomorrow," she said, feeling the start of a babbling attack. Maybe there was a self-help group out there. *Babblers Anonymous.* If not, then she could be the founder. She stifled an inappropriate giggle.

Laughter and tears. It must be kind of like the love-hate thing. Two emotions on opposite ends of the spectrum that weren't really opposite after all.

Why did the idea of demolishing the senior center suddenly make her feel so sad? A week ago, she wouldn't have blinked if she'd heard about the building coming down. But today...

"Have you decided what to do about your story? For the magazine?" Tom asked.

"I'll think of something." Then she put on her best smile because she certainly didn't want Tom Donalan feeling sorry for her. "I always do."

"I hope everything works out for you, Allie. You deserve nothing but the best."

"Thanks. You, too," she managed to say.

He nodded, but he didn't make a move to leave.

Oh God. They were having another *moment*. Only this one felt final.

She almost reached out to hug him. But of course, she didn't. You hugged friends or puppy dogs. You didn't hug Tom Donalan. Not unless she wanted a whole lot more than a hug.

Before she did or said something she'd regret, she took off across the parking lot. Good thing she had on her running shoes. She could feel tears welling up behind her eyeballs. But not because she was saying good-bye to Tom. It was the building. The ghost story. The agony of defeat. That's what it was.

She was so busy trying to get away that she ran smack into Roger Van Cleave, nearly knocking them both down in the process. "Oh! So sorry," she mumbled.

"Whoa!" Roger led her to a grassy area on the side of the parking lot. "You okay?"

"Perfectly fine. For a journalist without a story, that

is." She pointed to the camera slung around his neck. "That looks fancy."

"This old thing?" He grinned. "I thought I'd come out and record the demolition. For prosperity."

"Good idea." She almost hated to ask, but she had to. "So, how's your sister?"

"Phoebe's madder than a wet cat. But she'll get over it." He snapped a picture of the still intact building. "You know," Roger continued, "this place was originally built as a residential home by Earl Handy. He and Margaret raised their kids here, then after she passed on, he donated the building to the city. Pretty prime real estate, huh?"

She shaded her eyes to avoid the bright morning sunlight and looked at the building for what was probably the last time. A crane with a large wrecking ball sat poised on the edge of the senior center, ready to take aim. She'd known about the building's original owner, of course. Everyone knew old Earl Handy, grandson (or was it great-grandson?) of Cyrus Handy, one of Whispering Bay's original founders. Heck, half the town was practically related to him, Mimi and Lauren included.

A horn blared, making her jump.

"Everyone, clear the premises!" Hard Hat yelled into a bullhorn, followed by the sound of heavy machinery going into action. Allie and Roger stepped behind to a marked-off area, where a few other spectators looked on as well. Roger began recording the process with his camera.

Allie had never seen a building demolished. The roar of the cranes combined with the sound of smashing bricks produced what appeared to be a well-orchestrated production.

Allie glanced over at Tom, who seemed oblivious to his audience. There was no doubt that he was the guy in charge. He looked bigger than life. Handsome, confident, and totally in control of everything around him.

This is what he does. He tears things down, and then he builds things back up. She shuddered.

"It's sad," Roger said, seeing her reaction. "Watching something with so many memories come down. It's like each and every brick has its own story."

She nodded. Endings always made her feel melancholy, too. "Do you think Concerned Citizen sent me that anonymous letter with the hopes of delaying or even postponing the demolition? Maybe there was some ulterior motive for not wanting the building to come down. I mean, obviously, there's no ghost here."

It was depressing to think that her entire trip had been for nothing. Except, if she hadn't been here she'd never have known Mimi and Zeke were having marital difficulties. And she and Tom wouldn't have had their "closure." She glanced his way once again. How could he think that after all these years they could somehow have a future together? It was ridiculous.

"You sure about that?" Roger asked.

"You were at the séance. What do you think?"

"I think ghosts come in all shapes and forms," he said, following her gaze. "Maybe yours has some unfinished business."

Eyes off Tom, Allie. She felt herself blush. "Oh, no, that's definitely finished."

"Nothing's ever finished. Unless you want it to be."

"Generally, I'd say that's good advice, but in this case…" A breeze danced in from the gulf, bringing with it the warm smell of salty air. And something else. It was faint, but still enough for Allie's nose to pick up. Lemons. No, not lemons, Jean Nate. She sighed.

"Look what I found." Roger bent over and picked up a small bright object from the ground. "Penny for your thoughts?" He held up the shiny copper coin as if he'd found a winning lottery ticket.

"Some people would say they're not worth picking up anymore."

"Good thing I'm not some people." Roger pocketed the penny. He motioned to his camera. "I think I got what I need here. You hungry?"

"Starved," Allie admitted.

"Good. Because I make a mean omelet. How about you let this old man make you some breakfast? Maybe between the two of us we can figure out who wrote that infamous email."

Chapter Twenty-Seven

"I HOPE YOU LIKE grocery-bought coffee," Roger yelled from the kitchen. "I don't keep any of that fancy *Star Wars* stuff here."

Although he couldn't see her, Allie still smiled. "Regular coffee is fine." She walked around, inspecting his home.

The living room was surprisingly modern. Leather furniture, hardwood floors, and lots of black-and-white photographs on the walls. Mostly landscapes, a lot of them foreign looking—pictures of snow-capped mountains and deserts, but Allie recognized a few of them as local shots. There was a picture of the gulf at sunset that took her breath away. And lots of pictures of a pretty woman with dark hair and sparkling eyes.

Was Roger offering to help her with Concerned Citizen because he missed his wife and didn't have anything better to do? It occurred to Allie that she didn't care what fueled his motivation. She liked Roger. Having him make her breakfast was no hardship on Allie's part.

He came up behind her and offered her a cup of coffee, then set two plates down on the table in front of the couch.

"Did you take all these photos?" she asked, unable to tear her gaze from the images on the walls.

"Yep. With an old-fashioned camera. Like the kind I used today. Remember those?"

"I do remember those. Still use one myself from time to time, too."

"Well, how about that?" He grinned and took a sip of his coffee.

Allie stared down at her mug. "How did you know I take it black?" She actually preferred some cream in her coffee, but she'd learned over the years not to be fussy where her caffeine was concerned. She took a sip. It was strong and surprisingly good.

"No self-respecting journalist takes their coffee any other way. I should know. I used to be one myself. If you count twenty years working for *Life* magazine," he said.

"You worked for *Life*?" She went back to studying the photos. Of course he had worked for *Life*. "And *National Geographic*, too, I bet."

He winked at her. "Among a few others."

Allie's voice softened. "She was very pretty."

He followed her gaze to a picture of a woman sitting on a large rock. She wore khakis and hiking boots and a knit cap. Her straight, dark hair hung well below her shoulders and her smile was…breathtaking. Like she was the happiest woman on the planet.

"I met Janice when I was fifty. She was thirty-five and divorced. I was a confirmed bachelor but I still married her after our third date. She died last year. Cancer. We never had any kids."

"I'm sorry." She wished there was something better to offer than that, but she knew from experience that there simply wasn't. "Three dates, huh?"

"When you know, you know." He cleared his throat

and pointed to the omelets. "Food's getting cold." They sat on the couch, side by side, eating their breakfast. "Let's get down to it. You want me to help you figure out who Concerned Citizen is?" Allie nodded. "Then start thinking like a journalist. Who had the most to gain from you investigating that old building?"

"I don't know. Maybe someone who didn't want it to come down?"

"We all voted on it. The whole town. We need a new rec center. Kids need a place to play basketball. A community swimming pool. It's best for everyone." He set down his plate and pulled a photo album from a nearby bookshelf and handed it to her.

Allie began leafing through the pages. The album was full of pictures of the senior center. She recognized a few of the pictures that Betty Jean had given her from the *Whispering Bay Gazette*. "You took pictures for the *Gazette*, too?"

"Just a few. After Janice and I got married, we moved here to live on the beach. I had some family money and was tired of traveling. Phoebe lived nearby so we thought it would be a good place to raise kids. Never had the kids but we had a good life."

Allie lay the album down. "Mr. Van Cleave—"

"Call me Roger."

"Okay, Roger, what do you think about your sister's theory that the ghost is male?"

"She's got a fifty-fifty shot at being right." His blue eyes sharpened. "And you think she's full of it."

"I didn't say that, but I don't know how she can be so certain."

"Are you asking me if my sister's a fraud?"

"I wouldn't put it that way, exactly."

He looked her over as if trying to decide how much

to tell her. "After Janice died, I had trouble sleeping. Common enough, I was told, for someone who was grieving. Doc Morrison prescribed some sleeping pills...and something for depression, as well, but I didn't want to go that route, you know?

"So one night I had a couple of beers. More than a couple, to tell the truth. I must have passed out on my living room couch because I woke up in the middle of the night to, um, relieve myself. While I was washing my hands, I glanced up in the bathroom mirror...and there was Janice's reflection staring back at me. Smiling at me, just like she'd done in real life."

Allie held her breath.

"When I turned around, she was gone. I chalked it up to those beers and tried to get back to sleep. Eventually, I did." He stared at her hard. "I never had any problem sleeping after that."

Roger was quiet for a few long seconds and Allie wondered if it was the end of the story. She sensed it wasn't, but it also seemed as if he were hesitant to go any further. She laid her hand over his. She thought he might pull away, but he didn't. "And?" she urged softly.

"And that's when I started finding the pennies. Janice used to always use that expression, 'penny for your thoughts.'" Roger shrugged like he was embarrassed. "I found pennies all over the place. I'd go to the Piggly Wiggly and find a penny in the parking lot next to my car. Or I'd go out and get the morning paper and there would be a penny lying on the sidewalk. I knew intellectually it was just a coincidence. People drop pennies all the time. But, a part of me wants to believe that it's Janice. Telling me to hang in there. That I don't need those sleeping pills because she's watching out for me."

Then he stood and went to the kitchen. He returned

with a large glass vase filled to the brim with pennies. He set it on the table in front of her, stuck his hand in his pocket and produced the penny he'd found in the senior center parking lot, and dropped it into the vase.

Allie stared at the pennies. Like Roger, a part of her wanted to tell him that it was a coincidence. That people found pennies all the time. Especially if they were on the lookout for them. But who was she to tell him that? If the pennies gave him solace, then they were a good thing. And on the chance that they were somehow linked to his deceased wife, then...

She tried to find a delicate way to word it. "Roger, do you think that maybe...it's Janice who's haunting the senior center?"

"Nah. I would know if it were her."

Allie felt a moment's disappointment. She shook it off and handed him back her empty cup. "Thanks for the coffee. And for being so honest. I guess I'll never find out who wrote that email."

"So that's it. You're giving up?"

"You said yourself, the whole town voted for the new rec center. If someone secretly doesn't want the old senior center to come down it could be anyone. It's like trying to find a needle in a haystack."

"What about a more personal reason? Maybe Concerned Citizen doesn't care if the building comes down or not. Maybe they just wanted you to be involved in it somehow."

"Involved is putting it mildly. I've practically staked my career on this story." Allie told him about the job opening at *Florida!* magazine, and about Chris Dougal and his immigration piece and the competition the two of them had been forced into.

"Illegal immigration, huh?"

Allie didn't have to ask what he thought her chances of landing a job against that were. Not with a ghost story that was proving to be as flimsy as air. "I thought maybe I'd write an article about my experience at a séance."

Roger looked even more skeptical.

"Or maybe not." She thought about what he'd said, about Concerned Citizen having a personal reason to want her in town. But the only person she could think that would want her in town would be...

"You know, maybe there is someone who would want me here badly enough to write that letter. My sister-in-law's always going on about how much she wants me to move back home. But if Mimi wanted me back in town all she'd have to do is ask me. Not write a letter under the guise of some ghost haunting."

"You sure about that?"

"If I've learned anything this week, it's that I'm not sure about anything."

"All those years in the business taught me that when my gut tells me something, it's usually right. I've been watching you. You got those instincts, too." He winked at her and Allie caught a glimpse of the man he'd been at fifty. No wonder Janice had married him after just three dates. Roger Van Cleave was not only smart, he was charming.

"Thank you." She reached out and hugged him.

Correction: You hugged friends, puppy dogs, *and* kindred spirits.

Who would have thought Roger Van Cleave would turn out to be all three?

"So, no ghost story?" Allie hated hearing the

disappointment in Emma's voice but it was way past time she filled her editor in on the latest sad development.

"No ghost story. No séance," Allie said. "Sorry, but it just didn't pan out."

"What are you going to do? Ben is expecting your portfolio by the end of next week."

"I'm not giving up on the job, if that's what you mean. I'll figure something out."

"You're so good at connecting with your readers. Write from the heart, Allie. It's what you do best. You'll find your story. You know I'm rooting for you."

"Thanks, Emma. That means a lot."

At noon, Allie met up with Zeke as planned and they headed off to the courthouse in nearby Panama City. Thankfully, the process of getting her license reinstated was relatively simple. Expensive, but not complicated.

"I hope this teaches you to read the fine print from now on," Zeke said, dropping her back off at the house.

"Yes, Daddy."

"Don't be a smart ass." He glanced at his watch. "Tell Mimi I'll meet her at the football game."

Yikes. Allie had almost forgotten about tonight's game. And more importantly, what would be happening *after* the game. As in, Claire's big confession. "You're taking separate cars?"

"Mimi has to get Claire there an hour early. Plus, she's manning the refreshment booth so she's got to set up."

"Wow. Mimi really has her hands full, huh?"

"Tell me about it. And now she's come up with this cockamamie scheme to run for mayor."

Allie felt her hackles bristle. "I think Mimi would make an awesome mayor."

"Sure she would. When they invent a forty-hour day."

"When did you become such a Cro-Magnon?" She'd actually wanted to call him a prick, but considering all he'd done for her, it wouldn't have been very gracious. Still. Her brother was turning into someone she hardly recognized.

"Just being realistic," Zeke said. He waved good-bye and took off in his cop car.

"Men," she muttered. She made her way up the driveway back to the house, stopping briefly to pat her little VW bug on the hood. "I'll never take you for granted again," she said. Four days without a car had taught her a valuable lesson. She went in through the garage and into the kitchen to find Mimi up to her elbows in cupcakes.

"God, it smells awesome in here."

"My Bunco group is manning the refreshment stand tonight. Half the proceeds go to the non-profit organization of our choice." Mimi's eyes glittered. "Which, coincidentally, happens to be *me*. I've decided to run for mayor and campaigns don't come cheap. Not even in little ol' Whispering Bay."

Before Mimi could stop her, Allie grabbed a cupcake off the cooling rack. "That's the best news I've had all week."

"Zeke doesn't think so, but yeah, I'm pretty excited."

Allie picked up a spoon and dipped it into a vat of vanilla icing and smeared it on top of her cupcake, then licked off what was left on the spoon. "What does Zeke know?"

"He hasn't said so directly, but I think he thinks the

That Thing You Do

city will fall apart if I'm at the helm. Plus, if I do get the job, I'd sort of be his boss."

Allie nearly choked on the icing. "*Ha!* No wonder he's going ballistic."

Mimi picked up a cooled cupcake and began icing it. "What did he say? And tell me the truth."

Uh-oh. Allie hadn't meant to rain on Mimi's parade. Especially not when her sister-in-law needed her support. "Who cares what my dumbass brother thinks? I think it's great. The kids will, too. And Zeke will come around. You'll see."

"You think so?"

"Of course!" Allie decided to change the subject. "Roger Van Cleave is a pretty cool old guy."

"You saw his photographs?" Mimi smiled like she'd known a secret that Allie was just now discovering.

"Why didn't you tell me he worked for *Life* magazine?"

"I didn't think about it. I mean, all those Gray Flamingos are pretty interesting if you ask me."

Allie laid down her spoon. "Mimi, after Buela died, what happened to all her stuff?" Just two weeks after Buela's death, Allie had gone off to college, dazed and heartbroken. Mimi had taken on the sorrowful task of closing up the little house Allie shared with Buela. Allie had returned home to Whispering Bay for Thanksgiving break to find that Mimi and Zeke had made a place for her in their own home.

"You mean photos, things like that?" Mimi frowned. "You've seen them. They're all over the walls. Plus, I have a few dozen albums in the den closet. You're welcome to any of them, you know."

"Thanks. But I mean…the other stuff? Her furniture, things like that?"

303

"I think most of her furniture went to Goodwill and to the church bazaar. I kept a few things, though, like her china and her wedding dress. It's very cool, you know. Very retro. It would fit you perfectly."

Buela's wedding dress would fit her? Allie had never even entertained the idea. Of course, in order to wear a wedding dress you had to have a groom first.

"Why do you suddenly want to know about Buela's things?"

"I don't know. Seeing Roger's house, all his knickknacks, stuff from his trips, it made me a little nostalgic, I guess." She studied her sister-in-law carefully and said, "He gave me some insight into who might be Concerned Citizen."

Was it a figment of Allie's imagination or did Mimi's cheeks go pink? "He did?"

"Roger thinks Concerned Citizen had a sneakier reason to write me that email. He thinks maybe someone wanted to delay the demolition. Or maybe...someone just wanted me here in town."

"Leave it to those Gray Flamingos to turn this whole thing into some conspiracy theory." Mimi raised an iced cupcake in the air to inspect it. "Do you think I'm putting too much icing on these?"

"There's no such thing as too much icing."

"Agreed." Mimi placed the cupcake back on the tray and looked up to find Allie staring at her. "What? You don't think *I* wrote that email, do you?"

"You didn't? I mean, you seem pretty happy to have me back home."

"Why on earth would I write your editor an anonymous email when I could just speed dial you and tell you I needed you?"

Mimi was right. All she had to do was ask and Allie

would have come running. There would have been no need for subterfuge. Still, Mimi couldn't seem to make eye contact. She was hiding something. Allie was sure of it.

"So maybe you didn't write the letter yourself, but...you know who did."

Mimi's eyes widened.

"Busted!" Allie said.

"Okay, so I had no idea she was going to actually write it. We'd talked about different strategies, and if I'd known you were going to pin your hopes for a new job on that ghost story I *swear* I would never have gone along with any of it."

"*She*? Who exactly are we talking about here?"

Mimi sighed and wiped the icing off her hands with a kitchen towel. "Lauren Donalan, who else?"

Chapter Twenty-Eight

LAUREN DONALAN WAS CONCERNED Citizen? It made no sense. "Start from the beginning, please."

"You know that Henry and Cameron have become fast friends," Mimi said, "and Lauren and I have become friends, too." She made a pleading face. "Please don't be mad, but we kind of thought it would be neat if we could get you and Tom back together."

"Did you ever think of maybe just setting us up on a date?"

Mimi rolled her eyes. "As if you'd ever agree to that."

"Of course not, but—"

"I know what we did was wrong. Sort of. But to tell you the truth, I'd do it all over again in a heartbeat. If you'd seen your face when Tom came to pick you up the other night, well, you can tell yourself whatever you want but I've known you since you were thirteen. Whether it's a good thing or a bad thing, he's the one you want. So while I feel bad that this might have interfered with your job, I'm glad Lauren had the balls to do it."

Allie pulled her car into the last parking space and

killed the engine. The Bistro by the Beach was hopping, as usual. She studied the entrance to Lauren's shop, Can Buy Me Love. Gone was the Partridge family window display. In its place were two mannequins dressed in retro Halloween costumes. She peered in through the glass window.

There was no sign of Lauren. Which didn't mean anything. There was no sign of anyone, actually. Compared to the buzz of people coming and going through The Bistro's door, the little retro shop practically looked like a graveyard. How did Lauren make a living with this place?

Allie placed her hand on the doorknob and hesitated. Mimi had made her promise she wouldn't make a scene and she intended to keep that promise. She wasn't mad at Lauren. More like confused. She understood Mimi's rationale for wanting her and Tom to get together, but Lauren's? *That*, she didn't understand. Not one bit. But she wanted to.

She'd told Lauren she'd visit the shop before she left town so she had a legitimate reason for being here. But she suddenly felt...shy. And nervous. Talking to Tom's ex about the weather was one thing. But talking to her about Tom himself was something else entirely.

Allie stepped inside the shop, setting off a chime. Although she didn't usually frequent boutiques of any kind (Target was more in line with her current budget), she had to admit the place had a certain appeal. Racks of clothing were strategically placed along the weathered hardwood floors and each wall was painted a different color. It didn't take but a few seconds to realize that each "section" held clothing from a different decade. Allie had thought the place was a sixties retro shop, but she recognized clothing from the fifties and seventies as well as the eighties, too. The Shirelles' "Will You Still Love Me Tomorrow" played in the background.

Goosebumps erupted along her arms. Allie shook off an eerie feeling of...what? An odd sort of familiarity?

Lauren emerged from a back room carrying a hanger with a pleated skirt. By the expression on her face, she seemed genuinely surprised to see Allie. Good to know Mimi hadn't forewarned her partner in crime.

"It's you! I'm so glad you're here!" She hung the skirt on a side rack and pulled Allie into a hug.

Allie awkwardly hugged her back. "Well, I did promise I'd stop by before I left town," she said, feeling squirrelier by the minute.

Lauren's face momentarily fell, but she rapidly composed herself. "You're leaving town? Right now?"

"Tomorrow. I'm going to the big football game tonight."

"Along with half the town. It should be fun. Kind of like old times, huh?"

Allie nodded absentmindedly. Old times meant Tom playing first-string quarterback, Lauren leading the cheerleading squad, and Allie sitting in the bleachers, watching.

"So, what can I show you? There's an adorable navy blue pencil skirt that I think would look awesome with those legs of yours. What size are you? A six?"

"Look, I know you're Concerned Citizen. Mimi told me all about the plot the two of you hatched up."

Lauren blinked. "She did?"

"I kind of guessed. At least, I guessed Mimi's involvement. But yours? Sorry, but I don't get it."

Lauren walked over to the shop door and flipped the OPEN sign backward, then turned the lock. "Just in case anyone should come by." She glanced nervously to the back of the shop, then at Allie. "First off, I just want to say that I'm sorry for the mystery but I'm not sorry I wrote that letter. I meant every word of it, you know."

Allie stilled. "You're really a fan of my Perky the Duck story?"

"How could anyone not be? I *love* that story."

Of course this was something Allie would never get tired of hearing. "Thanks, but what about the other stuff? The stuff about a ghost?"

"Okay, so maybe I let my imagination run away with me a little, but there really has been some strange stuff going on around town. It all started when..." She frowned. "When I bought that record player over there."

Allie followed the sound of The Shirelles to the back of the store, where a beat-up old record player sat on a brightly painted wooden table. She stared at the black vinyl 45 turning round and round. A dozen or so album jackets lay stacked next to the player. Allie picked up the jacket on top. It was The Beatles' *The White Album*. In the corner, written in faded blue ink, was the name Barbara Alvarez. She quickly flipped through the albums—there it all was, Jim Morrison and The Doors, Franke Valli and the Four Seasons. Even Buela's favorite salsa singer, Celia Cruz.

"Oh my God. This is Buela's old record player. But...what are you doing with it?"

"I bought it at a garage sale a couple of months back, along with that stack of records. I figured it would be a great novelty for the shop, but the record player wasn't working. Not until Tom fixed it."

"Tom fixed this?"

"Oh yeah. He's terrific with his hands, you know." As a matter of fact, Allie did know. Was Lauren making a double entendre? Her smile was vague enough that

Allie couldn't tell. But she could certainly see why Lauren and Mimi had become friends. There was something so dang nice about her. But there was also this quirky side that Allie had never known about.

This woman had been Tom's wife. She was the mother of his child. Allie couldn't help but feel jealous, even though she had no right to.

She eyed the record player again. She remembered it, of course. It had sat in their little living room for years. Mimi said she'd saved all the photos and the heirlooms and the rest had gone to Goodwill. A scratched up record player would have probably seemed like a piece of junk. But where had it been all these years? Doing the garage sale circuit? How strange was it that it landed in Lauren's hands? And that Tom was the one who'd made it work again.

"Of course, if you like, you can have it. I didn't know who Barbara Alvarez was. Not until Mimi saw it and told me."

Allie shifted from foot to foot. "The thing is... I know it sounds crazy, but—"

"You've been hearing some of this music. Like, in your head," Lauren said with a completely straight face. If Allie was being punked then Lauren should be up for an Academy Award. "I have, too! Well, just a few snippets of it here and there. Isn't it awesome?"

Allie felt the blood rush to her ears. "I don't understand."

Lauren gently took her by the elbow. "Let's go to my office where we can sit down."

Lauren handed her a cup of tea. Allie wasn't a hot tea

drinker but she gratefully took it. "Thanks." She took a long sip, letting the warm liquid soothe her frazzled nerves. This was definitely turning out to be the strangest week of her life.

Lauren sat on the edge of her desk, facing Allie. "A couple of weeks ago, Tom was working at the senior center site and I decided to surprise him by bringing him lunch. He works way too hard, you know."

"That was...nice of you."

"I know what you're thinking. We're divorced. What the hell am I doing bringing him lunch? But it's not like that between us. I love Tom. Not in the I-want-to-spend-the-rest-of-my-life-having-hot-sex-with-you kind of way, but in the let's-be-friends-and-raise-a-son kind of way."

"O-kay," Allie muttered.

Lauren tried to hide her smile. "So there I was handing him a Bistro by the Beach tuna melt—that's his favorite, in case you might need to know for future reference—when all of a sudden I started hearing that old song, 'Where Did Our Love Go?' in my head. You know, by The Supremes? At first I chocked it up as a side effect of listening to all this great old music all day long, but the thing was... I only heard the song whenever I'd run into Tom and I began to wonder if the universe wasn't trying to tell me something. That maybe we'd made a mistake by getting a divorce."

Allie felt her stomach roil over. "And...was it?"

"No! That's the thing. Our marriage was the mistake, not the divorce."

Allie let go of the breath she didn't know she'd been holding. Not until now, anyway. "All right. But I still don't get it. Why the phony ghost email?"

Lauren's face scrunched up. "That was initially

Mimi's idea. Like I said, we've become good friends and I told her about the music thing. How it seemed too weird of a coincidence that it began with the salvaging of your grandmother's record player. Don't you see? The song wasn't about me and Tom. It was about *you* and Tom. It's like the universe is trying to get you and Tom back together. With some help from your grandmother, of course."

Allie laid her mug down on the desk. "Sorry. You've totally lost me here."

"Mimi and I knew that if we tried to fix you up with Tom you'd never go for it. Not with your history. But she thought you wouldn't be able to pass up on a ghost story. And what with Tom in charge of that building, it seemed inevitable that it would throw the two of you together. I had no idea you'd prove so stubborn. Mimi wanted to give up when you never responded, but I just couldn't, so I sent it on your editor hoping you'd eventually get it."

"I get why Mimi wants me and Tom together, but, sorry, I don't understand why you'd go to such lengths."

Lauren's cheeks pinked up. "Would you believe me if I told you the song was driving me crazy? And that it didn't stop until I sent that email? It's like someone was compelling me to write it."

Could she believe it? Ha! If Lauren only knew.

"Look, I know we don't know each other well, but this is what I do know. Tom is the best guy I've ever known. The absolute *best*. We got married because I was too afraid of being a single parent, and because I couldn't stand letting my parents down. It was a dumb reason, but twelve years ago it was the best decision we could come up with. I knew Tom was into you. Way more than he ever was into me. But he gave up everything to try to make our marriage work. And I love him for that. And because he's the best dad ever. When Tom takes something on, you get one hundred percent of him."

Allie cleared her throat. "So what happened? If Tom is such a saint why didn't the marriage work?"

"I know this sounds like a big cliché, but one day I looked at the calendar and realized that in a year I'd be turning thirty. And I knew that if I didn't do something, I'd be forty, and then fifty, and I would have spent half my life with someone I shouldn't be with. So I put on my big-girl pants and asked Tom for a divorce."

"I bet that was one interesting conversation."

"Yeah." Lauren grinned. "When Tom makes up his mind it's like moving a two-ton boulder uphill. But eventually, he caved in. And I moved back home to be near my parents."

"Mimi told me your daddy's been having some health problems."

Lauren nodded sadly. "Tom was terrific about it. According to our divorce settlement, he didn't have to agree to the move. Taking Henry out of state was a no-no. But you know what? He helped me pack up and settle in, and then for nearly a year straight he drove down almost every weekend to see Henry. Because that's the kind of guy he is. Tom doesn't go around telling you he loves you. He proves it with his actions."

Allie swallowed hard. "Can I ask you a question? What do you think is making us hear the music? I mean, do you think maybe..."

"Do I think your grandmother is using her old records to communicate with us? I don't know. I just think there's too many unexplained things in the universe to rule anything out. It's like the idea of an afterlife. I don't have to have proof to know one exists." Lauren smiled. "Maybe there's just some things we aren't meant to figure out."

For a long moment, neither of them said anything. Then Lauren glanced down at her watch. "I should open the store back up. In case any customers decide to show up."

Allie jumped from her seat. "Oh, yeah, of course."

"Look, Allie, for what's it worth, I'm sorry. I didn't mean to mess with your professional life. It's just, Mimi was convinced that you still had feelings for Tom. And I'm convinced he still has feelings for you. And all I know is that any woman lucky enough to be on Tom Donalan's radar would be an idiot to not give him a shot."

Chapter Twenty-Nine

IT WAS PERFECT WEATHER for a football game. Cool, crisp, and blessedly dry for a change. The air was heavy with excitement and the smell of hot boiled peanuts. Toss in a packed stadium and life didn't get much better in small town Florida.

The Whispering Bay Wolverines were facing their cross-state rival, the Old Explorer's Bay Conquistadors. Old Explorer's Bay was a small town south of St. Augustine located on Florida's east coast. Both schools had won the state's 2A football championship in the past and both desperately wanted to beat each other tonight. Small town pride was at stake, along with a chance to get into the playoffs.

Thirteen years ago, the Wolverines beat the Conquistadors 28-3. Tom had thrown a near-flawless game. Afterward, Lauren had given him his first blowjob. It had been the perfect end to a perfect night. Tonight, he sat next to her with Henry on his other side. His parents were here, too, along with half the town. He stared down at the top of her blonde head. A lot had changed in thirteen years. He wasn't the same guy who'd gotten her pregnant. And she wasn't the same girl who'd come to him in tears worried about how her parents would react to the news. They were both on a different course now, each of them trying to eke out a new life.

Are you happy? A week ago he thought he was. But tonight he knew different.

He wondered how Lauren would answer that question.

Then he wondered how Allie would answer it. He hoped the answer would be yes. Even if it meant being happy without him. Which definitely seemed to be the case.

"Want something to drink?" he asked Lauren, nodding toward the concession stand where Mimi Grant and Kitty Pappas were selling cold Cokes and hot nachos.

"Sure. I'll take a Coke. And a hot dog. You know how I like it." She turned to their son. "Henry, go help your dad."

Henry stood and waved to someone on the far right side of the bleachers. "Can Cameron spend the night?" he asked.

Tom followed his gaze. It was hard not to spot Zeke Grant. Harder even to ignore his sister, sitting next to him. Allie wore jeans and a maroon and gold Wolverines sweatshirt. Her long brown hair hung loose and straight down her back. Tom couldn't tell from this angle, but he'd bet she had on those blue cowboy boots, too. He'd like to see her in those again. In just those and nothing else. It was unlikely that would ever happen. But a guy could dream.

Man, he had it bad.

In that instant Zeke Grant turned and caught Tom staring at his sister. Grant's eyes hardened. *Yeah, asshole, good thing you can't read my mind.*

"I think that's a great idea," Lauren said. "As long as it's okay with Cameron's parents."

"Mimi's working concessions. We'll ask her." He led his son to the bottom of the bleachers. Within seconds, Cameron joined them. Both boys seemed happy to see one another.

Mimi smiled at him. "What can I get you?"

Tom placed his order and Kitty began filling the cardboard cups with ice.

"Henry wants to know if Cameron can spend the night," Tom said. "He's with Lauren tonight."

Cameron turned to his mother. "Can I, Mom?"

"I don't know. Don't forget you have that science project to turn in on Monday."

"I'll spend all day tomorrow working on it. Promise," Cameron pleaded.

"O-kay, you talked me into it," Mimi said, clearly having a little a fun at her son's expense. She handed Tom his order. "And just so you know, part of the proceeds from tonight's concession are going to my mayoral campaign."

"Finally, this town is going to get a mayor who really cares about what's going on," Kitty added proudly.

"So you're giving Bruce Bailey a run for his money, huh? Good for you," Tom said.

"Does that mean I have your vote?"

"Depends on how you feel about commercial zoning," Tom halfway joked.

"Actually, I'm working up a platform on that. Kitty has agreed to be my campaign manager and Lauren is going to help with my first official fundraiser."

"Oh, yeah? Good for her, too." Lauren hadn't told him her plans but Tom nevertheless felt a twinge of pride. They might not be married anymore, but he was happy to see her spread her wings. It would be a lot of work, and she already had the shop and an ailing father to help look after, but it was good for her to become civically involved. It set a good example for Henry, too.

He glanced back up in the stands and caught Allie staring at him. Their gazes held for a few long seconds before she looked away. She didn't look happy, that was for sure. Not that Tom derived any satisfaction from that.

Now that he was back home they'd probably run into each other from time and time. And no matter what he was certain he saw or didn't see in her eyes, he'd play along. He'd do whatever it took to make her feel at ease. And if that meant he had to smile and make nice and pretend they were nothing more than an old fling, then so be it.

Allie watched as Tom made his way back up the bleachers. He distributed the assorted drinks and snacks out to his family, then sat down next to his son. It was a cozy picture. One Allie vowed to imprint on her brain.

Once again, Tom caught her staring at him. Allie placed her hand up in a weak wave, then turned in her seat before she could see if Tom waved back or not.

They'd already said their good-byes. No need to draw anything out. Every few years they'd run into one another. They'd smile politely. Make some chitchat. Tom would eventually get a girlfriend. Maybe he'd even remarry. Heck, maybe he and Lauren would get back together. Despite the ex-Mrs. Donalan's protests to the contrary, it could happen. And it might be the best thing for everyone. Especially Henry. Maybe Allie would find someone, too. Get married. Pop out a few kids. She tried her hardest to envision it. But nothing came to her. It was definitely time to change up that Chunky Monkey fantasy.

The game went by quickly, but Allie was too focused on watching Claire to pay much attention to the score. She seemed so happy tonight in her maroon and gold cheerleader's uniform, all smiles and long legs (and those boobs!). She was growing up so fast. Her little Claire Bear. Drinking (or not drinking as she'd claimed) beer at a party with a boy that Allie was certain neither Mimi nor Zeke knew of.

She had to admit Claire's back flip was impressive. She could see how hard the team worked. It was almost more gymnastics than straight cheerleading. She hoped Zeke would take Claire's confession well, because Allie hated to think that this could be Claire's last game.

In the end, the Whispering Bay Wolverines beat the Conquistadors 14-7 in an exciting finish that had the entire stadium rocking. The players ran off the field, with the cheerleaders and the band following them into the gym, playing the school fight song.

Allie and Zeke made their way down to the concession stand, where Mimi and Kitty were finishing clean-up duty.

"I told Cameron he could spend the night with Henry," Mimi told Zeke. "They'll be at Lauren's house."

"Sure," Zeke said politely. Too politely as far as Allie was concerned. It was like the two of them were skating around each other, afraid to get too close for fear of crashing. Maybe a crash would be good. At least then they could pick themselves up and start over.

"See you in the morning?" Cameron asked Allie.

"I'll probably leave pretty early," Allie said. "How about you give your old aunt a hug till next time." Cameron hugged her and then ran off into the stands to find Henry.

Kitty locked the concession stand door. She handed Mimi an envelope and the two of them made plans for next week's Bunco game. Allie was tempted to ask how much money they'd raised for the mayoral campaign, but considering Zeke's feelings on that particular subject, she decided to keep her mouth shut. She'd ask Mimi later.

Gail from The Blue Monkey had called this afternoon asking what shifts she wanted to work next week. Soon, she'd back to her old routine. Waiting tables at the restaurant, dodging Jen and Sean at the apartment, and trying to find time to write her articles for the magazine. Same old, same old world. Funny. She'd been back in Whispering Bay less than a week, but her regular life seemed like it belonged to someone else.

Just five nights ago, she'd told Jen Whispering Bay was home. And in a way it was. She thought about what her life would be like if Mimi got her way and Allie were to move back permanently. Despite Allie's objections to the contrary, it was shockingly easy to envision. She could write anywhere. She could wait tables anywhere, too. What she couldn't do from just anywhere was help Mimi with the mayoral campaign. Or help her brother with his shaky marriage. Or get close to her niece and nephew again. Those were only things she could do if she lived right here.

Zeke stretched his arms above his head and yawned, interrupting Allie's thoughts. "Get Claire and let's head on home," he said to Mimi.

"There's a party tonight. I said she could go, as long as she's home before midnight."

Allie froze. Claire was supposed to tell her parents about the Grayton Beach fiasco after the game. Not run off to some party.

Zeke frowned. "Where's the party and who's driving her home?"

"One of the other cheerleaders. I think," Mimi said.

"You think? You don't know for sure?"

Mimi turned to Zeke, eyes blazing. "What's your problem?"

"I don't have any problems. At least that's what you told that quack you're making me see."

Oh no. Maybe crashing into one another was a bad idea. Best to keep them still skating around. "Um, guys, do you want me to find Claire and tell her she can't go to the party?" Allie offered.

"That would be great," Mimi said, snapping back into polite mode. Zeke stood there, his lips drawn tightly like he was having trouble keeping his mouth shut.

A little bit of Allie felt like dying. If Zeke and Mimi got a divorce, it would be like… It would be like losing Buela all over again. Her little family would disintegrate. She didn't want to think about that happening ever. Best to concentrate on finding Claire and diverting any possible disaster.

"I'll search for her in the gym," Allie said.

The Whispering Bay High gym was packed with excited teenagers and their parents, making it difficult to find her niece, so Allie tried Claire on her cell. It went directly to voice mail.

Talk about déjà vu! She suppressed a shudder. Surely, Mimi had heard wrong about this party. Claire had learned her lesson. She wouldn't be stupid enough to

323

lie to Allie. Would she? Not when she'd promised Allie she'd come clean with her parents tonight.

No, everything was fine. She'd just wait till the crowd thinned. Then she'd spot Claire and they'd rendezvous with Mimi and Zeke.

Football players high off tonight's victory strutted out of the locker room, freshly showered. Families made their way out the exit doors. The crowd died out, but there was still no sign of Claire.

The overhead gym lights blinked twice. It had been twelve years but Allie still remembered what those flashing lights meant. The gym was about to close up.

She scanned the dwindling crowd and spotted a few girls in cheerleading uniforms. "Excuse me," Allie said to one of the girls. "Have you seen Claire Grant?"

"Sorry." The girl shrugged. "I'm not sure where she went to."

"Well, can you tell whose house the party is at tonight?"

The girl looked confused. "Tonight?" The cheerleader standing next to her tried to discreetly elbow the girl, but Allie still caught the not-so-subtle movement. Did they think she was an idiot? "Oh! You mean the *after-game* party? Um, I think it's at the house of one of the football players. Sorry," she mumbled, "but I can't remember the exact details." Both girls scurried away before Allie could question them further.

A sour fuzzy feeling crawled its way into Allie's stomach and settled itself straight down to her toes.

"That was some game, huh?"

Allie turned to find Tom standing behind her. He wore jeans and a T-shirt and a brown leather jacket. She caught the subtle scent of cologne. The overwhelming urge to bury her nose against that jacket was so strong she had to concentrate on keeping her feet planted firmly to the gym floor.

"Yeah, it was great."

He stilled. "What's wrong?"

No use asking how he knew there was something wrong. "I'm waiting for Claire to come out of the locker room. You haven't seen her, have you?"

"Not since the game ended. She hasn't gone MIA again, has she?"

"Of course not," Allie said.

"You sure about that?"

She thought about putting him off, but there was genuine concern in his voice and Allie had to admit to herself that Claire had once again duped her. She couldn't even feel stupid about it. Or mad. She tried to tell herself it wasn't personal. This wasn't Claire against Allie. But it felt as if Claire had turned into some alien creature that Allie couldn't begin to understand.

"You're right. I think Claire has gone off to parts unknown again."

"Is she suicidal?" Tom asked.

"What's that supposed to mean?"

"Have you met your brother?"

"He's not that bad."

"Not unless you've boinked his sister."

Allie raised a brow.

"Trust me, the guy would love nothing more than to meet me in a dark alley some night."

"The thing is... I never told Mimi and Zeke about the other night. Not the boinking," she clarified quickly. "Thanks to Madame Gloria the whole town knows about that. But they don't know about the party at Jordan's. And before you say anything, I know what you're thinking. I should have told them. It was irresponsible of me. I'd never make it as a parent. I—"

"I wasn't thinking any of those things," he said.

Before either of them could say any more, Lauren walked up to them, her usual cute self. She wore black leggings and a maroon silk top. "Hey!" she said brightly. "I was just about to round up the boys and grab a pizza on the way home." Upon seeing their expressions, her smile faded. "What's wrong?"

"We need to find Claire Grant," Tom said. "Before Mimi and Zeke find out she's somewhere she's not supposed to be."

"Where do you think she is?" Lauren asked.

"I'm pretty sure she's at a friend's house in Grayton Beach," Allie said. "At least…it's a place to start looking."

"How can I help?"

"Just keep this to yourself," Tom said. "And if you don't mind, I'm going to skip out on the pizza and help Allie track her down."

"I know this looks bad," Allie said. "But Claire's a good girl."

"No worries. Hey, we were all teenagers once, too." Lauren gave Tom a hug. "See you later." She gathered the boys and headed out the gym door.

Allie took a deep breath. "Tom, you don't have to help me. I mean, there's no reason for you get involved in all this."

"Yeah. There is." And with those three simple words, he offered her his hand.

She should turn him down. Not because she wasn't grateful for his help but because involving him would mean letting him back into her life. This morning should have been the end. But she was beginning to think that as far as she and Tom were concerned there was never going to be an end between them.

She should take a minute and think about what she was doing. Go over the pros and cons of it all. But she didn't. She just simply took his hand, and that was that.

Allie gave Zeke and Mimi a bare-bones version of Wednesday night's activities.

"What do you mean Claire took off from soccer practice to go to a party? And you didn't tell us?" Zeke shoved a hand through his dark hair. The stadium parking lot was empty except for the four of them. "I know this Jordan kid. The DEA arrested her older brother last year for selling coke."

Mimi's jaw dropped. "Claire is involved with someone who's selling *cocaine*?"

"No, no, no," Allie said quickly. "There was some underage drinking involved but no drugs, at least not that I could see."

"Not that *you* could see? Brilliant," Zeke shot back.

Allie could kick herself. She deserved this. Why hadn't she told Mimi and Zeke the entire story the other night? How could she be so naïve? "I'll tell you everything. Later. But right now, let's just make sure Claire is all right," she said, trying to reason with her brother.

"Look," Tom said, "let's not waste time laying blame where it doesn't belong. I say we break up and go search for her."

Zeke looked as if he'd forgotten Tom was still there. "Who invited you to the party? This is between family. *My* family."

327

"Tom has offered to help and we'd be stupid to turn him down," Allie said.

"She's right, Zeke." Mimi grabbed the car keys from her purse. "We can sort this out later. We'll go search the beach and you two go back to this Jordan's house. See if her mom knows where they are."

"Good idea," Tom said.

Zeke didn't say anything. He climbed into the minivan and he and Mimi took off.

Chapter Thirty

THE HOUSE IN GRAYTON Beach was dark with just a few scattered lights visible toward the back of the house. The driveway was empty. Allie couldn't help but feel disappointed. If Claire wasn't here, then she had no idea where she might be. "It doesn't look like there's a party going on."

"Looks can be deceiving," Tom said.

True enough.

They made their way up the driveway. It was nearly midnight but despite the late hour, Allie had no qualms about ringing the doorbell. Jordan's mother looked surprised, but not unpleased to see them. She wore a short black cocktail dress and full makeup. She took one look at Tom and smiled. At least, the parts of her face that weren't surgically frozen, smiled.

Not nice, Allie.

"Remember *us*?" Allie said.

Tom placed his hand against the small of her back. It was a subtle, intimate gesture that Allie appreciated. Right now she needed all the support she could get. "Is Claire Grant here?" he asked.

"Is that one of Jordan's friends? Jordan's at a football game."

"The game ended two hours ago," Tom said.

"You were there? I was going to go, but I had a previous engagement." She glanced away. "Two hours ago, huh? I'm sure the kids are just somewhere having fun." But from the look on her face, it was obvious she didn't believe her own words.

"Yeah. I used to have that kind of fun, too, when I was in high school," Tom said.

"I grounded her after the party the other night and told her she was to come home directly after the game. I called her cell phone a few minutes ago but it went straight to voice mail."

Despite her previous behavior, Allie couldn't help but feel sorry for Jordan's mom. "That voice mail virus seems to be going around. Thanks, anyway."

They went to leave but she stopped them. "If you find them, will you please tell Jordan to come home?"

"Sure."

"Where to next?" Tom asked once they were back in the truck.

Allie sank into her seat. "Honestly? I have no idea. Let me see if Mimi and Zeke have had any luck." She pulled out her cell phone and made a call. Unfortunately, Mimi and Zeke weren't having any better luck than they were.

"I say we try the beach ourselves. It's dark out and they could have missed her," Tom said.

They searched in all the usual places. The burger hangout by The Harbor House. The beaches, not only once, but twice. Claire was nowhere to be found.

Tom pulled his truck onto the side of the road and killed the engine. "I'm all out of ideas here."

"I'm sorry to have gotten you involved in this. It's late. You can drop me off at my brother's anytime."

"Don't worry, she'll show up. It's not like she's run away from home." He stared at her a moment. "Is it?"

"Of course not. But I do think this is Claire's last hurrah before she gets grounded for life...and I'm just worried she's going to do something really stupid."

"You're kidding, right?"

Allie sighed. "You saw how Zeke reacted back there? He's a good dad and I know it sounds irrational but I think he's trying to make up for the fact that our own dad was a complete slacker. It's like he's changed somehow. He's always so tense and he and Mimi, well, they're having marital problems." She felt a moment's disloyalty, but it was a relief to finally share it with someone.

"Is that why you didn't tell Mimi and Zeke about the party the other night?" he asked quietly.

"I've never seen them this way before, Tom. It's like one minute they're polite strangers and the next..." She shook her head. "I think they're having *big* problems. Except neither of them wants to own up to it. Teenage drama isn't helping the situation, you know?"

"And you thought that by keeping it from them, you'd be helping?"

"I thought that Mimi and Zeke were the one couple on this planet who could make it. Don't you see? If they can't, then no one can."

"No relationship is perfect, Allie." She got the feeling that he wasn't just talking about Mimi and Zeke. He started up the truck. "Don't give up yet. There's one more place we haven't checked." He eased into the driving lane, then made a sharp U-turn.

"Where's that?" Allie asked. Then she saw the direction he was taking and she didn't need an answer.

331

They were heading to the last place on earth Allie wanted to revisit.

The bridge over the Choctawhatchee Bay was under construction. At least, part of it was. Being that it was past midnight, however, the construction area was deserted. Tom drove his truck over the bridge toward the mainland. On the left side along the water, a lone car sat parked among the sparse grass.

Allie swallowed hard. This had been their special place. The place she and Tom used to make out. The Night of the Great Humiliation Part Two. Did he remember?

"Popular spot," he muttered.

Of course he remembered.

He parked directly behind the car and turned on his brights. Two heads immediately popped up from the front seat. "Got 'em."

"Are you sure it's Claire in there?" Allie asked.

"Only one way to find out." Tom got out of his truck. Allie followed behind.

A tall, lanky teenage boy jumped out of the driver's side of the car. "What the hell's going on?" It was the hipster from the Grayton Beach party that Claire had been "drinking" beer with. The boy Claire claimed she hardly knew. *Ha*!

"Claire," Allie shouted, "come out of that car this instant."

Claire slowly emerged from the car. Her hair, which had been up in a high ponytail, was mussed. She smoothed down her cheerleader skirt and nervously licked her lips. "I can explain," she began.

"Perfect," Allie said. "So start explaining on the drive back to your parents' house."

"You don't have to go with them, Claire," Hipster boy said.

"Oh yes, she does!" Allie opened the truck door wide in invitation. Luckily, Claire meekly stepped up into the cab. Allie slipped in alongside her niece. She watched from inside the truck as Tom spoke to the boy. Quiet, low words that Allie couldn't make out. The kid shoved his hands into his pockets and nodded. Allie couldn't be sure if whatever Tom was saying was sinking in, but at least the kid seemed respectful.

"I'm sorry. I know I was supposed to come home after the game, but Mom said I could go to the party—"

"I don't think *this* is what your mother had in mind when she gave you permission to go to a party."

Claire began to sniffle. It might have worked, if Allie hadn't already been bamboozled by it once before. "Are you going to tell my parents?"

"You better believe I'm going to tell them."

Claire was too smart to respond to that. She pursed her lips tightly and craned her neck to see the exchange between Tom and the boy.

"Who's your boyfriend?" Allie asked, noticing the hickie on Claire's neck. "And don't tell me you hardly know him because it's obvious the two of you know each other pretty darn well."

"His...name's Adam and he's a senior. We've only been out a couple of times. Mom and Dad don't know about him."

"Why not?"

"Dad said if I wanted to have a boyfriend then I had to bring him to the house to meet him first."

"That sounds reasonable."

"Yeah. If it was the last century. He probably wants to fingerprint him and run it through the FBI database."

"Oh, c'mon, Claire."

Claire crossed her arms over her chest and stared out the window with a stony expression. After a couple minutes, Tom came back to the truck. "In case you're wondering, Adam is very sorry and won't take Claire off again without her parents' permission."

"Good to know," Allie said.

Adam lingered by his car like he was reluctant to take off. His gaze kept skittering back to the truck and Allie actually felt a little sorry for him.

"Can I go say good-bye to him?" Claire asked. "It's the least I can do considering that I'm never going to see him again."

"Sure, why not?" Allie said.

It was all the encouragement Claire needed. She jumped out of the truck and ran into Adam's arms.

"It's like they're Romeo and Juliet," Allie muttered.

"Don't you remember what it was like? Being their age?"

"God, it was…awful."

"Not all of it."

Tom was right. First love was painful, but it was also brilliant. It was one of those bridges you had to cross in life so that you could move on. "True. Not all of it."

He looked surprised by her admission.

The glare of oncoming headlights made her turn in her seat. A familiar-looking blue minivan pulled into the grassy area a few yards away. Claire and Adam immediately jumped away from one another, like the guilty teenagers they were. The minivan had barely stopped when both Zeke and Mimi came barreling out of the car. Allie and Tom joined them by the water's bank.

"I was so worried about you!" Mimi said. She grabbed Claire into a tight hug. "Please tell me you aren't doing cocaine."

Claire took a step back, her mouth half open in shock. "*What*? Oh my God. Mom, I'm not on drugs!"

Mimi took Claire's face between her hands and stared into her eyes for a moment. "Thank God."

Zeke took a few seconds to take in the situation. Right now he looked more cop than father, but Allie had a feeling that would be only be temporary. "What's going on here?"

"We found her with Adam." Allie nodded in the boy's direction. "But before you say anything—"

"Here? By the water? Parked in that car?"

"I know it looks bad," Allie began, "but they're just kids, Zeke."

It took Zeke two long strides to get to Adam. He grabbed the boy by the shirt collar. "What the hell do you think you're doing with my daughter?"

Tom placed his hand on Zeke's shoulder. "Calm down, man. Allie's right. They're just kids."

Adam shook himself loose from Zeke's grasp and scrambled away as far as he could.

Zeke turned to Tom, eyes blazing. "What the fuck do you know about it? The last time I looked you didn't have a teenage daughter."

"I know that you need to step away before you do or say something you're going to regret."

"Tom's right," Allie said. "Let's go home and talk about this like civilized adults."

Zeke pointed a finger at Adam. "You," he said. "Be at my house tomorrow afternoon. One o'clock sharp. And don't think I can't find you."

Adam nodded hastily. He threw a tortured look at Claire then took off in his car toward town.

"Thanks, Daddy," Claire said in her little girl voice. She'd managed to get her hair back in the ponytail but her cheeks were wet and her eyes were puffy. It was a look Allie was becoming all too familiar with.

"Don't thank me yet. You're grounded," he said.

"For...how long?"

"For as long as I say."

"I knew it!" Claire turned to Allie. "Didn't I tell you he'd ground me for life?"

"I'm afraid I'm partially responsible for what's happened here tonight," Allie said.

"No, Aunt Allie, it's my fault. Not yours." Claire looked at her with eyes that looked so much like Mimi's. But she was all Zeke's daughter. Headstrong, impulsive. Why hadn't Allie seen that before?

"Well, it's somebody's fault," Zeke said, looking at Allie. "How about you fill us in on all those details you conveniently left out earlier?"

Allie spilled her guts about everything. Except the part about nearly being arrested by Rusty for a second time. But she told them about Claire's duplicitousness the night of the soccer practice, the party at Grayton Beach, and Allie's decision to let Claire be the one to tell her parents after tonight's game.

Mimi shook her head in confusion. "So, the minivan didn't break down? That was all a...cover up?"

Zeke glanced between Allie and Tom. His shrewd eyes took in everything. "What I want to know is how lover boy's involved in this?"

Allie could feel the instant tension emanating from Tom's body. "If it wasn't for Tom, I would have never found Claire. He helped me track her down and he...he thought I'd told you everything. So please don't blame him for any of this mess."

"Great! So some fucking stranger knows more about what's happening in my family than I do."

"Calm down, Ezequiel," Mimi said. Using his full name had been a trick of Buela's. Usually, it helped bring Zeke's temper down a notch, but not tonight.

"Claire, get in the van. We're going home," Zeke said.

Claire crossed her arms over her chest. "Not till I know how long you're grounding me. Even prisoners deserve to know the length of their sentence."

Uh-oh. Yep. Definitely Zeke's daughter.

"Okay. You're grounded for life. From everything. Happy now?"

"*Everything*?" Claire's voice quivered.

"Obviously your father and I will talk to you about this in the morning," Mimi said.

"You can talk to her all you want," Zeke said. "She knows we're done here."

Claire got in the minivan and made a big show of slamming the door. Allie whipped around to stare at her brother. Who was he? Not the same Zeke she'd known and loved all her life, that was for sure.

"Claire told me about the marriage counseling. She says you and Mimi are on the brink of divorce. Cut her some slack, Zeke. She's sixteen and going through a rough time."

Zeke looked startled. "Claire's the one who told you about the counseling? We never told the kids. How did she know?"

Allie rolled her eyes. "For a cop, you're pretty clueless."

"We haven't used the word divorce," Mimi said softly. "At least, not yet."

"You're damn right we haven't," Zeke said. "No one's getting a divorce here. Everything's fine."

"Really? Because from where I sit, it doesn't look so fine. I've never met two people more meant for each other and if you don't know what you have then..." *Then what?* "Then you don't deserve one another!"

For a second, no one said anything. It emboldened Allie to go on. She reached out and touched Zeke on the arm. "Remember what an asshole Dad was? Is that the kind of relationship you want to have with your daughter? One based on fear?"

Instantly, Allie realized it was the wrong thing to say.

Zeke's entire face changed. He laughed, short and bitter-sounding. "Who made you parent of the year? Yesterday you couldn't even drive because your license was suspended. Get your own life together before you come around here preaching crap you know nothing about."

Allie winced. She should have never compared her brother to that worthless sack of nothing that had been their father. "I'm sorry, you're right. You're nothing like Dad—"

"Damn straight I'm not."

Tom stepped in between them. "I think we should all go home before we start saying things we're going to regret."

"Yeah? Thanks for the advice, buddy. Here's something I definitely know I'm not going to regret." Zeke made a fist and punched Tom in the face, landing him flat on the ground.

"Zeke!" Allie yelled. "Have you gone crazy?" She helped Tom get up. Blood squirted from his nose and down his T-shirt. Oh God. Why did there have to be *blood*?

"I've been waiting twelve years to do that." Zeke rubbed his knuckles. He smiled for the first time tonight. "Damn if that didn't feel good."

"Are you all right?" Allie asked Tom.

He pulled up the edge of his shirt to staunch the blood dripping down his nose. "I'll live." He looked at Zeke. "I probably had that coming. But don't hit me again. Got it?"

"Got it," Zeke said calmly.

The two men stared at each other for a second as if they'd come to some sort of understanding. Good. Glad they got that settled, but Allie would never understand the male psyche.

"Give me your keys to the truck. I'll drive you home," Allie said.

"How are you getting back to the house?" Zeke said.

"I'll figure something out."

Zeke wisely kept his mouth shut.

After a few long seconds, Mimi broke the silence. "Thank you for everything, Tom. Even though he might not act like it, Zeke and I appreciate your help." She ignored her husband's glare and gave Allie a weak smile. "So I'll see you later tonight?"

Allie nodded, then she remembered the promise she'd given Jordan's mother. "Can you give Claire a message? While she still has a cell phone in her possession, can you tell her to call her friend Jordan? Her mom's worried about her and wants her to go home."

"Will do," Zeke said. He followed Mimi to the minivan and they took off down the road leaving Tom and Allie alone.

"Are you okay?" Tom asked.

"Me? I'm not the one who just got pulverized by my brother."

"I mean, are you okay with this?" He pointed to his nose. Blood oozed down his chin.

"Oh, yeah, I'm...okay. Just don't go hemorrhaging on me or anything. Then I can't make any promises." She went to his truck, hoping to find a rag or an extra set of clothes to act as a pressure bandage. As usual, Tom's truck was spotless. "Why can't you be like most guys and have a messy car?" she muttered.

"Huh?"

"Never mind. Take off your shirt," Allie said.

"Here? Now?" he joked. "I'll take mine off if you take off yours." But there was no heat behind his words.

"Pretty brave talk now that my brother's gone."

Despite the swelling that was beginning to form, he managed a smile. He slipped off his jacket and pulled his T-shirt over his head and handed it to her. Allie wadded it up in a tight ball and placed it against his nose. She stood back and sighed. The blood was making her a little dizzy, but a shirtless Tom Donalan was just too pretty a sight to not admire. "We better put some ice on that before the swelling gets too bad."

She drove the truck to his place but before she could get out, Tom opened his door. "Stay here, I'll be right back." He returned a few minutes later wearing a clean T-shirt and holding a frozen bag of peas against his nose. He motioned for her to scoot over into the passenger seat. "I can drive now."

"Are you sure?" Allie gulped. Tom was right. What

was she thinking? That she'd stay the night again? He drove her back to her brother's house in silence and parked the car in the driveway.

More déjà vu. Just five nights ago they'd made this same drive. Parked in this same space. "Have a safe trip home, Allie."

It was a dismissal. A polite one to be sure, but one nevertheless. They'd already said their good-byes. It wasn't fair to him to drag things out any longer. But there was something Allie needed to know.

"Why did you let Zeke hit you?" she asked. "And why on earth didn't you hit him back?"

"Hit him back?" He said it as if the idea had never occurred to him. "For the record, I didn't let him hit me. He took me by surprise, but I would never have hit him back."

"Why not?"

He turned and stared at her. "Because he's your brother and—" He shook his head. "Never mind. Let's just say, he's right. I deserved it." He paused. "I've thought about what you said last night. And you're right. I did have a responsibility to you."

Allie stilled. "Tom—"

"Let me finish. I told you before that looking at you made me think of a time in my life that I wasn't so proud of. But…that was only partially true. Looking at you makes me think of what my life could have been like if I hadn't screwed up. Dad taught me early on that a man always pays for his mistakes. I thought by marrying Lauren, I was doing the right thing. But maybe what I did was the wrong thing. I don't know."

"I think you did the right thing," she said softly, surprising both of them. "Henry is terrific, and who knows, Tom? You and I would have probably broken up eventually. That kind of situation would have put a lot of pressure on our relationship."

He nodded slowly. "It wasn't true, when I said I hadn't thought about you these past twelve years. I thought about you a lot, Allie. But it always made me feel so damn guilty, so I had to shove it away. Compartmentalize it someplace where it wouldn't interfere with the rest of my life. I thought it would be easy for you to get over me. I was a world-class dick. It never occurred to me... The thing is if it makes you feel any better, it wasn't just you. My heart broke that night, too."

If it made her feel any better? Maybe it should have, but it didn't. It just made her sad all over again. But this time, anger didn't follow. This time, she wanted to reach out and comfort him and tell him...

"Thank you, for everything," she said instead. Then she opened the door and ran inside the house.

Chapter Thirty-One

ALLIE PACKED UP HER bag and tossed it into the back seat of her VW bug. She said good-bye to Zeke and Mimi. Claire (thankfully) hugged Allie and made her promise to come back soon. Things were strained. No doubt about it. But there wasn't anything she could do about that. She'd said her piece last night. It was up to Mimi and Zeke to fix things between themselves.

She took a right on Ocean Avenue. Leaving Whispering Bay always made her feel a little nostalgic. She couldn't help wondering what she'd encounter the next time she came back for a visit. Would she run into Tom again? Would Mimi and Zeke still be together? How would Claire feel if her parents split up? Or Cameron?

A part of her didn't feel right leaving this time. There were too many unanswered questions. Too much woo-woo out in the universe. But what could she do to change anything? She had a life back in Tampa. Maybe it wasn't a big life. But it was her life and it was high time to get back to it.

She stopped at The Bistro by the Beach to grab a cup of coffee. As usual, it was hopping. Saturday morning meant tourists, which meant business. Allie ordered a coffee and a bagel and was on her way out the door when she spotted Roger sitting alone at a table near the back window overlooking the water. It was a beautiful day. Clear, crisp, and still cool. Tampa could wait a few minutes longer.

"Mind if I have this seat?" she asked, pointing to an empty chair.

"I thought you'd already left town."

Knowing Roger, she took that as a yes, so she sat down and arranged her food on the table. "I had to find out who Concerned Citizen was first."

He raised an eyebrow, clearly waiting for her to go on.

So Allie told him how it had been none other than Lauren Donalan who'd written that infamous letter, and how she and Mimi had tried to fix Allie up with Tom, and how Lauren had Buela's old record player in her shop. If Roger found any part of the story incredulous, he didn't show it.

"That's one hell of a dating service," he mused.

"Agreed." Allie took a bite of her bagel. "How did those pictures turn out? The ones you took of the demolition?"

To her surprise, Roger reached into a satchel to produce a bundle of real-life photos. "Thought you were going to see them on some digital device, huh?" he said, seeing her reaction. "I developed these myself."

Allie flipped through the pictures. There was a sadness about them. An ethereal quality that could only be captured by an artist. And that's what Roger was, she concluded. A real, honest-to-goodness artist. She remembered the pictures Betty Jean had shown her the day she'd visited the *Whispering Bay Gazette*. She'd been drawn to those pictures and she was certain other people would be, too. The pictures were in her satchel, along with all the notes she'd taken about the senior center and the ghost story that never was.

An idea suddenly occurred to her. "Roger? Do you think you might be willing to sell these? To the right medium, of course."

"And that would be?"

"*Florida!* magazine. I was thinking… Maybe the article I'm supposed to write isn't about a ghost haunting the old senior center, but about the building itself. You know, how it started off as this regular house for a regular family, and then how it was donated to the city and…" She could hear the excitement in her own voice. "What it meant to the people who spent time there and the friendships that developed and those special friendships that became something more."

He nodded. "Gus and Viola."

Her heart began to race, the same way it did whenever she got an idea for a story.

"I've got more pictures," he said. "Photos of the place in its heyday. I showed you them when you were at the house. Remember? You could use those, as well. And I could help you with the article. We could interview old Earl; he's living out in Mexico Beach. We could get some good stories from him. Hell, we could get lots of good stories and I know just who to interview, too."

"You mean it? You'd help me? I could give you a byline," she said.

"Nah. Just credits with the photos is what I'd want."

"Oh my God," Allie said, "this could so work. But… *Dang it*, I already said good-bye to Mimi and Zeke and I promised my manager at The Blue Monkey I'd swing by today to fill out my schedule for next week."

"The Blue Monkey?"

"It's a restaurant in Tampa. I waitress there for extra money," she admitted.

"You a journalist or a waitress?"

"A journalist who clearly likes to eat," Allie said, motioning to her empty plate.

He glanced meaningfully toward the busy counter. "Seems to me you could waitress anywhere, though."

He had a point. But she was reluctant to stay in town longer. For one thing, Mimi and Zeke needed some family privacy.

It was as if Roger could read her mind.

"Since we're going to work real intensive-like on this piece, it might be easier if you just stayed at my place. I got a big old guest room that only Phoebe uses from time to time, but it's empty now and yours if you want it." He looked away, as if suddenly shy.

Allie glanced down at her coffee. She was touched by Roger's gesture but it was too much. She hated inconveniencing him. He was a photojournalist. And a highly experienced one, at that. He was more than likely out of Allie's league. But at the same time, she didn't think he was offering strictly out of charity. Tom thought Roger was a lonely old man looking for a cause. Well, she was certainly a cause, all right. Maybe he needed her just as much as she needed him.

"I accept." She leaped from her chair to give Roger a hug. "You're wonderful, do you know that?"

"On one condition," he added gruffly, disentangling himself from her arms.

"Anything."

"You can't fall in love with me." He shrugged. "Because that's what usually happens when two people work together under these kinds of intense circumstances."

"Too late," Allie said with a grin. "I think I already have."

Roger finished his breakfast then gave her a spare key to the house and told her he'd meet her back at his place. "Be ready to work harder than you've ever worked before," he warned.

"Absolutely," she said, saluting him.

She waited a few minutes after he left, then texted Emma with an update on the article.

A piece on the senior center itself? She texted back.

Allie hesitated a moment. She shouldn't read anything into a text but she couldn't help but feel that Emma seemed disappointed. She thought back to her Perky the Duck article. If she had outlined that piece ahead of time, instead of simply writing it, would Emma have been excited?

I'm going to write an article about a duck that was supposed to be dead, but when the hunter's wife opened the freezer and found it alive, she took it to the animal rescue and guess what? Now it's alive!

Ha! Emma would have probably laughed in her face and told her to try to sell it to the National Enquirer. Instead, Allie had gone ahead and written the piece and the rest was history. She'd trusted her gut then. Roger was right. She needed to trust her instincts once again.

I promise you, it'll work. Allie texted.

Then go for it. Emma texted back.

Next, she called Jen. "Hey, something's come up and I'm going to stay up here a little longer."

"How much longer?" Jen asked.

"Probably at least a week. Or maybe two."

"I was going to save this for later, but what the hell. Sean's moved in some more of his stuff."

"How much is some more?"

Jen laughed nervously. "All of it. I didn't think you'd mind since you're back home in Whispering Pines."

"It's Whispering—oh, never mind. Jen...do you think Sean wants to move in permanently?"

"You'd be okay with that?"

"You know the saying, two's company, three's a crowd."

"I thought three was a *ménage a trois*," Jen said.

Allie got something stuck in her throat. "Well, yeah, it's that, too. The thing is... I'm totally willing to give up my lease if Sean wants it."

"Damn, that's nice of you, Allie. I know Sean and I have been moving kind of fast, but when you know, you just know."

"Absolutely," Allie said. And she meant it. Sean and Jen were perfect for one another in that way that two people who seem so totally un-perfect for anyone else could be. *There's someone for everyone*, Buela used to say.

"So when can you move your stuff out?" Jen asked.

"I'm working on a piece right now, but maybe sometime later next week?"

"Great. Um, I hate to ask, but can you cover your portion of next month's rent? Just till we make the lease switch official. Because after all, you do owe it."

Allie slowed down as she approached the senior center, or rather, what was left of it. Despite the fact it was a Saturday, there appeared to be a small construction crew on site. More than likely making up for all the time they'd lost this past week. Big yellow cranes moved the rubble into oversized trash receptacles. Out with the old and in with the new. Progress was coming to Whispering Bay and Tom would be a big part of it.

She got out of her car. Like before, Tom was easy to single out. At least, for her he was. A lump formed in her throat. He looked so handsome. So in charge. How was she going to stay in town and not want to see him? Not want to talk to him? It didn't feel right that the two of them would be back in Whispering Bay and not be a part of each other's lives. She thought about Roger and how he was taking a leap of faith to work on this project with her.

Maybe it was time she took her own leap of faith.

Tom spotted her and jogged over to her side. He took off his hard hat and ran a hand through his hair. "I thought you'd be gone by now."

"I changed my mind," she said quickly, before she chickened out. "I wanted you to hear from me that I'm going to be staying in town."

There was a spark of hope in his eyes that made her heart skip a beat. "For how long?"

"A few weeks, probably. Or maybe... I don't know, forever?"

Before he could respond one of the crew members waved Tom over to the work trailer. "Hey, Tom, can you come take a look at this?" It was Hard Hat. He spotted Allie and his face split into a grin. "God Almighty, it's the Flaky Biscuit. Hey!" he shouted. "See that?" He pointed to where the building had once stood. "It's all gone! What do you think about that? Huh?"

"I take it he doesn't like me," she whispered to Tom.

She smiled and waved to Hard Hat. "Thank you for your help the other day, Keith! I really appreciate it!"

Hard Hat frowned, like he was confused by her friendliness.

Tom grinned. "Oh, it's not that he doesn't like you. He thinks you're, um…interesting."

"Right."

Tom turned serious again. "So, what do you mean maybe forever?"

She found herself shuffling from foot to foot. Any second now, she'd start her babbling. "The thing is I think I might have a story after all. I'm going to work on it with Roger Van Cleave. Actually, I'm going to move in with him."

Tom raised a brow at that. "Go on."

"And, it just doesn't feel right leaving now, what with Mimi and Zeke and their current situation."

"That's it? That's why you're staying?"

She took a deep breath. And there it was. Lemons. Jean Nate. Despite the fact that no one else seemed to smell it, it was *there*. Sure as Allie had a nose to sniff it out with. Maybe the Jean Nate was like Roger's pennies. Wishful thinking. Like believing that the music in her head had been put there by Buela. But who's to say it hadn't been? What had Lauren said? That maybe some things weren't meant to be figured out.

If Roger thought the pennies were a sign from his late wife telling him that everything was okay, why couldn't the Jean Nate be a sign from Buela telling Allie that it was time to get on with her life? That she'd forgiven Allie for shutting her out in those last couple of days? And that it was way past time Allie forgave herself.

"You know, your ex is a really smart woman."

Tom narrowed his eyes. "Because she divorced me?"

"Remind me to thank her for that one day." Roger told her she should go with her instincts. She was doing that with her story. Now it was time to put those instincts to work on her personal life, as well. "The real reason I stopped by is that I never told you the fourth part to my life plan."

He stilled. "The one you don't tell anyone?"

"Do you want to hear it?"

He nodded slowly.

Here goes everything.

"I want to tell someone I love them again. And I want to mean it, with all my heart. Like I did with you twelve years ago. I loved you, Tom. I really did. And I know I was only eighteen and so damn stupid—"

He slapped his hand over her mouth. "*Shut up.*"

Allie could feel her eyes widen.

"Sorry to ruin your part four, but I'm not going to let you be the first one to say it again. So, here goes. I love you," he said. "I think I loved you all those years ago, too, and I think a part of you knows that. The minute you showed me that ghost detector app? I was already gone. Head over heels. I've got it bad, and whatever it takes, no matter how much time you need, I can wait. Hell, I'll wait another twelve years if you need it, but I hope it's not going to take you that long." He went to take his hand from her mouth, then stopped. "And you want to know the real reason I didn't hit Zeke back? I mean, yeah, I deserved it, but more importantly, I don't think it's good form to hit your future brother-in-law." He removed his hand. "You can start talking now."

"I can't believe you told me to shut up. *Wait.* Was that a proposal?"

"Did it sound like a proposal? When I ask you to marry me, you'll know all right."

351

"Oh, okay, just checking."

"I thought we could start by going out on a date. Maybe tonight? There's this new seafood place I've been wanting to try out." He reached out and cupped her chin and stared into her eyes with an intensity that nearly buckled her knees.

He loved her. *Tom Donalan loved her.* And she loved him back.

"All right," she squeaked, "but only if you take me parking afterward. There's this little place I know over by the bridge…"

He smiled and it was like no smile Allie had ever seen before.

Epilogue

IT HAD BEEN A long time since Allie had visited her mother and Buela. They were buried next to each other in what most people in town called the "new" section of Whispering Bay Memorial Gardens. Fresh flowers adorned both graves. Pink roses on her mom's, and daisies on Buela's. Allie felt a renewed burst of love for her brother.

A cold burst of air swept through the cemetery, causing Allie to tighten her jacket. It was January and according to the weatherman, temperatures were supposed to drop into the low thirties tonight.

She opened up the advanced copy of the March issue of *Florida*! magazine to the story in the middle. "I came by to show you this," she said, not caring who might see her talking to a couple of tombstones. "It's my story on the old senior center. I hate to brag, but my editor says it's the best thing I've ever written. There's a picture of you, Buela, right here on page ninety-four. You're playing shuffleboard, and...you look really happy." She gently laid the magazine down on Buela's grave, right next to Zeke's daisies.

"I thought you might want to know that I got offered a full-time job with the magazine. I was in a competition with this other guy and his story is in here, too, right after mine. His name's Chris Dougal and they offered him the job first, but he turned them down. He's working for Newsweek now." Allie couldn't help but smile at that.

"And while he did get the job offer first, my story got the cover for the magazine," she added proudly. "So, in my eyes, I think I kind of won. But... I didn't take the job. I decided to stay here in town. Roger Van Cleave, you remember him, don't you, Buela? He and I are taking over the *Whispering Bay Gazette*. I know it's not much compared to being on permanent staff with *Florida*! magazine, but I think we're both going to be really happy."

She glanced and waved at Tom, who was waiting patiently by his truck in the parking lot. He waved back.

"That's Tom Donalan. And I *know* you remember him. We're on our way to a basketball game at the high school. Claire is cheerleading and we don't want to miss that. Mimi and Zeke, well, they've had their share of problems these past few months, but I think they're going to be okay. You'll keep an eye out for them, right?"

Allie took a deep breath and got down to the real reason behind her visit.

"So, back to Tom. He was my first boyfriend and well, it's kind of freaky, but he's actually my fiancé now." She raised her left hand to show them the diamond engagement ring Tom had given her last night. "I know what you're thinking. Because believe me, three months ago he was the last man on earth I ever thought I'd want to marry, but now, I can't imagine being with anyone else. He's the best man I know."

Another gust of wind came through, causing the

magazine to topple over. Allie bent down to straighten it and that's when she smelled it. *Jean Nate*. The last time she'd caught a whiff of Buela's perfume was that day at the senior center when she'd gone to tell Tom she wasn't leaving town. That had been three months ago, long enough for her to be afraid that it had all been a figment of her imagination.

But now, standing here above the graves of the two women who'd been everything to her, she knew that she'd smell the Jean Nate again. Maybe it would be on her wedding day. Or the day her first child was born. Or any other time she needed her grandmother's love. Maybe it was like Roger's pennies. It would come when she needed it most. A sign from the universe that everything was going to be all right.

It didn't make sense, but thank God not everything in life needed an explanation.

THE END

Thank you for reading!

I hope you enjoyed Tom and Allie's story as much as I enjoyed writing it. For news on upcoming books, sign up for my newsletter at http://mariageraci.com/subscribe/.

WHISPERING BAY ROMANCE
A NOVEL

maria geraci

Then
He Kissed Me

About

Then He Kissed Me

WHISPERING BAY ROMANCE BOOK 2

LAUREN DONALAN WAS ONCE Whispering Bay's golden girl—the rich, bubbly blonde cheerleader who married the high school football star. When her mediocre marriage falls apart, she returns home and starts a vintage clothing business, determined to prove she's more than just a pretty face with a trust fund.

Nate Miller may have been a nerd in high school, but now he has a beautiful girlfriend and is set to take over Doc Morrison's medical practice. Still, the good folks of Whispering Bay find his no-nonsense approach more than a little unsettling, leaving his future in town a great big question mark. And things go even further downhill when his well-intentioned marriage proposal goes awry.

Lauren doesn't need a man to complete her, yet when she finds herself set up on a date with Nate, she can't help but notice how sexy and confident he is. In fact, every time the former introvert kisses her, she sees fireworks. But, only a big love will make Lauren change her mind about commitment. As Nate attempts to win Lauren over, a real estate co-op threatens Lauren's business—and Nate's ex still has a thing or two to say about their previous relationship. Now Lauren has to decide to go big or go home, in business, as well as in love.

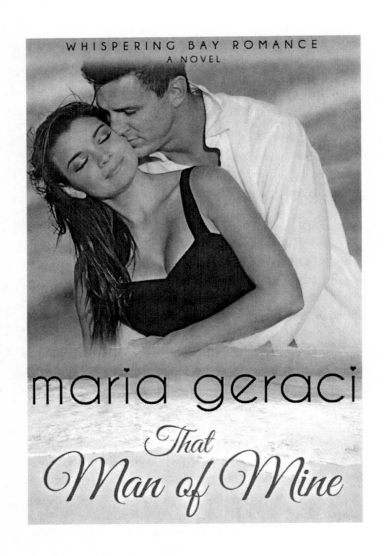

WHISPERING BAY ROMANCE
A NOVEL

maria geraci

That
Man of Mine

About

That Man of Mine

WHISPERING BAY ROMANCE BOOK 3

WHEN MIMI GRANT BECOMES mayor of Whispering Bay, she gets a whole lot more than she bargained for. Her biggest concern? The city's annual festival is in financial ruin and the former housewife doesn't have a clue how to fix things. But, she's determined to bring the sleepy beachside town into the twenty-first century.

Hunky Police Chief Zeke Grant isn't happy that his estranged wife Mimi has just become his boss. But for the town's sake, he's willing to swallow his pride and let her order him around—to a point. Everything aside, he doesn't count on someone from his past coming back to haunt him, forcing him to reevaluate what's really important.

While Mimi and Zeke continue to butt heads on how to get things done, there's one thing they can't help but agree on: their chemistry is hotter than ever. However, when a robbery threatens to derail the annual festival, some of the town's residents question Mimi and Zeke's ability to keep Whispering Bay safe—as well as keep their war-torn personal life out of civic business. Mimi and Zeke must team up to solve the crime, and decide once and for all if it's time to move forward with separate lives, or if true love really does conquer all.

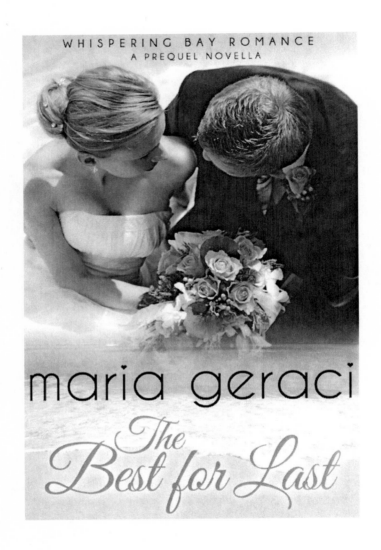

WHISPERING BAY ROMANCE
A PREQUEL NOVELLA

maria geraci

The
Best for Last

About

The Best for Last

WHISPERING BAY ROMANCE BOOK 4
A prequel novella

KITTY BURKE'S BIOLOGICAL CLOCK isn't just ticking, it's gonging. But who wants to be tied down by marriage and a minivan when you have an amazingly sexy boyfriend who worships the ground you walk on? Sure, Steve has never said those three magic words. But, Kitty knows he loves her. Some guys just have a hard time expressing their feelings, right? Right.

After three failed marriages, Steve Pappas is in no hurry to walk down the aisle a fourth time. As a matter of fact, he has no desire to ever say "I do" again. He's a successful self-made millionaire, but despite the best of intentions, marriage is one arena he's been unable to conquer. Kitty is funny, sexy, and whip smart—everything Steve has ever wanted in a woman and more. Their life is perfect the way it is now. So why rock the boat and ruin everything with a piece of paper that doesn't mean anything?

When Kitty's aging playboy father unexpectedly decides to tie the knot, Kitty realizes she's been fooling herself. She does want it all—marriage, kids, but most especially, a man who isn't afraid to openly declare his feelings. Can she convince her commitment-phobic boyfriend to take the ultimate chance? Or will she be forced to settle for Happy For Now instead of Happily Ever After?

About the Author

Maria Geraci writes contemporary romance and women's fiction with a happy ending. The Portland Book Review called her novel, *The Boyfriend of the Month Club*, "immensely sexy, immensely satisfying and humorous." Her fourth novel, *A Girl Like You*, was nominated for Romance Writers of America's prestigious RITA ® award. Her current addictions include watching the STARZ adaption of OUTLANDER to drool over Sam Heughan, hitting the beach on the weekends, and searching for the perfect key lime pie recipe (but not the kind they served on Dexter). Visit her website for more information on her books: http://mariageraci.com/

CPSIA information can be obtained at www.ICGtesting.com
Printed in the USA
LVOW11s2321070816

499402LV00002B/137/P

9 781534 866966